Mystery at Maplemead Castle

Also by Kitty French:

Knight & Play
Knight & Stay
Knight & Day
Genie
Wanderlust
The Skeletons of Scarborough House

Writing as Kat French:
Undertaking Love
The Piano Man Project

THE CHAPELWICK MYSTERIES 2

Mystery at Maplemead Castle

KITTY FRENCH

Bookouture

Published by Bookouture
An imprint of StoryFire Ltd.
23 Sussex Road, Ickenham, UB10 8PN
United Kingdom
www.bookouture.com

ISBN: 978-1-78681-131-8
eBook ISBN: 978-1-78681-130-1

This book is a work of fiction. Names, characters, businesses,
organizations, places and events other than those clearly in the
public domain, are either the product of the author's imagination
or are used fictitiously. Any resemblance to actual persons, living or
dead, events or locales is entirely coincidental.

This book is for the brilliant, funny Kim Nash, officially the bee's knees of the book world. Thank you for everything you do.

CHAPTER ONE

Every now and then someone tells me how lucky I am to be able to see ghosts and I bite my tongue and sit on my hands so I don't accidentally punch them in the face. Honestly, I know it might seem interesting, fun even, from the outside looking in, but if I could trade places with a regular Joe I'd do it in a heartbeat. It's a gift and a curse in unequal measures, but one I'm determined to make best use of by building my fledgling business empire around it.

'Hey, Bittersweet.'

I look up as Marina bounces a balled-up chewing gum wrapper off my head to get my attention.

'That's the third time I've said your name.' She folds the stick of gum in half before she puts it in her mouth. 'What's got you so distracted?'

I shrug. 'Just thinking about this afternoon's meeting at Maplemead. I can't remember the last time I went inside an actual castle.' I avoid places steeped in history on account of the fact they're usually also steeped in ghosts who want to hassle the hell out of me, but this is for work purposes so I'm breaking my own rules. We're meeting later today with the American couple who recently moved lock, stock and barrel to England after buying Maplemead Castle over the Internet. *I know.* Who does that?

'Do we need to buy caps to doff?' Marina asks, her dark eyes dancing. She's not one for taking things too seriously, unless someone winds her up or threatens us, in which case she morphs into a crazy woman and you don't want to be the one she's gunning for. It's her Sicilian heritage. Luckily for us, she also has a Sicilian nonna, or gran to you and me, who is a stonkingly good cook. Therefore, Marina comes in most days armed with something fabulous in her vintage biscuit tin.

'A quick tug of our forelocks should suffice,' I say, pulling ineffectually at my fringe.

We both look up as our assistant Artie comes through the door, all long legs and wide, nervous eyes.

'Morning.' He grins, then drops to his haunches to greet Lestat, my utterly uncivilised pug. He hasn't been with us very long, but he already has his paws firmly under my table, his ass in my bed, and his furry flat face in Nonna's biscuit tin too if he can find a way to get at it without being seen. He's a ninja when it comes to food, but it'll take a faster pug than him to come between me and my next sugar hit.

I'm not a girl with that many vices, but sugar is definitely near the top of my addiction list.

'What time are we due at the castle?' Marina asks.

Glenda Jackson, our part-time secretary, taps the end of her pencil against the diary that's open on her desk. 'You're due at Maplemead Castle for two o'clock.' She glances at her watch. 'It's going to take you approximately forty minutes to get there in pre-rush-hour traffic, so you'll need to leave immediately after lunch.'

Glenda doesn't even look up as she imparts this information, because her fingers are flying so fast over her keyboard that it's a wonder her hands don't levitate. She's worked for my family for more than a decade, and she now does a couple of hours each morning here at the agency before going back to her regular job next door with my mother and gran at Blithe Spirits. Some people would find it difficult to be the sole administrator for two businesses at once. Not Glenda Jackson. Monday to Friday she packs her curves into sexy little power suits, piles her red and gold curls on top of her head, then steers both of the Bittersweet ships whilst doing the cryptic crossword in her downtime.

We are an unlikely company, all round. Glenda Jackson, aka superwoman in a sexy power suit. Artie, snake-charmer, tea-drinker, trainee ghostbuster. Marina, my wisecracking, loyal right-hand girl since we were scabby-kneed kids; a gum-chewing, fiery Sicilian beauty queen.

And then there's me. The short, quirky girl in jeans and Converse who sees dead people, fantasises about superheroes and prefers sugar to sex. Actually, that is a complete and utter lie. I don't prefer sugar to sex, but I'm not getting any of one so I overindulge on the other. God, imagine if I could combine the two! For a moment I let myself imagine being boffed by Fletcher Gunn – the local hot-shot reporter who I have a love–hate relationship with – whilst eating a Curly Wurly, and it's so frickin' fabulous that I feel my cheeks heat up and wonder if the others can tell I'm suddenly on the brink of a saccharine orgasm.

'Stick the kettle on, Artie,' I say, reminded of my need for caffeine as he pulls a little plastic Ziploc food bag from his pocket and deposits his weekly supply of tea bags on the tray beside the jar of coffee. He's an oddball in all the best ways, our Artie. At first glance he seems gawky and awkward, and actually he is both of those things, but there's so much more to him too. He has his own special way of looking at the world; pragmatic to the tenth degree and a knack for stating the obvious in a way that cracks me up.

It strikes me suddenly that Marina has yet to produce Nonna's special biscuit tin from her bag. I go icy-cold with fear. Please don't let this be the day Nonna Malone has decided we don't need her sugar fix to set us up for ghost-hunting because, as far as I'm concerned, that day will never come.

'Coffee, Marina?' I say, hoping to jog her memory without needing to ask outright. If she doesn't get the hint, I'll face-plant myself in her cavernous suede hobo bag and wear it as a hat to snout out those biscuits.

She nods, looking at me coolly. 'I don't know how to break this to you gently, so I'm just gonna be fast and blunt. Brace yourself. Nonna's gone back to Sicily for a week. There are no biscuits.'

I gulp, and stare at her in wide-eyed horror. 'You must have known she was going,' I whisper hoarsely. 'You could have prepared me.'

She looks at me with a helpless shrug, which might mean there was a family emergency prompting Nonna's trip but, more likely, means she was too chicken to tell me.

Artie plonks his lunchbox down on my desk and opens it. 'You can have my egg sandwich if you want,' he offers. I appreciate the gesture of solidarity. He feels the same way about his mum's egg sandwiches as I do about Nonna's biscuits.

'I'm going to cry now,' I say. 'Because my life is practically ruined.' I shoot Marina a dark look. 'Glenda, cancel the appointment at Maplemead. I'm going to go to bed for a week. Wake me up when Nonna Malone comes home again.'

Glenda watches me have my sugar-free meltdown with calm, doe-like eyes, then silently reaches into her desk and hands me an unopened box of shortbread. It's quite fancy, as it goes; proper Scottish stuff dipped in white chocolate for good measure. I feel my blood sugar start to rise in anticipation and decide that perhaps I don't need to hit the sack after all. See what I mean about Glenda Jackson? She's Wonder Woman without the Spandex.

Lestat barrels across the room as I pick the end of the biscuit box open and our eyes meet as he ducks under my desk, skids to a halt and puts his stubby little foot on my knee.

'Not a chance, Mutt-Face,' I growl, as protective of the shortbread as a mamma tiger with her newborn cub. 'Go hunt your own kill.'

I feel absolutely no guilt as he slinks away across the office to his bed, shooting me daggers as he stomps around his cushions in ever-decreasing circles to get comfortable.

'I've printed out the recent sales particulars of Maplemead Castle.' I pause to hand the copies I made earlier around. 'It's worth us all taking some time to familiarise ourselves with it. There's also a potted history attached at the back, although we're going to need to go deeper after our initial assessment this afternoon.'

'It's quite a place, isn't it? I always hoped they'd open it up to visitors but the family were very private,' Glenda murmurs, admiring the moat and handsome facade. She isn't wrong; it's a beautiful sandstone brick building that has been cared for and modified over the years to keep it in service in various guises, and its many-mullioned windows glint in the sunlight behind the grand stone steps leading up to the entrance.

Marina flips the top image of the castle over and whistles as she glances over the details. 'Seventeen bedrooms!'

Aside from the numerous bedrooms, the castle has a library, a billiards room, various attics, cellars and an old dungeon.

'I vote we don't set foot in the dungeon,' I say. I'm not the bravest when it comes to the dark.

'Lois and Barty Letterman have been living at Maplemead for a month or so now, and in that time they've witnessed an array of paranormal activity; objects being moved, thrown, that sort of thing, that they attribute to ghosts,' Glenda says, reading through the notes from the booking-in telephone conversation. 'They're not unduly bothered for themselves, but a film crew are due in at the beginning of next month and the leading lady has already made it clear that she won't step foot inside the place while there's so much as a sniff of ghosts and ghouls.'

From what I can gather, the Lettermans are planning to run the castle as a business, hiring it out as a party venue and film set.

Privately, I'm hoping the first movie being made at Maplemead will have a distinctly superhero vibe; I mean, it isn't a deal-breaker that it *has* to star Robert Downey Jr as Iron Man, but it sure would help oil the wheels. Or would it? I'm not sure I'd get much done, mainly because I'd be stalking him and trying to cop a feel of his iron helmet. That's not even a euphemism. I like his actual helmet; all of that wizardy gadgetry stuff makes me come over all Gwyneth Paltrow and want to be his Girl Friday. Or maybe just his girl. Anyway, you get the idea. I'm not exclusive to Iron Man though. I'm a superhero junky; I'd be just as happy to see Captain America or Spidey rock up to the portcullis at Maplemead.

Surreptitiously scribbling on my jotter block, I clear my throat and whip quickly through the other bare-bone details we already know about Maplemead, mostly just the basic timeline of the castle that I've dug up from the net. There's not very much to go on yet; we need to get over there and try to assess what's going bump in the night before Hollywood descends and all hell breaks loose.

Glenda rules a neat line to close off the morning meeting in the diary and, as we slowly disperse back to our relative perches, Marina leans over my shoulder and reads my scrawl in the jotter block, then rolls her eyes.

Buy Curly Wurlys.

CHAPTER TWO

'Holy shit.'

I turn the engine off and Marina, Artie and I all sit and stare, goggle-eyed, at the magnificent castle frontage. We've just driven in across the drawbridge and through the huge wooden gates set into the thick castle walls and it's like entering a secret fairy tale. At least the public might get more of a chance to see the castle now; as Glenda said, it's always been in private hands and cloistered from prying eyes.

'I don't think the gatekeeper liked the look of Babs,' Artie says, stating the obvious from the disdainful way the uniformed guard had eyed Babs, our 1973 Ford transit. Perhaps it's the fact that it's two-tone buttercup yellow and off-white, or triple tone if you were feeling unkind enough to count the rust. Maybe it's the fact that we were gawking at him through the windscreen like the three wise monkeys from the front bench seat, or it's possible it had something to do with the in-your-face Ghostbusting Girls' Agency logo that Marina lovingly hand-painted on the side. Sure, it echoes back to the glory days of Charlie's Angels, but Babs is a seventies hippy chick so it's entirely in keeping with her retro style. She wears her slightly rusty chrome bumpers with jaunty panache, and her juddering and backfiring is the biggest thrill my nether regions get all day, which is more of a sad reflection of me than her.

'It's bigger than it looks on the pictures,' I murmur, leaning forwards until my face is almost pressed flat against the glass as I peer up at the crenelated roofline above the third-floor windows.

The facade is bedecked with several tiers of stone-mullioned windows, seven abreast set across the wide, almost mellow pink stone. It's actually very pretty, if a castle can be considered as such. It's certainly a far cry from the austerity of the ruined grey castles Marina and I were hawked around on rainy school trips as kids. It was difficult to listen to the teacher or tour guide when a bevy of beheaded prisoners from the 1500s were bustling around you with their heads underneath their arms indignant at their fate, or on another memorable occasion when the ghostly inmates of a lunatic asylum swamped me so badly that Marina caught me as I'd passed out.

I developed a twenty-four-hour sickness bug on trip days after that, which I expect came as a relief all round. I was universally known at school as the latest in a long line of weirdos from Chapelwick's resident crazy family. I was saved from being bullied only by the fact that some of them had seen *Carrie*, the Steven King movie where the telekinetic kid goes nutso and burns the school down with them in it. Oh, and by Marina, of course. To get to me they'd have had to come through her, and the Malone family are also well known in Chapelwick – for different reasons. Sicilian reasons. I'm sure I don't need to elaborate.

'Do you think we just knock on the door?' Artie says, gazing across the deep expanse of the gravel forecourt. I don't know why I've instinctively parked as far away from the castle as the forecourt permits; maybe because Babs is like an out-of-place canary here when there should be only sleek ravens. A sweep of wide, shallow steps lead up onto a stone porch inset with grand double oak doors.

Marina grins. 'Nah. I reckon we should just sit here and wait until a knight rocks up and bangs his rod on the window or something.'

'His rod?' Laughter bubbles up in my throat. Trust Marina to be inappropriate.

She shrugs. 'See if I'm wrong.'

On that, one of the front doors swings back on its hinges.

'You were wrong,' Artie says.

All three of us watch the small birdlike woman flutter out onto the top of the steps. She shields her eyes with her hand to peer at us and the huge jewels on her fingers catch the sunlight and bounce tiny rainbows around her, as if she is the actual rainbow queen in her own rainbow-themed Disney movie. Only this queen has switched her turquoise velvet cloak for a turquoise velvet jumpsuit and her ethereal crown has been exchanged for a white sun visor that loudly proclaims that she's a fan of the Kansas City Chiefs.

'And that must be Lady Lois Letterman,' I murmur. 'Time to get out and say hi, people.'

Marina pulls a fresh packet of gum from her jeans pocket and unpicks the foil seal, miffed that there will be no knight banging his rod on her windows today.

The tiny turquoise rainbow queen starts flapping both of her arms over her head.

'I think she's recognised us,' I say.

'That or she's trying to land a plane,' Artie says, watching her wide-eyed.

Marina laughs and I slide the driver's door back and jump out of Babs onto the gravel with a satisfying crunch. I raise a hand towards the turquoise jumping bean as I round the front of Babs and join the others in the warm early July sunshine.

'She looks like a manic smurf,' Marina shoots out of the corner of her mouth as she glides effortlessly over the uneven gravel in her beloved skyscraper heels, whilst I link arms with her to stop myself from stumbling even though I'm in my regular uniform of Converse. I let her go as we reach the safety of the sweeping stone steps and I glance across and flick an encouraging wink at Artie. He grins back, a slash of sunshine over his perpetually anxious eyes.

He's coming out of his shell a little more every day and I'm enjoying watching him unpack his personality in front of us. I don't think he even realises that he's funny or that he's smart, because no one besides his parents ever took the time to see beyond the awkward long-limbed boy in the thick glasses.

'That van is a riot!' Lois hoots, stilling her crazy arm motions as we come to a standstill on the top step. Close up, she looks like a bit of a nut. I don't mean she looks crazy, I mean she reminds me of an actual nut. A walnut, to be precise, in that her skin is deep-beige tan and criss-crossed over with fine wrinkles in all directions. She has been crazy-paved by too much exposure to sunlight, but nonetheless she exudes an almost child-like energy and excitement. Her skin says seventy and her behaviour says seven and, in actual fact, I know that she is mid-fifties. I know this because I researched her because, as I already said, I am a badass businesswoman. Or because Glenda Jackson gave me a file with all of the details. Thanks to the file, I also know that Lois is Oklahoma born and bred, as is her husband Barty, three years her senior.

'Melody?' she says, looking uncertainly at Marina, who in turn nudges me forward sharply enough for me to almost stumble into Lois. I smile, wide and professional, as I thrust my hand out and, at the same time, I flick my other elbow back into Marina's ribs in retaliation. I don't think Lois notices our minor girl fight; she's too busy arching her eyebrows at the fact that I'm the boss rather than the much slicker, more put-together Marina.

'I'm Melody Bittersweet,' I announce at the same time as Artie and Marina both say, 'She's Melody.' Have they never seen Spartacus? My stretched smile is hurting my face, so I plough on. 'I'm guessing you must be Mrs Letterman?'

Her bright-blue eyes twinkle with trouble. 'Aw, call me Lolo, honey, everyone does. Or Lady Lolo, as Barty has decided to call me!' She cackles loudly, amused by her own grandiose. 'What gave me away? The accent? The American tan?'

I'm tempted to say I've seen her photo clipped neatly into the file Glenda prepared, but I just nod and look enthusiastic. 'All of those things. It's so great to meet you.'

'What a place!' Marina steps up beside me, all smiles, her arms spread wide to indicate the castle.

Lois laughs with obvious delight. 'Isn't it? You buy a castle on the Internet and, trust me, you have your fears that you're gonna roll up and find a pile of rubble.' She lowers her voice and leans in conspiratorially. 'I mean, who does that, right? Only crazy Americans!'

We all nod and then shake our heads at the same time, confused. *Is it a test?* I can feel myself getting hot and flustered even though I'm only wearing a skinny pink T-shirt. I've deliberately erred away from my usual wardrobe of character or statement T-shirts to meet our prospective customers, because you never know who you might offend with Frankie Says Relax emblazoned across your bajongos. No one needs to know that I'm wearing my Wonder Woman knickers under my jeans. That's strictly between me and Lestat, the only male to lay eyes on me undressed in recent times.

'This is Marina Malone and Artie Elliott,' I say, introducing my motley crew.

'Lady Lolo. I feel as if I should curtsy!' Marina says, holding her hand out.

'Aw, honey, there's really no need!' Lois flaps, but all the same she doesn't take Marina's hand and her wide eyes and expectant toothy smile say, 'Go on then, English girl. Drop for me on the steps of my castle.'

Marina flicks me a look that says: 'must I?' and I respond with a bland smile that very clearly says: 'why yes, you absolutely must.'

I can barely contain my snort as I watch her daintily grip the edges of her imaginary tutu between her fingers and thumbs and bend her knees outwards like a frog. Lady Lolo looks taken aback, that big, flashy smile faltering.

'Where I come from, a lady always keeps her knees together, honey,' she sniffs and Marina shoots me a WTF glance.

'I'm so interested to see inside the castle,' I pipe up, shiny-eyed and enthusiastic. 'I don't know how you don't get lost in a place this size.'

'Oh I do, honey, all the time,' Lolo breezes. 'I've got a pretty impressive holler for a tiny thing though.' She stops suddenly and throws her head back, then lets out a blood-curdling scream. 'BARTY!'

She snaps her mouth shut and then starts to count him out with her fingers like a boxing referee, clearly amused with herself. We all watch her, slack-mouthed and transfixed, and she doesn't get past six before a tall, mahogany-tanned guy with a shock of white hair barrels out of the door and screeches to a halt beside her, his hands on his knees as he pants for air.

He's as robustly built as his wife is fragile, and dressed as if he's about to play tennis, except his build suggests he's more a spectator than a player. It isn't that he's fat; he's just tall and rangy with a gut that demonstrates he enjoys the good life.

'Barty, will you come look at this! Our ghostbusters have arrived in the most fabulous little van,' Lolo coos, laying her hand on her husband's bent back and completely ignoring the fact that he looks as if he might have a heart attack any minute.

'Did you need to yell out quite like that, honey?'

She looks surprised. 'You guys, this is Lord Bartholomew Letterman the first, otherwise known as plain old Barty to the likes of you and me.' Lois raises her hand to her mouth so she can speak confidentially to us, even though she speaks more than loud enough for her husband to plainly hear. 'Although I have other names I call him, depending on the circumstances, if you see where I'm heading with that. If he's in my good books I might call him my big sweet turkey cock.' She leans towards me. 'I won't tell you what I call him in the bedroom, but it rhymes with King Kong with a big dong. Oh wait, that *is* what I call him. Don't tell him I told you that.' She cackles and bats her hand, even though we are all perfectly aware that he heard, because she whisper-shouted it loud enough for the gateman to know their bedroom habits, let alone us.

For a second we all lapse into silence and Lois and Barty just kind of look at us with their big, expectant smiles, almost as if they're waiting for us to invite them into our castle rather than vice versa.

'Shall we?' I nod politely towards the open doors, deliberately leaving my question open-ended for Lois or Barty to pick up the baton. It does the trick, shaking them out of their King Kong with a big dong reveries and back to the matters at hand.

'Of course! Come on in, honey.' Lolo extends her arm expansively towards the entrance for us to go on ahead of her, and I shoot Marina and Artie a quick 'stay with me' look before I lead them inside the castle.

Oh my God. It's an actual castle. I mean, I knew it was from the outside, but inside it's the real deal. We're in a wide, dark-panelled vestibule and a grand reception hall lies to the left-hand side and a formal library to the right. The floorboards creak with age and atmosphere and a suit of armour stands stoic in one corner. Marina's heels clatter against the wood and I feel her fingers twist into the back of my T-shirt the way she does sometimes when she's unsure.

Lois ushers us sideways into the grand reception hall, where all three of us take a moment to gaze around in silent wonder. It's huge and double height and all of the mahogany-panelled walls are rich with carvings and inlaid glass-fronted display cases. Chandeliers hang from the raftered ceilings and there's a huge, luminous oil painting in pride of place over the broad, heavily lintelled fireplace. The room has been sympathetically furnished to allow for modern comforts; two deep, wood-trimmed sofas face each other across an oversized coffee table set on an oriental rug and the wooden shutters have been pinned back from the walk-in bay windows to allow sunlight to stream through and dapple the room. I'm pretty sure that you could fit my entire flat in this room. It's breathtaking.

'Oh goody. More badly dressed gawkers.'

No one takes any notice, because no one except for me can see or hear the woman staring at us moodily from beside the fireplace. I don't reply to her, because she doesn't realise that I know she's there and I haven't yet sussed how Lord and Lady Letterman feel about the whole ghost issue.

I try to look her way casually, as if I'm just checking out the fascinating architectural details, but it's incredibly hard not to stare because she's a dead ringer for Sophia Loren in her heyday. She's spectacular; all the more so because she is dressed in a cap-sleeved ivory leotard that flares at her hips with a filmy net under-layer that appears to be made from boned parachute silk. She's svelte but curvaceous, and she obviously knew how to accentuate her assets when she was alive given the way the encrusted neckline and skinny belt of her leotard glitter with delicate, eye-catching rhinestones.

I deduce from the nude pink ballet slippers laced around her well-turned ankles that she was a performer of some variety, and her lustrous midnight black hair is set into rippling, chin-length finger waves. From the neck up she's a decadent, carefree flapper and then a taut, lithe performer from the shoulders down; a potent combination I'm finding hard to look away from. So much so that it takes a sharp jab in the ribs from Marina to alert me to the fact that Lois and Barty are both staring at me, expectant once again. They must have said something, but I'm totally clueless. I flick my eyes nervously at Marina and try to relay a silent SOS and, thankfully, she picks up on my help-me cue and fans her face with her hand as she blows her fringe out of her eyes.

'I think it might be too warm for coffee. Something cold, maybe?'

Ah, so we're still on the formalities.

'Just water would be great, thank you,' I murmur. 'Or maybe you could give us a tour of the place and explain how we can help you as we go?'

I'm keen to have the ghostbuster conversation out of earshot of foxy-leotard girl; I'd rather introduce myself to ghosts in a less-confrontational way if possible. You ghost, me ghosthunter is never an easy conversation to have.

Barty bounds forward, practically rubbing his hands together, and Lois rolls her eyes.

'You might regret asking for a tour,' she mutters. 'I hope you've got your walking shoes on.'

She glances at my feet, then raises her eyebrows at Marina's skyscraper heels. Marina shrugs, thoroughly unconcerned.

'Trust me; there isn't a thing you can do in those that I can't do in these.' She waggles her ankle delicately and nods towards Lois's neon green running shoes.

She isn't lying. On our last case, she used her stilettos to pick a lock and whack an attacker; they're practically on the payroll.

Lois crosses to the window and furls herself delicately into an armchair. 'I'll wait on here for y'all, I've taken this tour pretty often now,' she smiles, waving us away with a flutter of her glittering rings.

I notice the way the woman beside the fireplace rolls her eyes, as if this is not unusual behaviour on Lois's part. I'm beginning to suspect that beneath that turquoise velour workout gear beats the heart of a closet couch potato. Don't get me wrong; I'm on her team. I was always the last to be picked for netball at school, mostly because I am openly rubbish at anything that involves coordination and speed.

'As you can see,' Barty says, already walking tall and directing our attention with his big tanned hands. He turns us to look towards the library on the opposite side of the entrance hall. 'This, folks, is the library.'

Okay. So Barty likes to state the obvious. There's probably a thousand books lining the walls, all leather-bound and clearly antique. I ignore the slow clap from the ghost ballerina in the other room and focus my attention instead on an elderly couple playing some sort of card game at a small table. Their clothes and hairstyles place them around the 1920s and they exude wealth and permanence, as if they belong here. They probably do, given that they must have died quite a few decades previously and are peacefully ignoring us and enjoying their game. Based on my research of the castle so far, I'd hazard a guess that they must be members of the Shilling family, the clan who'd been in possession of Maplemead for centuries up to the recent sale. I tune them out and try to keep my concentration on Barty.

'To be honest with y'all, Lois and I haven't yet pulled a book out of those shelves. We've been kept kind of busy, you know?'

Artie shakes his head, gawking around. 'My mum would go mental if she saw this. She loves history and old stuff.'

'You should bring her over, Mr…'

'I'm Artie.' Artie sticks his hand out. 'Artie Elliott.'

He's been known as Artie since Marina christened him with his first-ever nickname a few weeks back. I don't miss the shimmer of pride in his voice as he announces himself now.

'Artie…' Barty ruminates on it. 'Kind of like King Arthur, right?'

For a second Artie stares at him blankly. 'My mom has a round table,' he says, eventually.

'A round dining table,' Barty says, nodding with a slow smile of appreciation. 'You're a sharp one, Artie Elliott. I can see we're going to get on. You're the boss, right?'

He turns away and starts to walk away down the hall and Artie turns his big, troubled eyes towards me. Artie isn't the boss of anything. He was bullied out of school, is smother-mothered at home and he's fourth out of four in the pecking order at the agency. There's me, Marina is my wing woman, and Glenda Jackson is Glenda Jackson. Quite frankly, she might be the actual boss. If she tells me so, I'm not going to argue. The only thing Artie is conceivably the boss of is Lestat and making coffee, not necessarily in that order.

'Er, Mr Letterman,' he pipes up as we file along the panelled, narrowing corridor.

'Hmm?' Barty turns, but his attention is immediately snagged by a carved stone inlaid into the wall behind my head.

'See this? It was laid here by the first Lord Shilling, the dude who originally had the castle built.'

We all dutifully inspect the stone and then Marina leans in and peers closely at it.

'Randy sods back then, weren't they?'

Artie tips his head to the side as he studies it and then looks away quick smart from the image of the lord taking his lady in no uncertain terms from behind. Poor Artie. Only a week or two back he was subjected to the sight of an octogenarian vagina. It's been a baptism of fire and, to his credit, he's taken to it like a duck to water.

He clears his throat before he speaks up. 'I'm not the boss, actually, Lord Letterman. Melody is.'

Artie nods towards me and Marina and she, in turn, jerks her thumbs in my direction as if Barty really should have known better.

'You guys sure have some cool names.' Barty smiles genially. He glances towards me for a split second, dismisses me and focuses his attention on Marina. This is something that has happened lots of times over the years, mainly because Marina is jaw-droppingly gorgeous and I'm more of an acquired taste.

Don't get me wrong, I have my charms. I inherited my dad's round, dark eyes, the exact shade of early morning espresso brewed in a backstreet Italian coffee house. I know this because my mother tells me every so often. Rome was one of the few trips she got to experience with my dad and, back then, she marvelled at how the deep chestnut-brown brew was a perfect Dulux match with his eyes. When I was a child my gran used to call me her perfect pocket peach, because I'm pint-sized and I have a classic peaches and cream complexion, not to mention that a certain rock pool-eyed reporter recently told me that the need to have wild sex with me is keeping him awake at night.

So yeah, I'm not without my charms or low on self-confidence, but Marina… she's a visual feast. Tall and foxy, all curves and teeth and Sicilian drama. She knows how to work it too. Never seen in public without her heels and her fire engine red lippy, Marina doesn't buy jeans unless it looks as if someone applied them with a spray gun.

'And you are?'

Marina watches him shrewdly. 'Marina Malone. As in the ocean.'

'A beautiful tropical reef,' Barty schmoozes.

She nods, laughs lightly, in a way the uninitiated might take as friendly. 'Just when you thought it was safe to go into the water.' She sweetens the unmistakable *Jaws* tagline with a perfect smile, but her warning is clear.

'Then you must be Melody.' Barty turns to me, adding, 'As in a song.'

He breaks into a few bars of 'Unchained Melody' and I fix my smile because I've only heard that joke about a million times in my life already. After a few tumbleweed seconds he dries up and shrugs, then turns to push open a broad, heavy door to his left.

'Get a load of this.' He inclines his head for us to go inside, so I lead the way. *Holy frickin' moly.* I feel as if I am Hermione Granger walking into an enchanted Hogwarts ball. Our collective jaws hit the floor as we come to a standstill and gaze, awestruck, around the vast ballroom. Now, I'm not a girl given to soppy movies or romance novels, that's Marina's bag but, oh my God, where are all the princes? I can't dance to save my life, but right this second I want a dashing hero in full military dress and sash to appear and formally request my next dance. I could waltz. How hard can it be?

It really is the prettiest of rooms. The walls are the same pale blue as fragile song-thrush eggshells with frescos of waist-height summer flowers detailed in a pastel palate of pinks, yellow, mint and lavender. It feels as if we have walked into a wild meadow so lush and perfect that I can almost smell the honeysuckle, so unexpected that I can almost hear bird song.

It reminds me of a movie that Marina made me endure once, one where animated bluebirds land on the heroine and do all of her cleaning for her while she prances around and warbles a happy song. See what I mean about Marina? She's nails and then she's cotton candy.

'I feel like Cinder-fuckin'-rella,' she mutters under her breath, thankfully loud enough for only me to hear.

'We're thinking of throwing a welcome party, try out the space for size,' Barty says.

I badly want to come to that party.

'Fancy dress?' Marina asks, hopefully.

Barty begins to explain some of the room's fascinating history, including how the beautiful frescoes were commissioned as a wedding gift from Lord Alistair Shilling for his bride Eleanor, but my attention is pulled instantly away from him and towards the extraordinary man who has just materialised through the wall at the far end of the room.

He strides towards us like a matador, and I'm surprised that no one else can hear the staccato click of his heels as they hit the well-polished parquet. He's scowling, a full, dark simmer of an expression that gives him a monobrow and sends a shiver down my spine. You know those black and white yesteryear posters for strong men at the circus? The ones with a stocky, handsome man with greased back hair, a twiddly moustache and a stripy vest? He looks as if he just stepped out of one of those because he's furious that someone stole his dumbbell. He's closer now, and I have to admit he's quite a looker. Brooding and charismatic, he marches right on up to Barty and halts, banging his heel hard against the floor for emphasis even though no one can hear him. His trousers are skin-tight, leggings almost and, okay I admit it, his extremely defined package caught my eye. Don't judge me. I'm in a dry spell and the man is clearly hung like an elephant.

'I wish you to leave! You and that awful little woman, go now and leave us alone!'

He is properly squared up to Barty, fists clenched, while Barty is completely oblivious and giving us too much information about the restoration of the no-less-than-four whopping ballroom chandeliers. Artie is, at least, attempting to interject pertinent questions while Marina half-heartedly nods whilst probably imagining herself disco dancing dressed as Rizzo from Grease.

The ghost must know that Barty cannot hear his rage, yet still he continues, waving his fist sometimes. It's difficult to follow the fast, angry flow of his words as English is clearly not his first language; going on the scant visual and audio clues, I'd say he was probably Mediterranean? Italian, Spanish, Portuguese?

I wonder if his beautiful lady is the bombshell from beside the fireplace in the lounge. They sure would have made a striking couple in their heyday. I'm getting a performers' vibe from them both and I'm left in no doubt at all when a second, taller, equally furious man bursts through the wall; his scarlet red coat with brass buttons and black and white striped trousers leave me in no doubt as to his profession. This guy is every inch the ringmaster, right down to his mirror-polished shoes and his equally shiny brass-handled whip.

'You've gone too far this time, Dynamo!' he bellows and then he cracks his whip down as hard as he can on the floor with a terrifying snap. His eyes flash bright with fury and then he opens his mouth and shouts again.

'Goliath! KILL!'

CHAPTER THREE

'Goliath! KILL!'

I swing frantically around at the ringmaster's bellowed instruction and my feet start to run as an involuntary yell bubbles up in my throat.

'LION!' I shout, already making for the open ballroom door. 'Run!'

I don't stop running until I've belted through the castle's narrow passageways and made it safely back outside into the sunshine. I can barely breathe and my heart is banging so hard against my ribs that I'm almost certain I'm going to die. Marina and Artie barrel out a few steps behind me and she lays her hand flat on my back as I bend double, winded.

'I've never seen you like that before,' she says, perplexed. 'You know there wasn't a real live lion in there, right?'

'He looked bloody real to me,' I manage, wiping damp beads of sweat from my brow. The rational side of my brain knows it was a ghost lion and couldn't have actually harmed me but, you know what? He was still one heck of a shock, because I don't see ghosts as wishy-washy phantoms. I see them as living flesh and blood or fur and teeth and claws and, five minutes ago, my eyes were telling me there was a high likelihood of being mauled to death by a bloody great big beast of a lion.

I've been to the zoo plenty and I've watched lions prowl the plains of Africa with David Attenborough but, sweet baby Jesus, that's nothing like unexpectedly coming across one in an almost-empty ballroom. You know how intense a nightmare feels even though you know it can't really hurt you? That's how I feel about Goliath.

'Melody?' Marina's giving me a look like she thinks I'm crazy, which I don't often get from her – everyone else, maybe, but not her.

I try to slow my breathing. Now I'm outside, I'm clearly not in mortal danger. And I wasn't before. And I won't be when I meet the lion again. I have to get my act together – make like my gran would if she found herself in this situation. Or my mother. They're both pretty kickass and, given that they can see ghosts too, they're the closest thing I've got when it comes to role models.

'I really wish I didn't have to go back in there,' I say, hating the obvious shake still in my voice.

'You don't have to do anything you don't want to,' Marina soothes, instantly on my side.

'Maybe the ghosts will come out here and talk to you instead if you ask them politely?' Artie suggests, trying admirably to salvage the case from the jaws of collapse.

From what I've seen of the ghosts inhabiting Maplemead Castle so far, I highly doubt they're going to stroll out on the steps and accept their fate. There's a hot-tempered Italian trapeze artist, a beautiful, silk leotard-clad acrobat and a haughty ringmaster with a killer pussycat for a pet. Clearly circus performers when they were alive, death doesn't seem to have robbed them of their love of performing for an audience, even one they don't think can see them.

I sit down on the top step and take a few deep, calming breaths. It's peaceful out here; there is an air of calm and serene grandeur.

'Water, honey?' Lois appears behind me with a glass of iced water and I accept it with a small, apologetic smile. I'm over my attack of the vapours now and am starting to feel ever so slightly foolish. What kind of a badass businesswoman am I if I run around like a five-year-old girl shouting LION? I must have looked like a complete wacko. I gulp the water down gratefully and then get to my feet and wipe my clammy hands surreptitiously on the backside of my jeans.

'Lois, I'm so sorry,' I say. 'I never normally behave like that, I promise you.'

'She really doesn't.' Marina jumps to back me up. 'She's usually the coolest cat on the block.'

I shudder at the mention of cats, and Artie nods then shakes his head, unsure of the correct head gesture to offer support.

'Am I going crazy, or did you just say "lion"?' Lois frowns.

I shudder and nod. 'So far I've spotted five human ghosts and then, er, the lion. It just caught me off guard for a second, that's all. From what I can see, they're members of some kind of circus.'

Lois genuflects. 'You saw five ghosts in there already? Oh my gaaard! Barty, get out here!'

How can she be more disconcerted by the human ghosts than the lion? Barty appears in the doorway a few seconds later, winding up a telephone conversation.

'Interesting,' he says, still looking thoughtfully at the receiver in his hand as he clicks to end the call. 'That was a TV company. Have you guys ever heard of anyone called Leo Dark?'

Just when I thought my day couldn't get any worse. Artie winces and looks at Marina, who lets out a low-frequency growl.

I shrug, non-committal. 'We've come across each other, yeah.' I cringe at my own euphemism, because we *have* come across each other in the past, usually in the back of his car.

Leo and I have a complicated history, but if you wanted to sum it up, you might say that we were friends, then lovers, and then he dumped me when he thought he was going to be the nation's favourite ghosthunter on morning TV.

I guess you might call us frenemies these days. I'm mostly over him but, every now and then, there's that old sizzle and it confuses the hell out of me. Marina, however, cannot stand the sight of him; even the mention of his name is enough to send her a tiny bit feral. It's that loyalty gene again; he pushes her kill buttons.

'Say no. Whatever Leo Dark wants, say no,' she says.

'He's coming over to see us tomorrow with his producer,' Barty says. 'They mentioned a weekly feature on TV. Imagine that!'

Lois's ecstatic face tells me straight up that she's a media whore. This is not going to end well. Leo is going to swashbuckle his way in here tomorrow and bewitch the Lettermans with his glossy black waves and promises of stardom that he cannot keep. There's nothing for it; I need to get this job back on track and show them that I'm their woman.

'Can you just excuse me for one tiny minute?' I say. 'I left my phone in the van and I'm expecting a call. Be right back.'

Marina shoots me a quizzical look, because she knows full well that my phone is dead on my desk back in the office. I smile brightly and ignore her completely, then turn and make a quick dash across the gravel towards Babs. Throwing myself inside, I lie across the seat out of sight and whack the glovebox hard. It pops open obligingly; Babs is a good-time girl, she appreciates a firm hand. I reach inside and pull out my beloved magic-8 ball, clutching it to my chest for a second with my eyes screwed tight.

'Should I go back inside the castle right now, even though there's a ghost lion in there who almost made me pee my pants ten minutes ago?' I whisper, knowing the answer in my heart already. I turn the ball over once and peer into the window to receive its wisdom.

It is decidedly so.

'I know,' I say, sighing heavily. 'You're right, as always.' I push the ball back into the glovebox and slam it shut, pull up my metaphorical big girl pants and slither back out on to the gravel, running my hands over my hair to smooth it as I jog back up the steps.

'Sorry about that. All sorted.' I rub my hands together in a way I hope suggests that I'm chomping at the bit to get on with the job. 'Let's get back inside and finish that tour, shall we, Barty? We'd only just got started.'

The Lettermans exchange glances as he clears his throat then looks at his watch. 'Actually, honey, I've got a tennis lesson in a few minutes. I guess I should run…' He tails off and looks to Lois to take over the conversation.

'We're just not sure this is gonna work out, darlin',' she says, in a kind but steely way.

I'm stricken. This is only our second job and I've blown it within fifteen minutes of getting here. I feel the weight of failure press down heavily on my shoulders and I'm one hundred percent furious with myself for acting like a batshit crazy fool instead of the level-headed, cool, calm lady-boss I want the world to think I am.

'Wait, please. It was just the lion…' I mutter and then clear my throat and turn my voice up from mumble to clear. 'I'll go back in now and I won't turn a hair. I see ghosts all of the time. This isn't my first rodeo, Lois; I can get this done quickly and thoroughly.'

'I've known Melody for over twenty years and I've never seen her react badly to a ghost before,' Marina says, stoic beside me. 'She's usually as cool as a cucumber.' She stops and then starts again on the same breath. 'No, cooler than that. She's ice.'

Artie half raises his hand as if he's in the classroom and doesn't actually want the teacher to see him. 'I haven't worked for Melody for very long, but I think the same. She's an icy cucumber.'

Marina flicks sharp eyes towards him and he shrugs and grimaces helplessly. He's doing his best.

Barty moves alongside Lois and slings his arm casually over her narrow shoulders and suddenly they don't seem quite as fabulously friendly and welcoming. In fact, I think they're subtly barricading the door. I decide to make a tactical withdrawal.

'Well, it was terrific to meet you both.' I glance up at the castle facade. 'It sure is a fascinating old place.' I shoot them a warm, sincere smile. 'Why don't we head back to the office and research what we've found so far and maybe I could give you a call in a day or two? No obligation, of course.'

I watch them consider my words. I've deliberately left them without any polite option but to agree and let us leave, and they have the good manners to nod and make positive noises as I lead Marina and Artie down the steps and across the gravel to Babs.

We pile in and all three of us raise a hand of farewell as Barty and Lois wave us off with fixed, cold smiles.

'I'm sorry,' I start as soon as we're safely back over the moat and on regular roads again. 'I totally blew that.'

'You didn't,' Marina lies. 'It could have happened to anyone.'

We all know that's not true. The buck stops with me, and I acted like a startled goat. A goat who'd just spotted a lion and didn't fancy being its dinner. There is only one thing keeping the flame of hope alive in my head right now.

'You know, Leo's nan had this really evil cat when he was a kid, some huge thing that would most probably be illegal these days,' I say, flinging a right at the lights back towards Chapelwick. 'It took a chunk out of his leg. Left him with a scar he still bears and a pathological fear of cats. Even kittens make him sweat.'

Marina and Artie digest the implications of this nugget of information and start to nod in slow unison and a tiny smile curves my lips as I start to hum 'In the Jungle' under my breath.

As we come to a halt outside Artie's mum's house, he reaches for his lunchbox from behind the bench seat and climbs down onto the pavement.

'Does your mum really have a round dining table?' Marina asks as he opens the latch on the garden gate.

He grins and shakes his head and she laughs softly as we belch off back towards the main road in a cloud of exhaust fumes.

* * *

It's closing-up time when I get home and I'm hot, bothered and miserable. Not especially in the mood for my own company, I bypass the stairs up to my front door and head into the apartment my mother shares with my gran at the front of the building. We're a pretty fortunate bunch to have had this place in our family for generations; it's big enough for me to live separately from them but still stay close, which is a good thing most of the time. My mother feeds my addiction to sugar; she's my pancake dealer. They're crazy, but they're my crazies, and they see the dead people too, which makes them comforting for me to be around. Blithe Spirits is just about the only place I can truly relax and let my guard down, the only place where I'm not set apart from everyone else by my ability. Or my disability, as it feels like sometimes.

I push their ever-unlocked door open and step inside Mum's farmhouse-style kitchen and the familiar scents and sounds are like a soft blanket around my shoulders. Lestat is snoozing in the pillowy bed my mother insists she found in a jumble shop despite the fact that I know full well she bought it for him from an online pampered pooch store.

She looks up from reading the newspaper as I come in, sliding her glasses down her long nose and rolling her shoulders.

'I see Fletcher Gunn is at it again,' she grumbles, tapping the article with the arm of her glasses.

I look over her shoulder at the paper, my mouth suddenly dry. 'What's that?'

She sweeps her bone-straight silver hair to one side of her neck and sniffs with disdain. 'Casting aspersions on our industry, as usual. He's obviously picked up on that Maplemead Castle story you're involved with.' Oh crappola. 'They mentioned it on the local radio news this morning too.'

'They did?' My heart sinks even further into my Converse. I'd foolishly been hoping to keep the story on the down-low,

but it seems that Barty and Lois have wasted no time in court-
ing the publicity machine in order to boost the castle's profile.
I skim-read Fletch's article; it's a pretty standard story about
the castle having changed hands over the net, accompanied
by a smiley photo of the new lord and lady toasting their new
home with frothing champagne flutes on the grand front steps
of Maplemead.

Fletch goes on to detail their ambitious business plans to rent
the place out as a film location and how 'their first prospective
Hollywood A-lister is refusing to come near the place because
she's read the place is notorious for its ghosts'. I can almost hear
his scathing laugh as I read his derision-loaded words.

Word on the street is that the movie is slated to be the
blockbuster horror of the next summer. Rumours of the
location being haunted will no doubt be welcomed by the
production company and the local whackos, regardless of
the fact that they are completely baseless and even more
fictitious than the movie itself.

In other words, it's a load of baloney and bunkum made up
to create interest. I've no doubt that that is exactly what Fletch
thinks; if he cannot see something with his own eyes, then he
doesn't believe it exists. It's a fundamental difference between
us and not one we could ever agree to disagree on and try to get
along. Needless to say, my mum and gran can't abide him; he
never misses a chance to take pot-shots at us and our industry in
the press. Take just now: by local whackos, I know he is referring
to us and Leo.

'He'll never change,' I say tonelessly, because I don't want to
talk to my mother about Fletch. She's got a sixth sense for sniffing
out stuff I don't want her to know and I definitely don't want
her to know that Fletcher Gunn sometimes makes me go weak

at the knees. It's difficult; he gets under my skin by calling me a whacko in print and then, when he's in front of me, he gets under my skin with his clever words and his hot eyes. It's unsettling.

Lestat makes a grumble-grunt as he sits up, his eyes trained on the door. A moment later it opens, and in wafts my gran, or Dicey Bittersweet, as she's known to the world in general. Lestat has a crush on my gran. It's probably because she eats like a bird, passing most of her food to him under the table in order to leave room for her never-ending supply of champagne.

'Cup of tea?' I ask, crossing the room to kiss her perfectly rouged cheek. She glances at her Swarovski-encrusted watch and narrows her eyes.

'It's after five, darling. Let's have a glass of bubbly instead.'

The time is actually irrelevant; it's all theatre. She drinks champagne from a teacup before five in the afternoon and then in a crystal glass afterwards. You'd think it might addle her brain or weaken her heart, yet it seems only to increase her joie de vivre and couldn't-care-less attitude.

To be completely fair to her, she doesn't actually drink a great deal and she never touches anything other than champagne. It's just part of her glamorous persona to sip fizz as sparkly as her personality. She really ought to have been born French. She's a force of nature almost entirely sustained by champagne, daytime American soaps and the occasional prawn.

I go to decline, but then why would I? I've had a crapshoot of a day, and an evening of repeats on TV with a flatulent pug lies ahead of me.

'Have either of you ever come across any unusual animal ghosts?' I ask as I pour us all a glass of fizz from the refrigerator. It's a big double-door American job, with one shelf almost entirely taken up with corked green bottles. The rest is filled with all sorts of weird and wonderful ingredients, because my mother is what you might call an experimental cook. Don't get me wrong, she's often spectacularly good, but it's always fraught with that edge of danger, because she doesn't take criticism very well.

Mum takes her glass from me and screws her nose up as she considers my question. 'Believe it or not, I dealt with a ghost tortoise once. He'd been passed around in the same family for over a century and when he finally died no one realised for a good two years.'

It's a sad story, but not what I'm looking for. 'Neither of you have ever met a lion, then?'

They both look startled. 'A lion?' Mum says.

I nod. 'As in fully grown male, angry and roaming around Maplemead Castle this afternoon.'

'That's highly unusual,' Gran says, frowning. 'What's a lion doing getting stuck in a castle?'

'By the looks of the human ghosts I saw today, I'd say there must have been a circus there of some kind. The lion appeared to be with the ringmaster.'

'Fascinating,' Mum says, keen-eyed as she always is when it comes to learning something new. 'What did they have to say for themselves?'

I hang my head. 'I didn't get as far as speaking to them.'

Lestat shuffles underneath the legs of the table and plonks his backside down on my foot, a very belated hello.

Gran pats my hand. 'What's the matter, darling?'

My mother leans back on her chair, snags a cupcake from the work surface and pushes it into my fingers.

'Is it a man?' She makes a bad job of keeping the note of hope in her voice. She's desperate for me to find my Prince Charming.

I shake my head, my pride in my boots. 'I made a right bloody fool of myself today.'

'Oh, Melody, we all do that sometimes.' Gran squeezes my fingers. 'Look at me crashing around on TV a few weeks ago in that suit of armour.'

On the scale of making a fool of yourself, that was actually quite impressive. A misguided attempt to help me win our first case that went spectacularly wrong, this is actually the first time Gran has expressed anything other than righteous indignation about the fact that her meddling almost cost Leo his TV job and landed me with so much huge humble pie to eat that I almost threw up on my own shoes. He still holds it over me.

'Not like this,' I sniff. 'Barty Letterman was giving us a guided tour of the castle and the lion appeared out of nowhere and scared the pants off me. He just looked so…' I pause and make shapes with my hands to demonstrate the size of him, finishing off by clawing the air and a silent little roar. 'He looked real.'

They both watch me through narrowed eyes.

'Did you run?'

I lay my forehead on the table at my mother's quiet question. 'Yes. As if the building was on fire. Whilst yelling "lion" at the top of my voice and waving my arms as if I was having a fit.'

They lapse into thoughtful silence, so I carry on mumbling into the pine table top until my mother speaks with unexpected authority.

'Enough. Lift your head up this instant, Melody Bittersweet.'

I'm surprised enough to do as I'm told.

'I don't need to remind you about my reservations when you decided to open the agency,' she says.

She's right. She was vehemently set against it.

'But you went right ahead and did it anyway, because you have Bittersweet backbone, Melody. Haven't I…' She pauses and looks at Gran. 'Haven't *we* taught you more tenacity than this? Since when did a Bittersweet woman roll over and give up at the first sign of trouble?'

Her words seep slowly into my brain. All three of us around this table have lived our lives outside the lines because of our gift and it's made us independent and strong. I might not have my gran's devil-may-care attitude down pat yet and I'll probably never achieve my mother's Zen-like calmness, but I'm Melody goddamn Bittersweet and I don't give up on something that matters this easily.

'So you reacted in a way that you aren't especially pleased with. You can't change that, but you can put it behind you and come back fighting.'

'They sort of fired me,' I say.

'Pah,' my gran puffs. 'They just don't know you well enough yet, darling.' She takes a glug of fizz. 'To know a Bittersweet woman is to love her. It's our gift and our curse, Melody.'

I laugh a little bit, despite my mood. Gran has the supreme confidence of a twenty-one-year-old beauty queen and I love her for it.

My mother presses on. 'Being defeatist will get you nowhere except defeated.'

I split the last of the champagne between our three glasses and lift mine in a silent, resolute toast. They clink theirs against mine and I nod. Message received. Hauling Lestat out from beneath the table, I kiss my mother and Gran farewell and head on up the stairs to my flat.

En route, I text Marina and Artie.

Bring your A-games in the morning, people. We're going back to Maplemead and, tomorrow, we play to win.

CHAPTER FOUR

It's as well that I have good people in my life, because I also have Lestat.

I was awake researching Maplemead until the small hours, yet still here he is, bang on six a.m., with his pudgy face shoved into mine and his tongue up my left nostril.

'Get off me.' I use both hands to lift him bodily, because he doesn't respond well to polite requests. He doesn't respond to requests at all, actually; he's quite like Babs in that a firm, hands-on approach works best.

'Is there any chance I could train you to make coffee?' I ask him as he sits pointedly watching me shuffle my feet into my slippers and pull on the mint green floor-sweeping silk robe my gran gave me last birthday. It is fabulously, absolutely not my style, yet somehow Gran got it spot on. Whenever I slip my arms into it and knot the belt I expect someone to shout 'Action!' or hand me an Oscar and today is a day when I need all of the good old gumption I can muster.

A couple of minutes later I follow Lestat's furry ass down the stairs barefoot with my mug of coffee in my hands, as I do every morning now he's in my life. I don't walk him, exactly. We walk together and although I'd categorically deny it, I've come to enjoy it the tiniest bit as a quiet ten minutes to marshal my thoughts for the day ahead.

My entrance door is at the back of Blithe Spirits and it opens onto a broad cobbled cartway that runs between us and our neighbours, so I'm safe to swan up and down there in my robe without someone calling the local nuthouse to see if anyone with a Greta Garbo complex has escaped.

Lestat is on form this morning, prancing closer to the street end of the alley than usual. I shout-whisper his name quietly, mindful of my folks and everyone else who lives on Chapelwick High Street. Too quietly, obviously, because a ginger cat sticks its inquisitive nose into the alleyway and hisses at him and he hares off, impressively fast for one with such little legs and a fat ass.

Bumholes. I put my coffee down by the wall and dash barefoot across the cool cobblestones. At the end, I poke my head out and glance left along the High Street.

'I believe this belongs to you, ghostbuster.'

I close my eyes for a second, because I know that voice. Fletcher Gunn, otherwise known as the last man on earth I should go anywhere near, otherwise known as the man who sometimes presses me against the wall in alleyways and kisses me delirious. I can't explain it; he's a cynical hack and my family nemesis and I want to hate him, but every now and then he looks at me with those heartbreaker green eyes of his and makes my brain feel as if there's a unicorn cantering around inside it farting glitter. He's mostly thunder and lightning, but every now and then he dazzles me like sunlight in my eyes on the hottest day of summer.

When I turn the other way to look at Fletch, I find him holding a jiggling, ecstatic-looking Lestat.

'A girl could be forgiven for thinking you were hanging around here just to see her, Fletcher Gunn.' I'm horribly aware that I sound like a bad Mae West impersonator.

He deposits Lestat in the alleyway and I bend down and give my mutt a swift double-handed shove towards the safety of home again.

Fletch laughs as if my words were preposterous and his eyes drop as he registers what I'm wearing.

'I wouldn't have imagined you in something so…' He wafts his hand around towards my robe. 'Girly.'

My hackles shoot up. Just because I've carefully cultivated my edgy look, it doesn't mean I want to be predictable. 'I can wear girly stuff if I like. And, anyway, I'd rather you didn't imagine me in clothes at all, thank you very much.' Okay, so that came out all kinds of wrong.

'You want me to think about you naked?' he asks, amused. 'Because I do that a lot. And I'm usually naked too and we…'

'Stop!' I hold up a hand and roll my eyes. 'I haven't had breakfast yet. You'll put me off my muffin.'

His eyes glitter. 'I'm losing sleep over your muffins, ghostbuster.'

I hate it when he does this, because I love it when he does this. 'Scintillating as this is, could you go now? I've got work to do, places to go, people to see.'

He nods and shrugs one shoulder. 'Maplemead?'

I don't reply, but I don't need to.

He winks. 'Thought so.'

'You're too cocky, Fletcher Gunn. You'll trip yourself up one of these days.'

Fletch grins wide. 'Would you like me to crack the obvious big cock joke?'

Fucking hell! Why does this always happen round him? So far I've told him I want him to think about me naked and that I think his cock is big enough to trip him over.

I go to turn away and then I stop short because Fletch has pulled a key from his pocket and slotted it into a door between the shops.

He's well aware that I'm watching him and he glances my way casually.

'What?' he asks, shrugging nonchalantly.

Please, lord, tell me Fletcher Gunn isn't my new neighbour. The grotty little flat over the sandwich shop a couple of doors down has been to rent for a while now. I flick my eyes up and see with a sinking feeling that the To Let sign has gone.

'Nothing,' I mutter, refusing to give him the satisfaction of seeing me riled. 'Did you know that the previous tenant died in there?' I ask, glancing towards the dirty upstairs flat window. 'No one found him for at least three weeks. There's probably bits of him rotted into the floorboards.'

He just laughs and shakes his head. 'That would be the same guy who I met in the pub last week to sign the lease. The one who's alive and well and gone travelling in Asia for a year.'

I shrug. 'Similar story.'

He winks as he opens his door. 'See you around, neighbour.'

I'm in the office just after nine o'clock and you'd be forgiven for thinking that there was a kids' birthday party about to kick off. The coffee table is groaning with Krispy Kreme doughnuts courtesy of Marina, three catering-size bags of fun-size chocolate bars from Glenda and the tallest chocolate cake I've ever laid eyes on, which has been made especially for me by Artie's mum. I'm overwhelmed, both by their kindness and by the need to plant my face into the cake and eat my way down to the plate.

I make us all a drink and Glenda picks up the box of doughnuts to make space for me to set the tray down. When I reach out to take it from her she grips onto it tighter than I'd expected. For a second it really is like being at a kids' party; someone stopped the music and we both want to be the one who wins the parcel. In most situations, I'd defer to Glenda Jackson, but this is a sugar-related incident on the back of a very bad twenty-four hours, so I hold on tight. She narrows her eyes before she concedes and allows me to take the box from her hands before we tear the box in two, spill the doughnuts and everyone loses.

'Okay,' I say, with renewed, sugar-induced valour. 'Today, we're heading back to Maplemead and this time we're going to make them want us so badly that they're going to beg us to stay rather than ordering us off the property.'

Glenda's eyebrows rise, her pen poised over the meetings book. 'They ordered you off the property?'

'Well, no, of course not,' I say, throwing in a carefree little laugh and rolling my eyes as if I've wildly exaggerated when in fact it is pretty much what happened. I badly want Glenda to think I'm up to this job I've created for myself.

'They formed a human barricade across the door,' Artie says, lifting Lestat onto his lap to share his doughnut.

Turncoat! I bristle with hubris. 'You say barricade, I say…' Then I pause, because what the hell can I say instead of 'barricade'? 'Banana. I say banana.'

They all regard me as if I am a nutter. Even the damn dog.

Marina laughs. 'Banana?'

Oh, right. So she's on #teammockmelody this morning too. Why did I have to go and say banana?

'Yes, banana. As in banana split or Bananaman.'

'Even you must struggle to get excited about Bananaman.'

She's right, of course. Bananaman has never yet featured in any of my superhero fantasies.

'Can we please get back to the point?' I say, as if my errant employees are distracting me rather than the other way around.

Artie raises his hand. 'You could have said barracuda. It would have made more sense.'

If his mother hadn't supplied me with an orgasm-inducing chocolate cake I'd be thinking about sacking him about now, mostly because he's right. You say barricade, I say barracuda would have made a whole lot more sense than banana. I swallow a few times as I stare at him and, from the side of my mouth, I inform Glenda that none of this conversation is to be recorded in the book.

'Anyway,' I say, rising above their level. 'Today we go back and we're going to show them why they need us.'

'And how, exactly, do you plan to do this?' Glenda asks and they all look at me for the answers.

'We stage a triple-pronged attack,' I say because I planned all of this in the shower this morning. 'I'm prong one. I see the ghosts and this time I don't freak out.' I look at Marina. 'You're prong two. Leo will have his fembots with him. You need to go uber-fembot.'

Leo's twin assistants bring a whole new meaning to the word 'stalker'. They seem to serve little operational purpose beside making him look as if he has a permanent entourage; they chiefly feed his growing army of Twitter fans with shots of him looking moodily into the distance and updates of what he had for his lunch. The one thing they are is eye-catching though and, when it comes to men, they have instant kerb appeal.

'You want me to out-fembot the fembots?'

I nod. 'Marina, you're foxier, smarter and funnier than the pair of them put together. You bring the charm and the sizzle but you also bring brains and actual skills to the party. Wow them, help me make them realise that we're the team they need on the job.'

She's nodded throughout my pep talk and she picks up a pen and grins.

'Sign me up.'

'Artie, you're prong three, aka our secret weapon. Leo might have his TV slot and his production team, but he doesn't have an Artie Elliott.'

Now who's regretting that barracuda quip? He looks massively alarmed. I let him stew for a second before I carry on.

'Remember our last job? You were crucial in helping us gain the Scarboroughs' trust. People relate to you in a different way to me and Marina.'

Marina curls her lip but doesn't argue because she knows I'm right.

'They do?' Artie frowns.

I nod. 'You bring the respectable. Just be the best version of you, Artie, that's all I need.'

He looks mollified. Proud, even.

'I'll do as much as I can to be their ghosthunter of choice and you guys show them that my backup team are their dream team. Teamwork makes the dream work.'

Glenda fires me a look over her glasses and Marina chokes on her second mini Mars Bar.

'Have you been reading that 1970s handbook of hippydip-pyshite management phrases again?'

I shake my head and mutter, 'Late-night re-runs of *The Office*.'

I watch Glenda switch to her red pen and write *Melody is strongly advised not to draw management advice from David Brent* in the meetings book.

I take a glug of coffee, then stand up and half yell, 'Action!', whilst making clapperboard motions with my forearms.

Glenda makes a point of ruling off the meeting and closing the book, Marina salutes me, and Artie lowers Lestat to the floor and sits up to attention. Oh my God. I think I'm actually turning into the boss and it's got hardly anything at all to do with David Brent.

Approaching Maplemead is slightly less clean-cut. We were expected yesterday; this time round we're going to be slightly less-welcome arrivals. The gatesman scowls as he recognises us and grants us access over the bridge, barking an order to park at the back of the forecourt out of the way. It's not as if I'm turning up with armfuls of new information; last night's research so far hasn't unearthed any new details about a juicy secret circus from the past who all died there mysteriously. There must have been, though; they're stuck haunting the castle because it was presumably the scene of their demise. My first thought was that there might have been a fire for them all to lose their lives together, but I can't find any reference to a notable fire at the castle. It's perplexing; I've pretty much established the timeline of the castle's inhabitants and I'd love to get into the library again to speak to the card-playing couple. Going on their appearance and the approximate era of their clothes, I've pinned them down as most probably Lord Alistair Shilling and his wife Eleanor. They seem to be the least volatile of the castle's ghostly inhabitants and therefore a good place to start investigations.

I'm disheartened but not surprised to see that we're not the only visitors at Maplemead today. I'd hoped we might get there before Leo and wow Lois and Barty with our renewed enthusiasm and pronginess, but his flashy black 4X4 is already parked in pride of place at the bottom of the stone steps.

'We could always just wait until he's gone?' Marina suggests.

'We could, if we're cowards,' I say, reasonably. 'Are we cowards?'

Marina nudges Artie beside her on the double passenger bench seat.

'Glovebox.'

He obliges, smacking it with his knee twice until it flies open.

'Magic-8.' Marina nods for him to grab it and it's handed along the front of the van until it reaches me.

I roll my eyes, turn the ball once and ask my question out loud with a sigh.

'Should we be brave and go inside before Leo leaves?'

Yes.

I hold it out for them to see. Even though the odds are the same for all of the random answers to pop up, it's statistically quite rare for the single yes to appear. Unlike some of the other answers, it's unequivocal; not open to interpretation or ambiguity. I pass the ball silently back along the line to Artie, who places it back in the glove compartment and closes it. He isn't violent enough with it and it drops open again and Marina reaches over and slams it hard.

'For the record, I wasn't being a coward,' she grumbles, using the camera on her phone as a mirror to re-apply her lipstick because the one in Babs's sun visor is missing. 'I just don't trust myself not to murder his fembots and I don't want a stretch in prison.' She slides her phone back into her bra and jerks her head at Artie.

'Get out, prong three.'

He rolls the door back and unfolds his gangly limbs out onto the Tarmac, then turns back to offer Marina a hand down.

'Who do you think I am, your gran?' she scolds, harsher than she'd normally be because she's still in a grump.

'The drive's uneven,' he says, abashed, looking at her electric-blue high heels. 'I thought you might like some help.'

I cough like I'm dying to alert Artie to the fact that Marina isn't the only damsel who might require a hand. Chivalry and Converse clearly don't go together though, because he just scratches his head and then digs in his pocket.

'Polo?' he says, offering the pack to me.

'What am I, a Shetland pony?' I bark and then jump down from the driver's side without assistance and round the van to join them.

Marina sticks a fresh stick of peppermint gum in her mouth and pops another button on her blouse. It's the same colour as her shoes, a stark contrast against her loose dark curls and fresh slick of red-for-danger lipstick.

'Eyes on my face at all times, prong three,' she says, shooting Artie a dark look.

'Message received, prong two,' he says, looking awkwardly at the sky. 'You definitely don't look like my gran now.'

Marina's shoulders start to shake with suppressed laughter. 'I'd rather be your gran than a midget horse,' she says and I find I'm laughing too. Artie is laughing with us too out of sheer relief at having not upset either of us really.

'Sorry, Artie,' I mumble, poking the gravel with the toe of my Converse.

He glances at Marina, who flicks her eyes to the skies and then apologises too.

We start to walk and, beside me, Marina uncharacteristically stumbles on the uneven stones. She turns to Artie on her other side and crooks her elbow.

'Well, take my arm then,' she demands and he falters for a second and then does as he's told.

'I'll never understand women,' he mumbles as she hangs onto him until we get to the safety of the steps.

'Don't even try,' someone advises him, and I wish I had a Taser in my pocket because, for the second time today, it's Fletcher sodding Gunn.

CHAPTER FIVE

Fletch has just strolled out onto the shaded portico with a tall iced glass of water in his hand and his laughing eyes tell me that he's having a whale of a time. If there's one thing Fletch finds more amusing than taking the piss out of me, it's taking the piss out of Leo Dark, so he's found himself in a BOGOF situation here and is a proverbial pig in muck.

'Are you stuck on my knicker elastic?' I snark.

'In my dreams.' He shoots me a lazy wink. 'News just seems to follow you around, ghostbuster.'

'Or Leo's TV company tipped you off about the possibility of a story,' Marina says, rolling her eyes.

'And they weren't wrong,' he says, unruffled. 'It's turning into quite the party.' He makes a half-hearted attempt to not look down Marina's cleavage. 'Dark and his blow-up dolls have only been here for ten minutes and he's already passed out on the sofa.'

'Leo's passed out?' I say, mildly concerned despite myself.

Fletch nods. 'Stone-cold out.' He flips the page of his pocket book and consults it. 'Last seen being spritzed with cold water and muttering for his mummy. Derek Acorah would have been proud.'

I have a sneaking suspicion that Leo has just encountered Goliath. I may not have covered myself in glory yesterday, but at least I stayed conscious; maybe Leo's reaction will help strengthen my case. Is that mercenary? Probably, but was it mercenary of him to drop me faster than a hand grenade when the bright lights beckoned? Yes. Yes it was and I dropped my loyalty to Leo at the exact same moment. Put it this way; if there was a fire and I had to choose between saving Leo Dark or my beloved Converse collection, I'd have a tough time deciding.

So I perk up a bit, ignore the Acorah reference and politely ask Fletch to move aside.

'Haul ass, hack. You're in my way.'

Did I just come over all Clint Eastwood? Should I draw an imaginary pistol and point it in his smug face?

He takes a long, slow drink and my eyes are drawn to the movement of his throat. Half of me wants to slit it, the other half wants to lick it. If I ever meet Mother Nature in a back alley, I'm going to pin her to the wall and shout 'WHY? Why did you do this to me? Why does my body insist that it wants to tangle up the sheets with Fletcher Gunn when my head knows it's highly likely to end up with one of us needing to emigrate or do prison time?' Opposites doesn't even begin to cover what we are. He's the ocean and I can't swim a length. Or else I can, but not without feeling like I'm going to drown, which actually is how I feel most of the time around Fletch. Completely and utterly out of my depth.

He looks as if he's going to laugh, but then shrugs and clears away from the doors to sit on the stone balustrade around the porch, leaning back against one of the columns with his leg bent. He reminds me of a black and white poster from a teenage girl's bedroom wall, Jimmy Dean without a cigarette. I can feel him watching me and it takes superhuman effort to not turn back around and shove him right off that wall onto the gravel below.

Inside, there's a commotion. Leo is indeed prone on the sofa with the fembots offering him first aid, which seems to consist mostly of fluttery strokes of his cheeks and blowing on him with tiny little puffs of breath. Lois is also there, spritzing the air around him with a fine mist of water. It's like watching *Sleeping Beauty* in reverse, until he mumbles at Lois to kindly quit with the water because it's playing havoc with his curls.

My sympathy cup does not runneth over. I'm not saying he's faking it, but he's definitely milking it. No one has even noticed we've come into the lofty entrance hall yet, so I clear my throat and speak.

'Er, is everything okay in here?'

You'd be surprised how quickly Leo makes a full recovery at the sound of my voice. He bounds up from the sofa, all damp-shirted, with his hair in disarray. I'm reminded that I've seen him look that way in far more intimate situations than this and I squash the thought like an ant under the toe of my shoe.

'Melody, darlin'!' Lois squawks, more pleased to see me than I'd expected.

On that, Barty appears from the hallway. He looks a little put out to see us, until Marina steps forward and leaves a lipstick kiss on his cheek.

'So good to see you again,' she vamps, branding him as her kill for the benefit of the fembots, who start to twitch. 'Barty, we feel just awful about not finishing the tour yesterday.'

I nod, even though he hasn't looked my way once. Marina glances towards Lois, including her, because she's too smart to alienate Lady Lolo in her mission to cut the fembots off at the knees.

Barty beams at Marina's cleavage. 'I guess I could spare the time to show you kids around some more.'

Leo's face is thunderous, so I turn away and look towards the library. Fleetingly, I catch a glimpse of the woman from beside the fireplace yesterday watching us keenly, but as soon as she appears she disappears again. Has she realised that I can see her? Or that Leo can, perhaps?

'Now, where did we get to?' Barty murmurs.

'The bit where Melody saw a lion in the ballroom and ran out of the castle screaming,' Artie inserts.

Jeez, does he *have* to be so friggin' literal?

'And what a beautiful ballroom it is,' I enthuse, while sending Artie a slow, simmering look that suggests he might like to button his lip.

'You saw it too then,' Leo breathes, raking his hands through his flattened curls to fluff them up again. 'The lion.'

'She didn't pass out though,' Marina quips. Her lipstick smile says light-hearted banter, but her kholed eyes say don't mess with us.

'It was the heat,' one of the fembots murmurs, standing to the left of Leo.

'Overwhelmed him.' On his right, the other nods.

Leo shakes them off. 'I better come on that tour.'

I bristle with annoyance. How can I stop this from happening? He strides towards me, turning to Nikki and Vikki as they make to follow him. 'Stay here and keep Lois company, ladies,' he says and their heads twitch as if their batteries are short-circuiting.

Fletch picks his moment to saunter back inside and places his empty glass down on the table.

'I'm sure I can keep the ladies company while you guys go and do your spooky mcdooky thing,' he schmoozes, crossing the rug to sit down in the centre of the sofa. The twins press their reset buttons and perch either side of him and I don't know who's more wound up, me or Leo. It's turning into a stage farce where everyone is pissed with everyone else and smiling inanely to cover their rage.

Leo would probably like to kill Fletch in his sleep; they never miss the chance to take pot shots at each other, Fletch's usually in the press for all to see. The fact that I've been involved with both of them only makes matters worse.

Fletch would probably choose to kill Leo while he was awake so he could enjoy the fear in his eyes.

Lois is probably disturbed by the fact that Barty is having a mid-life crisis over Marina's cleavage.

The fembots are shooting me daggers because they know Leo and I have history and they're threatened by it.

And then there's me, spitting tacks because Leo has tagged himself onto our tour and spitting feathers because Fletch has stretched his arms out along the back of the sofa with a fembot cosied up on either side of him. He shoots me a mocking grin and I surreptitiously give him the finger as I turn to follow Barty and everyone else into the depths of the castle.

'No TV crew with you today then?' I snip at Leo as we bring up the rear.

'They wanted to be here, but I put them off.'

He's deliberately offhand, as if he calls all the shots with the production company, which likely means they cancelled because they had bigger fish to fry. 'Thought I should come and see the place on my own first, get a feel for it.'

'Lucky really, if you passed out from the heat,' I say with faux sympathy.

'Lion,' Marina fake coughs, unsubtle.

Barty is oblivious to the tit for tat going on behind him because Artie is doing a sterling job of asking all the right questions about the castle. I tune in, listening to him enquire about the castle's spell as a nunnery and then again about its time as a convalescence home for injured soldiers after the Great War. I get a small inner glow that he's remembered the information from my initial case research notes. I'll give it to them both. Prong two and three are keeping up their ends of the bargain. It's up to me now, prong one, to keep up mine and be the best ghostbuster in town. I don't want to tell Leo anything he doesn't already know, but by the same token I don't want him to have anything over me.

'It's fairly obvious that you've come across the lion, then,' I say, tucking my hair behind my ears. 'Bit of a shocker, isn't he?'

'You could say that,' he mutters.

'And his… companion?' I say, plying him for information.

'You mean the ringmaster,' Leo says. So he's sussed the circus connection, same as me then.

Barty leads us into a small side chapel. 'This was a private chapel for family use only,' he whispers. 'Devout, from what I can gather.'

I'm listening, but I'm distracted as a ghostly pair of nuns drift to the front and kneel before the stained-glass window. They don't speak to each other or look our way; they seem caught up in their prayers and contemplation. I slant my eyes towards Leo and find him watching the ghosts too.

'This place is full of them, isn't it?' I whisper.

He nods. 'I dread to think what we might find in the dungeons,' he mutters.

'Shackles?' I say.

He looks at me oddly for a second, as if I suggested something kinky. I cast my mind back to when we were together, but there was none of that stuff; I'm pretty sure I'd remember. The closest he came to tying me up was when the sleeves of my coat got caught in the car door when we were making out on the back seat; he didn't notice that I was stuck and I didn't like to mention it while he had his tongue in my ear because it seemed like the height of bad manners. If I'm honest, the edge of danger because he might break my arms was a bit of a turn on.

Barty leads us from the tiny chapel and down some steps into the vast quarry-tiled kitchens, still very much the working heart of the castle. He introduces us firstly to Marilyn, the castle's cook and housekeeper, and then to her young assistant, Belinda, or Hells Bells as he refers to her for reasons that go unexplained. They're making pastry to top what looks like a huge meat pie on the scrubbed table and I'm struck by how this scene must have played out here countless times over the centuries. For now the kitchen is a ghost-free zone, so we turn to troop back up the steps.

As we file past the table where the cooks are at work, I notice Belinda push a plate of chocolate-coated biscuits towards Artie with a shy smile. He turns as red as Marina's lipstick, glances over his shoulder to check if she might have meant the smile for someone else, then takes one of the offered biscuits with a whisper of thanks. Behind him, I look hopefully at Belinda, but she drags the plate of sugar goodness back slowly towards her and glowers at me from under her thick copper fringe. Hells bloody Bells indeed.

Barty takes us up the sweeping, portrait-lined grand central staircase and proceeds to show us so many cavernous bedrooms that I lose count.

The Shilling family must have had a bob or two; the interior design is quite lavish and in keeping with the age of the place and it's packed to the rafters with heavy, dark pieces and huge framed oil paintings. There're more rugs here than in Afghanistan and enough chandeliers to illuminate one of the smaller Greek islands.

So far, so quiet.

'Did you come across any other human ghosts this morning?' I ask Leo.

'I glimpsed a woman, but she disappeared in a blink,' he says. 'And the ringmaster, obviously. You?'

I shouldn't have asked him, because now I have to show my cards or tell an outright lie, which I'm not great at. I sort of shrug and mumble 'same', but I feel a bit crappy, so I add, 'and another guy, fleetingly.'

We're back at the top of the staircase and Leo looks down and says, 'This one, by any chance?'

The furious ghost from yesterday stalks towards us and squares up to Barty, just as he did yesterday.

'Go now! Why don't you people ever listen to me?' He prods at Barty's gut. Barty doesn't know, yet still he brushes an absent hand over his belly as if soothing an itch. The ghost throws his arms in the air and yells in anguish. 'You wouldn't have dared ignore Dino the Dynamo when he was alive!'

I cannot help but think how much he sounds like Gino D'Campo; I'm very glad this man isn't armed with a kitchen knife. As it is, he uses all of his might to shove a large gilt-framed painting on the wall to make his presence felt and he's remarkably successful. Moving inanimate objects is a skill that takes some mastering for ghosts, and one that shows that this one can be quite powerful when he needs to be. Barty is lucky that ghosts can't transfer the same skills to humans, because I'm certain Dino would have shoved him down the stairs by now.

Barty, Marina and Artie all jump back in surprise and then swing to look at Leo and me for an explanation as to why the painting is all jangling and skewed.

'Ghost,' I confirm quietly and Dino the Dynamo pauses, obviously shocked. 'Yes, I can see you,' I say, addressing him directly for the first time.

'So can I,' Leo butts in, keen not to let me get ahead.

Dino stares at us. 'And these?' He flicks his hand towards the others and I shake my head.

'Just us.'

'But you're living peoples, yes?' He steps forward and tries to touch my arm, but his hand passes straight through. He snatches it back again with an angry sigh and I try not to shudder because I'm not fond of the barely there chill his touch left behind in my bones.

'Bit of an odd way to phrase it but, yes, we're alive,' Leo says.

Dino narrows his dark eyes at Leo. 'Are you laughing at Dino the Dynamo?'

Great. Leo's managed to alienate the first ghost we talk to within three sentences. I shake my head and speak in a low, soothing voice.

'Of course not. We'd love to talk to you though, if you wouldn't mind?'

Dino points viciously at Barty. 'Tell this florid-faced bastardo to get out of this house before nightfall or I push him down the stairs!'

His eyes blaze with challenge and I almost feel sorry for him, because we both know that it's an empty threat. All the same, I look at the others and smile diplomatically.

'Do you think we could have a moment here, please? We'll be back downstairs in a few minutes.'

Marina and Artie don't question me. Barty, on the other hand, frowns sharply. 'I'll stick around. It's my ghost.'

It's enough to make Dino throw his head back, howl and go on another picture-whacking rampage. 'The Dynamo belongs to no one!'

'It really would be better if you waited downstairs with the others,' Leo insists. Barty clearly takes instruction more easily from a man, because he huffs and stomps off after Marina and Artie.

'Why you not tell him?' Dino demands.

'Why are you so angry with him?' I counter his question with one of my own.

Dino spits on the floor. 'He is a hog. They come here and now they want to bring all kinds of odd people into our home and turn it into the movies? Britannia, she speak of nothing else since they arrive!'

'Britannia is your…?' I prompt.

He slams his hand over his heart and is about to answer when the lady herself appears beside him, ravishingly pretty as she lays a hand on his arm.

'Don't, Dino,' she says and it is as if neither Leo nor I exist for the dynamic one. He has eyes only for Britannia.

'I'm his trapeze partner.' She directs her words towards us. Her answer surprises me. She's clearly much more than just a workmate, for him at least.

'And she's my wife,' someone else says and I brace myself because the ringmaster is strutting up the staircase and, once again, he isn't alone.

'It isn't real,' I whisper to myself and to reassure Leo, because he's just stiffened beside me at the sight of the lion and we both need to keep our shit together. 'It can't hurt us.'

It looks bloody real though and it takes everything I have not to bolt. 'Don't you bloody dare pass out again, Leo Dark, you'll fall down the stairs and die,' I mutter when he plasters himself against the wall as the lion advances towards us. I'm breathless, literally without any breath in my body, because he's level with me now and I'm not kidding when I say he's paused and is staring right at me. Oh dear God, dear God, oh shit. His velvet fur nose is twitching and I can't be sure but I think he's growling at me.

'He's not real. He can't hurt you,' Leo repeats my words over again, low and steady, and then he feels between us for my hand and grips it tight.

'Do you think you could possibly call your lion off please, sir?' I squeak, sounding like a terrified four-year-old girl. I close my eyes because the lion has inched nearer and he's baring his incredibly sharp, as big as my head, yellow teeth at me. I death-grip Leo's hand; please don't let any wee come out in my Batman pants. Superheroes don't take kindly to that kind of behaviour.

At last, when Goliath's face is no more than a hand span from mine, the ringmaster lays his hand flat on the lion's broad head and leans down to whisper something I can't quite catch into the animal's thick mane.

It seems to have the desired effect, because Goliath slowly closes his mouth and stops growling. I can still see his eyes though and what I see there is regret, regret that he doesn't get to have me for afternoon tea. That's the problem with animal ghosts; they mostly don't realise they're ghosts or that they can't hurt people. More benign animals don't realise that they can't feel a hand fuss them or a scratch behind the ears. It strikes me that I'd quite like to give Lestat's furry belly a tickle in that way that sends him gaga right now and it's enough to make me give myself a good shake and pull myself together. Sentimental thoughts and Lestat are two things that cannot go together in my head.

'Thank you,' I mutter as the huge cat appears to lose interest in us and lies down on the landing to wash his paws. I pass my hand over my forehead and find it clammy. 'I'm Melody Bittersweet and this is Leo Dark.'

'Bohemia Lovell.' The ringmaster inclines his head formally as he introduces himself. He's tall and elegantly put together, with fine, sandy hair and serious grey eyes. He holds himself with the air of an aristocrat, which is a stark contrast to Dino's Latin heat and fire. There is a bomb-like quality to The Dynamo; he simmers and seethes and seems always on the edge of a lethal outburst.

'Britannia Lovell.' The woman steps forward, her arms folded across her chest as if in defiance. Her tone is distinctly careless, as is the tiny, almost invisible, superior sneer on her face. I get it. She's in parachute silk and I'm in jeans, her hair is set in perfect ripples and mine is scraped back in a messy bun. She's a bird of paradise and right now I'm a sparrow, but I'm breathing and she's not so I still wouldn't trade places. Bohemia. Britannia. Is there anything about these people that isn't theatrical?

She tips her head to one side and smiles up at Leo. 'Do you see me too, Leo Dark?'

I glance up at him too and I recognise the expression on his face as he nods and swallows hard, because he used to look at me that way. *Don't be so completely and utterly bloody stupid, Leo Dark. She's been dead for almost a hundred years.*

'We should go,' Dino declares, glaring hard at Britannia. 'We have practice to do.' He doesn't even look our way before he vanishes.

Britannia smiles impishly at Leo. 'No rest for the wicked, and I'm very wicked indeed, Mr Dark.'

'Britannia…' her husband chides, holding her elbow. There's an edge to his tone, weariness, and I wonder about the dynamic of their marriage. I cannot imagine that this bird of paradise would have been easily caged; he must have grown accustomed to trying to clip her wings around other men. Even as a ghost, waves of sexual energy emanate from her; she must have been quite a force to be reckoned with when she was alive. Lock up your husbands or, in my case, I might need to lock up my ex-boyfriend for his own good.

Britannia lifts her fingers to her lips and kisses them lightly, then looks from Leo to her husband and back again, as if she's deciding which of them deserves her kiss. In the end she blows it towards Bohemia, then wiggles her fingers in farewell towards Leo with a delighted little laugh as she disappears. That woman is going to be hard bloody work.

The ringmaster shakes his head, his knowing, steely eyes on Leo. 'Don't even think those thoughts. She's dead, and she's mine.'

Leo blinks a few times, as if he's just come up for air after holding his breath under water. 'I wasn't thinking any thoughts.'

'You have no idea how many sacrifices I made to be with her, or how many blind eyes she asked me to turn over the years,' Bohemia says. It's much more revealing than I'd expected, a glimpse straight into the fractured heart of their marriage. I feel an unexpected pang of sympathy for him; being one side of an eternal love triangle must be incredibly tiring.

Behind him, the lion stirs and I cannot help but flinch.

'He killed five men before he came to me,' Bohemia tells us flatly, his eyes on the beast. His words do nothing to ease my fears, nor does the expression on his face when he looks our way.

'Don't come back here again.' His words are stark and ominous. Then he moves to stand behind his animal, lays his hand on its back and they both vanish into the air.

Leo and I don't speak for a moment, then we drop onto the stairs and sit side by side.

'That was intense,' he says, pushing his hands through his hair, his elbows on his knees. I don't know if he means the lion or Britannia Lovell. He had a strong reaction to both of them.

I'm a well-bought-up girl and I know when to use my manners, even if it is to someone who has caused me pain in the past.

'Thank you, for… you know.' I splay my hands and look at my fingers. 'The hand-holding thing.'

He laughs under his breath and brushes his fingers against mine, catching hold of them for a second. It's a flicker of the past, comforting because we are both coming down from our encounter with Goliath. It means nothing, or very little at least, but I don't pull away and at that exact moment Fletch appears at the bottom of the stairs and looks up at us.

His eyes take us in, the way we are sitting close together and holding hands. I pull away, confused, and he shakes his head and makes a sound in his throat, a whatever huff, an 'it means nothing to me who you mess around with' sound.

'You'll be glad to hear I'm off,' he says. I don't know whether he's speaking to Leo or to me; probably both of us.

I watch him slam out of the broad entrance doors and sigh.

'Tell me you're not involved with him,' Leo says quietly, even though he has absolutely no right to ask me.

'I don't think that's any of your business.' I get to my feet and push my hair out of my eyes.

'He's trouble,' Leo mutters.

'So were you,' I shoot back and instantly wish I hadn't.

Leo stands too and looks down at me, then shakes his head and takes off down the stairs.

I don't follow straightaway, and I definitely don't let any stray thoughts into my head about love triangles; new ones or centuries' old. I need this job, but this case, *this castle*, is already messing with my head. I reach into my back pocket and slick on some cherry lip-gloss for an emergency sugar fix, roll my shoulders, then head back downstairs.

I intend to join the others, but then a thought strikes me and I detour into the library in the hope of finding the elderly couple I'd seen playing cards in there yesterday. I'm in luck; they're there again, chatting and laughing quietly over their game, in a world of their own at the small table by the window. They don't pay me any attention; no doubt they're used to people milling around them without having a clue they're there.

I pretend to be interested in a book for a moment while I watch them out of the corner of my eye. I'd place them in their eighties or thereabouts. She exudes a quiet pearls-and-twinset glamour that speaks of a life well spent and he holds himself in the upright manner of a man who dedicated years to the armed forces. Lord Alistair Shilling, I think, and his wife Eleanor, for whom he had the frescoes in the ballroom painted as a romantic wedding gift.

Closing the book in my hands, I tuck the hair that's worked free of my bun behind my ears and walk slowly towards them. When they don't react, I move to stand right beside their table. Still nothing. Alright then. Walking behind the guy's chair, I survey his cards and then do the same to his wife.

'Don't play the ace, he's waiting for it,' I murmur in her ear and she jumps out of her skin. Or else she would have, if she had any.

'Goodness, dear!' She slaps her cards face down on the table and looks up at me as I come round to stand by the table again. 'You gave me the fright of my life there!'

Her husband gives me the once-over. 'Apologies for our rudeness,' he says. 'You looked like a breather.'

'A breather?' I murmur.

'It's our little name for the living, dear,' she says, recovering her composure.

'Oh, right. That's probably because I am one. A breather, I mean.'

He lays his cards face down, just as his wife had. I'm impressed; even when startled, these two don't show each other their hand.

'But you can see us? And talk to us?' he frowns. 'Did you hear that, Eleanor? This girl can see us and breathe at the same time.'

Eleanor; bingo. I was right.

'And hear us,' Eleanor murmurs, wide-eyed.

I get this sometimes. The dead are startled because I'm not dead too. It's the same way the living are creeped out by the fact I can see dead people; they usually lump me in with the undead, like zombies and vampires. You can imagine how popular I was at Christmas parties as a kid.

I wait a beat to let them take me in. Eleanor reaches out a hand slowly and pokes my forearm with one bony finger. We all watch her finger sink effortlessly through my flesh and she retracts it with a delicately disdainful look, as if she's just stuck her hand inside a raw chicken. I hold my smile in place, even though that's the second time this morning I've been ghost-prodded.

'I'm just a normal human who can see and talk to ghosts.'

'Why?' he asks, suspicious.

I shrug and steal a line from Lady Gaga. 'I was born this way.'

They don't know what to say to that and I pull out a chair. 'Mind if I sit?'

They shake their heads and watch me carefully as I lower myself into the chair, as warily as I watched Goliath earlier.

'Well, this is nice, dear. We don't get many visitors,' Eleanor says, polite and strained. I'm unsure what to say to that; she's been stuck here in this library playing cards for God knows how many years watching the breathers come and go around her without even knowing she's there. Thank goodness they have each other.

'*Any* visitors,' her husband corrects, still assessing me. 'Can't offer you a cup of tea, I'm afraid, young lady, on account of the fact that we're dead and the ruddy servants can't hear a word we say.'

I glance down and smile discreetly. An army officer in life and death too, given the way he barks his words and the brace of medals pinned to his blazer.

'Are you from the church?' Eleanor asks suddenly, her pale eyes clouding as her eyes rake my neck, presumably searching for a cross.

I pause. Why would she ask me that? I'm about as godly as my hairbrush.

'No, I'm afraid not.'

She smiles, her hand fluttering at her throat. 'Thank goodness for that. I thought for a moment that you'd come to exorcise us or whatever it is that those people do.'

Jeez, I hope she doesn't look out of the window and spot Babs. Not that I'm about to flick holy water around and start muttering incantations; my job here is to free trapped, disruptive spirits and these two seem to be neither of those things; I'm perfectly happy to leave them alone. If they promise to play nice, no one will even know they're here.

'So... may I call you Eleanor?' I ask and her face relaxes into a smile.

'Oh you must, my dear, you must. And this is my husband—'

'Lord Alistair Shilling,' he interrupts, straightening his shoulders as he introduces himself.

My night-owl Internet research is proving useful; I unearthed a family tree for the Shilling clan last night which is now printed off and Blu-tacked to the white board in the office. From what I can remember, Alistair Shilling was the last but one lord to live at Maplemead, not counting Barty Letterman.

'I can't tell you how interesting it is to be able to talk to a breather,' Eleanor says.

'Yes, I can imagine it must be tricky, just the two of you,' I murmur, nodding sympathetically as I let my words trail off.

'Oh, there isn't just us,' she says hurriedly. 'You'll no doubt meet my niece soon enough.'

'You mean Brittania?'

A wistful smile touches Eleanor's lips at the mention of Brittania's name. 'We didn't even know she was still here with us for all of those years after she… well, after it happened.'

I'm on red alert now, almost holding my breath because the sound of it seems incongruously loud in the quiet library. Come on, Lady Eleanor, I think, using the silence tactic to urge her to keep speaking and tell me something useful.

Her fingers worry the edge of her sleeve in a nervous way, but just as she seems about to speak Lord Shilling coughs and shakes his head, a tiny but noticeable signal to not spill any family secrets.

Perturbed, I change tack.

'She's very striking,' I say, admiringly.

'Like her mother,' Eleanor murmurs.

I wonder whether she means her own sister or Lord Shilling's, and I'm about to ask when both Lord and Lady Shilling's attention is snagged by something behind me. I turn and find Marina in the doorway.

'Just checking you haven't been eaten by the lion,' she says, taking in the way I'm sitting at the table and no doubt realising that I'm not alone. 'Glad to see you still have all of your limbs.' She hesitates and then wanders away again.

Lord Shilling pointedly picks up his playing cards and, after a pause, Lady Eleanor does the same.

'Bad show about that ace,' he mutters at me, a clear signal that we're done here as he tosses down a card.

'Come and visit us again if you'd like to,' Eleanor whispers as I stand up and I shoot her a tiny smile and leave them to their game.

I'm surprised to see Lois and Artie playing chess at a table in the main hall or, rather, Artie appears to be instructing Lois in the basics of the game. He looks up and beams at me when he realises that I'm there and his expression is pure joy. I don't know if he's teaching Lois to play chess as part of his prong three attack or if it's just a lucky break, but I don't think that the fembots could have brought that to the table. Speaking of Nikki and Vikki, they're clustered around Barty and Marina by the fireplace.

It's double unfortunate for them that Marina knows quite a lot about art and she's leading a lively discussion about the work of the artist who painted the portrait that hangs over the fireplace. Go, prong two, go. Leo has flopped down in an armchair, feigning interest whilst trying to do his hair in his reflection in the glass china cabinet beside his chair.

'Melody,' Lois calls, raising her glass, any lingering reticence towards me washed away by the gin in her tonic and Artie's easy companionship. Her call alerts the others to my arrival too, and they drift away from the fireplace.

'Y'all know each other pretty well, right?' Lois looks enquiringly from me to Leo, her eyes sparkling. I give the slightest of nods and Leo shrugs, neither of us willing to commit. 'Only I've been thinking how much better it'd be to have y'all work on these ghosts together, you know? Two heads are better than one, many hands make light work, and all that.'

Not when those heads and hands belong to Leo and me, I think darkly.

'There's really no need,' I say. 'It's sort of duplicating work.'

'And cost,' Leo throws in, clearly as horrified as I am by the idea of us working together.

Lois lets out a tinkly laugh and bats the air. 'Hang the expense. You guys are all such a hoot, we insist. Don't we, Barty, honey?'

She looks over at her husband and catches him gazing longingly down Marina's blouse. I don't think he even heard what his wife said. He looks caught out, like a naughty schoolboy and, as a result, he booms, 'Absolutely, darlin'!' in a robust way that brooks no argument.

I know what Lois is thinking. She wants the best of both worlds. That spot on the TV is too alluring to pass up, but I suspect she's realised that we're the better bet when it comes to actually getting the job done. Lois Letterman is a have-your-cake-and-eat-it kind of girl and right now she wants the entire Key Lime Pie, or whatever the equivalent is in Oklahoma.

I make a mental note to ask Lois about this another time, because someone who can educate me on new things about cake is a good thing, especially American cake, which has to be the top of the cake tree in anyone's book. Some people want to go to visit the States for Disneyland, some yearn to see New England in the fall. My overriding interest would be doing the USA Dessert Trail. Florida for its Key Lime Pie, New York for its cheesecake, Georgia for its oozy warm peach cobbler. Every state has something fabulous to offer on the pudding front and I'm more than ready to be the woman who taste tests them all and picks an overall winner.

Nikki and Vikki look from Leo to me as if they're watching tennis, while Lois bolts across to the corner of the room, picks up a mallet and whacks it against a huge brass gong on a stand near the wall. The sound is sudden and deafening, and Lois staggers backwards with the weight of the mallet still in her hands. The fembots cower with their hands over their ears as if a jumbo jet is passing over their heads and Artie looks dazed as Hells Bells, the cook's young assistant, appears in the doorway.

'You rang, m'lady?' she says breathlessly, wiping her hands on her apron.

Lois taps the glass face of her watch. 'Forty-six seconds,' she says, and the look of consternation on Hells Bells's face tells me forty-six is not a good number.

Lois looks at me, faux-pained. 'We're aiming for under thirty seconds. It's a work in progress.' She speaks with indulgence, and flicks her eyes in a 'you just can't get the staff' way that pisses me right off. I'd like to see her make it from the kitchen to the reception hall in less than a minute, this place is huge. She's clearly watched far too much *Downton Abbey* and this upstairs–downstairs gig has gone right to her head.

'Champagne all round please, Belinda. We're celebrating.'

Hells Bells smiles politely and starts to back out of the room. 'Very good.'

Lois stares at her and rolls her hand in the air, clearly waiting to hear more.

'Very good, m'lady.' Hells Bells fidgets with the lace collar of her dress and flickers a momentary glance at Artie before she darts from the room.

'I'm afraid we can't stay for celebrations, we've got another appointment in half an hour,' I say quickly, glancing at my watch-free wrist and nodding so hard that Marina and Artie start doing it too even though they know perfectly well that I'm lying. The last thing I feel like doing is celebrating the prospect of working with Leo.

'But you'll be back in the morning, right?' Lois's eyebrows knit together and her forehead lines up like a musical score. 'Because this needs doing pretty darn smart. The film crew are due in eight days and then, trust me, this place really *will* be a circus.'

'Not to mention the small fact that their precious star is refusing, point-blank, to even get on a plane unless it's certified spook free,' Barty adds. 'And if *she* won't come then the whole project is up the wazoola, along with our reputation and our business plans, most likely.'

Nothing like a good dose of emotional blackmail. My shoulders slump; these two sure know how to get what they want.

Leo looks like I feel, like a petulant child backed into a corner.

Marina sighs because she knows what needs to be said and that neither Leo nor I can find bring ourselves to utter it. Fixing her features into a toothpaste advert smile, she reaches out and shakes Lois firmly by the hand.

'We'll all be here, bright-eyed and bushy-tailed, one big happy ghostbusting family. You can count on us.'

Lois's brow smoothes out instantly and she sees us chirpily out onto the portico.

We smile and wave and the second we're over the drawbridge and back into reality I thump my forehead against the skinny black steering wheel.

'One big happy family?' I groan.

Marina fastens the button on her blouse and starts to laugh. 'Yeah. Like the Mansons.'

CHAPTER SIX

Back in my flat, I lie flat out on the sofa and idly wonder whether it would be too dramatic to kill myself. It'd save Leo's fembots a job; they gave me a look back at the castle that left me in no uncertain terms of their malicious thoughts. Lestat obviously thinks so, because he's just noisily shoved his food bowl all the way over to me from the kitchen with his flat face and is now clanking it against the floor in the same barely suppressed rage style often displayed by Marco Pierre White. He's not at all bothered when I roll from the sofa and scuttle to the kitchen on all fours; I'm going in the right direction so he's content. I briefly consider shoving my face in his kibble and chowing down just to piss him off, but when I drop my head he pauses and rolls his eyes back in his head to eyeball me and the message there is crystal clear: *Come any closer and you won't need to worry about killing yourself, because I'll sink my teeth into your soft throat and puncture you like a tyre, Bittersweet.*

I growl at him as I use the fridge door to pull myself up to standing. If he's refusing to share his kibble and I'm too pissed off to cook, there's only one thing for it. I don't even bother putting any shoes on. I just shuffle out of my flat, haul my sorry ass down the stairs, and amble through my mum's ever-open door.

It's unexpectedly noisy in there this evening. My mother and my gran are having a heated discussion, which in itself is unusual, and they both shut up and look shifty when I go in. I eye them as I pull out a seat at the dining table and collapse into it.

'What's going on here, then?' I ask. I direct my question at my mother because she is marginally the saner of the two. She doesn't answer, just glowers at me. Okay, we'll do this the hard way.

'Gran?' I say. She picks up her champagne glass and eyes me moodily over the rim and, for a second, I know how Saffy must feel in *Absolutely Fabulous*.

'This email came today,' Mum says, slapping a printout down on the table in front of me. 'From the *Shropshire Express*.'

The beginnings of unease stir in my gut. Fletch works for the *Shropshire Express*.

'They want to send a reporter to shadow us for a couple of days for an in-depth feature.'

'They do?' I skim-read the email and it does say pretty much exactly that. They produce a glossy quarterly pull-out on local businesses and as the next one is due out in autumn they're thinking of making a splash with Halloween features and ghost-related pieces. 'And you don't want to do it?'

'Our entire business is based on one-to-one consultations. Privacy is the cornerstone. You know that, Melody.'

I'm confused. 'So why the argument?'

Mum's eyes skitter away and then she opens one of the pine wall cupboards and extracts the waffle iron. 'Hungry?' she asks, already reaching for her mixing bowl. My mother makes waffles to die for. She turns to me with the maple syrup in her hands and she may as well have been swinging a fob watch for how mesmerised I am by it.

'Stop distracting her with sugar, Silvana.' Gran clicks her fingers at me. 'Melody, focus.'

I tear my eyes from the syrup. 'I don't see what the big deal is. If you don't want to do it, just say no.'

'Which will leave them free to make up as much rubbish and hocus-pocus as they like and we'll have no recourse because they offered us the chance to be fairly represented. Or they'll offer Leo Dark the opportunity instead and all of the precious publicity that could have come our way, *your way*, will go to him instead.'

Because my gran drinks champagne for breakfast and still sleeps with my grandpa's randy ghost even though he's been dead for twenty years, it's easy to forget that she's also been a businesswoman for over fifty years. She can see that this is something that needs to be done, but I understand my mother's reticence too. Their consultations are as confidential as a doctor's visit; how many patients would be comfortable with a reporter sitting in while they have their piles examined?

They're both looking at me as if they expect me to side with them. Mum pours batter into the waffle iron on the Aga and she may as well have said, 'don't bite the hand that feeds you'.

Gran narrows her eyes and then pulls a carton of fresh ruby red strawberries from the fridge and places them triumphantly on the table in front of me. She even goes so far as to flip the lid up and waft the sweet smell towards me with her hand.

This could get really interesting if I just sit here long enough. Who knows what they might offer me next? My empty stomach grumbles in appreciation at the exact same moment my brain short-circuits. Or else that's what must have happened, because that's the only feasible explanation for the words that leave my mouth next.

'We could offer to let them shadow me instead?'

Am I drunk? Has Gran slipped me a roofied strawberry? Bad, bad words, get back inside my head this minute! They don't though. They hang around in the air laughing at me while my mother and gran consider the new possibility.

'Well, I'd certainly rather Melody get the publicity than Leo Dark,' my mother says, opening the waffle iron with an expert hand. Within seconds she's slid the waffles onto a delicate china plate and served them up to me with a shake of cinnamon and icing sugar.

Gran nods. 'They'd find it harder to do a hatchet job on us if they meet Melody.' She smiles sweetly at me. 'To know you is to love you, darling.' She turns to my mother. 'Email them, Silvana. Tell them they can have access to our Bittersweet baby.'

'On the condition that under no circumstances do they send Fletcher Gunn,' my mother mutters darkly.

I'm not convinced that my gran is being one hundred percent genuine, in fact I think she just played me like a violin, but she passes me the can of squirty cream from the fridge when she tops up her champagne glass so I don't call her on it. I build a cream version of the alps on top of my waffles instead, and it's almost distraction enough to keep my mind off the fact that I've potentially just thrown myself into the path of Fletcher Gunn, and he's far more dangerous for my health than any sugar overload.

At half past nine the following morning, I find myself back outside the castle with Marina and Artie, jostling with Leo and the fembots to be the one who knocks on the door. We must look like the cast of some oddball movie. Leo is over six foot to my five three and he shoulders me to the side at the last minute as the door swings open and Lois greets us, dressed today in billowy white harem pants and a flamboyant rainbow silk turban fixed in place by a huge costume diamond. Huge dark glasses cover a good two-thirds of her face, as if she's had a night on the tiles and cannot bear to look into the sunlight.

'People, my people,' she croaks. 'Come in.'

I dodge around Leo and slide in in front of him. 'Are you alright, Lois?'

'Difficult night,' she murmurs, touching her turban with her fingertips. Barty appears, rolling a huge suitcase along the hall flagstones behind him.

'Are you going somewhere?' I ask, surprised.

'Only to the B&B in the village, darlin',' Lois says and when I catch Barty's eye he frowns and shakes his head to stop me delving deeper.

'I'm detecting a different vibe in here to yesterday.' Leo strokes the air with his palms like a stage medium. Everyone else probably thinks he's referring to ghostly vibes, but I know he means Lois and Barty because, so far today, the ghosts are conspicuous by their absence.

'The damn ghosts went crazy on us last night,' Lois mewls suddenly and she flops violently to the side. Marina lunges forward and catches her quick smart.

'Easy there, Lady L,' she says, guiding her down into the nearest chair.

I drop to my haunches and lay a hand on Lois's knee. 'What happened?'

She takes her sunglasses off and without her makeup she looks her age and then some. Her face is pinched and even her suntan doesn't stop her looking tired and drawn.

'They wouldn't give us a minute's peace,' she says, knotting her fingers in her lap. 'Everywhere we went in, they followed and threw things around. Broken glasses. Tipped-up chairs. Spilt drinks. Smashed photos. Poor Barty, one of them even took his dinner plate and tipped it up on his head, right there at the table while we were eating dinner.'

I look across at Barty, who nods ruefully. 'No way that spaghetti stain's ever comin' out.'

'Every time I poured myself a gin, they knocked it right over,' Lois says, shaking her head in distress. It's clear that the gin was the final straw. 'They obviously want us to leave, so that's what we're going to do.' There's drama to her delivery; I think it's just the kind of woman she is. Yesterday she was the hostess with the mostess, today she is the damsel in distress.

'You really don't need to do that,' Leo says, frowning. 'Or at least not until my camera crew arrive this afternoon.'

Trust him to have his TV show at the forefront of his mind.

'I can't possibly be filmed today,' Lois wails. 'I haven't slept in two days. My bags have bags.'

Leo kneels beside Lois's chair as if she's his grandmother in a care home. 'There, there,' he says, holding her other hand.

Who says that, really? No one, that's who. It's a good job he didn't go into medicine; his bedside manner would need some serious work.

'You look radiant, Lois,' he lies. 'The camera will love you and it'll make gripping footage if you can recount to them what you've just told us. You'll have everyone hooked and wanting to come and see this place for themselves.'

Oh, he's good. Flattery and the suggestion of extra press coverage. I don't have any such tools to tempt her with… or do I? I don't really want to go down the flattery line, but the press… just maybe.

'I have a bit of news that might cheer you up too,' I say.

'Are you leaving the country?' one of the fembots tinkles in the background. I take great satisfaction from the way Marina turns her head, slow and raptor-like, gives her the death stare and draws her finger across her neck in pure menace.

'The *Shropshire Express* want to shadow me at work for a couple of days for a big feature in their autumn supplement. The castle will feature heavily and we'll make sure they highlight the tourism aspect for you.'

Lois smiles bravely. 'That's great news, honey,' she says.

Leo doesn't seem as impressed though. 'Tell me this isn't just some thin ruse to spend more time with your boyfriend,' he sneers and I shoot icicles at him from my eyes. In my head they fly towards him pointy end first and stab him all over his smug, superior face.

Lois perks up. 'You're doing the hot patootie with the reporter guy?'

The hot patootie? I know Lois isn't from these parts, but I expect that's a phrase even native Oklahomans don't chuck around on a daily basis. You don't have to be a rocket scientist to get the gist though and I'm incensed.

'No, I'm absolutely not doing the hot patootie or anything else with Fletcher Gunn!' I say hotly and then I want to take one of those icicles and thrust it through my own heart because he's just walked in through the open castle door and heard every word. He's like a genie in reverse; he keeps popping up whenever I don't want him to. If I ever find the lamp he pops out of I'll personally take it to the nearest scrapyard and feed it into the jaws of the crusher.

'Did someone mention my name?' he drawls, smirking.

Artie nods. 'And something about jacket potatoes.'

Marina rolls her eyes and I close mine for a second to regroup. This morning is already spinning off plan so I refocus my attention on Lois and try to pull things back on track.

'Why don't you have a cup of tea and I'll go and see if I can talk to the ghosts? I'm sure there's no need for you to do anything as drastic as moving out.'

Leo is on his feet in a flash. 'I'll talk to them.'

Fletch laughs to himself, delighted, and pulls out his notebook. When everyone looks at him, he just glances up and waves us away. 'Don't mind me, folks. Just making notes.'

I seethe, but force myself to ignore him as Lois shakes her head and gets to her feet, gripping onto the fireplace for support.

'My mind is set,' she says, in a grim, determined way that Scarlett O'Hara would have been proud of. 'I will not stay in this castle another night until those ghosts are gone.' She looks across at her husband for moral support. 'Barty?'

He nods. 'Lois and I have booked into the B&B,' he says. 'And we'd appreciate it if you folks moved in for a few days while we're gone, be here around the clock until the job's well and truly done.'

I'm aware that my jaw is clenched almost tight enough to break my teeth. 'I can't stay here,' I say, because the last thing I want is to play house with Leo. 'I have a dog to look after.'

'So bring him,' Lois says, wiping out my only real excuse with a wave of her hand. My only other reasons; I love my own bed and I don't want to stay here with Leo because he's my dastardly ex-boyfriend don't sound very professional, do they?

'We'll pay you for the inconvenience, of course,' Barty says, and then he mentions a figure that's considerably more than double the fee I quoted, and one that any fledgling business would be crazy to knock back. I look towards Marina for guidance, but she shrugs helplessly back at me.

'I really couldn't stay over,' she says. 'I'm needed at home.'

I knew that already. Marina watches over her elderly nonno, grandpa to you and me, most evenings while her mum works, especially so at the moment with Nonna Malone back in Sicily.

I know without asking that staying here is out of the question for Artie, too. He keeps this job on the understanding that his mother thinks he works a desk job and, in any case, he needs to get home to tend to Pandora, his python. Somehow I don't think Lois would be so fast to invite him to bring his pet to work as she was with me. Although she hasn't met Lestat yet, at which point she'll probably rescind his invitation too. I would.

Fletch raises his hand.

'My boss tells me that I've been assigned as Melody's shadow for the next couple of days, so if there's a room around here with bunks…?'

My cheeks flame. 'I think you'll find that you're the one person we stipulated *wasn't* invited to shadow me at work.'

He shrugs with a smug smile that tells me he's well aware of the fact he's unwelcome and it only made the job more enticing.

'Well, I'm the only one available, so suck it up, buttercup.'

If I wasn't at work and therefore behaving like a professional in front of Lois and Barty, I'd pick up the nearest heavy object and take him down.

'Fine,' I say, faux-breezily. 'That's just fine. But office hours only.'

He scrubs his hand over his chin. 'Your office hours are my office hours. If you're working around the clock, then so am I.' He shakes his head ruefully. 'Looks like we're camping out, ghostbuster. Would you like me to call *Most Haunted* and see if they want to send Yvette Fielding over too? We could have ourselves a big old ghostly sleepover in the ballroom. I'll bring a sleeping bag.'

'No need. There's tons of rooms up there,' Barty interrupts, cutting us off. I really hope that Fletch's wisecracks about calling in sensationalist TV crews went over his head. 'You kids can take your pick.'

I cannot actually believe this. Isn't it bad enough that I have to share this job with Leo? Now I have to live with him as well and, not only that, Fletch is coming to the pyjama party too? I want to be resolute and demand that he doesn't get to stay, but the fact that he's living in that crummy flat lingers in my mind and I know that a few days here would be a world away from cockroach city so I hold my tongue and curse my streak of decency.

'My team and I will gladly stay on site,' Leo announces grandly, backing me into a corner. 'Whatever it takes, Mr and Mrs Letterman. I always do whatever it takes to get a job done properly.'

I'm a tiny bit sick in my mouth at his obsequious sucking up. He always has had ideas above his station, so to get to be lord of the manor for a couple of nights is pretty much his fantasy. It will definitely be a smoking jacket-worthy situation. I'm not even joking. He ordered one from America when we were still together; it's one of the many things I don't miss about him.

Lois blinks up at him like a mole emerging into sunlight. 'You're so kind, Mr Dark.'

Barty ferrets about on a side table and then presses a key into Leo's hand. 'The key for the left turret.' He points out of the window to a turret set into the far corner of the moat. 'It's all decked out with the latest fancy kit; TVs that rise from the bedstands and all that fuss. I want you guys to have it while you're here.'

His arm gesture incorporates Leo and the fembots. Leo frowns, obviously not happy with being relocated from the main building into one of the turrets, even though it sounds pretty darn fabulous and Barty bestowed it upon him as a favour. The main house rooms are grand and super traditional; it sounds as if the previous owner had a teenage son who was allowed to go tech crazy in the left tower.

'You and your team can take rooms in the house, Melody,' Lois sniffs. Me and my team? Me, Fletch and Lestat are going to play wacky families in a whole castle?

A horn toots out on the drive and Lois scuttles to the windows.

'It's our cab, honey,' she breathes with clear relief, glad to be getting out of Maplemead. Up to this morning I'd got the impression that Lois and Barty were made of pretty stern southern stuff, so I can only assume that the ghosts, or Dino most probably, put on quite a show last night. Within five minutes I find myself standing on the stone portico with everyone else watching Lois and Barty clamber into a silver people carrier.

'The staff will be on hand if you guys need anything,' Lois calls, already far chirpier because of her imminent escape.

Barty rolls his window down and shouts to us as their driver starts the engine. 'I'll call to see how your first night went.'

We wave them off, smiling bizarrely like their children seeing them off on their holidays, and then we all stand and stare each other down.

'It's a bit like *Big Brother*,' Artie observes. 'Lots of strangers suddenly living in a house together.'

'Or an Agatha Christie murder mystery,' Marina says, scowling. 'Melody did it, in the library, with a candlestick.'

Fletch laughs dirtily, clearly taking Marina's words in a very different sense to how she intended. '*Big Brother* works for me. I'm off to choose the best bed and then drink vodka naked in the Jacuzzi.'

He saunters off and we all watch him go. I notice one of the fembots tip her head to the side to watch his arse and feel all stabby again, so I moodily suggest we all take a bit of time to get our accommodation sorted and then gather for a lunch meeting in the dining room later.

Leo casts a miffed glance at the stairs, then struts out and away across the gravel towards the left tower with the fembots behind him, stumbling to keep up on the gravel in their high heels. He sighs loudly and offers them each an elbow to cling to and they waddle off like a six-legged monster and disappear into their new abode.

'That just leaves us then,' I say, leaning my back against the cool stone wall beside the castle doors.

'Are you sure you're going to be okay with this?' Marina asks, serious now we're alone.

'Honestly? No, of course I'm not,' I say, scrubbing my hands over my face. 'It was a bloody ambush from the second we stepped inside, wasn't it?'

Marina grimaces. 'It was a bit.'

'At least you'll have Lestat to guard you.' I think Artie intended this as genuine comfort, which just shows how much he has to learn.

I huff and consider punching the wall. In the end I don't, because that sort of stuff is the remit of characters like Biff from *Back to the Future* and I am a well-put-together businesswoman with dignity, but I really, really wanted to.

CHAPTER SEVEN

We troop back inside and head straight up the staircase to sort out my sleeping arrangements.

'I still can't believe I'm doing this,' I mutter, pushing open the first door I come to. The room is small but functional with a single bed and it has a pretty outlook over the gardens. A flash of movement out there catches my eye and, when I cross to the windows to check it out, Brittania Lovell emerges slowly from behind a huge rhubarb plant. She's alone and not looking anything like the sassy, confident woman I've met in the castle so far; I'd go as far as to say she seems forlorn as I watch her trudge up the path.

'This room will do.'

Marina pokes her head inside and then pulls the door closed again. 'Nope.'

'What?'

She looks at me as if I'm stupid. 'Just because you don't want to do this, it doesn't mean you have to pick the smallest bedroom in the place just to cut your own nose off. This is the closest you'll ever come to being a princess, Melody, and me by default. You're having the grandest bedroom in the joint, no arguments.'

There's no point in arguing with Marina when she's like this. Artie and I trail her along the corridor as she flings doors open and looks in them all in turn. A few doors from the far end she stands there and gawps. 'This is the one.'

We all troop in and check out the furnishings and I have to admit that she's right. The first room had been quite small; pretty, but nothing on the scale of this. The huge carved four-poster bed stands central in the room, draped in heavy gun-metal silk. Two tall windows look out over the grounds and the eiderdown on the bed looks to be about three-foot deep.

'Fit for a princess,' Marina breathes. She'd love the chance to stay here; it ticks all of her romantic movie boxes and then some.

'Or a prince,' Fletch says, appearing from what must be the en suite bathroom. 'Sorry, ghostbuster, this one's taken.'

I sigh, resigned, but Marina laughs in his face and jerks her thumb towards the door.

'Out of here. You're only here because Lord and Lady Letterman were too polite to say no. Melody's the one on the payroll, so she gets to call the shots.' She turns to me. 'Am I right or am I right?'

'I think you're right,' Artie says, because he's learned that that is always the appropriate response in this type of situation.

Fletch looks at me and I realise that it would be a good thing to have some ground rules and laying this one down early will be to my advantage. He needs to know that I am the boss and that for as long as he is here shadowing me, then he does what I say, not the other way around. It's easy to be bold when I have Marina next to me though; no one argues with her around.

'I'd like this room, please,' I say stiffly, feeling mean which is ridiculous given that he's got the pick of God knows how many other gorgeous places to rest his handsome, annoying head and none of them will involve cockroaches. He looks for a moment as if he's going to dig his heels in, but then he just throws me a jaunty grin and makes for the door.

'I'll go and find myself a cupboard under the stairs then.'

I lace my laugh with sarcasm. 'Harry Potter? I don't think so. Voldemort, more like.'

'I've warmed the bed up for you.' He tosses a look over his shoulder and I'd like to toss something heavy at the back of his head as he disappears.

'He's funny.' Artie grins, taking a seat on the blanket box at the end of the bed.

Oh well, that's just great. A spot of bromantic hero worship is just what I could do without. 'The man writes cracker jokes for a living,' I say, more pithy than a navel orange. Artie lifts his eyebrows as if he isn't sure if I'm lying and, worse, as if he's even more impressed by Fletch if I'm not.

Clicking my phone, I check the time. 'We have a couple of hours before lunch. Let's run through what we know.'

Marina kicks her heels off and wriggles her painted toes in the sheepskin rug.

'Mind the head,' I say and she looks down a second before she steps on the sheep's skull. Jumping off the rug, she rams her feet back into her shoes and shudders.

'Who does that?' she mutters darkly, eying the sheep's head as she walks around the edge of the rug to get to the bed.

'So, we have three principal circus ghosts plus the lion,' I say, pacing back and forth by the window. 'And there's a couple of nuns in the chapel and Lord and Lady Shilling in the library.'

'This job gets more and more like Cluedo every day.' Marina settles herself back onto a mound of pillows as we recapped the case so far.

'My instinct is to leave the Shillings where they are. They're not bothering anyone,' I say, glancing out over the drive as Leo appears briefly outside the tower. He is much more suited to this place than I am; I wonder if there's a place in the world that would be just right for a girl like me.

Artie reaches into his back pocket and pulls out a piece of A4 that he's folded several times.

'I found this on the Internet last night,' he says, smoothing it out on the blanket box beside him.

Marina crawls to the foot of the bed to take a look and I cross to stand beside them.

'It's the Shilling family tree going back to when this place was built,' he says, holding it flat at the edges for us to see. Artie is turning himself into our resident genealogy expert, based mainly on the fact that his mother is mad into all that stuff and has subscriptions to all those fancy websites.

'Lord Alistair Shilling.' I trace my finger across the name as I spot it printed beside Lady Eleanor Shilling. Counting back through the generations, I can see he was the fifth Lord Shilling to inherit Maplemead, succeeded by his son Rupert, who presumably is the one who made the decision to end the family connections with the castle.

'So we know that Britannia is Lady Eleanor's niece,' I muse, feeling in my pocket for a pen. Marina reaches into her blouse and hands me the one she keeps stashed in her bra, shrugging when I raise my eyebrows and jot the ghosts down on the paper.

'Good work,' I say, smiling at Artie as I grab a file out of my bag. Flipping it open on the blanket box lid beside the family tree, I recap my research into the castle's chequered history. The Shillings gave it over several times to be used by the community including a spell in the early nineteenth century as home to an order of Benedictine nuns.

'That explains the silent nuns, anyway,' I murmur. I don't plan on trying to oust them either; silent nuns who confine themselves to the chapel are about as benign as it gets when it comes to paranormal activity.

'Yet there's no mention at all of a circus meeting its grisly end here,' Marina murmurs, scanning the text.

'Come on, let's go take a look around,' I say, closing the file for now. 'See what we can unearth.'

We've searched the many bedrooms, annoyed the cook by being under her feet in the kitchens, and we've climbed and descended enough stairs to give me cramp. We're just checking out the grisly dungeons when someone bongs the gong at exactly one o'clock.

'Lunch?' Artie suggests. I can see he's conflicted, because if it is he might not get to have his beloved egg sandwiches. Given that he's just allowed himself to be strapped on to a torture rack by Marina, it's testimony to how good his sandwiches must be that they're the thing uppermost in his mind right now.

Marina crosses her arms across her chest and nods her head towards him.

'I vote we leave him here and send Hells Bells down to find him.'

'And I vote you leave him down here so I can twist those handles until his guts burst like spaghetti.'

I spin around and find Dino behind us.

'Dino.' I greet him aloud to inform the others of his presence.

'I don't think so,' I say, answering his macabre suggestion lightly. 'He's quite tall enough already.'

That's an understatement; I barely come up to Artie's armpits. Dino shrugs, his face like thunder.

'Maybe it will help you decide to leave us in peace.'

'If I could be so bold, you don't seem all that peaceful,' I say, tipping my head to one side to study him. I'm not keen on how full of fury he is.

'Dino was fine until the Americans came and now the peacock with his eyes on her all the time too. I want to wring all of your scrawny necks!' He makes throttling gestures as he prowls towards Artie and lunges for the handle to stretch his arms.

'We need to get Artie down this second,' I whisper urgently to Marina and she gasps and sprints across the bare earth floor. I'm a second behind her and we scrabble with a leather wrist strap each as Dino battles to make the rusted handle turn. Alarmingly, he seems to get it moving slightly and Artie whimpers, 'Help me,' in panic under his breath.

'Nearly there,' I tell him with a tight smile and when he gasps painfully a second time, Marina abandons her strap and turns instead to the handle Dino is desperately trying to crank. Grabbing hold of it, she drags it backwards as Dino redoubles his efforts to pull it forwards, snarling like a rabid dog. Oh, he's picked a fight with the wrong Sicilian. Marina kicks her shoes off and plants her feet wide on the earth as she hangs onto the handle for dear life and lets forth a string of fast, furious Italian that makes Dino double-take in shock. He falters and she gains the advantage, then he's right back at her with an unintelligible string of what must be expletives of his own.

'I've got it, I've got it, I've got it,' I chant under my breath to Artie and then I almost shout with relief because I actually have got it and one of Artie's arms is thankfully free.

He almost sags with relief and then quickly twists and finishes off the job of unfastening his other wrist himself as Marina continues her high-decibel row with a ghost she can neither see nor hear.

Shit. I don't know what she's just said, but Dino is bloody fuming. He's still cranking that handle for all his worth and his eyes are bulging.

'Why are you doing all of this?' I say, my heart still banging behind my ribs. If he'll just talk to me, give me some new insight.

Dino looks at me, aggrieved, and then makes an angry rattle in his throat and spits on the bare earth. Well he didn't, obviously, but he makes the motion and the ugly threatening sentiment is the same. It's plain that I'm not going to get anything useful from him right now, so I grab hold of both Artie and Marina to make a hasty retreat. She pauses to grab her shoes and as we leave she turns back and yells another insult. That's so Marina; she always has to have the last word, even with a ghost.

'Okay?' I say, turning anxiously to Artie as soon as we're safely back up in the main hallway of the castle.

He nods, already regaining his wonky smile.

'Never done that before,' he says, rubbing his wrists.

'Don't do it again, either,' Marina scolds, hanging onto my arm so she can put her shoes back on.

I look sideways at her. 'Er, you strapped him to the wall, remember?'

'She wasn't to know that the ghost of an Italian trapeze artist would come and try to stretch me,' Artie reasons, scratching his chin. 'It was a tiny bit exciting as well as terrifying, actually.'

'All in a day's work, ghostbuster,' I say, grinning with relief.

'You know to file this in the "never tell your mother" folder, right?' Marina says, tucking her black and green chiffon blouse back into her skinny jeans and fluffing her hair back into place. From She-Woman to supermodel in a blink. That's my girl.

As we pass the chapel I catch the quiet murmur of voices. I know it can't be the nuns as the Benedictine were a silent order, so I press my finger to my lips and tiptoe close to the door to see who's in there.

I peer around the edge and, sitting on the back pew head to head, I find Leo. And, even though they have their backs to me, I know the woman with him is Brittania Lovell.

I jump back and press myself out of sight against the heavy door as the nuns glide into view and it seems to rouse Leo and Brittania too because I can hear movement in there. I haul Marina and Artie flat against the wall too and, thankfully, they hurry from the chapel without glancing our way.

'What was he up to?' Marina asks quietly.

I shake my head. 'I don't know. He was with Brittania,' I murmur. I wasn't able to catch their hushed conversation, but I couldn't miss the intimate tone or the closeness of their bodies. What was it Dino said in the dungeons just now? The peacock can't take his eyes off her? It doesn't take a rocket scientist to put two and two together here and I don't like the answer I'm coming up with one bit.

We troop into the reception hall and find Hells Bells, gearing herself up to strike the gong again. She looks like she's warming up to throw the hammer at the Olympics.

'Umm, hello?' I say, and she looks our way.

'Oh there you are.' She pauses, flagging, with the hammer clutched in both hands. 'Where are the others?'

'Still over in the turret, I think,' Artie jumps in. 'I don't think they'll hear that from there.'

Hells Bells looks at us, counting heads like a schoolteacher. 'Three here, three there. There's one more. Lady Letterman said seven guests.'

'It's only Fletch,' I say quickly. 'He'll come when he's ready.'

She shakes her head and starts to limber up with the hammer again. 'M'lady says I have to keep bonging until everyone has heard it. 'Scuse me.'

Artie bounds forward and takes the bonging stick from her small hands.

'Let me,' he says and they both turn so red it looks as if their heads might spontaneously combust. Marina looks at the oak floorboards to hide her smile and I cover my ears in readiness as Artie spins a full revolution before striking the gong as if his life depends on it.

'Wow,' Hells Bells mouths. 'That's the biggest bong ever.'

'Said the matron to the bishop,' says Fletch, jogging lightly down the stairs to join us. 'You rang?'

'Lunch is served in the dining room,' Hells Bells says, formal once more, straightening her skew-whiff little white hat. She skips across to the huge bay windows, flings one open with both hands, then pulls a loud hailer from down the back of one of the sofas.

'Lunch is served in the dining room!' she yells, hanging out of the window and her little voice roars and echoes around the courtyard towards the turret. She hauls the top half of her torso back inside and drags the window down again, returning the loud hailer to its hiding place and dusting herself down.

'It's m'lady's,' she explains, with a tiny smile. 'She uses it to find m'lord.'

'Well, it certainly works,' I say, watching the twins emerge from the far tower with a sinking feeling.

'Shall we?' Fletch asks, holding his elbow to me formally.

'Piss off,' I say, walking straight past him.

'You're even more beautiful when you're angry,' he murmurs so only I can hear and I close my eyes and ignore the fact that he's just pressed that brain-bypass button that makes me want to rip his shirt off. I know he was being sarcastic, but he's filthy hot and he's just called me beautiful and I haven't had sex for so long that I think the next brave soul might need a pick-axe to hack their way in. I hate that I have a brain-bypass button that he seems to be able to find at will and I vow to never, ever tell him because he'll press it hey-willy-nilly and I'll have to be his sex slave for eternity.

Hells Bells leads us into the dining room, which is at the rear of the ground floor looking out over the grounds. It's another vast, high-ceilinged affair with dark panelling and oil paintings and the French doors have been opened wide to allow the cooling summer breeze to freshen the room. I take a second to stand there and gather my thoughts and I can't be certain but I think I caught a flash of ivory silk moving down behind the bushes again; Brittania Lovell if I'm not mistaken. She seems to oscillate between being a vixen in the house and a lonely maiden in the garden. It's an odd juxtaposition.

Turning back to the long, central dining table laid with fine china and gleaming silver cutlery, Hells Bells and the cook stand quietly at one end as we all file around it and take a seat.

Leo is already in there, papa bear at the end of the table, and I end up at the other, mama bear. I have Fletch on my left and

Marina on my right with Artie beside her, as he most often is. I think he has a little case of hero worship going on for her too; but then it's very easy to be in awe of Marina Malone. She's effortlessly charismatic and always has a smart answer on the tip of her tongue. You know those times when you think back over a situation and think of all the things you wish you'd said? I don't think Marina ever feels like that, because she's always said something clever straight off the bat.

'Soup?' Cook asks, serving me first.

I nod and say thank you, because even if it's cauliflower and cold sick soup, we're eating it. I don't like this being waited on malarkey one bit, it makes me feel like a twat, and I vow to have a quiet word with Cook and Hells Bells once this meal's over to tell them they don't need to do this for us. We all sit in awkward silence whilst they move around the table ladling clear broth into our bowls. If I had a pearl necklace, I'd flutter my fingers over it about now in an affected fashion and I find myself touching my bare neck instead. I catch Fletch watching me. His eyes follow my hand and then he glances away quickly as if I've caught him doing something he shouldn't, which is at odds with his usual behaviour. Christ. He can press my brain-bypass button without even using words. I am in serious trouble here.

'Bread, m'lady?'

'It's Melody,' I say, hoping to put Hells Bells at her ease around me, but it seems to have the opposite effect because she looks at the floor and stammers. 'Sorry. I thought it was pronounced m'lady. That's how they say it on *Downton*, anyhow.'

'No,' I say. 'Just call me Melody, please. It's my name.'

Her expression clears with understanding. 'Very good, M'lady Melody.'

Marina grins. 'That must make me M'lady Marina,' she says, taking a bread roll from the basket in Hells Bells's hands with a polite thank you.

'Malady means diseased,' Artie says. Fletch starts to laugh and raises his glass in appreciation.

'And we're right back to those cracker jokes again,' I mutter.

One of the fembots looks over, faux concerned. 'Melody has a disease? Is it fatal?'

I'd just picked up my soup spoon and I lay it down again slowly.

'I don't have a disease and I don't wish to be addressed as m'lady.' I look towards Cook and Hells Bells who, having served everyone, have returned to their spots by a side table.

'Please, you don't need to wait on us like this, we can perfectly well take care of ourselves.'

Cook shakes her head. 'Orders is orders, m'lady.' She pauses and then, with difficulty, corrects herself. 'Malady.'

I sigh, too stressed to rise to it, despite the fact that even Leo is finding it funny.

'Perhaps someone should call you a doctor?' he suggests, his face a picture of supercilious amusement. 'I can handle things here if you need to go home sick.'

I'd really like to start an undignified food fight by bouncing a bread roll off his head, but I settle for picking up my spoon and eating my soup in silence. Everyone follows suit and, for a moment, silence reigns as we all realise that the stuff in our bowls is actually bloody divine. It's chicken consommé, I think, flavourful and delicious.

Fletch draws his pocket book and pen out and lays it beside his bowl. On it he writes: 'chicken soup is good for invalids recuperating from fatal diseases', so only I can see.

In the food fight going on inside my brain I have just upended my soup bowl on his head.

'People from the TV production company are coming to scope the place out this afternoon,' Leo says, addressing the table. 'Nikki, Vikki and I will handle them and I'd appreciate it if the rest of you could make yourself scarce.'

I bristle with annoyance. 'Well, I'm planning a full walk through the castle this afternoon with my team. Perhaps you could make sure you stay out of our way instead.'

Leo eyes me. 'This doesn't need to be a battle. We're all on the same page here and everyone's getting paid.'

I refrain from telling him that everything between us will always be a battle, because he's the bastardy bullshit-peddling hippocrocotwunt who broke my heart and I don't have to listen to his twatwaffle any more, but I keep the crazy words in my head just by the skin of my teeth.

Maybe I do have a disease after all, one that makes me want to say exactly what I think.

Cook and Hells Bells move quickly around us to replace our empty soup bowls with individual little tiered stands laden with dainty sandwiches and a selection of cakes and little desserts. Is it too late to retract my statement that they don't need to cater for us? This is bloody heavenly.

Leo picks up a salmon sandwich and waves it airily down the table. 'Don't you think it's taking this shadowing thing too far for you to stay in the castle at night, Gunn?'

We all look at Fletch, who takes his time over a teeny rare-beef-filled Yorkshire pudding.

'I don't mind protecting Malady from things that go bump in the night,' he says, studying his stand again and selecting a mini quiche.

I roll my eyes. 'If anyone is going to need protecting, it's you.'

Fletch's eyes flash with interest. 'Worried you're not going to be able to keep your hands off me, ghostbuster?'

'I think she meant that the ghosts might try to kill you in your sleep,' Artie says, then sticks a sandwich into his mouth whole.

'Or she might sleepwalk and do it herself,' Marina says, with an evil glint in her eye. 'Melody did it, in the bedroom, with a poker.'

'I'd pay good money to see that,' Fletch murmurs, effortlessly hovering his finger over my button again.

At the other end of the table, Leo slams his fork down on the table with unnecessary force, making both of the fembots jump like startled rabbits. He doesn't say anything, but I get the message. He doesn't appreciate watching Fletch flirt with me. Well, well, well. An admittedly mean-spirited flush of 'in your face, sucker, what's good for the goose is good for the gander' enjoyment warms my bones and that's the one and only explanation I can offer for what I said next.

'I sleep naked.'

Fletch almost chokes on his butterfly cake, Marina claps her hand over her laugh and Artie hums and looks at the ceiling. The fembots are both staring at me and blinking really fast, as if they cannot compute the relevance, and I notice that Leo's hands are clenched into fists on the table.

'No you fucking don't,' he says. 'You sleep in fluffy pyjamas.'

I look at him, and it becomes apparent that I am still in stupid mode because I say, 'My tastes have changed. I've grown up. These days I can't sleep unless I'm completely naked. I'm like Marilyn Monroe.'

They all contemplate this unusual revelation.

'I bought a dress just like that white one she wore,' Marina says, valiantly keeping up with me. 'On ebay, from China, for ten pence or something.'

'Let's hope you don't die the same terrible death as Marilyn with the telephone in your hand,' Leo spits at me.

'Leo did it, in the bedroom, with the telephone receiver,' one of the fembots says, with a rare display of wit.

'Not on my watch,' Fletch says, quiet and serious. My stomach does a slow backward somersault and for a moment Leo and Fletch stare each other down across the cake stands.

'Is that the heady whiff of testosterone I smell?' Marina sniffs at the air and at the other end of the table the fembots each lay a hand over one of Leo's clenched ones.

Artie catches my eye and holds it. 'Have some cake, Melody. The pink one tastes like the fresh strawberries I picked with my dad one summer.'

I think I might actually love Artie Elliott. He's a lad of spare words, but he always chooses them carefully, right now being a case in point. Not only was he distracting me with cake, he's unwittingly reminded me to focus on what really matters. I swallow, try to recover my tattered dignity, and do as he suggested and take a bite of the perfectly rectangular pink-iced slice. He's quite right, it's an explosion of fruit in my mouth, and the sweetness of the cake, along with the sweetness of Artie Elliott, is enough to ease my mood. I've got this. For now at least, anyway.

I risk a glance towards Fletch and hope like hell I'll be able to hang onto my poise and dignity tonight when we're alone in the castle.

CHAPTER EIGHT

I decide not to deliberately tangle with Leo and his production meeting; I begrudgingly admit to myself that he was right about the fact that we have actually both been employed to work here at the same time. It's not a competition like the last job I pretty much stole from beneath his nose, so I lead my crew away from the ground floor and up the stairs.

Pausing on the first floor-landing, I try to get my bearings.

'What are you looking for?' a voice says and I turn to find Britannia Lovell beside me.

'I saw a small back staircase somewhere here earlier.' I answer her, unguarded as I scan the corridor, and then I remember that not only can Marina and Artie not see her, I've got Fletch to deal with here too. I make a quick decision; the only way I can do this is to behave exactly as I would if he wasn't here, so I turn to the others and say, 'Britannia Lovell is here with us.' I nod to my left to indicate where she's standing.

'About time,' Marina mutters. I can't blame her. For a haunted castle, these guys have so far been pretty selective about their appearances around us.

'Rather rude,' Britannia says, with a flick of one perfectly arched dark brow. 'The stairs are behind the last door on the right. Nothing up there though, just dull storage.'

'Can I talk to you about what happened here last night?' I ask and she laughs in the mean way of a cool but vicious schoolgirl who enjoys the odd spot of playground bullying.

'Dino decided he'd had enough of the Americans.'

'Were you having an affair with him? With Dino, I mean? When you were alive?'

I didn't intend to ask that quite so directly, but she annoyed me with her uncharitable attitude towards Lois and Barty.

'Oh don't be so dull, darling,' Britannia says and her appraising glance settles on Fletch. 'Are you having an affair with *him*?'

'No,' I say quickly, glad no one else can hear her.

Britannia laughs. 'Why not? He's terribly handsome, don't you think?' She's circling Fletch now and she stops in front of him and strokes the back of her hand down his face. 'Don't you ever wonder how this stubble would feel when he kisses you, Melody?'

I shake my head, grit my teeth, and refuse to rise to her goading.

'Liar,' she whispers, and she leans forward and touches her lips to his.

'Just pack it in, will you?' I say, sharper than I planned to because, to me, she looks like a gorgeous living and breathing woman kissing Fletch. Even though he isn't aware of her, he's just parted his lips slightly and skimmed his tongue over his bottom lip and it looks for all the world as if he's responding to her kiss.

Britannia laughs with wicked delight. 'I think he senses me, Melody.'

'Don't be so bloody stupid,' I say, but she does it again and Fletch passes his hand over his mouth as if a butterfly had landed on his lip and he was brushing it away.

'What's she doing?' Marina asks.

'Being a cow,' I mutter and Britannia slants her sly eyes at me as she runs a hand down Fletch's chest.

'I bet he's firm and warm to touch,' she sighs and I know where her hand is heading next.

'Okay, you win. Yes, he is, okay? He's all of those things,' I snap. 'He's as firm as a racehorse, he's as warm as morning bed sheets and his stubble grazes your face when he kisses you. Now can we stop this stupid game and move on, please?'

Britannia claps happily. 'Ah, so you *are* lovers! I knew it.'

'No, we are not,' I say, and I don't want to say the next bit loudly, so I lean towards her and hiss in her ear, 'Just because he's kissed me a couple of times, it doesn't make us sodding lovers, okay?'

Britannia's smile brims full of wickedness and in a blink she disappears, leaving me practically face to face with Fletch. He's staring at me and I can tell from his expression that he's trying to assess what's happening here and frame it in a way that makes sense to his black and white mind. He reaches for his pocketbook, takes out his pen and I watch as he writes:

MB wants me so badly that it's sending her crazy. Also, buy a razor.

I take a deep breath and realise that we need to establish the ground rules of this shadowing malarkey pretty damn quick or else he's going to enjoy himself then do a hatchet job on me in the paper.

'Marina, would you and Artie please head on up to the top floor and check if there's anything that strikes you? I just need a quick word with Fletch and then we'll be right up.'

As soon as they're gone, I turn on Fletch.

'The lengths you'll go to to get me alone, ghostbuster,' he drawls.

'Do you have to be a cock at every possible chance you get?' I ask, exasperated. 'This shadowing thing… we need some ground rules.'

He grins. 'You're cute when you're bossy.'

'Rule number one. Stop flirting with me. I don't like it and it's unprofessional in front of other people.'

He huffs softly and looks at the floor. 'Says the woman who just said I was as firm as a racehorse and as warm as morning bed sheets. Does my stubble really graze your face when I kiss you?'

I'm not sure, but I think he's stepped closer and my back is against the wall so I can't move away.

'I can't remember,' I mutter, looking down the length of the empty corridor rather than into his sea foam eyes.

'I could remind you,' he says, and his voice has dropped to that sex octave. My skin prickles with awareness as his hand lands flat on the wall beside my head. Oh shit. I wanted this to be a me talk, you listen situation and he's turned it into a me swoon, you kiss me situation without even really needing to try.

'Rule number two?' He prompts me, which is useful because it seems that I've lost the power of autonomous thinking.

I cast around in the flotsam and jetsam inside my head. 'It was something about you not taking the piss out of me, or making a fool out of me or trying to destroy my reputation,' I manage.

Fletch spans his other hand flat over the base of my neck, stroking my collarbones with his thumb and little finger. It's so very unexpected that I don't ask him to stop.

'I promise not to make a fool of you,' he murmurs, and his hand slides up the side of my neck until his fingers massage into my hair. 'Or hurt you, or destroy your heart the way he did.'

Wait… that wasn't what I said at all, was it?

'No, Fletch…' his name catches in my throat, because the truth of the matter is I cannot hide the fact that his words have hit home. How does he do that? He spins from sarcasm to silver-tongued on a sixpence and every now and then he is so raw that he almost reduces me to actual real tears and it is well documented that I am not a crier.

'Hey,' he whispers, and he lowers his head and brushes his lips over my cheekbone.

'Your stubble is scratching my cheek,' I tell him and he slides his mouth down my face and then he's kissing me, pressing me into the wall, his body every bit as racehorse-firm and bed sheet-warm as I remember.

I know, *I know*. This is unprofessional and I should push him away, but he's just made that low, sexy noise in his throat and now he's pinning my hands above my head in one of his own bigger ones and his body is telling me how very turned on he is. I cannot be held responsible for this total lapse in control; Fletcher Gunn is to kissing what John Travolta is to dancing. It's so incredibly sensual and spine-tingling, and he's so tall and I love the way he dips his head down to meet mine, and I can't explain how my hands have threaded themselves into his hair to hold his mouth to mine in case he thinks about stopping.

'Jesus, Melody,' he whispers into my mouth. He so rarely uses my proper name and I love hearing him say it now, like this.

'Fletcher Gunn,' I murmur, then slide my tongue over his lips. In answer, he rocks his hips into me and palms my breast through my T-shirt and I put my mouth against his ear and tell him I want him to get me naked.

Both Fletch and I are too caught up to notice that the corridor is no longer empty. He rucks my T-shirt up and feels for my bra catch and it isn't until someone coughs, exaggerated and loud, that I turn and find myself being watched by a hulking great camera lens, a short, beardy cameraman who looks like he's enjoying himself far too much and an absolutely livid Leo Dark.

I automatically put my hand out and cover the lens. 'Get that thing out of my face!' I yelp as if I'm Kim Kardashian.

Behind Leo, the fembots observe proceedings with their dead-behind-the-eyes expressions, iPads in their hands as if they are actually useful assistants.

Fletch steps in front of me to give me a chance to straighten my clothes. 'Sneaking around to get your thrills again, Dark?' he drawls.

'Just doing the job I've been paid to do,' Leo says and his eyes laser into me as I step out from behind Fletch. 'Unlike some people.'

'I'm working,' I protest squeakily and then I realise that the only people who do what I was just doing for a living are prostitutes. 'I'm not charging you though,' I say quickly to Fletch, as if it makes it better that I just let him cop a freebie. I've gone all hot.

Fletch rolls his eyes as if my randomness is entirely to be expected. 'That footage better not see the light of day,' he warns.

'I'm looking for supernatural occurrences, not a cheap peep-show,' Leo snaps. 'There're seventeen bedrooms in this building. You could have picked anyone of them for your sordid little romp, yet you have to go and pick the public corridor.' He looks at both of us as if we're rancid teenagers on an eighteen to thirty holiday in Kavos, but Fletch just shrugs.

'What can I say? Heat of the moment. You know how it is. Or perhaps you don't.'

There's a strange, unreliable glint in his eye when he glances down at me and then, without warning, he bends down, lifts me as if I'm a damsel in distress and he's a fireman and flings me over his shoulder.

'What the… put me down!' I yelp, pummelling his back with my fists in shock.

'To bed with you, filthy wench!' Fletch declares robustly and, turning to the nearest door, he kicks it wide on its hinges. I'm outraged but powerless as he struts through the door. All the blood is rushing to my head and I catch a glimpse of the cameraman scrabbling to catch it all on film as I reach out and slam the door as hard as I can.

Inside the room, Fletch strides to the bed and tumbles me onto my back on the mattress. I spring to my feet like a jack-in-a-box and round on him.

'What the hell was that all about?' I whisper-shout furiously in case they're still outside the door listening, my hands on my hips and my chest heaving. I know this because Fletch's eyes have just dropped to look at it.

'That,' he jerks his thumb towards the door, and his words come out all urgent and hot, 'was to piss Leo Dark off. But this *thing* going on with us... we need to have sex, ghostbuster. I can't concentrate on work, or writing, or any damn thing else.'

I stare at him and he stares right back with those bold 'let me do you' green eyes.

'What do you expect me to do? Strip off right now and get into bed?'

He shrugs and then he softens his voice down to the danger zone again. 'I'd rather take your clothes off for you.' He reaches out and tucks my hair behind my ear and I untuck it again, just to make a point.

'Are you always this stubborn or do I bring it out in you?' he asks, tucking my hair back a second time. 'You look at me like you hate me, all flashing, angry brown eyes and then you look at me like you want me, all pouty lips and breathy. You're the queen of mixed messages.'

'And you're the king of bad intentions,' I hiss back, fluffing my hair around my face, affronted by the suggestion that I'm ever pouty or breathy.

His lazy grin tells me he doesn't mind the title as much as I'd hoped.

'Only where you're concerned.'

We eye each other and I become aware suddenly of how close our bodies are and how bunched his shoulders are as he looks down at me. He cups my face between his hands and I feel disconcertingly fragile and hyper-aware of his contained strength. I sense he's about to say something sexy in that honey gravel way he does sometimes, so I shake my head to dislodge myself from his clutches and step backwards.

'Fletcher. It might have escaped your notice, but it's three in the afternoon, Marina and Artie are waiting for us upstairs, and there's a daytime TV crew in the corridor.'

He looks towards the door. 'I'll wedge a chair under the handle if it makes you feel better.'

'It doesn't. We're both on the clock while we're here, Fletch,' I say, moving away from him in case he tries any of his cavemen tactics again. 'Let's just grow up and try to act like it, okay?'

I look down and notice that someone has slipped a note under the door or, to be more precise, someone has scrawled something on the back of a screwed-up receipt and shoved it halfway underneath. Curious, I bend down, pick it up and smooth it out so I can read the untidy writing beneath a mobile number.

Tip me the wink if you and your boyfriend want to put on another peepshow for the camera. You've got a nice little rack, love, and voyeurism goes down a storm on Pornhub.

CHAPTER NINE

'What took you?' Marina asks when we join them on the second floor a few minutes later.

'We ran into Leo and his camera crew. It didn't go well,' I say. 'Anything to report up here?'

'Not sure.' She pats a small, deep-set wooden door with a fancy latch and keyhole. 'This one is the only door I can't open. I think it leads up into that small turret at the back.' She leads us across to the diamond-leaded window seat and points up at the small, twisty turret at the outside end of the building.

'There's a window in it so there must be a room, which means there must be access somehow,' Artie says, peering out too.

On that, Brittania Lovell materialises through the locked door.

'There's nothing up there.'

I still, and place a hand on Marina's arm. 'Brittania.'

Brittania leans her back against the door, almost as if she is trying to barricade it.

'Do you know where the key is?' I ask and she bristles with impatience and then backs through the door again, disappearing as quickly as she came.

'Bugger.' I sigh. 'She's gone again.'

'Short and sweet,' Marina says. 'What did she say?'

I repeat her scant words and both Artie and Fletch make a note of it in their pocket books.

'The rest of the rooms on this floor appear to be bedrooms, mostly used for furniture storage and the like.' Marina recaps their findings for my benefit. 'Smaller than the grand suites on the first floor, probably servants' quarters back in the day.'

I nod, scanning the windowsills or picture rails for any sign of a key for the locked door. There's obviously something of importance in that turret and I badly want to know what it is.

'Want me to break it down for you?' Fletch asks casually and, much as I appreciate the offer, the last thing I want to do is smash a hundreds of years'-old door off its hinges.

'Perhaps we should just ask Lois and Barty if they have a key first,' I suggest.

He looks a little disappointed, like 'if I can't have sex then at least let me smash stuff up' disappointed. Of all the superhero costumes I'd have imagined Fletch in, the hulk isn't one of them. Not that I've imagined him in a superhero costume, of course. That would be weird. Although if he was to be a superhero, his superpower would be seduction, which technically would probably make him gigolo-man. I give myself a mental slap. If I cannot keep my mind out of the gutter while Fletch is around, I might have to cancel this shadowing thing altogether and let him make up whatever crap he wants to for his bloody double-page spread.

Heading back down to the ground floor again, I lead the way to the ballroom. It's the room where I first witnessed paranormal activity in the castle and I feel inexplicably pulled back there again now. I don't explain as much to Fletch of course; I can well imagine his derision at the fact that I count my gut instinct as one of my most valuable investigative skills.

Stepping inside, I stop and catch my breath, because my gut was bang on the money. No wonder Brittania disappeared so speedily upstairs just now; she was due down here to perform for her adoring, imaginary crowd. It's such a shame that I'm the only one amongst us who can see it, because watching Britannia and Dino soar from the chandeliers like exotic, swooping birds for the first time is a sight I'll never forget.

I lay my hand over my heart and whisper, 'They're here. Britannia and Dino are performing up there on the trapeze. It's so beautiful, Marina.' I feel her hand slide into mine as I watch and when I look at her quickly she's staring up towards the ceiling too, rapt, even though she cannot see them.

It's such a sweeping, epic room and without the constraints of preserving human life, they fly uninhibited by fear. Dino is a different man now to the one we encountered in the dungeons earlier. There is tenderness and grace in the way he reaches for Britannia's outstretched hands and catches her effortlessly, swinging with her as if they are lovers dancing on moonbeams.

They dip and then embrace, and then they fall apart and meet once more. Their hands clasp and every so often their lips almost touch for the most fleeting of romantic moments. The crystals on Britannia's silk costume catch the light like dancing fireflies and I can hear her laughter and his jubilation as I stand beneath them and watch them perform, awestruck.

What a sight they must have made back in their heyday; people would have flocked to marvel at their stunning bravado. Britannia reminds me of the beautiful girls from the turn-of-the-century dance halls, of the glamour and dazzle of *Moulin Rouge*; she's euphoric and ravishing and impossibly sophisticated. Up there, there is only the two of them and they delight in each other and the majesty of their private flight. I see her differently as she perches inside her spinning hoop and pirouettes; she is no longer petulant or spoilt. I can completely understand how both of the men in her life were so enamoured of her; she is magnificent, a triumph of femininity and beauty as she strikes a sensual pose, her head thrown back in abandon.

I watch them as Dino blows her a kiss across the room and releases a swing for her. She reaches out with one pale, elegant arm, catching it with practised ease, but as she clutches it and swings free of her hoop, the rope holding the trapeze bar snaps suddenly and she freefalls towards the floor with a hideous, blood-curdling scream.

I scream out loud too and I run to where she lies in a crumpled heap of tangled ropes, her limbs twisted to ugly, unsurvivable angles.

'Britannia,' I gasp, dropping to my knees, scrabbling at the air around her. Dark blood pools around the back of her head and Dino is beside us now, griefstricken as he gently turns her over. Her eyes flicker open for the briefest of moments and she looks at me, bereft.

'It always ends like this,' she whispers, and then he gathers her into his arms and clasps her to his chest before they both disappear.

I sag onto my knees and hold my face in my hands for a minute or two. Beside me, Marina rubs my back and waits until I'm ready. They all do. Artie has taken a seat on one of the chairs set around the edge of the room and Fletch has watched the whole thing leaning against the doorway. I can't even think what this must have seemed like for him, my heart is too busy breaking for Britannia and the tragic way she met her demise.

Covering my mouth with my hand, I realise I feel sick. 'I need a couple of minutes,' I say, pushing up onto my feet. 'I'll be alright after a few gulps of fresh air.'

I dash past Fletch without even looking up at him and I keep going until I'm outside on the stone steps. Thankfully I manage not to hurl my lunch over the side of the balustrade, and I grip the cool, rough stone and slowly, slowly, try to regulate my breathing as I concentrate on a planter of pretty summer flowers for distraction.

'You saw them perform then, I take it.'

It's not a question, more of a statement, and I nod as Leo comes out to stand alongside me. It's a measure of how shaken I am that I'm relieved to see him, because right now he's the only one around here who truly understands.

'I saw them earlier,' he says. 'Turned my stomach too, if it helps.'

It doesn't, really. My rational brain knows that I didn't just witness her actually die in front of me on the ballroom floor, but it sure as hell felt real, and the fact is that she *did* die in exactly that manner and it was a truly terrible way to go.

'She was so beautiful,' I say, looking out over the courtyard. 'Mesmerising.'

It's an accurate description for Britannia Lovell. She seems to mesmerise everyone in her orbit.

'Have you spoken any more to them today?' I ask quietly, hoping he'll reveal his earlier meeting with Brittania in the chapel.

'I *have* been rather busy with my production team,' he sniffs, which implies two things; he doesn't want to tell me about his meeting with Brittania and also that he's still pissy with me about the snogging incident in the hallway.

'About that incident in the hallway earlier…' I say, because I should probably attempt to clear the air.

'Please don't think that I'm bothered, because I'm not,' he says, too quickly. 'I couldn't care less what you do or who you do it with, in your spare time at least.'

And there he goes again, making me feel shoddy for getting my face snogged off while I'm on the clock.

'Good,' I huff. 'Because you have no right to.'

He looks steadily ahead, his profile etched like a Roman statue in the sunlight. 'I know that.'

'Well, I'm glad we've got that sorted,' I say stiffly and, after a moment's awkward silence, I sigh and head back inside to the library in search of Lady Eleanor. She's there at her usual table in the window with Lord Shilling and, by the looks of it, backgammon is the game of choice today.

'Would it be okay if I sit with you for a few minutes?' I say, when they glance up.

'Long as you don't expect to play,' Lord Shilling says.

Eleanor shoots me a little smile as I sit down. 'Busy day, dear?'

I nod, non-committal because hopefully she still doesn't know precisely what I'm doing at Maplemead.

'I wondered if you could help me with something, actually,' I say. 'There's a door up on the first floor that seems to be locked. I think it leads up the far tower?'

Eleanor goes statue-still, all apart from the tell-tale shake of her hand.

'Brittania loved it so up there.'

Lord Shilling sighed. 'Why would you want to get in the tower? Full of old junk as I remember.'

Eleanor shoots him a reproachful look, but I answer him all the same.

'It's the highest window in the castle, isn't it?' I improvise. 'I wanted to check out the view from up there.'

'Same as from the bedrooms,' he huffs.

'Is there a key?' I cross my fingers under the table. The fact that Brittania favoured the tower has only increased my gut instinct. I need to see whatever lies behind that door.

'Long-lost,' Lord Shilling declares.

No! I look at Eleanor, hoping he's bluffing, but she shakes her head too.

'I'm afraid it's been missing for ages, dear. I couldn't bring myself to go up there for a long time after Brittania died and, when I finally felt able, the key had disappeared.'

'Isn't there a spare?' I say, desperate. What kind of a castle doesn't have a big old bunch of spare keys?

'Bit odd, really. That's missing too,' Eleanor said. 'I always thought it was a sign that it was best left.'

I can't believe this. How can you live in a place for years with a locked room you can't access? I know it's a castle and all that, but it would drive me nuts. In fact it *is* driving me nuts, and

I'm only living here for three days. I bid them farewell and leave them to their game, hoping that Barty and Lois might be more forthcoming. If all else fails, there's always a locksmith.

I ease Babs to a juddery standstill and sit in the quiet cobbled alley at the side of the building beside Blithe Spirits for a few minutes before I head inside. I've come back to grab some things for my stay at Maplemead and to let my folks know I'm not going to be around for a few days. I won't lie; I know it's going to go down like a lead balloon. No, worse than that. Like a lead airship. It's a little before five o'clock, so my mum will still be up front closing up shop for the day and if I know Gran she'll be in the kitchen popping the cork on a bottle of champagne. Reaching over to the glovebox, I give it a half-hearted thump and pull out my magic-8 ball. Turning it over in my hands, I consider what it is I need an answer to.

Is it a bad idea to live with Fletcher Gunn at Maplemead for the next couple of days?

After a moment, the water clears.

Concentrate and ask again.

God, I hate it when it says that! I frown and try to work out what the real question is that I need an answer to. After a couple of quiet minutes, I spin it and try again.

Am I getting in over my head with Fletcher Gunn?

Signs point to yes.

Oh God. I think about re-shaking the ball, but what if it comes up with the same answer again? Or an even more decisive one? What will I do then? I know myself well enough to know that it won't make any difference to the outcome; I'll just throw myself headlong into disaster because that's what I always do. At some point in my life I might start to behave as if I understand that you can't keep doing the same thing and expecting a different outcome, but today is not that day. It can't be, because even though I know perfectly well that staying overnight under the same admittedly massive roof as Fletch is a bad plan, I'm going to follow through on it anyway.

I just need to go inside and break it to my mother.

'No way. Absolutely and categorically no.'

We are in my mother's kitchen, the setting of so many of my life's most important conversations, and I've just told them that I won't be around for the next few days because Lois and Barty have asked me to stay over at Maplemead. The conversation was relatively calm to begin with; in fact, I'd go as far as to say that Mum was quite keen on the idea.

'A mini-break in a castle! How lovely,' she said, flipping pancakes.

'So there will be just you and that dog in the whole castle?' Gran asks, sipping her champagne innocently.

That pancake is almost on the table. I draw the sugar bowl closer in readiness and lean back on my chair legs to grab cutlery from the drawer. Have you ever tried to shake your head whilst also saying yes in order to give out mixed signals? I try and do it now to throw them off the scent, at least until I have that pancake in my possession.

'Was that yes or no?' My mother demands verification, clutching the plate to her chest for leverage.

'It's a no,' I mumble, flipping the lid on the maple syrup. So what if it's going to be a double sugar hit? How can that be anything but a good thing? I've already eaten a massive wedge of Artie's mother's chocolate cake while I was throwing things into my overnight bag in my flat just now. I needed it to fuel up after the day I've had so far and I used it to distract me from the fact that I was packing for an impromptu slumber party with Fletcher

Gunn. I had a mini-crisis over whether to pack my fluffy black pyjamas. I like to think I channel Black Widow when I'm wearing them, but I fear I'm more like a small furry bat. Not Batwoman. Just a bat. Not that it matters, because there's no way Fletch is going to see me in my furry Black Widow slash fruit-bat costume, but what if there's a fire or something? I slipped my mint silk Hollywood starlet robe in too just in case, whilst trying not to remember my ridiculous claim to sleep in the nude like Marilyn Monroe. Seriously, what's wrong with me sometimes?

So the van is packed and now I just need to wrestle that pancake from my mother, tell her as little as possible without telling actual lies, and get out of there as fast as possible.

'You're not making yourself clear, Melody. Who else is staying at the castle with you?'

Oh man, that was direct. I almost wince and make a bit of a vague face. 'A few people. Couple of girls, couple of guys. It's going to be fine, Mum, honestly.'

She doesn't move a muscle, and the plate stays where it is.

'Who?'

Balls. Fine. 'Leo, Nikki and Vikki are staying there too.'

My mother starts to shake her head. 'Oh no. No, no, no. Those girls are *not* your friends, remember?'

Even Gran seems mildly perturbed. 'Sleep with one eye open, darling,' she warns.

'If it helps, they're not staying in the main building with me. Barty Letterman gave them one of the turrets. It's completely separate. They have their own front door and everything. In fact, they're technically going to be my neighbours, not housemates. I can lock them out.'

My mother's expression softens a fraction. She can't be blamed for not trusting the fembots; they've been fairly murderous towards me in the past and have been certified as crackerjacks by the police. She advances towards me with the plate and then, at the last moment, my gran tips her head to one side and counts slowly on her bony fingers.

'Couple of girls, couple of guys,' she lilts.

It's enough of a nudge for my mother, who narrows her eyes at me. 'Who is he?'

'Who is who?' I whisper and shoot Gran a death stare for coming between me and my pancake.

'A couple of guys, you said. Leo is one. Who is the other?'

I could practically lick the edge of the plate it's so close. 'Reporter,' I say, making quite an impressive job of not moving my lips. If this agency gig doesn't work out, maybe there's a future for me as a ventriloquist. I shoot my gran the evils again as I imagine her perched on my knee as my champagne-swilling, shit-stirring dummy. It doesn't help.

'What did you say?' my mother hisses, craning her neck forward.

'She said reporter, Silvana,' Gran says very loudly and shrugs at me when I bare my teeth at her.

My mother swishes her curtain of silver hair viciously over one shoulder. 'You better not be about to tell me it's Fletcher bloody Gunn.' My family hate Fletch with a robust passion; my crotch couldn't have picked a worse subject to feel amorous towards.

'It's Fletcher bloody Gunn,' I say, clear and loud to deny my gran the satisfaction of repeating me a second time.

'I *knew* this was a bad idea. Of all the reporters in all the world, why did they have to send him?'

I sigh. 'He said he was the only one available.'

And *that's* when my mother says: 'No way. Absolutely and categorically no.'

I could point out that I'm twenty-seven and don't even live with her any more, so she doesn't actually have any jurisdiction over what I do and who I do it with, but that will not help my pancake cause in the slightest, so I don't.

'It'll be fine,' I say breezily, as if it's nothing, nada, perfectly normal to be sleeping with the enemy. Not that I'm sleeping with him, of course.

'In which universe will it be fine, Melody? The one where Fletcher Gunn is not a megalomaniac hack intent on ruining us, column inch by column inch?' She isn't shouting, exactly; more loud, aggressive talking.

I feel my patience slip. 'In the universe where I offered to let a member of the press shadow me instead of them having to shadow you two, remember?'

She smacks the plate down on her side of the table, gripping the edges of it until her knuckles turn white. 'Yes! Shadow you at work! In the daylight, not in a castle on your own at night!'

'What do you think we're going to do?' I ask, exasperated.

'Play hide and seek?' Gran suggests, and we both glare at her.

'I think you're going to stay right here in this building until tomorrow morning,' she blazes, as if I'm fifteen again.

'No,' I say quiet and serious. 'No, Mum, I'm not. I'm a grown woman and when I say I'm going to do something, I do it. I'm not that keen on the idea myself, if I'm perfectly honest, but if staying under the same roof as Fletcher Gunn is what it takes to get the job done in time for Lois and Barty to welcome the film crew to a ghost-free Maplemead in a few days time, then that's exactly what I'm going to do.'

She knows that short of tying me to the chair, she cannot stop me, so she takes the only action available to hit me where it hurts. Stamping her foot down viciously on the pedal of the bin beside the kitchen counter, she upends the plate, and we all watch the pancake tumble and flip its way towards the bin. It's almost slow motion, and it takes everything I have not to hurl myself over the table to catch it before it lands, half in and half out of the bin.

Slowly, I flip the lid back down on the syrup and, with as much dignity as a girl can muster in pigtails and a Rainbow-Brite T-shirt, I shove my chair back and sweep out of the kitchen.

Bollocks. I forgot the frigging dog.

For a moment I contemplate leaving him behind, then I grit my teeth and fling the door open just in time to see Lestat dragging the pancake slowly out of the bin. He rolls his shifty eyes at me, a silent 'don't you judge me', as he tries to hoover it up. Furious, I haul his fat ass up off the floor and carry him, pancake and all, from the kitchen without a word.

'Would he like sugar on that?' my mother yells as I slam the kitchen door in temper, push the dog into the van, and pull out of the alleyway in a belch of exhaust fumes. Lestat grumbles on the seat beside me as I wind the window down, rip what's left of the soggy pancake from his jaws, and fling it at Blithe Spirits' window before I wheeze off down the High Street, turning the air inside the van blue as I go.

CHAPTER TEN

Fletch is sitting on the castle steps when I pull into the courtyard of Maplemead, his back against one of the stone columns
and his face turned up towards the low evening sunshine. He
looks as if he belongs there, as if the stonemason whittled him
to sit forever at the base of the column looking handsome and
inviting to castle visitors. With any luck Lestat will feel invited
to cock his leg and pee on him.

He gets to his feet and dusts off the ass of his jeans as I
drag my bag out onto the gravel and give Lestat enough of
a shove for gravity to send him tumbling out too. He's like
a hedgehog; he balls himself up tightly and rolls as far as he
possibly can before deciding if he can be arsed to use his stout
little legs and walk.

'Ghostbuster,' Fletch says, as I draw level with him.

'Hack,' I say, firing him a pithy look. I fish the huge brass key
from my back pocket and fit it into the oversized lock feeling like
Alice in Wonderland.

'Should I carry you over the threshold?' he says, close behind
me, and I pause, remembering that it wouldn't be the first time
he's carried me today.

'Pick me up again and I'll stick my foot so far up your backside
it'll come out of your mouth,' I say, battling with the monster key.

'Can I say that prospect isn't wholly without its appeal?' he
says as he leans over my shoulder and twists the key with embar-
rassing ease.

'Don't start,' I say, shouldering the door open with a creak. 'This is turning out to be one hell of a long day and I'm not in the mood for your particular brand of sarcasm, okay?'

He follows me inside, and I halt in the cool quietness of the reception hall. It's different being here as an inhabitant rather than a visitor. As a visitor I could marvel at the ornate carvings on the walls and be impressed by the huge windows and soaring ceilings. Now though, the vastness of these grand rooms engulf and overwhelm me, as if I'm alone at the funfair and got locked inside the haunted house. Or almost alone. Leaving the front door open for Lestat, I drop the dog bed down on the floor with my overnight bag beside it. I'm about to speak when my stomach lets out an almighty rumble.

'I was just about to ask you if you'd eaten,' Fletch says, drily.

'I'm not hungry.'

'Tell that to your guts. You're hungry alright.'

I shake my head, salivating at the thought of the pancakes I never got to eat because of him. Laying the key down on the side table, I notice a folded note with my name written neatly across the front of it.

There's dinner for two in the warming trolley in the dining room. Mr Dark and his guests have taken their evening meal in the tower. Breakfast will be served at 8 a.m. in the main castle.

Kind regards, Marilyn Foster, head cook and housekeeper at Maplemead Castle.

It's curiously formal considering we've already met, but I hand it to Fletch to read without comment. He glances at his watch.

'It's just gone seven. Shall I see you in the dining room at half past?' I must have looked sceptical, because he rolls his eyes. 'It's just food at the same table, Melody. I'm not asking you out on a hot date.'

He's successfully backed me into a corner where it would sound churlish to refuse, but all the same I struggle to say a civilised yes. I end up waggling my head like a chicken and he just sighs, picks up my overnight bag with his own, then makes for the stairs.

'I can carry my own bag,' I say, starting after him and grabbing for the handles. He doesn't fight me for it when I take it from him.

'Just trying to be polite,' he says as we reach the first-floor landing.

'Why change the habits of a lifetime,' I grump, half running to reach the door of my bedroom to get away from him. I hadn't noticed earlier, but there's a little plaque attached to the door that's engraved with Princess Suite. I don't feel very princessy at this very minute. I've got the weight of the world and the grime of the day on my shoulders; I want a shower and I need some dinner.

Across the corridor, Fletch pushes open the door of the room he's decided to sleep in. I glance along the whole corridor one way and then the other, then frown at him.

'There's at least five hundred bedrooms on this floor. Do you really have to sleep in the one right opposite mine?'

He taps the little silver plaque on his door. 'Every princess needs someone keeping guard, even sarcastic passive aggressive ones.'

I check out the plaque as he goes inside and closes his door. The Knight Suite. Jeez. Disney would have to be hard up to cast Fletcher Gunn as a knight and me as a princess. She'd be snarky and refuse to let him drag her from the jaws of the fire-breathing dragon and he'd shrug and pull out his camera to video her being eaten and make his fortune on YouTube.

I have one of those moments in the shower, a 'should I shave my legs just in case' moment, and then I stop and ask myself this: just in case of *what*, exactly? I pick up the razor and put it down again, because I cannot and will not shave my legs for

Fletcher Gunn. I shut off the water and then, just as I go to step out, it strikes me that I should shave my legs for *myself*, because I'm a thoroughly modern woman who likes to feel good, and that's exactly what I keep telling myself as I step back under the water and self-righteously whizz the razor up and down. There. Smooth, and all for my own pleasure and absolutely not for anyone else's.

I have a similar moment of uncertainty as I get dressed. I don't in any way want Fletcher Gunn to think I've dressed for him and our non-date, but it seems that all of the underwear I haphazardly threw into my bag is black lace, and I'd forgotten how the filmy fine-knit black sweater Marina gave me for Christmas clings to my waist, or how the wide neck keeps slipping off one of my shoulders. As I sit and apply a little make-up, I resolutely ignore the fact that I look more adult and feminine than I have in some time and I applaud myself for acting like a grown up who can handle herself and knows how to wing her eyeliner. A slick of mascara and a slash of nude lippy, and I'm as ready as I'll ever be to eat dinner with the man who is my business nemesis, a wind-up merchant, and who occasionally kisses me and turns my blood into fire in my veins.

'You're not seriously putting those on,' someone says as I sit on the edge of the bed and reach for my black Converse. I look up and find Britannia staring disdainfully at my shoes.

'Did I ask for your fashion opinion?' I ask, but I falter all the same.

'You actually look like a woman tonight. Don't blow it with those now.'

She crosses to a huge wardrobe, feels around on top of it for a second, then tosses a little key onto the bed. 'This was my room. Use whatever you need.'

'Your room? Did you live here at the castle then?'

She looks momentarily thrown. 'For a little while.'

'With your husband?'

I really want to get to grips with what they were doing at the castle at the time they died.

Brittania chews her lip. 'They were all here.'

'All?' I deliberately draw the word out in the hope of drawing more words out of Brittania too.

She wraps her arms around herself and smiles, faraway. 'Aunt Eleanor loved the circus. She used to let us spend our winters here, no one wanted to visit the circus in the snow. We'd perform for the villagers in the ballroom sometimes and, in exchange, she'd let the whole troupe stay here and prepare for the new season.'

I can't imagine that Lord Shilling can have approved of his castle being overrun with acrobats and elephants every winter. He must have loved Eleanor very much.

'Was that when the accident happened? When you were here for the winter?'

She looks at me, thrown. 'Accident?'

'The one where you hurtled to your death from the trapeze?'

Her shoulders sag. 'Oh. That.'

I know she's been dead for a long time, but surely she shouldn't need reminding? Unless, of course, it wasn't an accident? I file her response away to think about later.

I wait to see what she says next, but am left disappointed when she just taps the side of the wardrobe.

'Look inside. And, for the love of God, don't put those shoes on.'

And then she's gone, leaving only the little silver key on the bed as evidence that she'd been there at all.

Leaving my Converse on the floor ready to slip on, curiosity gets the better of me and I pick up the tiny key and cross to the mahogany wardrobe. It strikes me how much Marina would love to be me right now and then I turn the key and swing the door open.

Oh my God. Oh. My. God. The smell hits me first. It's female and seductive, like heady oriental flowers, instantly evocative of the woman who once owned these things. Exquisite clothes hang from ivory padded hangers; dresses that are little more than whispers of silk and satin, flashes of crystal hemlines, trails of silken ties, satin-lined fur stoles. My fingers slide lightly over them all, slippery soft and cool, and I pause and sigh with pure pleasure over a inky-purple floor-length halter-neck dress. I don't even wear dresses but, if I did, I'd want them to be like this.

One side of the wardrobe is fitted out top to bottom with shoe racks and there is not an empty shelf amongst them. Britannia was clearly a woman who adored fashion and she had the shoes to go with them all. Strappy, delicate sandals, gold dancing shoes, palest green and ivory T-bars, nude silk pumps. It's a treasure trove of heart-stopping yesteryear gorgeousness and I sigh as a pair of butter-soft black suede Mary-Janes almost fall out into my hands, mid-heeled and designed to fasten over the foot with sassy long satin ribbons. I stare at them and I can almost hear Britannia's whispers of encouragement in my ear as I wind the ribbons around my fingers. *Try them. Try them.* What harm can there be? I don't let my brain engage with reality at all. I just go with it, perching on the stool at the dressing table to slip my feet into them. They fit; of course they do. They were always going to. They're not massively high so even a heel novice like me can actually walk in them and, as I fasten the black silk ribbons, I'm overcome with a feeling of what I can only describe as *womanliness.* I'm not going to wear them tonight, of course. I stand up and catch sight of myself in the full-length wardrobe mirror and I hardly recognise the woman I see there. She's me, because she's wearing my trademark skinny jeans and she has my face, but she's not me, because the heels, ribbons and clingy sweater give her curves and there's a nervous glitter in her round dark eyes. She's me with flushed cheeks and a wave of Gok's magic wand and, all of a sudden, I have that same feeling I get whenever I put on my mint silk dressing gown. It's the shoes. I know I should change them, but I really don't want to take them off my feet and that's when I have another of those empowering moments like the one earlier in the shower. I glance at my black Converse beside the bed and then I think about the fact that I'm in a castle, for God's sake, and I know I'm not going to change into them.

I'm a twenty-seven-year-old woman and I don't dress for anyone but myself and, right now, I want to wear these to-die-for sexy shoes and that's exactly what I'm going to do. Emmeline Pankhurst did not burn her bra for me not to be a woman in charge of her own destiny and shoe choices. Buoyed by my own skewed-feminist pep-talk, I half run from the room before I can chicken out and change into my trusty flats.

I pause at the bottom of the stairs because I can hear the low murmur of voices. Intrigued, I move quietly towards the sound and then I stop and tuck myself behind the wall because Leo and Britannia are once more head to head beside the fireplace. They don't spot me, but I can see his face and I know that look in his eyes because he used to look at me that way. Bloody Britannia Lovell! The woman is to men what catnip is to cats. I can't catch their words, but somehow I don't think his line of questioning is going to be of any help to the case.

I jump as my text alert sounds loud in my back pocket and I regret letting Artie set the *Star Wars* theme as my ringtone because Leo seems to model himself on Kylo Ren and will no doubt think it's in homage to him. He'll conveniently gloss over the fact that Kylo Ren was a cold-blooded killer who murdered his own father and concentrate on the fact that he has good hair. Sorry for the spoilers. I'm left with no choice but to style it out with a nonchalant stroll from my spot behind the wall, as if I'd just chanced upon Leo and Britannia there that very second. I make a show of checking my phone as I stroll in, because that's how very relaxed and disinterested I am in their conversation.

Brittania turns around with an expression of panicky guilt all over her beautiful face, which clears quickly to relief when she sees it's only me rather than the ghost of her husband or her lover. God, it must be complicated being her.

She whispers something to Leo, then flees past me, murmuring 'nice shoes' slyly as she goes.

Leo looks at me and for a minute he seems disorientated, as if so very bewitched that he cannot focus on reality. I don't think for a second that I'm the one who bewitched him, but even so he does something of a belated double-take when he finally fixes on me.

'You look… different.'

I almost say different good or different bad, but then I remember this is Leo and his opinion is of no importance to me so I keep my mouth shut.

'I brought your dog back,' he mutters, by way of explanation of his presence. 'Nikki found him in her bedroom eating her prawn cocktail crisps. He'd ripped the bag open and was rolling around in them on her bedspread.'

It's such an overly detailed image that I don't know what to say. What I actually want to say is that Leo should know better than to associate himself with people who buy prawn cocktail crisps, especially people who eat them in bed. Fish and bed are two things that should never happen in the same sentence.

'Thank you,' I say, distracted because the text alert was from Marina, telling me to stop whatever I'm doing and check Twitter right now. I click it open and see why; the fembots have uploaded a photo of me and Fletch snogging in the upstairs hallway to the official Darklings feed. They've captioned it with something sarcastic about me working hard as usual and hashtags of #Leo-wouldnt and #allplayandnowork.

'Bollocks!' I seethe and scroll down to see Marina is locked in a furious running battle with them. Thank God my mother and gran aren't tech-savvy enough to be on Twitter.

'Did you know about this?' I stab my phone towards Leo and he glances at it then whips his own phone out to check what's going on. After a moment, he clicks it off and slides it back into his shirt pocket with a shrug. The look in his eye tells me he probably didn't know, but also that he's fine with the fembots' underhand attempts to discredit me. Times like this I see how very far apart we are these days.

'You better get over there and make them take that down right now,' I demand, my chin in the air. 'I've played fair with you so far and, trust me, you don't want me to let Marina at Nikki and Vikki after this. There might be two of them, but she's smarter, she's faster and, right now, she's ready to rip their heads off.'

He smirks. 'I'll see what I can do. You know how these things are though; it'll have gone viral by now.'

Thankfully, I doubt it. Leo might be popular these days because of his TV slot, but despite his over-inflated ego, he's not Kanye West. His followers probably have no clue who I am. I'm more worried that Glenda might be a Twitter ninja.

'Just deal with it,' I shoot back, and the supercilious smile on Leo's face renders him more Severus Snape than Kylo Ren.

'What did Britannia have to say just now?'

Hah. That wiped the smile off his face. Never before have I seen Leo Dark blush. He tries to bluff his way out of it, shrugging and muttering something about meeting her again tomorrow to discuss something urgent and then he takes his leave with a clatter of noisy leather soles on wooden floorboards and a swish of his glossy man-mane. I sigh as I close the heavy castle doors behind him to keep Lestat inside for the evening. I know from experience that getting attached to a ghost you're investigating is only ever going to lead to complications, but seeing as I'm standing there in Britannia's satin-ribboned shoes, I'm probably not in a position to judge.

CHAPTER ELEVEN

It's one of those perfect summer evenings and the garden is still sun-warmed and fragrant as I take five minutes to myself before dinner.

'Shouldn't you be in there on your hot date by now?'

I look up and find Brittania coming towards me along the garden path.

'It's not a date,' I say, distracted because I hadn't noticed her out here and wished I'd taken more notice of what she was up to. 'What were you doing out here?'

She glances over her shoulder quickly, a reflex check almost, and then shrugs. 'Pretending I could still feel the sunshine and smell the flowers.'

I feel momentarily guilty, because I'd just been idly enjoying both of those things.

'You seem to spend quite a lot of your time in the garden,' I venture.

Her face softens. 'It's one of my favourite places.'

She's such a difficult one to get a handle of. A sophisticated siren and then a lonesome waif wandering in the gardens. What draws her back out here so constantly? My gut instinct burbles again, telling me to tread carefully but that there's a piece of the puzzle here somewhere.

'Looks like you're late.' She nods towards the house and I spy Fletch through the open French doors of the dining room. When I turn back, she's gone.

I sneak back in through the kitchen to the dining room and inside I find Fletch lounging by the open doors with a glass of white wine in his hand. He's staring out over the lush gardens and he hasn't noticed me yet and I fight the urge to back out of the door again and run up to the relative safety of my bedroom.

On the table, a couple of bottles of wine rest in a chiller and a silver candelabra flickers. I'm not sure what to make of that; it feels a bit date-ish rather than dinner at the same table-ish, and that isn't the plan we agreed on. I consider blowing the candles out, but I don't because it'd look a bit over dramatic, wouldn't it? I plan on making a quiet entrance, but thanks to the clatter of my heels he realises I'm there and turns around as soon I make a move.

'Ghostbus…' his word trails off and he stares at me intently.

I freeze, awkward. 'What?'

'You dressed for dinner,' he says quietly.

'Did you expect me not to?' I quip.

He takes a sip from his wine and recovers himself. 'A guy can hope.'

My legs remember how to move again, so I head towards the end of the table that has been prettily laid for dinner for two.

'Well, I'm sorry to disappoint you,' I say lightly, noticing the small jug of freshly picked garden flowers.

Fletch lifts the open wine bottle from the ice bucket and pours me a glass. 'I didn't say that you'd disappointed me. I meant the opposite, actually,' he says. 'You look…' He pauses to choose his word carefully.

If he says different, I'm going upstairs to put my Converse and Little Miss Predictable T-shirt on.

'You look foxy as fuck.'

He just pressed that button again. Shit. I take the wine from him, down half of it in panic, and say the first thing I can think of.

'I'm wearing a dead woman's shoes.'

A smile kisses his lips as he shakes his head. 'You really need to learn how to take a compliment, ghostbuster.'

Resenting the suggestion that I'm gauche, I sip my wine and attempt to stand with one hip cocked, the way Marina naturally does, and I fidget awkwardly with the sloppy neck of my sweater like a teenager.

'I can take a compliment just fine.'

'Good,' he says. 'Then you won't mind if I tell you that I like the fact that your jumper stops me from having to wonder what colour your bra is and that you've got a killer ass in those jeans.'

'I'm not sure that knowing the colour of my underwear is a compliment, it's more of an letchy observation.' I frown. 'And as for my ass…' I look down. 'It's the dead woman's shoes. They make my legs look longer.'

Fletch pulls a chair out for me, watching me all of the time with amused eyes. 'For future reference, it's probably easier to just smile and say thank you when someone says something nice.'

I smile as advised. 'I'm not sure foxy as fuck counts as something nice, but thank you for the life advice.'

'You're welcome. It's probably appropriate for you to say something nice back to me now, too.'

'Don't push your luck,' I say, although, in truth, I've already registered the effort he's made this evening. His dark charcoal shirt looks expensive and fits him in a way that accentuates his body, which we both know I think is as firm as a racehorse and as hot as morning bed sheets. God alive, I can feel my cheeks starting to burn. For a non-date, all of this foxy as fuck chat about the colour of my bra and thoughts about his hot body are highly inappropriate.

'Did you see what happened on Twitter just now with Leo's fembots?' I ask, changing the subject.

Reaching into his pocket, Fletch pulls out a lurid pink mobile and lays it on the table.

I swallow. 'That's a bold colour choice for a man like you.'

'It's not mine. It's theirs. The crazy twins. It was like taking candy from a baby.'

I frown, not following.

'It wasn't just you who looked bad in that photograph,' he says. 'I've dealt with it.'

I don't even want to ask him how he distracted the twins for long enough to steal their mobile.

Clicking my own phone on, I see that the image has indeed been taken down and there's a new one up now, one of Leo passed out on the castle sofa in a dead faint after his first encounter with Goliath. It's accompanied with a #sleepingonthejob hashtag and a #pretentiousknob one for good measure.

I don't know whether to be impressed, amused or even more pissed off. Between Marina and Fletch, the fembots will have at least learned that if you poke a stick in a hornets' nest, you should expect to get stung.

'So, dinner,' I say nervously, getting up again fast although I've only just sat down. 'Let's see what there is.'

An old-fashioned hostess trolley sits close by and I slide the top open to reveal what appears to be a chicken casserole and a side dish of little herby roasted potatoes tossed with green beans.

'Mediterranean chicken and chorizo stew,' Fletch says, reading from a little handwritten menu card on the table.

God, it smells delicious. I hadn't realised quite how hungry I was until now. Reaching for a couple of warm plates and taking them out from the trolley, I spoon some food onto one and place it down in front of Fletch.

'Thank you,' he says, waiting for me to join him with my own plate before picking up his cutlery.

I steal a glance at him as I reach for my fork and catch my breath. The candlelight casts golden shadows across his face and I'm jittery because, all of a sudden, he looks like a sophisticated, grown-up, worldy man. I mean, I know I'm a proper grown-up woman too, but I feel about sixteen most of the time, and I try very hard not to think of Fletch as anything but the smart-arse hack who gets under my skin.

He glances up and catches me looking, so raises his glass. 'To your foxy ass and your dead woman's shoes.'

I touch my glass to his without comment. Under different circumstances, this could be wildly romantic. We're sharing a delicious candlelight dinner alone in a gorgeous castle and there is undeniable sexual chemistry between us.

'We should talk about what I'm hoping will happen here over the next couple of days,' I say, because I'm keen to steer the conversation towards work.

'That's refreshingly forward of you,' he grins. 'Would you like to go first or shall I? For the record, I'm a fan of girl on top.'

A butterfly unfurls its wings in my gut and takes flight behind my ribs.

'Can you just stop with the innuendoes, please?' I lay my cutlery down and look at him steadily, valiantly keeping all sex images out of my head. 'I didn't expect the paper to respond to the email about shadowing me so quickly, I didn't necessarily think it would be you, and I certainly didn't imagine in a million years that we'd end up spending a couple of nights together alone here like this.'

He eats slowly as he listens to me, taking a sip of his wine as he waits for me to go on. His expression is completely unreadable and I feel a fresh flush of panic scuttle beneath my skin.

'What I'm trying to say is just because we're two people sharing a delicious candlelight dinner alone in a gorgeous castle and there is undeniable sexual chemistry between us,' I pause for air and to wish that my inner monologue had not just become my outer monologue, 'it doesn't follow that we have to have sex, girl on top or girl on bottom.' I almost hum with panic because I think

I might have accidentally just offered him anal sex. 'One plus one does not always equal two, Fletcher.'

He frowns. 'It does.'

I shake my head. 'Nope. One plus one can still be one. Or three. Or sometimes it can even be five.' I don't have a clue what I'm jabbering on about.

'In the context of sex, Melody, one is masturbation, three is a ménage à trois and five is edging towards an orgy.'

Christ, now he's saying lots of sex words and I've gone so hot that I might need to take my sweater off before I pass out. This is going very badly and we've only been in the same room five minutes.

'You shouldn't have lit the candles,' I say, accusatory, looking to blame him for getting the evening off on the wrong footing. 'You know this isn't a date.'

'I didn't light them. I thought you did.'

'Funny,' I snark.

'He didn't light them. I did.' Britannia appears through the nearest wall.

I should have known. 'Did you pick the flowers from the garden too?' I ask.

'No,' he says.

'Yes,' she says.

'You shouldn't have. This isn't a date.'

'Will you stop saying that? I know it isn't, and I didn't try to turn it into one. You're the one who brought up sex, not me,' he says, exasperated.

'It looks a lot like a date to me.' Britannia laughs, then casts a longing look towards Fletch. 'Don't be such a schoolgirl, Melody. He's divine, and he wants you very much. Even I can feel his sexual energy and I've been dead for a century. God knows how he's keeping his hands off you.'

'Will you just piss off?' I mutter. 'This is difficult enough without you hanging around whispering clap-trap at me to wind me up!'

A pulse flashes along Fletch's set jaw and his cutlery rattles as he puts it down. 'Jesus, you're like a faulty air-conditioning unit. You blow hot, you blow ice cold. What the hell did I do so wrong here tonight?'

'Uh-oh. You've upset him now,' Brittania whispers, her coal-dark eyes flashing with glittery excitement. 'What on earth can you do to smooth his feathers, I wonder? I think drastic action is the only way.' She looks at him, her head on one side. 'Straddle him, perhaps?'

And then she disappears, laughing, and I'm quiet for a moment whilst I contemplate what she said. Is he really so pent-up with wanting that he's having a hard time keeping a lid on it? Or is Britannia doing what she seems to do so well, stirring the romantic pot for her own amusement? The word vixen could have been invented just for her.

He's staring at me. What was that about an air-conditioning unit? I'm confused. I reach for the wine and refill my glass and, while I'm about it, I top his up too.

'Sorry,' I murmur, aware that what I said to Britannia must have sounded rude out of context.

He shakes his head as if to clear it, then picks up his knife and fork again. We eat in silence for a few minutes, then I lay down my cutlery.

'There are ghosts from a circus here in the castle and one of them, Britannia Lovell, was here just then. She's a terrible flirt and she was being a pain in the ass so I told *her* to piss off, not you.' I take a good mouthful of wine. 'She's gone again now.'

'Will she be back, do you think, or can we finish our dinner in peace?' he asks mildly, and I think what he's really asking me is if I'm planning to be randomly rude to him again, as if I have a split personality and my head might start rotating three hundred and sixty degrees on my shoulders at any moment.

'I don't know,' I answer him truthfully, because he's here to shadow me and the ghosts, and he's going to find that pretty damn hard to do if I don't tell him they're there. 'She said that she could feel your sexual energy even though she's been dead for a hundred years, and that it's a wonder you're keeping your hands off me.'

He's staring at me again. 'Why are you doing this?'

'Because you can't see them and I can and I thought the whole bloody idea of you shadowing me is to know what I do, how I feel, what I see and what I hear.'

'Right. And did she say anything else or can we eat dessert now?'

I shrug. In for a penny, in for a pound, otherwise known as I've drunk two large glasses of wine in quick succession and my tongue is loosening dangerously. 'She said that I should consider straddling you to smooth your ruffled feathers.'

'And there you go again, flicking the switch over to hot,' he huffs, looking at the ceiling. He's breathing in that measured way people do when they're trying not to fly off the handle. 'So which is it to be, ghostbuster? Peach cobbler, or would you like to straddle my crotch first?'

I guess I asked for that.

'Pudding. Definitely pudding.'

I get up from the table, relieved to have something to do. It's an indication of how skittish I feel that even the idea of pudding isn't enough to relax me. I scoop dollops of the golden crunchy-topped peaches into a couple of bowls and carry them to the table, then ferry the accompanying jug of warm custard across and sit down again without looking at him.

'It's good,' I say, after a couple of minutes. And it is; fabulously sweet and comforting. I can feel the sugar whizzing around my blood and restoring my equilibrium.

'I don't really have much of a sweet tooth,' he says, laying his spoon down, his pudding half eaten. 'Frankly, I'd have preferred it if you'd straddled me.'

And he says *I* blow hot and cold; I feel as if he's just blow-torched my face.

'Fletch—'

'I know,' he sighs like a man resigned to his fate. 'It wasn't your idea, the dead woman told you to say it.'

When he puts it like that, I sound crazy. 'Is that really how you see me? As borderline insane?'

He looks as if he's struggling to articulate himself, which is unusual for him. 'You probably don't want me to answer that.'

'Yes I do.' I swallow and I wait because, actually, I really, really do want him to answer me.

'We're just very, very different people,' he says diplomatically, opening the second bottle of wine. 'I'm straightforward and analytical, and you're… you're neither of those things.'

'So what am I then?'

'Fishing for compliments?' he says, filling our glasses.

I pull my glass towards me and drag my finger down the chilled condensation on the side of it. 'I'm not. I just don't like the thought that I come across as bonkers.'

Fletch looks as if he's going to say something and then looks pointedly at the empty chair beside him.

'Stop pissing about, will you,' he hisses at it. 'I'm trying to have a conversation here.'

Turning back to me again, he smiles with an apologetic shrug. 'Sorry. There's the ghost of a merry monk from the castle's days as a monastery here and he keeps lifting his cassock and showing me his hairy knees. Oh, and he's just suggested that I ask you for a lap dance.'

I look at the empty chair and then back at him in horrified silence and then I push my pudding bowl aside and lay my head on the table and close my eyes, because he's right. For the last minute or so he looked like he'd completely lost his marbles, and that is precisely how I must appear to him and pretty much everyone else in the world, speaking to thin air and saying ludicrously random things that make no sense. How absolutely depressing.

I'm protected, lucky, I guess you could call it, because I'm insulated by the fact that I spend most of my time around people who either see the world as I do, or else people who believe in me implicitly and don't make me feel like a crackpot. Fletch isn't being deliberately unkind; he's just showing me what it's like to be him around me and I feel like a prize fool.

'I'm tired, Fletch,' I say, because I realise that I'm not just tired, I'm actually exhausted. Today has been a long and disjointed day, punctuated with some moments that I won't forget in a long time. Was it really only this afternoon that Fletch threw me over his shoulder? It feels a week or more ago at least.

'Get your head up off the table and defend yourself, you lily-livered ninny.' Britannia, right on cue.

I don't open my eyes or answer her, because I'm now acutely aware of how ridiculous I look through Fletch's eyes.

'It's half past ten,' he says quietly. 'Maybe we should call it a night.'

His fingers lightly smooth my hair back from my face and when I finally open my eyes, he's standing up.

'Come on.' He holds his hand out to me and the expression on his face is almost impossible to read; the closest I could get to a description would be longing. 'Let's go to bed.'

CHAPTER TWELVE

He leads me from the dining room, his fingers laced casually in mine. I can hear the low airplane engine-style rumble of Lestat's snoring coming from the direction of the kitchen, so I feel safe to assume that he's eaten the monstrously huge bone that Cook had left out for him as well as his usual fare and is now away with the fairies in his bed beside the gargantuan Aga. Castle living clearly agrees with him more than it does me.

'Okay?' Fletch catches me around the waist because I'm swaying a little thanks to the several glasses of wine in heels on stairs situation.

'I'm climbing the sweeping staircase of a stately castle with warm bed sheets man,' I whisper. 'Must not fuck up. Must not fuck up.'

'Are you talking to yourself?'

I nod, hoping he didn't catch my last words. 'To myself and no one else, Fletcher Gunn.'

He laughs under his breath and I'm aware of his fingers spanning my waist. 'You don't even need the ghosts to make you weird, you do a great job all on your own.'

He's aiming for light-hearted, yet I find his comment makes my heart anything but light.

'I know, I know,' I sigh, as we approach our doors. 'You think I'm weird and that the way I can talk to ghosts makes me look insane and I'm kooky and crazy and, oh, isn't she just bizarre! Don't you think I've lived my whole life with those kind of labels, Fletch?'

He looks disconcerted as I reach for the handle of the Princess Suite.

'I know what you're thinking,' I say. 'You're thinking here she goes again, turning the ruddy blower wotsit onto cold. Well, you're right, because I can't go to bed with someone who thinks I'm foxy as fuck to look at but batshit crazy on the inside. From now on let's keep it stuck on hell freezes over ice cold all the sodding time. Let's make it so ruddy freezing that the castle becomes an ice palace and your knob shrinks as tiny as a walnut pickled in a jar.'

At this point I try to show him just how small a walnut is between my thumb and forefinger, then I wave my hand in the vague direction of his walnut crotch. God I'm drunk. How strong was that wine? I'm no seasoned drinker, but I can usually hold my own better than this over a few glasses.

'Go to bed, princess.' Fletch doesn't react to my tirade, just presses his lips against my forehead. 'You need some sleep.'

'*Ice* princess,' I correct him, leaning against his chest. 'I'm practically fucking Elsa.'

He slides his hand down to the small of my back and laughs softly in my ear. 'Who's Elsa and can I watch?'

I frown. 'Do you kiss your mother with that mouth, Fletcher Gunn?'

'My mother's dead.'

'God, I'm sorry.' I look up at him, stricken by his flat tone and bald words. We stare at each other in silence for a few long moments. 'I really don't know the first thing about you, do I?'

He reaches behind me and pushes my door open. 'Go to bed, Melody. I'll be right across the hall if you need me.'

And with that, he turns away and leaves me standing alone in the hallway.

* * *

'I don't think this shadowing thing is going to work out, Fletch.'

He shakes the morning paper out on the breakfast table and scans the headlines, like a bored businessman before he leaves for work in the city.

'I don't give up on assignments,' he says, offhand. He turns the page as Hells Bells hurries in with a mammoth English breakfast and places it down in front of him.

'The dog has had some sausages,' she says breathlessly, winding one of her vivid orange plaits around her fingers as she looks at me. 'And some bacon. And black pudding. And a scotch egg.'

'Thank you,' I murmur, wondering if they've confused Lestat with a small, fat, really ugly horse and feeling glad that I don't have to share a bed with him tonight.

Once Hells Bells is out of earshot, I try again.

'You wouldn't be giving up on the assignment. It's me that's changed my mind, not you.'

He closes the paper and regards me steadily across the dining table. 'I'm sorry if my crack about the lap-dancing monk hit a raw nerve,' he says, spooning sugar into his tea.

'It did,' I say, honestly. 'And I'm equally sorry if my crack about your rude mouth was insensitive under the circumstances.'

'It wasn't,' he says shortly. 'You didn't know. No tea and sympathy required, it was a long time ago and I'm a big boy now.'

I've never stopped to think of Fletch as someone's son or someone's brother or someone's friend, even. It casts him in a different light, one I'm not sure I'm entirely comfortable with. He has a clearly defined role on the periphery of my life; he's Fletch the annoying hack, Fletch my verbal sparring partner, Fletch, the man who occasionally snogs me senseless.

'Think of it this way. If you pull me off the job, the supplement will run anyway. I'm obliged to file the report up to this point and then state that you asked me to leave because you weren't comfortable with being watched.' He cuts a sausage in half and makes 'aw shucks' eyes at me. 'Hate to say it, but it smacks of flaky, ghostbuster.'

Fine. If he's determined to stick this out, then I won't give him the satisfaction of seeing me interact with the ghosts again; that little performance of his at dinner last night hit home. I'll make sure he knows enough of what's going on to write his precious report, but no way am I going to look like a crackpot or have him portray me as such for the sake of column inches.

I flounce out of the open French doors into the garden and leave him there to chow down on his meat mountain.

Stomping around the paths, I pause once I'm out of sight behind the shrubbery and call Fletch a few choice names to make myself feel better. It doesn't, especially, but seeing as I'm out here on my own I use the time to have a poke around to see if I can work out what it is that draws Brittania out here so often.

There isn't anything obvious to seize on. Flower beds in fine summer bloom, lush rhododendron bushes, a herb garden with little wooden name sticks to guide the gardener.

I'm thinking of heading back inside when I spot what looks like the top edge of a wooden bench behind the bushes, and as I stand and study the foliage, I can just about make out a long overgrown path leading between the big, frilly rhododendron heads.

Glancing around to check Fletch hasn't snuck up on me, I push my way through the flowers and find myself in a small clearing and there is indeed an old, intricate bench. It strikes me as an odd site for it really; the castle grounds are so gorgeous, why would someone choose to hide themselves away behind here? The old wood groans a little as I take a seat, pushing my hands underneath my thighs as I survey the hidey-hole. The plant life isn't so abundant back here; it doesn't get much sunlight, so the ground is dry, patchy grass and not much else, and I'm facing the bottom of the garden wall a few feet away. There has to be something here, I know it. Dropping to my knees to inspect the ground, I scrub my hands methodically over the grass and crawl towards the tall tangle of weeds against the wall. The exposed, pale grey bricks are smooth to the touch and, as I clear away the plants, my fingers slowly work until they come into contact with something amongst the leaves. More carefully now, I keep going until I reveal a wooden cross bracketed flush against the wall. It's about a foot tall and quite chunky and it's been engraved with initials in an old-fashioned, curly script that makes me sit very still so my brain can connect the dots.

B. B.

It takes me less than a minute to deduce that they must stand for Brittania and Bohemia.

Acting on a sudden hunch, my heart races a little faster as I start to move the rocks lined up at the bottom of the wall aside. I daren't dig too deeply for fear of what I might unearth, but if I can just go down an inch or so I might be lucky. My fingers scrabble in the loose soil and I have a bit of a turn when I encounter a fat, wriggling earthworm, but after a few strenuous, unpleasant minutes mooching, my fingers finally close around the thing I'm looking for. My hunch was right. The key.

I pull my phone out and photograph the engraving for the file and then reach out and trace my fingers over the letters. What is this place? Try as I might, I can't shake the feeling that I'm sitting by Brittania and Bohemia Lovell's gravesides.

I've never been more glad to see Marina than I am when she and Artie turn up together just after nine. Having them here bolsters me because they're in my corner without question and I'm extra glad because she's carrying a clear-lidded box of prettily iced cupcakes. My fine-tuned sugar barometer suggests salted cara-mel; roll on tea break.

'Saw these and thought of you,' she says with a grin, pushing them into my hands. 'How was your night?'

I resolutely don't look at Fletch, who's followed me through into the reception hall. 'Uneventful.'

'Nothing went bump in the night,' he drawls. I don't know if he's referring to us or the ghosts.

I hand Artie the box of cupcakes. 'Artie, would you mind taking these down to the kitchen, please, and check in on Lestat while you're there?'

He nods, and as he draws closer I can smell aftershave, which is highly unusual on Artie. I almost pass a jokey comment on how it reminds me of a teenage locker room, but then I bite my tongue because I suspect that he's hoping to impress a certain little kitchen maid. He lopes away, pulling awkwardly at the bottom of his *Star Wars* T-shirt, and I catch Marina's eye and know that she's rumbled him too. I think we both feel nervous for him; I hope for Hells Bells's sake that she doesn't turn out to be a heartbreaker because I fear that Marina might choke her with her pretty orange plaits.

I'd dearly love to grab Marina for a catch-up right about now, but I'm thwarted by the squawky arrival of Lois and Barty.

'We come bearing happy news, my darlin's!' Lois looks back in fine form now that she's not terrified or knackered, back to her happy-clappy self as she and Barty breeze in, demanding our instant attention.

She's top-to-toe in peach velour this morning, with a matching terry towelling band sun visor and a face full of shiny make-up. Barty looks equally dapper in his anyone-for-tennis garb, although I've yet to see the man actually wield a racket.

'News?' Leo queries, draping himself carelessly over one of the armchairs. The fembots, as fresh as little daises in lemon mini-dresses and huge Jackie O sunglasses, perch either side of him on the chair's arms, their shiny knees crossed and their heads moving in jerky little movements to follow the conversation.

It totally wouldn't surprise me if they had those little battery panels on their backs like the dolls Marina and I had as kids. Mine is probably still in the attic at Blithe Spirits somewhere, but Marina's won't have been saved as a memento. I know this because she gave hers a crew cut within a week of owning her and, within six months, she'd lost a leg and had four fingers on one hand.

Lois is so jittery with excitement that she's practically bouncing on the spot by the fireplace.

'We're having ourselves a big ole party!'

As news goes, it wasn't that shocking a revelation really. But given how shaky she was about the castle when we last saw her, I was half-expecting her to say that they were selling up rather than planning a bash. The wonders of uninterrupted sleep.

'Party?' I say, with a small, enquiring, please-do-elaborate smile.

She nods and claps her hands, delighted. 'A ball, actually.'

'In the ballroom?' I venture, flickering a glance towards Leo, because he's the only other person who's seen the same macabre scenes as I've seen in the castle's beautiful ballroom.

'Of course,' Lois says, in the grand, offhand way that only people who own an actual ballroom can. 'A masquerade ball, naturally.'

'Someone's been watching *Eyes Wide Shut*,' Marina murmurs beside me and I'm a little bit sick in my mouth at the thought of being rogered over a sideboard by Barty in a snood and a phantom of the opera mask. I go quickly from queasy to hot and bothered as someone far sexier strolls into my head, head to toe in black with a black strip across his eyes that renders him superhero. He's tall, he's fit, and when he turns to look my way I see that he's—

'Melody?'

I tune back in when Lois says my name loudly, annoyed at not getting to know the identity of my sexy superhero. They're all staring at me.

'This Saturday seems a bit soon for the ball, don't you agree?' Marina clues me in. She knows that progress has been slow to non-existent so far on the case and is trying to buy me some time while I'm too busy daydreaming about being whisked off my feet by Tonto to pay attention.

Lois bats the air like Top Cat. 'Saturday is perfect. The cast and crew arrive in town on Friday, it's the perfect way to show them that this place is ghost-free and good to go, which it will be, right?'

Today is Tuesday. Saturday is five days away. There's no way I can guarantee that we'll have drilled down to the root of the problems here by then, but Lois has just morphed from kindly school teacher into the evil ice queen from Narnia in front of my eyes. She smiling at me, but she's emanating so much frost that I fear my nipples are going to freeze and drop off.

I want to object, to say it might not be enough time, but when I look at Leo I notice that Britannia has put in an appearance on his lap. Shit. She's trouble with a capital T, and he's completely distracted and unable to either disagree or reason with Lois because Brittania is whispering sweet nothings in his ear.

'Leo, what do you think?' I say, and they both look my way. Britannia's eyes dance with positive devilment, but his eyes couldn't be more serious and that scares the bejeezus out of me, so I decide not to wait for his very compromised opinion. This is going from bad to worse, I may as well go for broke.

'You know what, Lois? I hear the weather is forecast to be a mini-heatwave over the weekend,' I say, beaming at her. 'That sounds like pretty perfect party weather to me.' I throw her a cheesy double thumbs-up for good measure, and everyone else in the room beside Barty and Lois look at me as if I've completely lost my mind. I haven't, but if I don't do something fast I fear that Leo might be about to.

CHAPTER THIRTEEN

'Artie Elliott, your face is as red as my lipstick! What *have* you been doing down in the kitchens for so long?'

Artie has just appeared in the library with Lestat in tow, and Marina is absolutely right about the fact that his head resembles a pickled beetroot. If anything, he turns even more puce at Marina's observation, and she picks up a magazine from a side table and fans him as she laughs knowingly.

Artie shoots a nervous glance my way and swallows audibly.

'I haven't been doing anything.' He shrugs, rubbing his hand around the back of his neck. I think there are beads of actual sweat breaking out on his brow.

'Did Hells Bells make a pass at you?' Trust Marina to cut straight to the point.

Fletch stifles a half-laugh and pulls a book from the nearest shelf to look as if he's not listening, and I'm glad that the others are still in the main reception hall and out of earshot.

'What?' Artie yelps. 'No! Of course she didn't. She wouldn't! She's not like that.'

'There's nothing wrong with a woman taking control, Artie,' Marina says archly. 'Just because we're in a castle, it doesn't mean the kitchen maid has to be seen and not heard.'

'Or screwed by the master of the house as she peels the spuds,' Fletch murmurs, flicking idly through his book. He looks up when we all stare at him accusingly. 'Sorry,' he shrugs. 'Too many episodes of *Game of Thrones*.'

I send him the death stare. Artie is Fletch's polar opposite in terms of experience or worldliness and I feel my protective gene kick in hard.

'Not everyone's brain operates at your sewage level,' I hiss out of the side of my mouth. 'She's a very nice girl and that's an outrageous thing to suggest in this day and age.'

'Said the princess to the knight,' he shoots right back and chucks in one of his infuriating winks that makes me want to find something sharp to poke his eye out with.

'You're no knight,' I mutter.

'But you're every inch the princess,' he says softly, and my knees go unaccountably weak. God, I hate myself! There's something about the deep, gravelly tone of his voice that makes my ovaries twang. Please, someone, stop me. If I stay in this castle much longer I'll be asking him to crawl underneath my crinoline and kiss my Batman pants.

'She gave me a sausage roll,' Artie says, laying the linen-napkin-wrapped pastry down on a marble side table and gazing at it wistfully. It's bloody massive. 'She said she made it especially for me. What do you think that means?'

We all look at it with him and I really hope no one says anything stupid.

'Maybe she thinks you look like you have a good appetite?' I say.

'She wanted to give you a gift,' Marina decides.

Fletch grins. 'She wants your hot sausage.'

It was always going to be him.

'*Game of Thrones* again?' I snark.

He laughs. 'Not unless it was the triple X-rated version.'

Trust him to bring up porn over a sausage roll. I don't like that gloaty look on his face either; it says *I'm cool because I watch dirty things that you don't watch.*

'Don't look down your nose at me, Fletcher Gunn,' I say, thrusting my chin at him. 'You're not the only one who watches porn, you know. Sometimes I flick the adult channel on late at night when I'm alone… with the dog.'

Marina choke-laughs, Artie looks alarmed and Fletch nods seriously, interest in his mirth-filled, glass-green eyes.

I should never have said that. The closest I get to porn is rewinding *Poldark* to watch him doing manly things with his scythe, but I've started now so I brazen it out regardless.

'Go on,' Fletch says, crossing his arms over his chest and leaning on a glass-fronted bookcase. 'I'm riveted.'

Oh piss off, you supercilious twat. That's what I want to say and, on reflection, it would probably have been better than what I actually said next.

'Oh, I pay per view with the best of them. Brandy, the er, randy stripper, is practically on my payroll.' I attempt to crick my neck like I'm one of the lads for good measure.

Fletch laughs openly and Marina is trying so hard to keep herself together that a silent tear runs down her cheek.

'So you and your one-eared pug pay to view late-night lesbian porn?'

'Did I say she was a lesbian?' I say, hotly. I'm sure I didn't, and I don't like the way he's making assumptions about fictitious Brandy.

'No, but I figured that she must be if you're paying her to strip for you. Or maybe she isn't, but you are.'

'God, what is it with you?!' I half shout. 'Women can enjoy other women's company without being lesbians, you know!'

'I don't mind if you're a lesbian. It's sexy.' `

Oh God, this has gone badly off the rails. He thinks I'm a sexy lesbian who forces her dog to watch late-night porn.

Artie frowns, gazing at the sausage roll. 'I don't think I can eat it. It's too big.'

'I bet Brandy could manage it,' Fletch murmurs, so low that only I hear him.

'She doesn't get involved with food,' I whisper cattily. *I am actually insane.* 'Not since the tricky incident with, um, a yam. It was a special request from one of her punters.'

'Brandy sounds like a game girl. Can I have her number?'

'She's too busy to fit you in.'

He laughs. 'I imagine she must be, what with all those unfortunate vegetable-related sexual incidents and stripping off for you and the pug.'

'It was only one yam, not the whole vegetable aisle in Sainsbury's!' I'm hazy on what a yam looks like. I've probably suggested something anatomically impossible.

'I genuinely cannot fathom what goes on inside your head, ghostbuster,' he says. 'You're the most unusual person I've ever met.'

What the hell even was that? A compliment or an insult?

'I think you made it perfectly clear last night that you think I'm some kind of crazy nut,' I say, angry out of nowhere. 'And, for the record, you make me feel it more than anyone else I know, so quit with the unusual person crap, will you? I know I'm different. I'm painfully fucking aware of it, thank you very much.'

I stomp straight out of the library, out of the open castle door, and I don't stop until I'm hidden behind the hulking protection of Babs and can slide down on my ass and hold my head in my hands.

'Melody?' Marina's beside me on the gravel in seconds. 'What's happening here?'

I understand her concern. I'm not given to emotional outbursts. She's the one with the soft, sentimental spot a mile wide, I'm the tough as nails one who prefers blood and guts to hearts and flowers.

'I need to ask you a question and I want you to be completely honest with me,' I say.

She frowns. 'I've never lied to you. Unless it's about whether it was me who cut Susan Benson's ponytail off when we were fourteen because she kept taking the piss out of you.'

'I *knew* that was you!' I say, completely distracted. I've always had my suspicions, but it happened in a crushed corridor and it could have been any one of a number of suspects. Susan Benson was one of those girls who got on a lot of people's nerves with her big mouth and bad attitude; all flicky ponytail and too much electric-blue eyeliner, that is until someone hacked her hair off and left her with no choice but to have an unflattering mullet for a good three months while the brutal chop grew out.

'Better that you didn't know, then you couldn't be guilty by association,' she says. 'I'm still not sorry, the gobby cow. I think I still have her ponytail in a drawer somewhere.'

For a moment we sit and reflect on that macabre revelation. She's one step away from that nutter in *Silence of the Lambs* who makes dresses from his victims' skin.

'Do I look like a crazy woman when I'm speaking to ghosts?'

'What?' She looks at me, surprised, as if I actually am a crazy woman. 'Why would you ask that? Has Fletcher Gunn been winding you up when I'm not there to black his eye for him?'

'No,' I say, picking at my now untidy orange nail polish. 'Yes. Not exactly, not really. He just… I don't know, he made me see how it must be for everyone else to see me talk to empty chairs or vacant spaces, and now I feel like a bit of a fool.'

'A fool?' Marina looks mutinously towards the castle. 'Melody Bittersweet, do you have any clue how special what you can do is? Yes, it makes you different, but different good, not different bad! Jesus, are you seriously going to let some cynical bloke dull your shine or take away your pride and self-belief? So what if no one else can see what you can see or understand that the chair isn't empty? That's our loss, not yours. It's pretty bloody magnificent to watch you work and anyone who chooses to make you feel anything less than fucking brilliant needs my foot shoving up their backside, even if the backside in question is fit and attached to the bloke you seem to have decided is the next man you're going to go to bed with.'

She pulls a tissue out of her bra and shoves it into my hands, presumably in case I decide on a good old cry. She doesn't use the tissues to boost her cup size; Mother Nature already blessed her with a bosom that stops traffic. She's just one of those women who views her bra as additional on-board storage. Tissues, pens, gum, her phone, she's got the lot stashed down there. She used to put her lipstick in there too until the day it melted all over her cleavage and her mother thought she'd been shot in the chest at point-blank range.

'Did Artie's sausage roll tip you over the edge?'

I laugh softly at the stupidity of her suggestion, just as she knew I would.

'No.'

She squeezes my knee. 'Sudden onset of panic over whether we can get the job done in time for the party?'

I sigh hard. 'That's part of it. I don't feel as if I'm making enough headway.' I feel around in my back pocket and pull out the key. 'Although I did find this just before you arrived this morning. It's for the turret, I hope.'

Marina nods. 'Well there you go then! I know it feels like longer, Melody, but we've only been on the job for a couple of days. They've barrelled in here this morning demanding that you rush, but you can only do what you can do. It'll work itself out. And, remember, we're not the only ones on the case this time. Can Leo help out?'

She even sounds dubious herself, because we both know that the words 'Leo' and 'help' aren't generally good bedfellows. Leo is a fully paid-up member of the self-preservation society; his help is conditional on it being advantageous to him. That's under normal circumstances, anyway. These circumstances stopped being normal when he started going doe-eyed over Britannia Lovell, who is fully aware of what she's doing and revelling in her feminine power over a beating heart for the first time in a century.

'It's a bit complicated,' I sigh. 'Leo seems to have fallen hook, line and sinker for Britannia Lovell. He's like a lovesick puppy whenever she puts an appearance in.'

Marina rolls her eyes and her laugh is full of scorn. 'That's just *so* Leo Dark.' She narrows her eyes and suddenly clamps her hand hard around my knee. 'You're not jealous, are you?'

'God, no,' I shoot back, fast and furious. I'm genuinely not jealous, it's just messy seeing him so smitten. 'I don't think he's going to be an awful lot of help in getting rid of her, because he's enjoying having her around so much. That's all.'

'Sure?'

God, she knows me too well sometimes. Don't judge me on this because I don't harbour any hopes or rose-tinted delusions of a future for me and Leo, but it hits me in a soft, secret corner of my heart to see him melt for someone else right in front of my eyes. It's not as if he's being subtle; he's mesmerised. I'm sure the day will come when he meets a real, live woman who makes him feel that way and actually that will be alright, but I don't relish the idea that I've got to wade in and tangle myself up in this improbable, impossible romance he seems intent on throwing himself headlong into. He's a cock because, dead or not, her husband has a lion and her lover is a nutter. Fletch would have a field day with all of this if I told him.

'And what about Fletcher hot-ass Gunn?'

Marina enunciates his name with a hearty helping of derision and a sigh that says she knows that he is the main reason I'm on my backside in the gravel. She probably knows it better than I do, because I am in denial where he's concerned and she has eyes in her head.

'What about him?' I mutter like a grumpy, antisocial teenager who's been asked about her overdue homework.

Marina shrugs and turns her palms up in question. 'What gives? You could cut the atmosphere between you two with a butter knife.'

I shrug, wallowing in my own self-pity. 'Just for once, I'd like to be normal. A normal woman who sees normal things. Empty chairs, empty ballrooms and no goddamn lions. He thinks I'm an inmate from *One Flew Over The Cuckoo's Nest*.'

'You wouldn't like normal life,' she says. 'It's dull compared to your spookivision.'

'Dull sounds right up my street.'

'He wouldn't be interested in you if you were dull. It's all part of your allure.'

'That isn't evenly remotely reassuring, Marina. You're saying that he's attracted to me because my weirdness turns him on. It makes him sound even bloody odder than me, like those people who want to marry inanimate objects or do taxidermy.'

She takes a moment to process that. 'I watched a TV show once about a man who wanted to marry his hoover.' She laughs scornfully. 'It wasn't even bagless.'

This is why we are best friends; most people would struggle to think of a comeback, but she is totally on my wavelength. We have a shorthand that cuts through all the crap and lets us see inside each other's heads and hearts the way an x-ray machine sees broken bones. Right now, I think Marina is looking at my heart and she can see it's a putrid shade of green.

'I don't know why it even matters to me what he thinks,' I say. 'I don't want anything from him apart from a decent write-up in the paper.'

Marina looks at me out of the corner of her eye. 'And his sausage roll.'

I ignore that and lean my head back against Babs. 'It's all just made me realise that I'm kidding myself if I think I'll ever have anything even close to a normal life. A normal relationship.'

She rubs my knee soothingly. 'You will. We both will. Romance is no picnic, even without the spooks.'

I clutch her hand. 'Am I holding you back? If you want to go out and get a proper job with normal people and sandwiches and water coolers, you can you know. I won't be offended.'

She rolls her eyes. 'Nah. Watching you declare yourself a lesbian porn addict is far more fun.' She snorts. 'What *were* you thinking?'

I huff. 'That's exactly it, I wasn't thinking. I never do around Fletcher Gunn. My mouth is an entirely separate entity from the rest of me, it keeps saying things that horrify me.'

Marina picks up one of her curls and holds it up in front of her eyes to inspect it for split ends. 'Much as it pains me to say this, I think you're going to have to sleep with him.'

I glance up sharply. 'No you don't.'

'I do,' she nods. 'For the last God knows how many weeks, you two have been winding each other up to the point where you either have to have sex or else spontaneously combust. In unison, probably, like some weird suicide pact that neither of you has actually agreed to.'

I stare at her hard, trying to decide if she's joking.

'It's either that or I'll move in with you and your olds and we can all live together like the Golden Girls.'

I start to laugh a tiny bit. 'You'll have to be the slutty one.'

'Naturally. I quite fancy the way they have middle-of-the-night kitchen table conflabs.'

Much as I love Marina, the idea of sharing our spinsterhoods with my family is hideous.

'So, basically, I've got to sleep with Fletcher Gunn to save us all from wearing lace collar nightdresses and eating ice cream straight from the tub. Is that your point?'

She ums and ahs before she speaks. 'Not precisely, no. Let's be frank here for a second, Melody. When did you last have sex, aside from with Brandy the made-up lesbian stripper?'

I'm not answering that accurately on account of the fact that even a nun would fall to her knees and say a prayer for me. 'I had a really vivid dream last week that Green Arrow crawled through my bedroom window and showed me his quiver. Does that count?'

She shakes her head and sighs. 'My point exactly. You can't waste your life waiting for a superhero to come and sweep you off your feet. Your lady bits will fuse together from lack of use and then where will you be?'

'In A&E?'

We both titter and then she stands up and holds out her hand to haul me up too.

'Come on, Blanche. Pull yourself together.'

'You're Blanche, not me. She was the slutty one.'

I scrub my hands over my cheeks and she snaps a fresh piece of gum into her mouth and straightens her clothes.

'Just think about it. You're alone here together again tonight, you could boff his brains out and then come to work refreshed and ready to kick this case's ass in the morning. Think of it as taking one for the team, or as friends with benefits.'

'Don't ever apply for a job as an agony aunt,' I say, but all the same I'm turning over her advice in my head as we start back towards the castle.

'He's not my friend.'

She shrugs. 'Frenemy, then.'

'I won't respect him any more in the morning.'

'Do you respect him now? This isn't about friendship or respect, Melody. It's about switching off your emotions and swinging from the chandeliers; God knows, there's enough of them in this place to choose from.'

We've reached the castle door now and just as I'm wondering how to style out my earlier teenage girl exit, I'm saved the bother by the fact that Lestat starts going full on batshit bananas. He's morphed from Garfield to raging up and down the hall like a tiny snorting bull, crashing into things and sending a probably priceless vase crashing to the floor.

'Bollocks!' I half shout as Artie tries valiantly to catch hold of him. I break into a run to help, because I'm the only person present who can see that what Lestat is actually doing is brawling with an incredibly angry lion.

CHAPTER FOURTEEN

Attracted by the commotion, Leo strides into the hallway from the direction of the kitchens with the fembots and the Lettermans all following him at a frantic trot.

'What the hell's going on he…' he trails off and stares at Lestat squaring up to Goliath. It's almost comical in a fantastically stupid sort of way. What astounds me the most is that Lestat can even see Goliath at all. He's never reacted to any other ghost around me before, I can only assume that it's an animal-related glitch. Who knew? My one-eared little pug just became a Bittersweet by nature as well as by name and, bizarrely, it endears him to me even more.

Bohemia and Britannia Lovell are around too, but they're over by the grand fireplace in the reception hall and far too embroiled in their own argument to bother trying to intervene and, oh joy, from what I can gather, they're arguing about Leo. I didn't read *that* one wrong then.

'What the hell's wrong with him?' Marina shouts over the top of Lestat's howling, growling racket as Artie makes another failed grab for the dog.

'He's fighting with the sodding lion,' I mutter, wincing as Goliath lunges for him. I hurl myself between them and scoop Lestat's furious, panting little body as he twists in mid-air. He's practically foaming at the mouth and the only thing I can do right now is get him out of there, so I turn and run for the door.

Oh God, oh God, oh my bloody God. *Lestat.* He's stopped struggling at last and, as I sit down on the stone steps, he goes horribly floppy in my arms. Marina and Artie are either side of me in seconds, and we all stare, horrified, as Lestat seems unable to regulate his breathing.

'Come on, little buddy,' I whisper, over and again, and I berate myself for all the times I've called him names and, sheesh, I wish I'd let him eat that stupid pancake this morning.

'I'll make you a whole heap of pancakes all to yourself,' I promise him, holding his stubby paw in my hand as I cradle him like a baby.

'Don't leave me,' I whisper, and his charcoal, beady eyes lock onto mine.

'Oh God, might it be his heart?' I say, stricken. 'Is there a recovery position for dogs?'

'Melody.' Fletch strokes his hand over my hair and hunkers down to study Lestat. 'I think he'd be better on his side,' he says gently.

I nod, overwhelmed with gratitude that someone, anyone, is taking charge. Fletch lifts the dog easily from my arms and lays him down on his side on the shady top step. I can barely breathe as Fletch runs his hands lightly over Lestat's little body, tilting his head back and feeling carefully inside his mouth for his tongue. He lowers his head to Lestat's and listens intently and I know he's checking if he's still breathing.

Please let him be breathing.

Fletch lifts his eyes up to mine after what feels like an eternity and nods.

'I don't think he's injured, he seems to be in shock more than anything.'

I can barely bring myself to ask the obvious question of Fletch who, to all intents and purposes, has just elevated himself to fully fledged vet in my eyes. 'Will he be alright?'

He frowns. 'Obviously I can't say for sure, but I think so. Just sit with him and give him a few minutes to recover.'

Fletch puts his arm around my shoulders and that's how we all wait, quiet and observant, until, little by little, Lestat finally starts to rally. I watch his ribs move up and down and as his breathing pattern normalises, mine does too.

'I thought I'd lost him for a minute there,' I say, almost shivering with relief when Lestat reacts to my gentle fuss with a half-hearted lick of my fingers. Artie dashes the back of his hands across his eyes and nods, then gets up and lopes away across the gravel for a breather. Marina catches up with him and Lestat stoically gives his legs a go and shuffles himself into my lap.

'Looks like he knows where the safest place to be is,' Fletch says, and I feel a rush of emotion wash over me like warm rain.

'Thank you.' My words catch thickly in the back of my throat. 'I didn't know what to do.'

He shrugs. 'I covered a pet convention for the paper a while back. It was one of the demonstrations.' He rolls his eyes. 'I'm just glad he didn't need CPR.'

'You really are the man who knows everything.'

My defences are down and my face is turned up and it's as natural as breathing when he lowers his lips to mine and kisses me softly. It's not a 'God,-you're-hot,-let-me-drag-you-upstairs-by-your-hair kiss. It's a kiss borne from relief and gratitude, from a raw and unexpected moment of closeness. He's tender with me, thumbing a tear from my cheek as he lingers all too briefly, all the more sweet and exquisite for it. I barely taste him, scarcely register the touch of his tongue against mine, and yet I feel the slow life-affirming kiss in every cell and atom of my body.

'Better now?' he whispers.

'Think so.'

His laugh is low and intimate. 'Need me to kiss you some more until you're sure?'

Leo appears in the doorway of the castle and his eyes meet mine briefly over Fletch's shoulder before he spins on his heel and disappears back inside.

'Best not.' I push myself up to my feet, Lestat still away with the fairies in my arms. Marina and Artie amble back across the drive and I hand the still-snoozing dog over into Artie's care.

'He's fine, I think,' I say. 'Would you mind taking him down to the kitchens and settling him in his bed, please?'

Artie colours up, and I don't know if it's because he's been entrusted with Lestat or because he gets to go and visit Hells Bells again. Either way, he smiles uncertainly as he takes the dog, smoothing a nervous hand over his gelled hair as he heads inside.

'One of you two needs to talk to that boy about the birds and the bees,' Fletch says, and Marina and I both look at him, horrified.

'Don't look at me like that,' he says with a shrug. 'You know the chat I mean, the "when a daddy loves a mommy very much", one?'

Deadpan, he makes a circle with the forefinger and thumb of one hand and makes sex motions through it with his finger. He rolls his eyes when neither of us reply. 'Fine, I'll do it.'

'Don't you dare say a bloody word to him,' I say, hot and bothered at the thought of Fletch leading a sex ed class. In the space of half an hour he's been a vet and a sex educator, not to mention that he found the time to kiss me breathless too. No one could accuse the man of being lazy.

'Fine. I'll talk to him.' Marina sighs. 'He probably *could* use some romantic advice about Hells.'

'Really?' I ask, high-pitched. 'What will you say?' I can't think of many more squeaky-bum conversations to have with Artie than that one, he's like a gullible puppy and Marina's advisory style can err on the bolshie side. I love her, but just this morning she told me to shag Fletch. If she gives Artie the same advice we could end with the castle being more like a carry-on movie than a movie set.

'Not sure yet.' Marina shrugs. 'Don't make a mistake, cover your snake? It'll be much sweeter if you cover your Peter?'

'Marina, no!' I say, horrified on Artie's behalf. 'I don't think he needs sex advice, I doubt he'll even kiss her for a good six months!'

Fletch smirks. 'He'll kiss her before the end of the week, tops.'

'So at least teach him about kissing first. Don't go straight to sex,' I say, and Marina looks alarmed.

'You're not suggesting I snog Artie, are you? Because like no frickin' way, José.'

I pull a face. 'Of course I'm not telling you to snog him. Jesus, Marina, you'd scar him for life. He breaks out in a sweat every time you pull your phone out of your bra.'

'Looks like it's down to you to teach him how to kiss then,' she says, with a sly, mischievous grin.

Fletch coughs as if he's got a hairball in his throat. 'Chill out, ladies. Unless you want to be closed down for sexual harassment, kissing the tea boy is a bad idea.'

I bridle at Fletch's description of Artie. 'He's not the tea boy. Artie does lots of very important things at the agency.'

'Does he make the tea?'

'We don't even drink tea. We're sophisticated businesswomen. We drink only good Italian coffee.'

He smirks and shakes his head, heading for the castle doors. 'I need to go to the little boys' room. Later, ladies.'

'The little boys' room,' I mutter at his back as he disappears. 'Who says that?'

'Grown men who're hung like donkeys and being sarcastic?'

I tuck my hair behind my ear and try very hard not to think about Fletch's man bits. 'I wouldn't have a clue if he's hung like a donkey or a chicken or a… little pig. One of those tiny pigs that sit in tea cups.' I make stupid little snorting noises to demonstrate my point and make her laugh.

'Chickens are all girls, so we can rule that one out.'

'Pig, then. He's probably packing a tiny little piggy willy in his jeans. Now, do you think we can we stop this and get some actual work done?' I nod towards the castle pointedly and lead the way back indoors. Marina follows me and, as we join the others in the main reception hall, she leans in close and whispers in my ear.

'Pigs have curly ones. Like corkscrews, apparently. Imagine that!'

'I'd really rather not,' I shoot out of the side of my mouth.

'So, if he's not a chicken, and he's not a tiny piglet…' She leaves the sentence hanging in the air. I glance at her out of the corner of my eye and she winks, holds her hands about a foot apart in front of her, and mouths *donkey* at me.

Much as it pains me, I need to talk to Leo and, seeing as he looks across when we walk back inside, I seize the opportunity.

'Leo, could I speak with you in private, please?'

The fembots exchange distress calls, tiny little coos that I can only imagine are secret code for kill her, kill her, but I fix a small professional smile on my face and look him dead in the eye. I see there that he is still sniffy with me about the kiss he caught me sharing with Fletch outside just now, but he makes a point of sighing dramatically and steps forward.

'After you.'

I ignore Marina's quizzical look and lead Leo out of the hall and down the hallway. I don't actually know where I'm heading, but when I see Fletch coming towards us in the other direction I make a hasty decision and dip sideways through the first door I come to.

'Are we going to say our prayers?'

I let Leo have that cheap dig. The chapel wouldn't have been my first choice either, but we're here now so I shoo him into the back pew and perch alongside him.

We sit in silence when the two ghostly nuns who seem to be in charge of the chapel drift in and kneel in front of the pretty stained window at the end of the aisle.

'What the hell's going on between you and Britannia Lovell?' I hiss at him through clenched teeth, earning myself a sharp over-the-shoulder glance from one of the nuns.

Leo looks bored. 'What the hell's going on between you and Fletcher Gunn?'

'At least he's bloody breathing,' I spit.

He looks down at his hands and flexes his long fingers. 'I think it would be wise to keep this conversation strictly business.'

'This *is* business. Our business here, mine *and* yours, is to find out why Britannia, Bohemia and Dino are all tethered here and to help them resolve whatever it is so they can move on and leave Barty and Lois to enjoy their castle in peace.' I can hear my voice skittering up the octaves. 'Nowhere in that job description does it include the need to turn their love triangle into a love square and make matters a million times more complicated!'

He looks at me and shakes his head slowly. 'Is this all because you're jealous?'

What the? 'What, exactly, do you think I'm jealous of, Leo? Your current love interest has been dead for a hundred years.'

Bollocks. I'm not proud of what I just said, he really does know how to goad a reaction out of me. This isn't going very well. He still has that superior look in his eye, that 'we both know I'm better than you because of my flash-in-the-pan TV slot' look that he's so damn good at.

'You're pissing the nuns off,' he says, bowing his head as they both turn to stare at us.

'And you're pissing me off,' I whisper urgently. 'Have you got *any* useful information at all out of Britannia Lovell yet?'

'I'm working on it.'

Famous last words. 'Tell me, do you always find it helps you to work if the ghost sits on your lap and whispers in your ear? Only it's not an approach I'm familiar with.'

'At least I'm trying to communicate with her, rather than necking in hallways and snogging on the front steps,' he half shouts and on that the nuns turn in unison and glide soundlessly towards us.

'Crap,' I mutter, dipping my head. I don't even know what a Hail Mary is to say one. They hover at the end of our pew and emanate waves of disapproval and I'm instantly reminded of the many times Marina landed us both in detention when we were in high school. Thankfully these seem to be the sort of nuns who have taken a vow of silence, otherwise I'm sure they'd turf us out with a flea in our ear.

'Very sorry,' I whisper. 'So is he.' I jerk my head towards Leo. 'For the shouting thing, about er, snogging. Very bad form in church.' I can't think of any more apologies to make and after a few more long, painful seconds they move on.

'When are your camera crew coming to film again?' I whisper.

'Tomorrow,' he mutters. 'Shame it wasn't today. That scene with your dog would have been TV gold.'

Jesus, he's mercenary. 'Presumably because you can't think of anything else to fill your segment.'

He curls his lip. 'I've got plenty, actually.'

'Good, because so have I,' I say. 'Like whether or not Britannia's death was an accident or if someone murdered her.'

CHAPTER FIFTEEN

'What? Why would you say that?' he asks, doing a double-take. 'Has she said as much to you?'

She hasn't, of course, but it's a theory I've been turning over in my head since I spoke with her in my bedroom last night. She reacted oddly when I suggested that her death had been an accident; as if that was news to her.

'Not in those exact words, no, but think about it. We've both seen that scene in the ballroom where she falls. I can't help but think that there's something she's trying to make us notice. Something we're just not getting yet.'

He's probably just too dazzled by her long legs and lithe curves to see what's staring him in the face.

I don't like the idea one bit, but I realise I'm going to have to return to the ballroom and watch the performance again for myself, to look more closely for anything amiss in the run-up to Britannia's fall. It was such a shock first time around that I missed pretty much everything apart from the fact she was spectacular and then she was dead.

'When I saw it, right before she died, she looked at me and said, 'it always ends like this.'

He nods slowly. 'She said something similar to me.'

'Have you spoken to Dino or her husband?'

Leo twitches. 'The only conversation her husband is interested in having with me is about how I should back off from his wife, which is pretty fucking rich given the state of their marriage.'

'Meaning?' I frown. His conversations with Brittania must have been pretty intimate for him to say something like that.

An evasive look erases the crease from Leo's brow. 'Nothing, really. I just get the impression that she must have been deeply unhappy to turn to Dino in the first place.'

'Has she said anything about their affair to you?'

Leo develops a sudden interest in the ceiling for a few moments before he answers me.

'Do I ask you to share details of private conversations you've had with Gunn?'

I'm losing my temper with his constant comparisons between Fletch and Brittania.

'Like that's anywhere near the same thing! How can we work on this case together if you keep secrets? And given that you think I'm having some great affair with Fletch which, for the record I'm not, does that mean that you're having some kind of great affair with Britannia?'

It's worrying that he doesn't instantly jump in and shoot me down. I watch him, the way he closes his eyes and breathes a few steadying times before he speaks.

'I think we both know that there can be no love affair for Britannia and me.'

I'd been about to tell him of my discovery of the engraved cross and the buried key in the garden, but his words make me have second thoughts.

'I never mentioned love, Leo.' But he did, and that's most telling of all. We sit in the quiet confines of the tiny, peaceful chapel and I soften, because I can see that, however bizarre the idea would be to pretty much everyone else who cannot see ghosts, Leo is getting in over his head with Britannia Lovell.

'Maybe it'd be best if you pulled yourself off the case,' I suggest quietly, trying to offer him a way out. 'Invent a reason. Family emergency. No one else needs to be any the wiser.'

He starts to laugh under his breath, but I don't think he's even remotely amused.

'Yeah, that would suit you, wouldn't it, Melody? I do all the heavy lifting and you swoop in and resolve it at the last minute. I never had you pegged as a glory-hunter.'

Says the man who left me in a heartbeat when the bright, glorious lights of TV land beckoned.

'That's not fair and you know it, Leo. I'm trying to help.'

'To help yourself, more like. I'm not going anywhere.' He gets to his feet. 'Not while she needs me here.'

My shoulders slump at his last words and I sigh as he flounces out of the chapel. I don't even try to stop him because he's not listening to me at all. He's not going to listen, because this is actually much worse than I initially thought.

Leo has gone and fallen in love with Britannia Lovell.

'What a total and utter knobchops,' Marina says, when I relay my observation to her quietly a little later. We're catching five minutes respite at the wicker table and chairs set out on the castle's rolling back lawn with a quick cup of coffee and Marina's cupcakes. Artie has nipped down to check on Lestat, which is most likely code for going to gaze longingly at Hells Bells for a few blissful minutes. 'Trust Leo to enjoy having his ego massaged to the point where he's as useful to us as an amoeba. A dead amoeba at that.'

'I do feel a tiny bit sorry for him,' I admit. 'It's unusual to see him lose control like this. Don't mention it to Fletch, he'll have a field day with it.'

Marina's face tells me that she doesn't share my sympathy even one jot.

'Top-drawer twattery, that's what it is. I don't know why we're even surprised. He's proven himself a twat-master often enough now for us to expect it from him.'

She's talking about how he treated me, of course. Even if I've let go of ninety percent of my stabby instinct where Leo is concerned, she's probably only down to about fifty. Fifty-five on an exceptionally good day. Her ability to hold a grudge is all part of her Sicilian charm.

'Right, so, to business,' I say, glancing up at the tower in the top corner of the castle. 'We need to get up there to the tower and check if this actually is the key, and I need to go back to the ballroom and watch Britannia's final performance again.'

'Are you sure? Because the last time ended quite badly for both of you. She died and you cried.'

I nod. 'I'll try not to cry this time, but it's a fact that she's still going to die. I need to watch carefully and see if there's anything to indicate her death was anything other than a hideous accident.'

'Do you think that's what's holding them all here?'

I shrug. 'Potentially.'

'Can't you ask them outright?'

'Well I *could*, but asking a woman if one of her lovers offed her is likely to cause offence, and offended ghosts are unhelpful ones.'

'Okay,' Marina says slowly, thinking it through. 'And you can't ask her husband because…?'

'He has a lion.'

'Fair point. And you can't ask Dino the Dynamo because…?'

'Well, for one, he's like the scarlet sodding pimpernel to pin down. I've only seen him a couple of times, briefly, and he's always been highly emotional at the time.'

'And for two?'

'I saw his reaction when Britannia died. He goes to pieces.'

Marina picks the buttercream off her cake while she thinks. 'Guilt?'

'Could be.' How can Marina still have hardly dented her cake when I've eaten two and licked the wrappers? She knows I'm considering a third because she closes the lid and moves them out of my reach.

'You can't be in a sugar coma if you're gonna watch someone die a grisly death and then boff the brains out of Hack Attack.'

I frown. So much of that sentence disturbs me.

'One.' I hold up one finger, the middle one, naturally. I'm never one to knowingly miss an opportunity to flip the bird. 'It'd take more than three piddly cupcakes to put me in a sugar coma. Two,' I pause to hold up a second finger, and use the opportunity to flick her the Vs. This is fun. She rolls her eyes but gestures for me to go on with a flick of her hand. 'Two, I'm not going to watch a horror movie here, so a little more gravitas if you please about the grisly death bit. And three,' I pause, stuck for how to be offensive with three fingers. I settle on adding the middle finger of my other hand into the mix, which is surprisingly satisfying. Try it now, you'll see what I mean. Marina inclines her head in gracious acknowledgement of my double-swearing skills, and I know it's something she'll use herself in the future.

'Three,' I say. 'Hack Attack? Really?'

'Humour me. It was a last-minute thing. He's a hack and he wants to attack your love taco with his donkey dong.'

'Or his tiny little corkscrew piggy willy.'

She looks at me knowingly. 'I think we both know that it's not going to be tiny, Melody. Men don't get to be that arrogant unless they're supremely confident in the trouser department.'

'Leo's more arrogant than Fletch, if you want to play that game,' I say, purely to wind her up. Truth told, Leo has nothing to be ashamed of when it comes to the contents of his jockey shorts. I mean, he's not built to startle the horses or make women break out on a cold sweat on sight, but I bet he never worries about getting it out in the gents.

'Fine. He's the exception to the rule on account of the fact that he wears a cape and probably owns his own set of heated rollers.'

I can't help but laugh, because Leo is more precious about his hair than most women. There's every chance he does own some kind of curl-enhancing product for a discreet bouffe before doing his piece to camera. Lip balm with a hint of gloss too, I shouldn't wonder.

Belatedly, I pick her up on her other terminology. 'And love taco? Really, Marina?'

Her dark eyes glitter with laughter. 'Would you prefer the correct anatomical terms?'

I shudder at the memory of our human biology teacher trying to say the words 'vagina' and 'penis' to our class of rowdy twelve-year-olds.

'I think I'd prefer it if we didn't talk about genitals at all,' I say, trying to stealthily pull the cake box towards me on the glass table top.

She catches me in the act and holds onto the other side, just as Fletch saunters through the French doors and tucks his mobile phone into his shirt pocket.

'I'll talk about genitals with you if you like,' he says, silky-smooth, and Marina finds her first opportunity to try out my newly patented double-handed swear. She looks at me and grins approvingly.

'That feels good,' she murmurs, standing up. 'I'm going to go and save Artie from getting square eyes from all that mooning over Hells. Meet you in the ballroom in ten?'

I nod, full of dread at the thought of watching Britannia plummet to her death from the trapeze again.

Marina waltzes back into the castle, pausing to sniff Fletch as she passes him. He raises his eyebrows at her but she offers him nothing in the way of either feedback or explanation, and he shakes his head faintly as if he's learned better than to ask. Unhooking his shades from the neck of his shirt, he slides them over his eyes as he takes the seat Marina vacated.

He steeples his hands on the table in front of him. 'I've been called back into work.'

'What? Why? When?' The questions tumble from my mouth unchecked because he's caught me by surprise.

He glances at his watch. 'Now.'

'Oh.' By rights I should be thrilled, yet my overriding feeling is disappointment. I honestly don't know what to say, so I say nothing.

'Will you be alright here on your own tonight?' he asks softly.

I laugh breezily, as if it's a ridiculous question. 'What girl wouldn't love a castle all to herself?'

Fletch looks up at the imposing, iron-grey back wall of the castle. 'It's a big place. Sure you won't get scared of things that go bump in the night?'

'Bumping is pretty much guaranteed around here tonight,' I say, and then wonder if that came out wrong. Did I just tell him that sex was a sure thing? I wish I could see his eyes, his mirrored shades show me only my own sun-frazzled hair and pink cheeks.

'Then I'm even sorrier to miss out.' He pushes his chair back and stands up. 'I'll call you.'

And, just like that, he's gone.

I sit alone in the warm sunshine for a few minutes and try to make sense of how I'm feeling. Work-wise, I'm concerned but not yet at Defcon 1 levels, especially now I hopefully have the turret key in my back pocket. I'm burning to try it out, but something in me didn't want to go up there with Fletch in tow. It already feels like invading Britannia's private space, which is ridiculous given that she's dead and that's precisely what I'm being paid to do. The time frame is now terrifyingly short but I instinctively feel as if we're moving towards a breakthrough in time for the ball on Saturday.

It's not work that's got my stomach churning over like I'm making butter in there. It's Fletcher goddamn Gunn. He's pulled the rug out from under me. I've become accustomed to him making moves and me rebuffing him, and I guess I'm guilty of feeling that if at any point I change my mind, then he'll be there ready and willing to show me his piggy willy or whatever it is.

God, I really hope it's not a piggy little willy after all this build up. I'm pretty sure it won't be though, going on the more than one occasion now when he's been hot under the collar and pressed me against the nearest wall to snog my face off. I go all dry-mouthed at the thought; if Fletch was a superhero, sex would so be his superpower. Imagine that. What would his superhero name be, I wonder? Donkey Man? Iron Dong? Captain Sex Trumpet? It's no good. I need to get back inside and do some work. And I will, right after I eat another one of these to-die-for cupcakes Marina carelessly forgot to confiscate. Sugar coma my backside.

CHAPTER SIXTEEN

'This really is the most gorgeous of rooms.' Marina sighs wistfully when I reluctantly join them in the ballroom a few minutes later.

She holds her arms out and closes her eyes. 'Dance with me, Arthur Elliott.'

The look of panic he sends me shouts *help me, Melody* so loudly that I'm surprised that I can't hear him. He's frozen to the spot and Marina opens one eye and eyeballs him sharply.

'What are you waiting for?' she snaps. 'Music? I'll sing if it helps. We can waltz.'

'It doesn't help,' he whispers hoarsely.

She opens both of her eyes and puts her hands on her hips.

'Artie, there's going to be a ball in here on Saturday evening and we'll be guests of honour because Melody is going to nix those ghosts into never-never land and be the hero of the hour. If you're lucky, you might be able to waltz Hells Bells around this very dance floor. Won't you be glad you practised then?'

He looks conflicted, because I'm sure that somewhere in his head he's already imagined tripping the light fantastic with Hells Bells on Saturday night. The difference between imagination and reality has never been starker. In the end, Artie does what he always does; whatever Marina tells him. Stepping forwards, he places an uncertain hand into her outstretched one and the other stiffly on her waist. He's standing so far away from her that his arms are at full stretch.

'HAVE YOU EVER WALTZED BEFORE?' she yells.

He flinches. 'No. Why are you shouting?'

'Because you're standing so far away you're practically in Wales! Get over here and stop pratting about.' She hauls him inwards a few feet until he's standing ramrod-straight in front of her. I wonder why she's doing this; she can't really be that desperate for Artie to waltz her around the ballroom.

'Right. Now, listen to me and do exactly as I say. Melody, can you please clap out a waltz for us to follow?' She looks at me as if I'm supposed to know what the frig a waltz sounds like.

'Er, no?'

She huffs her fringe out of her eyes and demonstrates. 'For God's sake! Am I the only one around here who watches *Strictly*? Listen and repeat after me. One, two, three. One, two, three. Like that.'

'Got it. Count to three. I think even I can manage that.'

Marina scowls at me. 'With rhythm, Melody. With rhythm.'

I clap out the beat like a performing sea lion and she narrows her eyes at me suspiciously without comment.

'Okay, Artie. Lead me off.'

His eyes are as wide as dinner plates and a bead of sweat drips from his hairline into his eyebrow.

'Fine, I'll lead,' Marina sighs, resigned, and with that she starts dragging him around the room.

'Clap, Melody! Clap!' She has to prompt me in between shouting out instructions at Artie, because I'm too busy laughing at their clumsy dancing to remember what I'm supposed to be doing. And suddenly I know. I know *exactly* why Marina is forcing Artie into waltzing stiffly around the room with her. It's for me. She knows how much I don't want to hang around in here waiting for Britannia's macabre aerial show to begin, so she's taking my mind off it by turning herself into my very own comedic warm-up act. I don't know what I did in a past life to deserve a best friend like Marina Malone in this one, but it must have been something pretty damn magnificent. I start to clap. If Marina and Artie can waltz for me, then the least I can do is give them a beat to follow.

'I do believe you're getting the hang of this, Artie Elliott!' Marina laughs with delight. To give him credit, he does seem to have mastered the basics, as long as you ignore the fact that he's scowling with concentration and clearly counting under his breath. I mean, he's never going to give Bruno Tonioli a run for his money, but he could probably make it round the floor at an OAP tea dance without breaking anyone's toes.

'What's this, auditions for *Billy Elliott*?'

We all stop, as if we're playing musical chairs and someone pressed the pause button, and then I spin slowly and eyeball Leo.

'Can I help you with something?'

If I didn't know him better, I'd describe the look that momentarily crosses his face as vulnerable. 'Are you waiting for Britannia to perform?'

I don't especially want him to watch it with me. I need to concentrate and, given how he's feeling about Britannia at the moment, I don't have time to hold his hand and rub his back through it.

'Not exactly, but if they show up, I'm here and I'll watch closely.'

I'm hoping that he gets the message and leaves, but he doesn't. He heads further into the room instead and takes a seat on one of the high-backed chairs dotted around the walls.

'Then I'll wait too.'

I glance towards the door. 'Where's Nikki and Vikki?'

'With Lois and Barty back in the reception hall. I'd rather them not be here for this, to be honest. They're… easily disturbed by my emotions, shall we say.'

I mull that over. I'm not entirely convinced that they're particu-larly useful to him in any capacity besides making it appear as if he's constantly surrounded by his adoring fan club. They flap and they fawn, but I've never seen either of them wield a notebook or pen. On the other hand, they certainly have his interests at heart; they're sort of like his occasionally lethal kittens.

Marina and Artie have given up on the waltz and she's adopted something more like the march, all the way across the ballroom to Leo.

'You can't stay in here if you're likely to lose your shit, mush. You'll distract Melody while she's working.'

I highly doubt anyone's ever called Leo mush before. He looks deeply affronted, so I step forward and lay my hand on Marina's arm to smooth the waters.

'It's okay, Marina, he can stay. He might be helpful, an extra set of eyes and all that.'

She squints at him menacingly and then forks her fingers quickly towards her own eyes and then at his.

We're saved from having to keep this not very passive but really rather aggressive conversation going by the sudden appearance of Britannia Lovell amongst the chandeliers over our heads. I scan the ceilings and see Dino is here too, over on the far side of the room.

'They're here,' I whisper and Artie discreetly reaches for his notebook and pen from the back pocket of his jeans while Marina pulls her phone from inside her bra and clicks it onto record. They have different styles, these two, but they're both ready to help me capture as much detail as possible for us to pore over afterwards. They're limited, of course; they can only see and hear things through my eyes and ears and, unusually, in this instance, Leo's too.

Leo is out of his chair, his eyes trained on Britannia as she begins to perform.

'She's there.' I point Britannia out for Artie and Marina so that we can re-imagine it later from Marina's video footage. 'And Dino is at the other end.' I watch, enthralled, as Britannia's performance begins.

'She's laughing,' Leo murmurs beside me. 'How can she laugh when she knows what's coming?' He sounds like a little boy lost.

'I should think she's grown pretty accustomed to it after all of these years,' I say. 'She doesn't feel any pain.' We watch her closely as she swings with effortless grace. 'She looks more like an exotic bird than a woman,' I say. 'Freefalling. Swooping.' I follow her looping progress with my outstretched hand, sketching her movements in the air for Marina and Artie.

I must look as if I'm conducting an invisible orchestra; the performance is certainly enthralling enough to warrant musical accompaniment. If I *were* conducting a big band, I think they'd be playing something hauntingly beautiful, perhaps with a menacing, portentous underscore to herald the upcoming shift of mood. There's a jaunty air of carnival, of sickly sweet candy floss and poisoned toffee apples, a sense of euphoria walking hand-in-hand with darkness that has me clammy and laying my hand over my racing heart.

'It's not the same watching it when you know how it ends,' I murmur.

'Remember to watch the ropes. Look out for fraying, signs of tampering, anything suspicious.' Marina is my quiet prompt to stay focused, because she knows that if I don't, then I'll have to do this again until I'm satisfied that I haven't missed something crucial.

It's difficult to know if Britannia is even aware of our presence. I guess she must be, realistically, but she seems so in the moment, so at one with Dino and the trapeze, ethereal and otherly and magical, that she's in another place entirely.

'She looks like an angel,' Leo breathes. 'Doesn't she?'

It's awkward, really, listening to my ex turn himself inside out with admiration for another woman, even if she is long dead. I briefly consider admiring Dino's Lycra-clad package, tit-for-tat, but actually I'm more saddened than I am angered, because Leo seems genuinely unable to hold back either his words or his thoughts. He's as swept away by the performance as the performers themselves, leaving me to do the heavy lifting when it comes to looking for clues.

I walk slowly into the centre of the ballroom and, high above me, Britannia steps inside her hoop and begins to twirl. I watch her from every angle, narrating the scene for the purpose of the video as I go.

'It's soon,' I breathe. 'It's going to happen soon.'

Dino has moved across into position and I can see the trapeze in his hands as he prepares to toss it out towards Britannia. I make a dash because I want to get a look at the ropes before he lets go, but I'm a fraction too late to get a clear view.

'Bollocks.' I curse myself for being too slow, but then I gasp because, as I'm watching the empty trapeze swing overhead, I run my eyes up the length of the ropes and I'm almost sure I can see fraying about halfway up. I cry out 'stop!' a fraction of a moment before Britannia reaches out to grab the ill-fated swing, but it is as if she cannot hear me, because she's smiling, wide and triumphant, ready for her final flight that will bring the house down. It doesn't, of course. It brings Britannia down, hurtling, screaming, smashing to the floor in a jumble of bones and blood-soaked rhinestones.

Leo is beside me, on his knees, and now Dino is here too, his chest heaving as he gathers Britannia into his arms.

Just like the last time, Britannia opens her eyes, only this time she doesn't look at me. She has eyes only for Leo.

'I wish it didn't always have to end like this,' she breathes, blinking blood from her eyelashes. Leo reaches out and desperately tries to clutch onto her red-smeared hands as they fade, as if he can save her, or comfort her at least. And then both Brittania and Dino are gone, leaving us silent and shell-shocked, even though we knew what was coming. Leo holds his head in his hands and

I nod discreetly to Marina and Artie to head on out and leave us alone for a couple of minutes.

When we're alone, I kneel beside Leo and smooth my hand down the back of his dipped head. His hair is as warm and slippery thick as I remember it and I soothe him for a slow minute while he gathers himself together.

'Okay?'

He nods, then shakes his head with a tiny, helpless shrug.

'Why? Why does she keep performing over and over, when she knows how it ends?'

It's a question I've pondered too. 'The ride must be worth the fall,' I say softly, and then he looks up at me and I inhale sharply with shock.

'Leo…' I reach for his hands and turn them palm up and he sees what has me so rattled. His hands and face are covered in Britannia's blood.

CHAPTER SEVENTEEN

'How can that be?' Marina asks me, her eyes on stalks when I relay all of this to them in the library a little later. Artie is wide-eyed with wonder, although I'm not sure if it's because of Leo's lovesick stigmata-like episode or the fact that he's eating one of a batch of Hells Bells's homemade custard creams. They're similar in taste to the shop-bought version, only a million times nicer and about ten times the size. They look like they'd be the perfect bricks to build an edible house from.

I daren't let my mind wander too far down this particular road while I'm at work, because it's one of my ultimate, top-ten fantasies. I regularly construct houses made entirely of confectionary in my head and then I'm visited in my sugar palace by one of any number of superheroes and we mostly spend our time alternating between shagging like chocolate Easter bunnies and licking the sherbet-coated walls. It's pretty much perfect in every way, right down to the sweet cigarettes we smoke afterwards while lying on our bed made of marshmallows and gazing at the stars. We have a damn fine view of them too, because we've eaten the roof.

'It's very rare,' I say, dragging myself out of my sugar shack and back to the moment. 'Practically unheard of, to be honest. It only happens when there's an intense emotional connection between the living and the dead.'

Marina frowns. 'Is that why your gran can still get it on with Duke even though he's been dead for twenty years?'

'Thanks for that.' I shudder at the idea, but she's kind of right. My grandpa's ghost is happily tethered to their marital bed for Gran to make use of whenever the mood strikes. She might be well past pensionable age, but between Grandpa Duke and her daily observance of yoga, she's probably the fittest Bittersweet in Chapelwick.

'So could he feel her flesh when he reached out?'

'He said not,' I say, although privately I'm not sure I believe him. He went to pieces when she'd gone, even though he'll no doubt see her looking every bit alive and well and up to high jinks again soon enough. I knew he'd fallen hard and fast for her, but the fact that they connected so intimately has to mean that the feelings aren't all one-sided. That's potentially a huge, momentous spanner in the works as far as clearing her off is concerned. Bloody Leo. Marina was right earlier. He'd be better off out of the way, because all he's going to do is lose his shit. And his heart, by all accounts.

Fabulous. Just as we were beginning to achieve a friendship of sorts, he goes and falls in love with a phantom trapeze artist and leaves me with the messy job of heartbreaker as well as ghostbuster. This job just keeps on getting harder and harder.

I cave in and shove a custard cream in my mouth sideways.

'Cross your fingers,' I breathe. We've trooped up to the top of the castle and I'm hoping like hell that the key I unearthed in the garden fits the turret door. Artie holds up both hands to show me his tightly crossed fingers and Marina gives me an encouraging nod, so I push the key into the lock.

'It fits,' I whisper, feeling the notches on the old key slide into place. It turns with a good twist and, for the first time in years, the turret door swings open on its hinges.

'It's a good job I haven't got claustrophobia,' Marina says, right behind me as we pick our way up the narrow, winding stone steps.

There's another door at the top, thankfully not locked, and I step cautiously inside the room and pause as Marina comes to stand beside me.

'Wow,' she whispers, and I can only agree.

Shafts of bright sunlight slant in through the leaded window, warming and illuminating the quiet, circular room. Mellow boards line the floor and outfits, a dozen or more, hang all around the walls. Dazzling showgirl leotards and tutus; Brittania's, no doubt.

Silk ballerina slippers hang with each one, tied by the ribbons to the padded hangers. We walk slowly around the room, looking at them, and I can well imagine how beautiful Brittania would have looked in them to her rapt audience below. There's just one piece of furniture in the room; a wooden blanket box beneath the window and I come to rest in front of it.

'That's some view.' I follow Marina's gaze out of the window; it's a clear summer's day and from up here you can see for uninterrupted mile on mile. 'No wonder she loved it up here.'

I think it was more than the view that attracted Brittania to the tower. I've seen her perform, soaring like a bird, and up here was probably the closest she could get to being sky borne and free.

I bend and, as I'd hoped, the lid to the blanket box isn't locked.

It's full. Full of memories; programmes and circus memorabilia, scraps of a lifetime spent moving from town to town. A child's ballerina pumps, a battered picture book, a well-loved doll wearing a scarlet coat. It speaks of a normal little girl living an extraordinary life; I cannot help but see how it is almost the opposite of my own life as a different child striving to fit into a normal world. A photograph catches my eye; a woman, formally staged and dressed, but charismatic nonetheless. Was this Lady Eleanor's sister? Brittania's mother? I think she must have been; there is a shared devil-may-care look in her eyes that jumps out even from the black and white image in my hands.

'This must have been her mum.'

In my mind's eye it's easy to imagine Brittania as a child, wild-haired and innocent, clutching onto her mum's hand. God, I hope she had a happy childhood, because what I know of her all- too-brief adult life tells me that she was deeply unhappy. I sigh, heavy-hearted, as I hand the picture to Marina.

'She was beautiful. Are they very alike?'

I nod, looking at the image. 'Brittania has darker hair, but yes.'

The woman in the photo is about the same age as Brittania must have been when she died and there is the hint of a smile playing over her mouth even though she is trying to be serious for the camera.

A small linen-wrapped parcel lies at the bottom of the chest and I lift it carefully out onto the floor. It's feather light and I fold the cloth back to reveal something small made from pale ivory silk. Unfolding it on its linen wrapper for protection, I sigh.

'Do you think it's a memento from when she was a baby?' Marina asks quietly.

I study the tiny romper and try to imagine an infant Britannia. I wonder if her mum rocked her to sleep at night and told her stories as my mother did with me. I hope so.

'I don't know,' I murmur, leaning back while Marina photographs it for our case file. 'It doesn't look as if it's ever been worn, does it?'

Marina considers it and then is distracted by the bleep of her phone inside her bra. Pulling it out unceremoniously, she clicks the screen.

'Artie wants to know where we are. He says he's looking for us in the garden.'

She stands and peers out of the window. 'He's down there...' she squints. 'With Fletcher Gunn.' She slips the phone back into her blouse as I gently rewrap the linen around the baby romper and pack Brittania's belongings carefully back as I found them.

* * *

I hang up the phone. I don't know what possessed me to make the call; I should have at least consulted my magic-8 ball beforehand.

One by one, everyone has left me, scattering like a dandelion clock on a sudden five o'clock breeze. Marina offered to stay with me, even though I know it would be a complete pain in the ass for her mum to arrange for someone else to sit with her grandpa. Artie valiantly offered too, even though we all know that his mother will have a heart attack if he hasn't walked through the garden gate for his dinner by six. I turned them both down, of course, and shooed them out and Leo and the fembots speedily retired to their chambers to do whatever it is they do over there. I imagine that Nikki and Vikki probably need to plug themselves into the mains and, given Leo's behaviour, it's highly likely that he's hoping for a visit from a friskily gorgeous but inconveniently dead harlot.

As for Lois and Barty, they didn't stay much past lunchtime, because organising a shindig the size of theirs at short notice clearly requires lots of swanning round the county to discuss canapés and visiting dressmakers.

And that's more or less how I found myself home alone in a seventeen-bedroom castle, impulsively on the phone inviting my mother and my grandmother over for a spot of dinner.

I think I've been overcome with delusions of grandeur, as if I'm chatelaine of the castle and am bestowing an invite upon the lowly surfs of Chapelwick to come feast at my dinner table and gaze upon the bounty of my wealth. That, or I'm so hellishly lonely that I need to invite my family over or else eat my dinner on my knees with only Lestat for company. And the ghosts, of course, but they don't really count. I'm quietly hoping that my mother or gran might be able to help me crack the case open a little. It's like a tight little nut refusing to open and with only days to go to the deadline, I'm badly in need of a breakthrough.

Yes. There are many good reasons to invite my folks over and none of them are even remotely to mask my gnawing disappointment about Fletcher Gunn running out on me.

My mother drives a gun-metal grey 1968 Pontiac Firebird. It's so incongruously not her, but it was a gift from my father so she cherishes it almost as much as she cherishes her other gift from him. *Me.* He bought it for her on sight because it matched her silver hair and I spent a lot of years as a kid being embarrassed by it whenever she picked me up from school. I don't know why really; I've come to appreciate it as I've grown older and, God knows, people in glass houses shouldn't throw stones.

I watch through the reception hall window as she sedately parks her muscle car next to Babs, and I sigh as my gran climbs out of the passenger seat dressed in a full-length turquoise and violet wrap-around dress with a trailing jewelled belt. It wouldn't look out of place on J-Lo yet somehow, with her piled-up vintage curls and slash of cerise lipstick, she pulls it off. She has a knack with clothes; a curious mix of outrageous charm and couldn't-care- less that carries her seamlessly through pretty much any situation.

I'm more startled to see Glenda Jackson unfurl herself from the backseat, a picture of restrained elegance in a bottle green silk sheath dress and perfectly colour-matched high-heeled pumps. My mother rounds the bonnet and joins them beside the car, her black lace dress neither as restrained as Glenda's or as rock star as my gran's.

'Well, well. Who do we have here?' Britannia lets out a low whistle as she appears beside me in the bay window.

'My family,' I say. 'You're back, then.' I'm almost surprised to see her here when she could be over in the tower fraternising with Leo. I'm also more than a tiny bit pissed off with her for deliberately luring him in and rendering him next to useless.

'I haven't been anywhere but here for over a hundred years, Melody,' she says pithily.

'You know what I mean. I last saw you bleeding out on the ballroom floor and now here you are again without so much as a scratch on you.'

She shrugs. 'Would you prefer it if I were black and blue? Or if I let the back of my head hang open and my brains drip down the back of my neck? I can you know, if you want.'

'I'd prefer it if you didn't suck Leo into your already tangled web of a love life, if you must know.'

She laughs under her breath. 'Jealousy really isn't very becoming on a woman, darling,' she chides. 'Men get away with it because it makes them look manly, but on a woman it's shrew-like, and no one likes a shrew now, do they?'

I resent her implications. 'I'm not bloody jealous,' I hiss, watching my family approach the castle with their heads flipped back like a bunch of gawking sightseers.

'The lady doth protest too much,' Britannia quips and I wish she were flesh and blood so I could kick her in the shins.

'Melody?' My mother's voice rings out loud and clear even through the two-foot-thick wooden door. She waits a beat and then bangs the huge iron door knocker a few times.

'That's my cue to leave.' Britannia wiggles her fingers at me, cute as a super-annoying button. 'Places to go, people to see.' She's gone in a blink, leaving me in no doubt that the place she has to be is over in the far tower and the person she has to see is Leo.

I vent my frustrations by stamping loudly across the stone flagons and pause before I open the door to pull myself together into the hostess with the mostess.

As I swing the door open, I plaster a broad smile onto my lips. 'Do come in, do come in,' I say, sweeping my arm out grandly to indicate that the paupers are allowed to cross my threshold.

My mother shoots me an assessing look as she passes, but she is suitably distracted and impressed by the castle's grandeur not to grill me. Not yet, at least.

'Glenda, how lovely to see you too,' I say as she pauses and hands me a box of chocolates.

'Your mother invited me. I hope that's okay?'

It's a polite-enough question, but I read the subtext behind it: Your mother wanted me to come with her and check out what's going on here with her, because your gran's opinion and observations will very soon be addled by champagne.

'You're very welcome, Glenda. It's great to see you.' I smile, even though her direct eye contact is making me nervous and I fear that she's passing judgment on the furnishings of my new pad, even though they're not actually mine.

Lestat must have caught the overpowering, familiar sent of my gran's Chanel, because he comes galloping from the kitchens in a flurry of clattering claws to greet them like his long-lost pack members.

'I think it might be best if you take him back with you, if you don't mind,' I fret as he disappears underneath gran's dress. 'He had an awful fright earlier on with the lion, I honestly thought he was going to have a heart attack.'

'Well, he seems to have made a full recovery,' Gran says. 'I think he's trying to make whoopee with my ankle, dear.' She lifts the hem of her dress and reveals him and he rolls his little black eyes like a teenager caught with a copy of *Dazzle* before he slouches moodily away from her sandals.

'The dog could see the lion?' my mother asks, fascinated.

'I know, it's odd, isn't it? He's never reacted to any other ghosts before.' I shudder at the memory of Lestat attempting to take on Goliath.

'It's not unheard of,' Gran muses. 'Beefcake used to have a ghost girlfriend in the alley round the back of Blithe. I'm going back to the sixties, mind.' She pauses to think. 'Chloe the Chihuahua, if my memory serves me right.'

I sincerely hope that her memory hasn't served her correctly, because Beefcake more than lived up to his name and would have squashed Chloe the Chihuahua flat on sight. I can't help but wonder if Chloe the Chihuahua was alive before she encountered Beefcake.

The table has been laid for three at my request, so I quickly lay a fourth place for Glenda as they all head towards the open French doors and admire the rolling lawns and abundance of summer colour in the flowerbeds.

'It's bucolic,' my mother sighs. She loves this kind of thing. You only have to look at her farmhouse-styled kitchen and her beeswaxed surfaces in the shop to know that she's someone who admires the traditional look, and this place has it by the bucketful. She makes a much more appropriate lady of the house than I do in every way, given that she's willowy and elegant and I'm pocket-size with a beloved character T-shirt collection. I watch her fondly as she takes a seat at the dining table. She looks every inch the dowager Duchess of Maplemead with her upswept silver hair and discreet pearl and diamond necklace.

'So, tell me, darling,' she says as I ladle minestrone soup into our bowls. 'How did you manage to scare Fletcher Gunn away? We've been trying to shake him off for years without success.'

It's true. Fletch has sniffed around our business since he was a wet behind-the-ears intern at the paper, always looking to debunk mysteries or expose fraud where there's none to be found. He's a thorn in the side of anything with a whiff of the occult or the unexplained, which is precisely why our worlds are too different to ever collide without war. My mother's words make me pause for thought though. *Have* I scared him away? Did he make up the excuse of being called back to work to get away from me? I can't help but let that idea creep under my skin and it's like when you're given a general anaesthetic and you feel it run like ice through your veins. I crawl out from beneath the crushing weight of rejection and take my seat.

'He was called back to work,' I say, nonchalant. 'Or maybe he's too much of a scaredy-cat to sleep here again.'

'Whatever did you do to him last night, darling?' Gran deadpans, but her eyes sparkle with mischief and I send her a look that could kill ducks on the water. 'His kind never have any backbone, darling. No sticking power,' she adds in a vague attempt to placate me, popping the cork on the bottle of champagne in the wine cooler after she's looked approvingly down her nose at the label.

I feel an irrational urge to offer some kind of defence for Fletch in his absence, but why should I, really? He's done nothing to earn any loyalty from me, aside from several shockingly hot fumbles and, if anything, they're more frustrating than satisfying in the long term. He's ruining me for other men. Or ruining other men for me. I'm not sure which is the right way around, but you get the gist. He's scuppering my chances of a satisfying love life with my future husband by being all bone-melty.

'Actually, he did prove useful today. He sort of saved Lestat's life.'

Three sets of eyebrows are raised in my direction.

'He did?' My mother looks unconvinced. 'How?'

'Well... he laid him down on the steps to get his breath.'

Glenda narrows her eyes. 'Did he perform mouth to mouth?'

I shake my head.

'Heimlich manoeuvre?' Gran suggests.

Again I shake my head. 'He wasn't choking, Gran. Fletch just laid him flat on the step. But he did it in a special, life-saving sort of way, okay?'

I catch my mother's eye and she sends me a long, considered look that suggests she isn't entirely happy with my defence of

Fletcher Gunn or even the way I just referred to him as Fletch and I don't know what to say to wriggle off the hook.

'This is delicious, Melody.' Glenda spoons her soup, delicately changing the subject whilst also taking the piss. 'Did you make it yourself?'

She knows perfectly well that I didn't make it myself.

'Yes,' I smile, relieved to have moved on from my inappropriate spot of Fletch worshipping. 'From scratch. I've been inspired by the castle's kitchens to have a go.'

'Really?' My mother, bless her, is always keen to think the best of me.

'No, of course not really,' I relent, because I know that Glenda is about to drill down into my cooking methods and anything beyond opening a tin and upending it into a saucepan is beyond me. 'The cook is very precious about her ovens. No one else is allowed to cook in there or I totally would have taken over tonight.'

I send Glenda a secret little triumphant smile and she sends me one right back. No one ever gets the better of Glenda Jackson. She'll bide her time, but she'll strike back.

'How's the case going, darling?' Gran asks and I fill them in, relieved to be able to share the details openly with people who completely understand. They're as startled as I was when I tell them about the turn of events between Leo and Britannia, my gran in particular.

'You need to take care of that situation quickly,' she warns, suddenly serious. 'If she can connect to him physically, she just got a whole lot more powerful.'

I nod, troubled. 'I know. And he just got a whole lot less useful.'

'Perhaps you could show us the ballroom after dinner,' Glenda suggests. I don't know if she's being genuinely helpful or wants to imagine herself doing a frisky foxtrot with Colin Firth but, either way, it's a good suggestion. Instinct tells me that that's where this case is going to succeed or fail. I like the room less every time I go in there, but having my folks take a look is too good an opportunity to pass up. I clear away the soup bowls, all of them empty aside from my gran's, who eats like a ballerina.

'Chicken casserole,' I say as I open up the hostess trolley.

'Coq au vin,' Glenda corrects, behind me.

'Could I possibly have the vin without the coq?' Gran enquires sweetly, topping up her champagne flute.

'I think you'd be better off having just coq, actually,' I mutter and then feel slightly queasy, because so much is wrong about that sentence that I don't know what to say next.

I load our plates, including a small one for my gran, because despite her insistence on trying to prove otherwise, humans cannot exist on champagne and fresh air. Besides, I want her to soak up that champagne, because despite her age and apparent flightiness, she's actually the most gifted of all of us. We're like fine wine, us Bittersweet women. We get more powerful with age.

'Ready?' I say, as we all cluster outside the ballroom door.

'Geronimo!' Gran sways and wafts her champagne glass around. I tried to take it from her as we left the dining room, but she gripped it like an eagle might clutch a little mouse it's just caught for its dinner.

'An apt word choice, Dicey, given that the ghosts swing freely from the chandeliers,' Glenda says. Gran lifts her shoulders in a manner that suggests she knew that all along and I push the door open.

I haven't been in here at night before. Moonlight shafts through the tall windows, throwing long shadows and shading the corners for monsters to lurk in. I don't know where the light switches are. For a moment I feel engulfed by the inky-blue darkness, and icy fingers trail down my back. Fear isn't something I feel all that often;

ghosts and ghouls are just other people to me, so I'm thrown by my own irrationality. I spin and, at the same moment, the chandeliers blaze into life and Glenda strolls back in from the hall.

'Switches are by the doorframe,' she says, matter of fact.

My irrational fears settle now that the room is illuminated and I wait while they all experience that same gut reaction to the room that Marina and I did the first time we walked in here. It's different by night, a little less fairy tale, a little more sophisticated soirée thanks, in the main, to the glittering chandeliers, but it's still an awe-inspiring room.

They don't have much time to fancy themselves being whisked around the floor by Mr Darcy though, because Bohemia Lovell and his magnificent lion come blazing through the far wall towards us.

'Where is she?' he yells, ignoring everyone but me. Goliath let's an ear-splitting roar out to add emphasis.

I assume he means Britannia.

My mother, who up to now had been gazing dreamily around the ballroom, rears up like a cobra about to strike and steps in front of me. Have I told you that I love her? She's understated and demure, but cross her and she's a fearless warrior. I can only hope that I've inherited even half of her quiet moxie.

'Don't you dare speak to my daughter like that and kindly control your lion!'

Bohemia lays a hand on Goliath's mane to quieten him, momentarily pulled up short by the fact that she can see him.

'That's right, I can see you perfectly well,' she says, crossing her arms across her chest and eyeballing him.

'So can I, and that, sir, is a very fetching jacket,' my gran says, waving her glass towards his scarlet ringmaster's coat with gleaming brass buttons.

He looks towards Glenda. I do too and she must sense he's waiting to hear from her, because she shakes her head. 'Thankfully,

I cannot see you, although from what I gather, you're a rather pompous ass with a dangerous animal and bold sartorial tastes.'

Bohemia blinks rapidly. I doubt he's met the likes of Glenda Jackson before, even if he has been around for more than a century.

I step out from behind my mother to stand beside her.

'This is my mother, Silvana Bittersweet, and my gran, Dicey.'

I'm about to introduce Glenda when Dino hurtles through the wall at the same alarming speed as Bohemia a couple of minutes earlier.

'Where is she?' he shouts, tempestuous.

My mother looks at me with arched brows. 'Is it Groundhog Day?'

Gran sips her champagne. 'The Dynamo, I presume, going on the tights.'

Dino glares at her and then at me. 'Who is this old lady dressed in her mother's curtains to be so rude to me?'

'That's no way to speak about someone three times your age,' I say, jumping to Gran's defence.

'Barely twice, if that, darling,' Gran murmurs, more offended by my comment than Dino's.

'I'm one hundred and twenty-nine,' he spits, and Bohemia laughs nastily.

'And the rest. You were easily forty-five when you died.'

Dino barrels his chest out and puts his fists up in a way that looks curiously outdated to my eyes, but then I've grown up on a diet of Thor bashing people over the head with his hammer.

Dino suddenly drops his arms and narrows his eyes at Bohemia. 'She's not with you.'

Bohemia shakes his head. 'And she's not with you either.'

This is like pulling teeth. Surely they can put two and two together? But then, of course, I know something they don't know yet; or at least, I sincerely hope they don't. I know that Britannia Lovell has managed to go and earth herself to Leo Dark and there's every chance she's over in the tower right now reacquainting herself with the pleasures of the flesh.

'You've just missed her,' I say, trying to throw them off the scent. 'She was right here a few seconds ago and now she's… er, popped off again.' Man, that was lame. I wouldn't believe me. My mother flicks her eyes at me, a clear WTF, this isn't *Rentaghost,* that I hope Dino and Bohemia miss.

Even the lion must sense I'm lying through my teeth, because he's staring at me and has started to low-level growl, as if he wants to bite my head off. I'm not scared of him any more. Well, actually I am, I'm terrified, but I've got Mum and my gran beside me this time and I've never seen either of them run from anything in my life. Besides, Glenda Jackson's here too. The woman can't even see Goliath, but I've no doubt that she'd make an even better job of slaying him than David did if he puts a paw out of line.

'She popped off?' Dino says, confused.

'This isn't *I dream of Genie,* darling. Watch and learn,' Gran murmurs, handing me her empty champagne glass and stepping forward into the breach.

'What a fabulous animal,' she says admiringly, approaching Goliath as if he's a cute puppy.

Bohemia preens. 'A killer. I was the only man on earth who could control him.'

'What happened to him?' she asks, walking around him. It's horrifying to watch, because she's rail thin and wispy and he's a golden muscle-bound monster, but I school myself to stay completely still because Gran isn't in any actual danger. Or is she? Lestat wasn't in physical danger, but he still nearly died of panic.

A dark frown crosses Bohemia Lovell's face.

'How did he die? Your lion, I mean?' Gran elaborates, even though there's clearly no need. If I didn't know her better, I'd say she was goading him. Oh hang on. I do know her better. She *is* goading him.

'*He* shot him!' Dino declares, pointing at Bohemia like Columbo doing his big end of show reveal. 'He took his lee-tle pistol out and he blew out that animal's brain.' He pauses to wave both hands at the parquet. 'Right here all over this floor.'

I relay all of this quietly to Glenda to keep her in the loop. She scans the floor and then a look of frank admiration crosses her face. 'Well I don't know what they used to clear the mess up, but I want some. Not a speck of blood.'

My mother tips her head to the side and stares at Bohemia. 'You killed your own lion?'

Contempt pours from the ringmaster and, if he were able, I'm sure he'd be sweating profusely.

'It was kinder than leaving him behind,' he says.

'Where were you going?' I ask quietly and we all wait for his answer.

'To her, as always.'

He sighs and then he's gone, taking Goliath with him.

Dino's laugh is hollow and macabre. 'He always rode her coat-tails, but it was I who let her fly.' He stalks away, disappearing, leaving us staring after him, more confused than ever.

'I've never seen the likes of that lion,' my mother says, wonderingly.

I almost feel sorry for Goliath now I know how he met his end and I have to commend him on his unerring loyalty to the man who blew his brains out.

'So we know that Bohemia killed the lion, but how did Bohemia himself die? And what happened to Dino?' I seem to have come away with more questions than answers today. I can sense the pieces of the puzzle hovering around my head like hornets and I know that this case isn't likely to get resolved without someone getting badly stung.

Gran takes her glass back from my fingers. 'Such a shame to waste good champagne, darling. Anyone for a fizzy little nightcap?'

CHAPTER EIGHTEEN

Turns out it's distinctly odd being in a castle all on your own at midnight. I packed Lestat off home with my mother for his own good an hour or so back; if he stays here any longer he's entirely likely to either go in for another rumble in the jungle with Goliath the pug-slayer or else explode from the amount of food he's being fed in the castle kitchens. He was last seen being rolled towards my mother's Pontiac like a keg of beer, and then hoisted between the three women and thrown onto the back seat like they'd just purchased a heavy bag of potatoes from a dodgy farm van in a lay-by. They sort of swung him back and forth a few times to gather momentum before letting go, and then my gran and Glenda had a restrained lady fight about who was going to climb into the back with him. It goes without saying that Glenda won. I wouldn't bet against her, even if she was fighting Wonder Woman.

I locked the massive front doors behind them and laid the key on the table, then perched on one of the armchairs and just sort of gazed around me in the silence. I don't really go in for words like eerie, but I was suddenly very aware that I was on my own. Across the castle forecourt I could see a light on in the far turret; Leo must still be awake. I won't lie. I toyed with the idea of wandering across and asking to sleep on their sofa, but then what would that say about me?

One thing it wouldn't say is badass businesswoman, and that is very much the image I want the world to see of me these days. What would the fembots think when Leo switches them on in the morning if they see me passed out in their lounge? I'd have to do the walk of shame back to the castle, even though I'd have done nothing to be ashamed of besides proving myself to be a lily-livered scaredy-cat. My mind's made up for me when the light in the turret winks off and all I can see through the front window is unending darkness.

'Night-night, Leo,' I murmur into the silence. 'Night, crazy twins with murderous tendencies.'

I make the only possible decision I can in the circumstances. I pour myself a large brandy from the decanter in the corner of the main reception hall and head on up the stairs to bed.

'I miss brandy.'

I'm startled by the sound of Britannia's voice next to me as I make my way down the long hallway towards the Princess Suite.

'Yes, I think I'd miss it too,' I say, after a beat, as she follows me into my room; into her room.

'Were you with Leo this evening?'

'For a while.' She sits down on the bed and sighs. 'Before Bohemia came hunting for me and then Dino, of course.'

'Can I ask you something?' I say, kicking off my Converse. I don't mind her being here; in truth, I'm quite glad of the company.

'If I can ask you something in return,' she says, ever the coquette, even with me.

I shrug. 'Okay.' I pause and sip my brandy while I decide how to frame my question. 'So, Leo. Can you touch him?'

Ghosts don't blush, but I fancy she would if she could. 'Not yet, but I'm hoping I might be able to soon.'

This is good news. I'd assumed that she'd achieved contact by now given the blood on Leo's hands in the ballroom, but it's an incredibly difficult thing to master and she's obviously struggling to perfect it.

'My turn to ask a question,' she says. 'Do you love him?'

'Leo?' I have to clarify who she means because he's not the first man who came to mind when she asked her question. Let's just ignore that fact and hope it goes away. Britannia nods and I struggle to fathom out the subtext behind her question. Is she trying to decide if I'm her love rival?

'Leo and I were together for quite a while, but that was a long time ago now. I guess you could say that we're trying to be friends these days, professionally at least.'

She mulls that over quietly while I head into the bathroom and brush my teeth. When I go back through, she's moved to the tall, broad old chest of drawers beside the chimney breast.

'Look in here,' she says and she's suddenly child-like and excited.

I humour her and cross to join her in front of the drawers. She taps the second drawer down. 'This one, I think.'

I grasp the faceted crystal knobs and slide it open, and inside I see layers of silk, satin and crisp cotton.

'My trousseau,' she says. 'Get this one out.'

She gestures towards a snowy white broderie anglaise slip. I indulge her, lifting it out and shaking it straight. I have to concede that it's a beautiful thing. 'Spanish lace,' she tells me as I admire the scoop neck and tiny shell buttons on the pin-tucked bodice.

I'm reminded of the sweet baby romper Marina and I found in the turret and I'm about to ask her about it when the look in her eyes pulls me up short. I don't think I've ever seen anyone look so wistful.

'Try it on?'

I look up sharply.

'Please?' she wheedles, suddenly like a little girl who misses her most favourite doll. 'It's the next best thing to wearing it myself again. I just want to see it.'

I automatically go to refuse, but why, really? What harm is there in going along with it for her? Perhaps she'll reveal something while she's unguarded like this. Besides. My single secret girly chromosome really fancies a spot of fancy dress, even if all of the others are saying put your Snoopy onesie on and go to bed.

'Oh go on then,' I mutter and roll my eyes to show her that I'm not still entirely sure this is a good idea. 'Wait there.' I feel compelled to add that, because she's more than likely to trail me into the en suite.

I strip off in the bathroom and slide the nightdress over my head. As I pull the front together and button it, it hugs and boosts my chest. It's very fitted with a scoop neck and delicate straps; it brings to mind serving wenches and bodice-rippers. The mirror shows me cleavage and curves and I'm glad and sad at the same time that no one else can see me. The skirt falls to my knees; it's sort of filthy demure, like I should thread daisies in my hair and wear it with wellies at a festival and then dance around a campfire barefoot in the evening. All this from a nightie! That champagne has gone right to my head.

I wander out to show Britannia, but when I get back into the bedroom a sudden almighty banging downstairs starts up and she flees in wide-eyed panic. Oh shitty-shitty-shit-bollocks, what the hell am I supposed to do now? Sodding Dino! I might need to lie down. God, how I wish Marina was here, and I want my mum. No, what I really wish is that Glenda sodding Jackson was still here. But they aren't here. None of them are. I'm all on my own in this seventeen-bedroom haunted castle and the racket has just started up again now, loud and more horribly, ominously insistent. I look for my mobile on the bedside table but find it dead. Thump, thump. Thump, thump. Ohmagod, really loud thump. Oh crap, it's no good.

It seems as though Dino wants this out with me right now, and he's not going to let me rest until I've been down there.

I pause at the top of the sweeping staircase, keeping myself pressed against the wall in case Dino decides to try and play 'let's push Melody down the stairs'. It's not usually the case that ghosts can physically touch the living, but given Leo's bloody hands episode in the ballroom I'm not taking any chances.

I frown, groping for the light switches and finding nothing. My heart is beating so hard it's almost painful.

'Britannia?' I whisper her name in the hope she's still around somewhere, but she doesn't appear. Of course she doesn't. One thing I've learned about ghosts is not to rely on them to help you. I tiptoe slowly down the dark staircase. The banging has stopped and everything has fallen spookily quiet and still. I could go back to bed. A sensible person would scamper back up to bed and pull the covers over their head until daylight, but I think we've already established that I'm not a sensible person.

I'm halfway up and halfway down the stairs when the banging suddenly starts again. After a few seconds of being sure I'm about to have to face down a malevolent poltergeist, realisation dawns on me. It's not a ghost making trouble this time.

There's somebody at the door.

CHAPTER NINETEEN

My feet mobilise, carrying me down the rest of the stairs and along the cold-floored hall towards the doors.

'Ghostbuster!' someone shouts. 'Open the damn door.'

Fletch.

Oh God! Relief floods through my veins, a gut reaction to the realisation that I'm not about to be murdered, or worse.

'Bittersweet, can you hear me in there?' Fletch shouts, banging again, and I feel the vibrations as I lay my hand flat against the solid, smooth door.

'Stop banging, you'll wake the dead,' I say loudly and silence suddenly reigns. I imagine him waiting on the other side of the door while I consider whether to open it or not. I think we both know that I'm probably going to, but I really am trying to be a sensible person.

'What do you want?' I dilly-dally, half shouting because the door is so thick.

'Not to sleep on the stone steps like your bloody dog?' He's quieter when he bangs again, softer and muffled. I'm pretty sure he's bumping his forehead on the door out of frustration. 'I'm cold, ghostbuster.'

There's something in the tone of his voice that has me reaching for the unwieldy key and fitting it into the lock. He must be able to hear me grappling with it, because he waits silently until I manage to get the damn thing to turn, throw the bolts and slowly swing the door wide.

'They put me back on the job,' he says and then his eyes rove over me, taking in Britannia's nightgown. 'Fuck. You look like a Victorian waif.'

It's quite a charming description, until his eyes settle on my boosted cleavage and he adds, 'A waif with a really great ra—'

'Could you not keep more conventional working hours?' I pointedly cut him off.

'I'm not a conventional sort of guy.' He leans against the doorframe and sighs. 'Let me in? Please?'

I reason with myself that I really didn't care for being alone here all that much and, on that basis, I step aside and let him pass. I'm not saying that this princess needs her knight, but this ghostbuster will sleep a tiny bit easier for knowing she's not the only living soul in this hulking great castle.

I tussle with the bolts and keys for a minute or two, and when I follow him through into the reception hall I find him slumped into one of the fireside chairs with his head resting against the flared side wing. His eyes are closed and, for a second, he looks vulnerable and as worn out as I am.

'Drink?' I say, motioning towards the decanters when he opens his eyes.

He seems to wrestle with the decision for a few silent moments and then, eventually, he nods, resigned. I could be snarky and tell him to get himself one then, but I don't. I pour him a decent brandy and hand him the cut-glass tumbler. He accepts it with the briefest smile that doesn't get anywhere close to reaching his eyes; he looks off kilter somehow.

'You okay?'

He cups his glass between his hands and leans forward with his elbows on his knees. He doesn't answer me straightaway; his eyes are nailed on the deep bronze brandy swirling in his glass.

'I lied to you.'

I'm not sure what he means, so I perch in front of him on the heavy square coffee table, smoothing the crisp cotton nightdress over my kneecaps. I say coffee table; it's big enough to hold about ten thousand cups of coffee, but everything is scaled up when you live in a castle. Only the humans stay true to size. We're like dolls in one of those fancy dolls' houses where you can open the front and peep inside.

'I lied to you a while back too,' I say, casting around for something to lighten the mood. 'I said I had a dog and then I had to go and get one before you found out I was lying.'

'My mother isn't dead.' He knocks back a good half of his brandy and then shudders as it goes down. 'Not yet, anyway.'

I'm so out of my depth here that I'm drowning. 'Is she ill?'

His laugh is harsh and as brittle as the outback in a drought. 'Nothing that another bottle won't cure. I grew up watching her have whisky for breakfast, vodka for lunch and tequila for dinner. She's in the hospital again and still the only thing she wanted was for me to switch the mineral water in her bottle for gin.'

I realise now why he was called away so suddenly.

'Is that where you've been today?'

'Her neighbours found her face down on the front lawn in her underwear. They called an ambulance when they couldn't rouse her.'

Jesus. 'Does she live on her own?'

His bleak eyes meet mine. 'She does lately. Yet another reason for her to hate me. She has quite the list.'

That explains why he's rented the grotty flat on the High Street then.

For all my oddness, I've lived a pretty regular, Pollyanna lifestyle thanks to the two strong, positive women who've raised me. I know I joke about my gran and her love of champagne, but it's a world away from the life Fletch must have endured. She's a lightweight, someone who drinks a few glasses of champagne a day because it makes her feel like a sophisticated French movie star and because it adds to her fanciful image. Beneath it all there's a woman in her eighties who eats only good stuff, can out-yoga most thirty year olds, and has a sharp wit and a huge, warm heart that has held her family together through the decades.

I slide down onto my knees and cover Fletch's hands with mine around his glass.

'Do you have any brothers or sisters to share the load?'

He shakes his head, his eyes still hidden from me as he studies his brandy.

'And your dad?'

'She's always been proud of the father unknown status on my birth certificate.' He makes a derisory sound low in his chest.

'So it was just you and your mum, huh?' I murmur.

I can almost see the weight of his misplaced guilt pressing down heavy on his shoulders, years of not measuring up, and my hands reach out instinctively to soothe him. I hold his warm jaw, stroke my fingers over his hair, smooth and dark in the low-lit room.

He empties what's left of his brandy into his mouth like medicine and then places his glass on the table beside me.

'Would you do something for me, Melody?' he whispers, low and forlorn. At this moment, there isn't much I'd refuse him.

'Come up here and let me just hold you for a while?'

It's such a heart-achingly simple request, but wildly complicated too, because this isn't the Fletcher Gunn I know and understand. This man is different. This man needs comfort to help salve the hurt of his hellish day, is asking for a tiny sticking plaster on a lifetime of careless paper-cuts inflicted by the hands of his alcoholic mother.

I can't imagine his childhood. I don't even want to, so I crawl up into his lap and curl myself into his warm body, tucking my knees up and wrapping my arms around his shoulders. He gathers me in, cradles me, presses his face into my neck and breathes me in deep, as if he's inhaling me into his veins.

God knows what this is. It isn't a sex thing, exactly, although it's profoundly, deeply sexy to feel this needed.

He's holding onto me tightly, fiercely, the way you might hug someone if they were going to live on the other side of the world tomorrow. His defences are on the floor and he's just lifted me over them and onto his side because he's lonely and desolate and he needs someone, he needs *me*, to make him feel something other than shitty for a while.

I couldn't swear to it, but when he mouths my neck slowly, I think his cheeks are damp.

I can't bear it that he's so fucked up. It rebalances the scales in a way that puts me at a disadvantage, because that chip on his shoulder is all part of the Teflon wall he's built around himself so no one gets close and hurts him.

I drag a soft woollen rug from the back of the chair and settle it over us. Fletch helps me, tucking us in, his mouth moving against my hair as he shifts beneath me to get comfortable.

I can hear his heartbeat beneath my ear, steady and strong, soothing in the same way a train going over the tracks sounds if you close your eyes and let yourself nod. He's warm too, so very, very warm, kind of how it is when you step off the plane somewhere sunny and the heat envelops you and makes you feel like taking off all your clothes and ordering a cold beer and staying there for the foreseeable. I'm perfectly still, aside from my fingers stroking the back of his neck and he is the same, aside from his thumb rubbing slowly over my cheek as he cups my face. I suddenly realise I'm absolutely bone tired and peaceful, encapsulated in a place far from here, a place where there's a population of two. Fletch and me.

'Best ten minutes of the damn day,' he says, sliding his thumb over my mouth. I kiss it without thought, then catch his hand in mine and press my lips against his palm. His fingertips rest warm against my face and then move into my hair as he tips my chin back to touch his lips to mine.

It's the single most sorrowful, sensual kiss of my life. His lips are soft and he barely moves. It's a slow, intense coming together, a sigh into my mouth, both of us giving, not taking. It's powerful in a way I never knew a kiss could be. I'm spellbound, and all of the things that normally keep us mentally apart melt like snowflakes in Las Vegas. I don't have a name for this, or a handy shorthand way to describe what happens sometimes between Fletch and me. All I know is that here feels like the only place either of us should be tonight, and that this kiss is more than just his mouth and mine. It's kiss nirvana.

'Is this a private slumber party or can anyone join in? Not that I imagine anyone would want to.'

I jolt awake at the sound of Leo's sarcastic tone and open my eyes, disorientated. I'm tucked up in Fletch's arms on the armchair and he's still fast asleep. The blanket has slipped down onto the floor and I'm instantly aware of the heat of Fletch's hand pressed against my bare thigh exposed by Britannia's rucked-up nightdress. His other hand is in my hair. God, did we have wild, abandoned sex and I've forgotten?

It takes me a good few moments to re-live the last few minutes before I fell asleep last night and assert that, no, we definitely didn't. We're both still as dressed as when Fletch turned up, but my cheeks go hot at the memory of how unguarded we were with each other, and of how intimate falling asleep in Fletch's arms felt.

'Jesus, Leo,' I whisper, carefully sliding from Fletch's lap and clambering to my feet. God, I'm stiff. 'How did you get in here?' I distinctly remember locking and bolting the door.

'The staff entrance around the back. The cook let us in.'

By us he means himself and the fembots, who are looking at me and Fletch curiously from beneath matching army green berets. I feel like asking them if they've joined the Resistance, but don't bother because I know it'll go right over the top of their jauntily angled berets.

'Have you come especially early in the hope of catching me doing something you think I shouldn't?'

He sighs and rolls his eyes as if I bore him.

'Nothing could be further from the truth,' he says, and I'm confused because that sort of implies that he doesn't like seeing me with someone else. 'It's Thursday. My camera crew are coming, remember?'

I do remember, but I don't want to say so because I'm pissed off that he's caught me in yet another compromising position. Behind me, Fletch stirs and I turn as he opens his green eyes and assesses the situation. He pauses, then looks my way with a barely there wink.

'Morning, ghostbuster.'

His voice has an early morning thickness that feels too private for anyone else's ears but mine, so I turn and look at Leo.

'Could you give us a few minutes, please?'

He walks to the window. 'I doubt it. The camera crew have just pulled up.'

I can see the wagon turning around in the driveway and, behind me, I feel Fletch get to his feet and stretch with a wake-up groan. 'I ache,' he murmurs, dropping his arm over my shoulders.

'We'll get out of your way.' He's curt with Leo, earning himself a glare.

I feel weird, as if I've been caught doing something far worse than just snoozing. I guess it *was* something more than that, but even I don't know what it was.

'Actually, I wondered if I could have a word with you,' Leo says, looking at me, pointedly ignoring Fletch. I nod, acutely aware that I'm barefoot, bed-haired, and have a nightdress on that makes me look like I'm up for a good ravishing. Or like I've just had one.

'Let me just go and get dressed. I'll be back down in a few minutes.'

Fletch follows me up the stairs, his hand warm on the small of my back. I roll my shoulders as we walk down the hallway towards our rooms, still un-stiffening from a night spent curled in his arms on the chair.

'Stiff neck,' I mumble, when we reach my door. Fletch reaches out and curves his hand around my neck to massage it. It feels much, much too good.

'Maybe we should have gone to bed last night,' he says, quietly, and then he traces the tip of his index finger around the lace-edged scoop of my nightdress. He bites his top lip as his gaze follows his finger's path across the swell of my skin, and I can barely breathe.

'And maybe we shouldn't,' I say.

'Your skin feels like liquid-fuckin'-gold.'

Aw, man. He's doing that sexy swearing thing again and I want to rip this nightdress right off and let him touch me in all my shiny liquid-fuckin'-gold glory. How does he do that in so few words? Dear future husband, please talk dirty to me like Fletcher Gunn does.

Downstairs I can hear doors slamming and engines revving out on the drive, a bevy of voices and commotion. Leo's heavy-booted crew are making themselves known and the last thing I want is a camera shoved in my face again while I'm in my nightie and being idly turned on by Fletch.

'I need to get dressed,' I say, feeling behind me for the doorknob.

'I know,' he says, playing with the straining top button of my bodice. His knuckles graze my skin. 'Want some help? I'm good with buttons.'

I am one hundred percent certain that he could have me out of this nightdress in three seconds flat.

'I don't know if I'm coming or going with you, Fletch,' I say softly, because he perplexes, infuriates and melts me in a way that has me in a constant tailspin. We are so unalike and mismatched, yet our mouths and our bodies insist on feeling like matching jigsaw pieces.

'Coming,' he says. 'You'd definitely be coming.' A crooked Leo Dicaprio style smile tips his mouth and makes my nipples hard. He notices and I see his throat move when he swallows.

'Going would be more advisable, I think.' I push the door open behind me and step away from him. He drops his hand and studies my face, serious.

'We both know what needs to happen next, Melody.'

I'm starting to think that this castle isn't just haunted; it's bewitched. I feel as if someone, Britannia bloody Lovell, probably, has cast a spell over me and Fletch, causing a temporary glitch, a breakdown in hostilities, making us want to bump uglies so badly that it's sending us cuckoo.

It's all very well sharing secrets and late-night armchair smooches, but that isn't what he and I do best. We do snark and sizzle and I kind of need it to stay like that, because my heart is off the table as far as Fletcher Gunn is concerned. Oh, I want to be loved, and to love someone so much that my heart would literally stop if he's in trouble, but that man needs to be someone who gets me, not someone who gets me so mad I'm likely to end up incarcerated.

That man needs to be someone I can trust with my crazy, someone who understands and champions and celebrates me. For a woman with my quirks and foibles that's a pretty tall order and, for a fair chunk of my life, the only man who came close to ticking all of those boxes was Leo Dark.

Shit. Leo. He's waiting for me downstairs. I hightail it into the shower to go and find out what on earth it is that he needs to have a quiet word with me about.

CHAPTER TWENTY

'I think I've fallen in love with Britannia Lovell.'

No shit, Sherlock.

My feet had barely hit the bottom step of the staircase before Leo grabbed my arm and half dragged me out through the back of the house and into the walled kitchen garden, where we're now hidden from sight behind the giant rhubarb.

'Bloody hell, Leo.' I sigh, trying to hide my exasperation. 'Can you even hear how ridiculous that sounds?'

He's pacing in front of me, three steps left, three steps right, coating his mirror-shiny black leather winkle-pickers in a fine mist of dust.

'Says the woman who is clearly getting it on with Fletcher Gunn, of all people.'

Here we go again. 'How is that even *remotely* the same thing?'

He stops pacing to eyeball me as if I've asked a stupid question. 'He's just as inappropriate for you as she is for me.'

'How, Leo? How is someone who is similar in age, single and breathing, equally as unsuitable as someone who is one hundred and twenty-five, married with a lover, and dead?'

He looks down his nose at me. 'You've got about as much chance of going the distance with him as I have with her.'

That hit home. 'Meaning what?'

'Meaning that we all know that Fletcher Gunn is a man whore. He wants you this week because you're playing some bizarre game of house. And getting heavily into character, if this morning's ridiculous choice of nightdress is anything to judge by.'

A man whore? I don't think we all do know that, actually. In truth, I don't know the first thing about Fletch's romantic history. Because I'm feeling catty about Leo's wisecrack, I fire a round of bullets right back at him.

'It was Britannia's nightdress, not mine, if you *must* know. She asked me to wear it because she wanted to see it again. I think it might have been from her wedding night.'

He takes the bullet right between his dark, searching eyes. I don't feel especially proud of telling him that he caught his ex-lover wearing his dead crush's nightie. It's all kind of screwed-up, isn't it? I'm just sick to the back teeth of his judgmental attitude where my romantic life is concerned.

'I have to say this, Leo,' I say, hotly. 'You kind of lost the right to comment on my love life when you dumped me, okay? What I choose to do, or not do, with Fletcher Gunn, or with anyone else for that matter, has absolutely sod all to do with you. Have you got that?'

He scowls and shrugs his shoulders. 'It was just friendly advice. Take it or leave it.'

'I'll leave it, thank you very much.' I cross my arms over my Rugrats-emblazoned chest and glare at him. 'Now, if I'm not very much mistaken, we're lurking behind this bush because of problems in *your* love life, not mine. What the hell do you want me to do about the fact you think you're in love with a ghost?'

He passes both of his hands over his shiny hair and shakes his head, an out-of-character loss of composure for him.

'I don't know what to do.'

I pause to think. 'Well, I don't see as you can actually *do* anything, Leo. I'm sorry to be blunt, but Britannia's dead. There's no coming back from that.'

'Don't you think I know that? But I had her blood on my hands, Melody, *her actual blood*. You saw it with your own eyes, didn't you?'

He's not messing around here. He's borderline emo at the best of times, but right now he's more like borderline breakdown.

I nod and try to look tactful. 'I did, and we both know how incredibly rare that is. I'm not saying that you haven't forged an unusual connection with her because it's obvious you have but, Leo… it can't lead to anything. You do understand that, right?'

Unfortunately, Leo looks as if he doesn't agree. His brow draws down heavily over his eyes, stubborn and brooding.

'She's trying to achieve contact.'

'And she might manage it, briefly, in a day, or a week, or a year. Is that what you want? To watch her die daily on the off-chance that she'll achieve temporary physical form so you can shag like rabbits in springtime? Because that's a whole lot of ifs, buts and maybes to stake your future happiness on. And what happens afterwards, if it ever actually happens at all? You'll feel worse and then become one of her unlikely trio of suitors, except you're even more stupid than they are because you're actually alive and breathing and wasting your life.'

He's staring at me now. Or glaring at me, because the truth has obviously hurt. 'Of course that isn't what I want. God, I don't know what I want, okay? I thought you'd understand.' He shakes his head. 'As someone who's loved and lost, I expected more empathy from you.'

Hang on. Is he telling me that I should be a more sympathetic ear about his heartache because he made my heart ache? His self-smugness knows no bounds and, even worse, I don't think he's aware of the irony.

'Well, I don't,' I say, shortly. 'Here's what I think. You've fallen for the oldest trick in the book. One flick of her long eyelashes and Britannia has you right where she wants you on her hook, wriggling like a fish at her beck and call. Has it not even occurred to you that she might be doing all of this to try to put you off your job?'

It strikes me in that moment that she might be trying to befriend me for the exact same reason. I don't think so somehow though; I think she's genuinely lonely. She's gregarious and severely company deprived; I'm the first living female she's had to talk to since she died.

But then… isn't Leo the first real man she's had to talk to, too? Maybe she isn't the cunning, manipulative harlot I've just made her out to be. Perhaps she's just sparking off us and is as bowled over by our company as we are by her vibrant presence. God, I'm even confusing myself, which is of no help to either Leo or the case.

'I don't think I can extinguish her. She's so beautiful,' he says, downcast.

'Is that what you wanted to tell me? That you can't do your job?'

He snags a flower off a honeysuckle trailing over the garden wall and picks the creamy petals off one by one, unwilling to admit defeat in such bald terms.

'I just need your help more than I expected to.'

I read between the lines and know that what he actually means is he can't do this job, but he still wants to flounce about on TV and be paid for his efforts whilst I do all the actual work.

'Just go and do whatever it is you do with your TV people,' I say with a sigh. 'Leave me to have a think.'

I need to get out of this castle.

Marina and Artie walk in through the front door as I come back in from behind the giant rhubarb.

'Has it really been less than a day since you were last here?' I say, hugging Marina like she's a ship's mast in a monumental storm. 'It feels more like a week and we've got so much still to do.'

She extricates herself delicately from my clutches after a couple of moments and then shoots a filthy look at one of the TV crew who tries to drag an extension lead across the flagstones beneath her spike heels.

'Damage my shoes, I'll damage your camera,' she snarls, and he pushes his glasses nervously up his nose and scurries away.

Artie watches the exchange almost fondly; he knows Marina well enough by now to know that that was actually quite polite by her standards.

'I might just go and look in on Lestat,' he says, nodding towards the kitchens.

'He's not there. My mum took him back to Chapelwick last night.'

He looks utterly crestfallen, and I don't think it's because he's missing his furry amigo.

'I could kill a coffee though,' Marina says, pretending to splutter because her throat is so dry.

'Me too, come to think of it,' I say hoarsely.

He brightens instantly. 'On the case. Two coffees coming up.'

'What's the betting he'll come back with lipstick on his collar?' Marina murmurs as we watch him walk away.

'I hope not, for his sake. His mother would have a turn.'

I don't think either of us realistically expect Artie to engage in a kitchen table clinch with Hells Bells. He's more likely to send her a handwritten note asking to fill her dance card at the ball on Saturday.

'Long night?' Marina says, patting me on the back because I've just lunged in for a second quick hug. It's just that she's living and breathing and not trying to snog me or double-cross me, so she's becoming something of a rarity around these parts. I go to tell her about last night, but there's people milling around and then Fletch himself jogs down the staircase and joins us. I can smell his shower gel, citrus and fresh mornings, and his hair is still slightly damp and towel tousled.

If Marina is surprised to find him here she doesn't show it. She just watches us keenly, probably trying to assert whether I took her advice and let him wave his donkey dong around my love taco. I don't know if I'm disappointed or relieved that he didn't.

'I need to go back to Chapelwick for a while this morning,' I say, turning to Fletch. 'We'll probably be back on site after lunch. And it's non-work-related so, before you ask, no, you don't need to shadow me.'

This is a lie, but I don't care. If he shadows me at home he will no doubt come into contact with my family and that won't end well for anyone involved. There would be restraining orders.

'I should head into work this morning anyway,' he says, distracted by the TV crew milling around and turning the main reception hall into a makeshift TV studio. 'I might just go and grab some coffee first though.'

He nods curtly and takes his leave, leaning away from Marina this time when she sniffs him again. We watch him until he disappears out of view towards the kitchens; I do hope Hells Bells and Artie are decent.

'He exudes a manly scent,' Marina says, lifting a knowing eyebrow in my direction. 'Like a big fox on the prowl at midnight.'

'You mean like he's been sniffing around people's dustbins?'

'Like he's had his nose stuck where he has no business sticking it,' she snickers. 'So… did he?'

'Did he what?'

'Stick his nose somewhere he shouldn't?'

'Is that some sort of Sicilian mating ritual?' I snark, and she laughs it right off.

'If I show you the biscuits in my bag, will you tell me if Hack Attack is a donkey or a piglet in the trouser department?'

This is difficult. I want her biscuits. She knows my tastes run to the big and calorie-packed luxury end of the biscuit aisle; there's no way she's going to have a plain old packet of Rich Tea in her handbag. I need to make like a politician and be evasive so I nod, but try to shake my head a bit at the same time and she narrows her eyes suspiciously.

'Are you having some sort of fit?'

We both know that I'm not having a fit. She delves into her shoulder bag and pulls out just the very tippy top corner of the biscuit packet, flashing it at me as if she's a prostitute and I'm a kerb crawler who's just slowed down to check her out. I can't see enough to know exactly what they are, but I now know that they're in a matt black package that looks expensive and that they're definitely from the all-hallowed luxury section of the aisle. These babies aren't wartime stalwarts with sensible shoes, they're good time showgirls with frilly bloomers.

'Do they have big crunchy nuts?' I whisper.

'Does he?' she shoots back.

'Thick chocolate coating?'

She nods approvingly. 'Food play on your first night? Kinky.'

Someone stop me if I ever attempt to run for parliament. I intended to be evasive, and yet so far I've managed to imply that Fletch has big crunchy balls and coated me in Nutella.

Actually, that idea isn't wholly without merit. Any sex that includes chocolate has to be good sex, right? I'm not precious about it being Nutella, either. Maltesers. Matchsticks. Aero bubbles or Rolos. There isn't a single sexual activity that I can think of that couldn't be enhanced by a Double Decker. That sounds a lot ruder than I intended it to. For clarity, I'd only want to lie back and blissfully eat the aforementioned chocolate while Fletch (for instance) and his big crunchy balls did the necessary down the business end. Or whoever else it is that I happen to be doing the trouser snake dance with. I just used Fletch as an example to demonstrate that I don't want Munchies popping in any other orifice but my mouth.

We fall silent as Nikki and Vikki attempt to walk through the castle door, arm-in-arm. It's too narrow so they reverse, turn sideways, and then side-shuffle in, as if they went to bed and have woken up conjoined.

'We better go and rescue Artie.' I steer Marina away from the twins by the elbow. They've tried to get rid of us in the past and Marina holds a grudge. The twins have clearly picked up on this, because they've taken to making alarming yappy noises when she's around and she in turn tends to emit a low-frequency growl that probably alarms every cat within five hundred foot of her.

As we head down the hall towards the kitchen, she spins her head around and bares her teeth at them.

'You shouldn't let them wind you up so much,' I say mildly as we step down the couple of steps into the kitchen.

'I can't help it. I want to take a hot poker and shove…'

She trails off at the sight of the empty kitchen, frowning. 'Where's Artie?'

Cook appears out of the pantry with a catering-size tin of baked beans under each arm and puffs her fringe out of her eyes.

'For the crew,' she explains, although we didn't ask. 'If you're looking for the lanky chap with a bad case of the heebie-jeebies for Bells, he's in the garden with the sexy chap.'

Poor Artie. He isn't just wearing his heart on his sleeve. He's waving it around over his head the way women wave their knickers at a Tom Jones concert.

The cook nods towards two steaming mugs sitting on the side.

'He left those for you.'

Lanky chap. Sexy chap. I wonder what she calls me and Marina? Stubby lass and slutty lass?

'The sexy one?' Marina says.

The cook nods whilst grappling wilfully to get the tin-opener fastened onto one of the tins, then pauses and stares off into space.

'Reminds me of a young James Dean.'

Seeing as James Dean never made it to anything but young, I rather feel that's a moot point, but I let it slide. She means Fletch.

I know, because he sometimes reminds me of James Dean too; a charismatic rogue with do-me eyes and a smart answer always on the tip of his tongue.

'What do you think Fletch wants with Artie?' I say, half to Marina and half to myself as we grab the coffees and head out of the back door into the sunshine-filled kitchen garden.

'Let's go and find out, shall we?' Marina says as we spy Fletch and Artie ambling along the far path deep in conversation.

'At least they're not having a clandestine meeting behind the rhubarb,' I say, thinking back to earlier.

'Only fools would attempt to camouflage themselves with fruit,' she laughs, picking her way along the uneven path with her coffee mug in her hands.

I feel compelled to defend myself, even though I haven't told her about earlier yet. 'It is *giant* rhubarb, Marina.'

'Even giant rhubarb couldn't hide our Artie.' She isn't wrong. If he was sporty, they'd be queuing up to sign him as a basketball player.

'What do you think they're talking about?'

'I don't know, but I really hope it's not the birds and the bees, because Fletch is a big bloody bird of prey and Artie is more of a duckling.'

I sip my coffee as we walk and Marina slants her eyes at me in the sunlight.

'A big old bird of prey, huh? You mean, like a cock?'

She thinks she's so smart finding a way to work the conversation back around to whether or not Fletch and I got it together last night.

'A cock is literally no one's idea of a bird of prey,' I say.

'Just tell me already, will you?' she hisses, losing her cool and chucking what's left of her coffee in the nearest flowerbed. 'He wasn't even here when I left last night and then he's strolling down the stairs fresh out of the shower this morning. What gives?'

It doesn't escape my notice that we've come to a halt behind the giant rhubarb and are totally screened. I daren't mention it to her in case she whacks me with her mug. The problem is that what happened between Fletch and me is kind of personal. Moreover, it's *his* personal stuff and I'm one hundred percent certain that he wouldn't want it sharing with anyone. I don't think there are many other times he would have shared it with me, to be honest. It was just the right place after a shitty day all round and the right nightdress for a romantic armchair tryst.

'You do know we know you're hiding in there, right?' Fletch's voice carries through from beyond the huge, splayed leaves of the pink-tinged rhubarb plant. 'Because only a complete newb at investigating would imagine that hiding behind fruit is a good idea.'

Marina puts her hands on her hips and smirks at me, pulling an 'I told you so' face as coffee dregs drip from the upturned cup dangling from her fingers.

'We're not hiding, thank you very much,' I call out haughtily. 'We're, er, having a snack. A healthy rhubarb snack.'

Beside me, Marina mimes shoving her fingers down her throat and pulls a gagging face.

'Is that so?' he says loudly and I can practically hear him laughing. He and Artie follow the path around until they appear alongside us.

'Let me help you ladies out there,' Fletch says, snapping an offshoot off one of the monstrous stalks and handing it to me. It's as long as my arm and as thick as a piece of rope. I really detest rhubarb, unless it's bathed in sugar and hidden in a crumble.

I smile politely and go to pass it to Marina. 'There you go,' I say, and she shoves it straight back into my hands.

'You first, I insist.' She smiles, but her eyes say, 'Piss off, you said it, you eat it.'

I smile and say, 'If you're sure,' as if she's bestowing a great favour on me and bring the brute of a stalk towards my mouth slowly.

'Er, Melody, I don't think—' Artie starts, but Fletch shushes him and all three of them watch with varying expressions. Artie is doubtful, and rightly so. Marina has turned her mouth into a grim line, but her eyes tell me that she's laughing inside. *Cow.* Fletch, predictably, looks as if it's Christmas morning and someone gave him a book of blowjob vouchers.

Because there is nothing else for it, I shove the massive damn stalk into my mouth and take a far-too-sizeable bite. Oh God! I can barely get my teeth through it; it's as tough as Marina's attitude and sourer than goats' cheese left out for a month in the desert. How can something with juice in it make my mouth dry up as if someone made me eat sand? I think it's actually curdling my saliva.

'Is it… good?' Marina chokes. The fact that tears have started to stream down my face should be a goddamn clue to how good it is. It's like there's a sour bale of hay in my mouth and it's so big that I don't have a prayer of chewing it.

'Healthy?' Fletch smiles expectantly at me and I consider blowing the whole wad out of my mouth into his smug face. It could easily take his eye out.

I think I'm going to die from rhubarb. It won't go down, it can't come out, and I can barely breathe. I'll have to die and then they'll feel terrible and wish they hadn't been so ha-ha amused. Only Artie can walk away from this guilt-free; he looks like he'd love to help me but is clueless how. Then, and I cannot tell you how much I love him for this, inspiration strikes him. He winks at me, almost subtle, and then he executes a perfect comedy fall, as if an invisible person just shoved him over. Marina and Fletch jump to help him, and in the moment of distraction I bury my face in the giant rhubarb plant and gag out the lump of rancid string. I kid you not; it's the size of my fist. No. The size of the hulk's fist. It lands in the dirt with a thud, like a house brick.

By the time Artie has been hauled back onto his feet and has laughed off the incident, I'm standing nonchalantly sipping my coffee.

'Thank you, Fletcher. That was delicious.'

Marina and Fletch both put their heads to one side, suspicion in unison, and I just shrug helplessly.

'What can I say? I like healthy stuff.'

Fletch shakes his head, clearly not conned for a minute.

'What's next on your healthy snack list, ghostbuster? Want me to find you some lemons to suck?'

I give a forced, tinkly little laugh. 'That rhubarb has filled me right up. I feel so healthy, I could probably run a marathon without breaking a sweat.' He laughs and strolls away, whistling, and he's lucky I don't chase after him and ram that rhubarb up his fit sodding backside.

CHAPTER TWENTY-ONE

'So what were you and Fletch talking about?' I say, glancing at Artie as I pull Babs to a juddering halt at the traffic lights.

'Yeah, actually. You two looked thick as thieves,' Marina says from his other side. He's sandwiched between us on the front bench and he has to keep batting the Hawaiian garland hanging from the rear-view mirror out of his eyes every time I fling us around a corner.

'Man stuff,' Artie mumbles, turning pink and staring straight ahead.

I sigh. 'He told you to say that, didn't he?'

Artie nods. 'He knows a lot of things though, doesn't he?'

Oh yes. Fletcher Gunn knows a lot of things. He knows how to wind me tighter than a clockwork mouse, and he knows how to kiss me until I feel as if he's filled me up with moonlight and he knows how to make me want to shove a stick of giant rhubarb so far up his backside that it comes out of his mouth.

Marina folds a stick of gum in half. 'Like what?'

Artie shrugs. 'Like everything.'

She shakes her head. 'You're not going to tell us, are you?'

He pretends to think. 'No.'

'Was it about snogging Hells Bells?'

He makes a strangulated sound. 'No!'

'It was, wasn't it?'

Artie covers his purple face with his hands and shakes his head.

I want to tell him that if Fletch gave him snogging advice then he should take it, because he's a Jedi-snog master, but I don't.

I just keep driving, and hope that whatever lust spell Britannia Lovell has cast over me and Fletcher Gunn wears off when we leave Maplemead Castle.

It's so good to be home. Just pulling Babs into the shady cobbled alley at the side of the building makes me feel calmer; I hadn't realised quite how on edge everything back at Maplemead had me. It seems to have all become very romantically tangled very quickly over there, between both the living and the dead. Being away from there will hopefully help me gain a little clarity, as well as some respite from the pressure of being observed from all angles.

'I'm sorry I made you eat rhubarb,' Marina says, once I've turned the engine off. She roots in her handbag and withdraws the much-teased packet of biscuits.

'Peace offering?' She hands them solemnly to Artie, who hands them solemnly to me.

'Triple chocolate and candied pecan butter cookies.' I read the swirly silver writing as if I'm Charlie Bucket and I've just found the last golden ticket. Have I mentioned that that is my favourite movie in the world? Oh to live in a world where chocolate lakes are real and the trees are made from lollipops.

'You're forgiven,' I say. 'The biscuits outweigh the rhubarb.'

'And it was a very big rhubarb,' Artie says.

I feel better than I have in days. I hand Marina the office key and the biscuits as I slide Babs's door shut. 'Go on in and stick the kettle on, you guys. I'll run and grab Lestat and be right back.'

I love the bell over the door of Blithe Spirits. My mother's insistence on keeping the shop traditional is a warm blanket around my shoulders today, the familiar scents of beeswax, old books and fresh flowers is the welcome scent of home.

My mother is bent double behind the counter and her face breaks into a smile when she straightens up and spots me.

'Melody, darling. You're home.'

Glenda pops one arm out of the back office and waves, a jingle of gold bangles.

'Hi, Glenda,' I call through.

'Do you need me to come down to the office?' she says, popping her head around the doorframe and looking at me over the top of her horn-rimmed glasses.

I shake my head. 'We're only back for a couple of hours, so there's no need.'

My mother frowns. 'I do worry about you being there around the clock like this, Melody. Is there any sign of an end in sight?'

'That's kind of why I've come back. It's impossible to think straight over there, so we're going to go through everything and try to make sense of it. With biscuits.'

Turning her back on me, my mother opens a cupboard behind the counter and then turns back and places a cellophane-wrapped coffee cake on the counter. Absence seems to have made her heart grow fonder; she usually saves this kind of thing to use as bribery when she wants me to do something.

'Have some cake too,' she says, pushing it towards me. 'Be careful, won't you, darling?'

I pull the cake towards me so she can't change her mind. I'm still not over how easily she upended that pancake into the bin.

'I know. Eat it with a fork, don't put too much in my mouth at once. I'm a grown woman, Mum. I'm not about to choke on coffee cake.' My childhood was one long round of being warned not to shove sweet things into my mouth whole.

She flips her eyes to the ceiling. 'Not with the cake, foolish child.' She taps her heart with her fingertips. 'With this.'

I'm not sure if she means because of cholesterol or romance, and I don't dare ask, because neither are something I want to think or talk about. I'm rescued from needing to answer by the tinkle of the bell as the shop door opens.

'Melody, you've come home!' my gran cries, as if I'm Lassie and I've been missing for days and have turned up bedraggled and dirty. She's wearing a lavender Spandex all-in-one topped off with a wide-brimmed sunhat; it's a difficult look to pull off but she works it. Lestat barrels in behind her and makes a beeline for me and I find myself begrudgingly glad to see him back to rude health. I say rude because, as he stretches his stout little body up my leg and paws my knee, he lets out a volley of dog farts and rolls his eyes back blissfully.

'She's going back over there again in a couple of hours,' my mother says darkly. The knowing look she shares with Gran tells me that they've been talking about me. Gran heads behind the counter to stand beside my mother and then Glenda pops out of the office too and joins the other end of the row. They look like the now shot of Charlie's Angels in one of those 'then and now' picture features the trashy celeb magazines love.

'Are you auditioning for a police line-up?'

They all sigh and then cross their arms over their chests in unison as if they've rehearsed it. They have, in a way; these three women have been the stalwarts of my life from the moment I was old enough to hoard my first box of Mr Kipling French Fancies.

'Why do I suddenly feel as if I'm standing in front of the jury?' I joke.

'We don't think it's wise for you to spend another night in that castle,' my mother says. Oh no. She's wheeled out the royal we. They've formed an army and they're trying to stage an intervention.

'It's Thursday today. With any luck this will be the last one I need to spend there.'

They glance at each other like contestants on *Dragon's Den*, trying to decide which of them is best to speak up on behalf of the team.

'We think your judgment is being clouded by the unreasonable time expectations you're working under,' my mother declares, and they all nod sagely.

'And that they're asking far too much of you, expecting you to stay on site like this,' Gran adds, smiling at me the way she used to when I was eight years old. Indulgently, as if I am a child in need of guidance.

'And that you're highly likely to succumb to the carnal temptation of either Leo Dark or Fletcher Gunn and then regret it as soon as the job's over,' Glenda finishes, matter of fact and direct, and my mother and my gran both look at her sharply.

'There's not a chance in hell that I'd ever let Leo near me again,' I say, sounding scandalised because I am affronted. 'I'm offended that you'd even suggest it of me.'

Their alliance is in disarray and I take the chance to scoop Lestat up under my arm and stomp my way to the door. My fingers touch the handle and then I remember the coffee cake.

I turn and march back across to the counter, but my mother lays her palm flat on top of the icing and stares me down.

'I note that you didn't mention Fletcher Gunn, Melody.'

I'm flustered and I give the cake an exasperated little shove towards her. 'Keep your cake.'

She pushes it back to my side of the counter and I twist away because Lestat cranes his neck to try to catch hold of the cellophane and claim it as his.

'Take the cake.'

We stare at each other while I decide whether to do as she asked.

'And take care of your heart?' my gran says.

Glenda dips into the office, reappearing a few seconds later with a small box and pushing it across the counter at me. 'And take protection.'

It pains me greatly, but I leave the cake on the counter beside the box of condoms and hightail it out of there with my dog under my arm and nose in the air.

* * *

An hour later and I'm almost calm again.

Marina let me have unfettered access to the fancy biscuits out of solidarity after I relayed my encounter with the Witches of sodding Eastwick, and Artie made me a huge cup of coffee and has started to update the white board.

'What I don't get is what's holding the ghosts at the castle,' Marina says, cracking a cookie in half and picking the nuts out as she stares at the board.

I tap the end of my pen against my teeth. 'Their unresolved love triangle?'

We all consider that for a little while.

'Or maybe whether or not one of them cut the ropes on purpose?' Artie suggests.

I study the whiteboard. We have all of three names written up there, along with the information we've gathered from them and about each of them so far. It's frighteningly scant given that the ball is in a couple of days, but I know for certain that one of those three ghosts holds the key to this.

'The least likely to have cut the ropes, assuming someone did, has to be Dino,' I say, thinking aloud. 'I can't help but think that he's trapped in the castle by circumstance; he's fiery and besotted and his lover died a hideous death in his arms.'

'That's true,' Marina says slowly. 'Unless he was trying to commit dramatic suicide because Britannia had dumped him or they'd had a lovers' quarrel, something like that?'

Artie notes our thoughts down under Dino's name. Okay, right, so maybe I shouldn't write Dino off into third place so readily.

'Well, I think we can safely assume that Britannia didn't cut the ropes herself,' Marina says, pushing the biscuit plate towards me so I can hoover up her unwanted pecans.

'Can we, though? Can we be absolutely sure of that?' I'm questioning everything more deeply now. 'Maybe she needed to kill Dino off for some reason. Perhaps he was threatening to expose their affair to Bohemia?'

Artie jots the possibility down, then cracks open his Tupperware sandwich box and pulls out one of his egg sandwiches.

Marina tucks the bottom half of her head inside her shirt and murmurs 'mayday, mayday' into an imaginary walkie-talkie and even Lestat falls down flat on his belly and tries to shove his face up the skinny leg of my jeans. Usually, the smell would get me too, but not today. Today I'm Iron Woman. Artie helped me get out of swallowing giant rhubarb, the least I owe him is an egg sandwich free pass.

'And then there's Bohemia, the ticked-off husband,' I say. 'He's the obvious one, isn't he? Killed his wife by accident when he intended to murder his love rival?'

They both nod and Marina and I sway backwards on our chair legs when Artie waves his sandwich in our direction because an idea strikes him.

'Unless he actually *intended* to kill his wife.'

We all lapse into silence as Artie writes the new scenario down.

In some way this exercise has helped us, because we've crystallised our thoughts in black and white, but the truth is that we've still got far more questions than answers.

'We don't even know how Bohemia or Dino died yet,' I say, thinking. 'And we need to find out what happened to them after they died, too,' I say. 'Because if, and it's a big if, if Brittania and Bohemia are buried by the secret bench at Maplemead, who buried them there and why? And where is Dino's body?' I frown. 'We need to interview each of the ghosts in turn with all of these questions in mind,' I say, snapping a picture of the white board on my phone.

Marina gathers up the cups and dumps them in the sink, then grabs her denim jacket. 'Considering it's Thursday now and Lois and Barty's grand welcome ball is in forty-eight hours' time, we better get our asses back over to the castle.'

As we pile back into Babs, I notice a note has been stuck under the windscreen wiper. I open it and find a small sealed white envelope tucked inside. The handwritten note is from my mother to apologise for earlier, and to wish me luck with getting the case sewn up as quickly as possible. I huff under my breath, but I'm relieved not to be fighting with her all the same.

'What's in the envelope?' Marina asks, clicking her seat belt into place.

'Emergency gift from Glenda, apparently,' I say, scanning the PS at the end of the note. Ripping the envelope open, I tip out a four-finger KitKat onto my palm.

'Trust Glenda to send four fingers instead of two,' Marina grins. 'Over-prepared, as always.'

I run my fingers over the wrapper because it doesn't feel quite right, and then the penny drops.

'Yeah,' I mutter. 'She's a regular Girl Scout.'

I shove the KitKat back into the envelope before Marina or Artie can catch sight of the silver-sealed condom packet hidden beneath the red paper wrapper.

CHAPTER TWENTY-TWO

I'm glad to see that Leo's TV crew have cleared out for the day as we pull over the drawbridge at Maplemead. Fletch's dark blue Saab is also absent and I find myself relieved about that too. Taking time away to review the case has pressed home the fact that we're short on time and I'd much rather get on with the job without constantly wondering if he thinks I look wacko. I can't sensor myself and do the job justice and, at the end of the day, I'm on the clock here and trying to build up my professional business reputation.

Leo's blacked-out sedan is over by the turret. Even his car is attention-seeking. I think that's possibly the first requirement he asks of the things he chooses to surround himself with; they have to gild his life and add to his public image. I realise now that he applies the same criteria to the people he chooses to surround himself with too; perhaps that's why I didn't make the final cut. Not flashy enough, not quite eye-catching enough. It's a disquieting thought, and one I'm pissed at myself for allowing to creep in, because if there's one emotion I don't do well, it's self-pity. Given my quirks, it would be all too easy to allow doubt to creep in, to tell myself that I'm odd, and weird, and different, that I'll never quite be mainstream enough to be anyone's first choice. For the most part though, I don't feel that way and, for the most part, that's down to the women in my life.

Leo might surround himself with people who blow smoke up his backside and tell him that he's marvellous, but my cheerleading team are every bit as loud and they wave their pompoms just as fiercely. My mother. My gran. Glenda Jackson. Marina. They are my people and their hard line on self-pity has made sure that I've grown up walking as tall as a five-foot-three woman who sees dead people possibly can.

'Right then,' I say, determined as I look up at the castle façade. It's overcast this afternoon and the grey walls soar up and touch the troubled skies overhead. It looks a different place without sunlight glinting off its leaded windows. Less welcoming. Not forbidding, exactly, but cold and hard. I'm really quite glad that, one way or another, this will be my last night alone under Maplemead's castellated roof.

'Hang on, my phone's buzzing.' I reach into the back pocket of my jeans as I slide out of Babs. 'Crap, missed it.' My screen tells me that it was Lois and, a second later, a voicemail pops in.

'Just checking up on how things are going, doll!' Her voice belts out of my phone. 'Call me and wow me with good news!'

'Someone's turning the thumbscrews,' Marina says, tying her hair back with a band from around her wrist and sliding her sunglasses up her nose.

My nerves jangle louder than the car keys in my hand as we walk briskly across the gravel and jog up the stone steps. Lestat is with us, moseying along at his own pace, although he sticks close as soon as we go inside the castle. Once bitten, twice shy. Or, in his case, once mauled, twice terrified. A marquee company arrive and park up next to two black and white catering vans, jumping out and throwing their back doors open like a military SWAT team. It's obviously all systems go with the ball preparations and it's as busy inside the castle as it is outside when we walk through the open front doors into the cool reception hall.

'Mind your backs please!' someone says behind us and we move aside to allow a guy carrying a huge, precariously balanced, box of champagne flutes through.

'Looks like we're going to struggle to find some peace to talk to the ghosts around here today,' Marina says. 'It's like Grand Central station.'

Artie scoops Lestat up and we pick our way around hulking great amplifiers and crates of champagne and head towards the kitchens.

It's thankfully quieter in there and Hells Bells and Artie lock gazes and both flush the same shade as the summer pudding that Cook is assembling on the scrubbed table.

'The posey one was looking for you.'

I'm guessing 'the posey one' must be Leo. He got off quite lightly there in my opinion. I might have gone with the narcissistic, egotistical, self-centred, floppy-haired, twattish one, myself. It has a more truthful ring about it.

'Do you know where he is now?' I ask. I'm worried he wants to offload the fact that Britannia managed to successfully achieve physical form in my absence and that they've had filthy sex behind the giant rhubarb, seeing as that seems to be the clandestine meeting place *du jour*. Is it possible to get a ghost pregnant? Maybe I should slip him Glenda's emergency condom.

Cook shakes her head. 'No idea, but he had the creepy ones with him.'

Now *there's* a nickname I don't feel the need to correct.

I change tack. 'Are Lois and Barty around somewhere?'

'They were, but now they ain't.' Hells Bells's words rush out all on one breath. 'M'lady said she was going to have her eyebrows plucked, her hair styled, her nails painted, her tan sprayed…' She ticks them off on her fingers, then pauses and frowns in concentration. 'There was one more…'

'Back, sack and crack wax?' Marina suggests. 'Bleaching around the old hoochie-coochie-hoo-haa?' She wiggles her backside and I give her a sharp elbow in the ribs.

'And Barty?' I ask, to stop Marina from saying anything else.

Cook looks up from her mound of blackberries and, in unison, they both say 'playing tennis'.

The amount of tennis that man supposedly plays, he should be better than Andy sodding Murray. Given his robust frame, I'd say his arm gets more action lifting a pint of beer than it does lifting a tennis racket. Marriage is a bit like that though, isn't it? Little lies to keep the peace, and sometimes big ones.

Right. So the owners have done their usual vanishing trick, the castle is teeming with strangers who are going to get in our way, and Leo might be about to tell me he's boffed Britannia. This job is never, ever straightforward. We need to get out of the way of everyone to do our stuff and the only way to do that around here is to either head down to the dungeons or upwards to the bedrooms. I don't need to debate those two options for long, because I'm not a psychotic sadomasochist.

'Artie, could you settle Lestat down here in the kitchen and then meet us upstairs in the Princess Suite please?'

I'm not sure how many opportunities I can naturally create for him to ask Hells Bells to the ball; if he doesn't get the nerve up soon I'm going to give up and do it for him.

Upstairs, Marina and I drop down flat on our backs on the huge bed in the Princess Suite.

'You're not going to tell me if you and Donkey Dong got it on last night, are you?'

I laugh under my breath and study the ceiling. 'It's complicated.'

'I didn't ask for your Facebook status,' she grumbles.

'We didn't, okay?' I relent because Marina and I are so close, I don't like not being able to confide in her. 'He came by, we talked a bit, and then we fell asleep in the chair.'

She thinks this over. 'Together?'

'Yes.'

'Right.'

'Why did you say it like that?'

'Like what?'

'Slowly, like you don't approve.'

She lifts her hands up off the mattress. 'What am I, your mother? You don't need my approval.'

'Marina, you were the one encouraging me to fall into bed with him yesterday, remember?'

'Yes. For sex,' she says, as if that would have been better. 'Not for talking, and definitely not for falling asleep together with your pants still on. That wasn't what I meant at all. Tell me he kissed you, at least.'

I stay silent and she groans under her breath.

'Okay, okay,' I say, trying to make up ground. 'He did kiss me a little bit.'

She groans loader. 'That's worse.'

'How can it be?'

'Because it's romantic, Melody. I didn't realise that I needed to be so specific with my instructions.'

I pretend that I don't know what she's getting at, because I do know what she's getting at and I know she's right. 'So what you're saying is I should have wild-monkey-sex with Fletch but not let him kiss me or speak to me? Is that it? Because that sounds a little bit like you're suggesting I should be a prostitute. Shall I charge him twenty quid while I'm on?'

'Twenty quid? Jesus, Melody. Have some pride. Add a nought on.'

We both laugh a bit and carry on staring at the ceiling.

'Just let him do anything he likes to your body, but don't let him into your head or your heart. That's all I'm saying.'

'He's not all bad,' I say, thinking back to the vulnerable, emotionally battered man I held in my arms last night.

'They said that about Hitler.'

'Marina!'

'I like your handsome reporter. He's sexy.'

I didn't say that, and neither did Marina. I prop myself up on my elbows and find Britannia sitting at the dressing table rearranging her hair in the mirror.

'Britannia,' I say, both as greeting and to let Marina know to shut the hell up.

'Ladies,' she says, getting up from the stool. 'I hear talk of a ball on Saturday.' She catches my eye in the mirror. 'I've come to be your fairy godmother.'

'I need to talk to you,' I say, rolling off the bed and standing up.

Britannia wafts over to the wardrobe and opens the door.

'Take your pick.'

'She did that, right?' Marina murmurs and I nod. Then Marina catches sight of all the beautiful clothes hanging in there and bolts off the bed fast enough to break her neck.

'Oh my God, these things!' she says, awed. 'Can I touch?' Her hand hovers in the air, ready.

Britannia nods, so I do too. Britannia walks around Marina, assessing, and then tells me to suggest the silver dress. I pass the message on and Marina trails her fingertips over the padded hangers until she finds a silvery floor-length mermaid-like gown and pulls it out carefully.

She hangs it on the open door and we all gaze at it. Marina clutches her neck. The dress oozes vintage glamour; its dull-silver velvet bodice nips in at the waist and the gun-metal silk skirt, overlaid with a filmy mesh, flares to sweep the floor. A braid of flattened flowers trails over one shoulder and around the bust line, wrapping around the waist to form a delicate belt.

'That one wasn't mine.' Britannia sighs, wistful. 'It belonged to Aunt Eleanor. She kept most of my things in here after I…'

Even after all of the intervening years, Britannia still struggles to speak of her own death. I jump in to save her from the need to elaborate.

'She must have been very proud of you.'

Britannia looks more downcast than I think I've ever seen her. 'I hope so. My mother was her younger sister, the family tearaway. It's such a cliché to run away and join the circus, isn't it? But that's what she did, and by seventeen she was pregnant with me.'

'So that's how you ended up performing,' I say, piecing the jigsaw of her life together bit by bit. Marina has fished her phone from inside her bra and is recording me as I speak in the hope that I'll be able to piece the one-sided conversation back together again when we study it afterwards.

'Yes. I grew up travelling. My mother always said I flew before I walked.'

I smile, because right now Britannia isn't a troublesome, sexy harlot. She's a wild-haired, tiny child flying like a rare bird on a trapeze in those child-sized ballerina slippers in her blanket box and she's a wilful teenager who called this place home because she'd grown up on the road.

These insights help me because they fill in the colours of the broad-stroke image I hold of her in my mind, but they hinder me too, because the more real she becomes, the harder it is to detach myself from her and do what I need to do. I can see why Leo is struggling; I'm dazzled by her too and enjoy her company. God knows what it's like for him when you throw in the element of mutual desire too. Jeez, they're both so charismatic. A relationship would never have survived between them in real life, they're both the kind of people who need to be fêted and adored. They'd kill each other in a battle for control of the heated rollers.

'I know it's difficult, Britannia, but could we please talk about the accident?'

Her face clouds and the light of nostalgia in her eyes dulls as if someone has just blown out a birthday candle.

'It wasn't an accident.' She studies the contents of the wardrobe. 'You should try the purple.'

'How can you be so sure it wasn't an accident?' I breathe, because she didn't say that with any element of doubt.

'Because I know who cut the rope.'

CHAPTER TWENTY-THREE

'She knows who cut the rope?' Marina gasps as I relay the information a couple of minutes later. 'Who was it?'

Infuriatingly, Britannia winked out like a light bulb being switched off as soon as she made her revelation, leaving me with a head full of unanswered questions.

I drop down heavily onto the dressing table stool. 'I'm not sure. She didn't hang around long enough to tell me.'

An idea, small and stubborn, takes up residence in my head. I don't say anything yet, because it's an inkling, an instinct, a not quite fully formed thought. Artie, who arrived just as Britannia departed, is making furious, spidery notes in his flipbook.

'So if she knows who did it, then they can't all be trapped here by the unresolved mystery,' he says, looking up uncertainly as if he doubts himself. 'Is that right?'

I mull it over. 'Just because she knows, it doesn't mean that the others *know* she knows,' I say slowly.

'You sound more and more like Columbo every day,' Marina says. 'Never buy a mac.'

'I tried one once. I looked like a flasher.'

'I rest my case.' She glances at Artie. 'Don't put that in the notes.'

He turns his pencil around and rubs out the last sentence he wrote as I hang Lady Eleanor's dress back inside the wardrobe.

'Did she really say I could wear the dress?' Marina says, reaching out for it and pawing the air.

I nod. 'She said to help ourselves. Let's see if we can find Bohemia and Dino and, when we're done, we'll come back and do the Cinderella thing if you want.' I glance at Artie. 'Don't put that in the book either.'

'Here, kitty-kitty!'

I roll my eyes towards Marina. 'What are you doing?'

'Calling the lion.'

We're in Fletch's room, working on the assumption that if Britannia had laid claim to the Princess Suite, then it follows that the Knight Suite would most likely have been her husband's lair. It's similar in size to my room, but there is an air of masculinity to the pared-back mahogany furniture and steel-blue eiderdown. Fletch's leather holdall adds to the look, still left abandoned on the chair.

'Why don't you go the whole hog and fetch Goliath a saucer of milk?' I snark.

'I'll fetch it!' Artie pipes up, hopeful of yet another mission to the kitchens.

We both look at him long and hard.

'Artie,' I say. 'Do you genuinely think a ghost lion will drink a saucer of milk?'

He shakes his head and studies his fingernails. 'A bucket?' he suggests, clutching at straws.

Marina puts her hand on her hip. 'Have you asked Hells Bells to go to the ball with you yet or not? Because today's Thursday and the ball's in two days. If you don't do it soon, someone else might beat you to it.'

Artie is wide-eyed and slack-mouthed, a combination of horror that Marina has even bought the subject up along with fear that someone else might steal his girl from under his nose.

'She wouldn't do that,' he says. 'Would she?'

Marina shrugs. 'I hear that Lady Lolo has hired a hot waiter to be on gong duty on Saturday. He's going to have a lot of spare time and he's going to need a foxy date.'

Artie looks wretched.

'Go and fetch the lion a saucer of milk, Artie,' I sigh, and he hightails it from the room so fast he almost trips over his own feet.

I narrow my eyes at Marina when we're alone.

'What?' she says, shrugging her shoulders like a mafia don. 'You have to be cruel to be kind with some people. He'll be thanking me on Saturday night, trust me. Tough love and all that jazz.'

I hadn't really given any thought to taking a date to the ball. I flutter my eyelashes at her and dip my chin.

'Will you come to the ball with me, please?'

'Piss off, Bittersweet. This is the first ball we've ever been invited to. There's no way I'm going with you as if we're a pair of wallflowers in *Pride and Prejudice*. This arm needs a proper man.'

She crooks her elbow at me to emphasise her point.

'Well, Marina,' I say, snootily. 'I'm sure I don't need to remind you that today's Thursday and the ball's in two days' time. If you don't ask someone soon it'll be too late.' I smile sweetly and wish Artie was there to savour the moment. 'You'll wish you'd said yes to me then, won't you?'

'Oh, please,' she scoffs. 'I've already got my date sorted.'

I'm taken aback. 'Who?'

'Gong man.'

'Really? I thought you'd made him up to put the frighteners on Artie.'

'Nope. I bumped into him a day or two ago outside on the drive. Date secured within ninety seconds. He's fabulously handsome, I'm all-round fabulous, job done.' She clicks her fingers. 'I'm not all mouth and no trousers, you know.'

'Right.'

Bollocks. What am I going to do about a date? Because I'm not doing anything that involves the word date with Fletch. I wouldn't ask him, and it'll snow in hell before he asks me. It's just not who we are or what we do. I mean, he can ask me to shag like wild boars and that's okay; it's offensive and brash and I can mock him and refuse, but something as downright civilised as asking me to accompany him to a ball… no. Just, no. I'm already worried about what I'm going to wear for the date I don't yet have, because everything in Brittania's wardrobe is uber-glam and beautiful. Can you wear Converse with a ball gown? I reckon I could pull it off.

Something growls behind me and pure fear trickles cold down my spine.

'Goliath,' I murmur.

'Shit,' Marina mouths, stepping closer to me as if she's going to fend him off. 'Here, now?'

I turn slowly and there he is by the window with his owner alongside him.

'Bohemia,' I say, resolutely not looking at the hulking great lion.

'I presume you're looking for me,' he says. 'Unless of course you have an ulterior motive for being in a gentleman's bedroom?'

Is he having a flippin' pop at me about Fletch? I can't decide.

'I need to talk to you, if you have five minutes?'

Something close to a sneer curls his lip. 'I'm not sure I can fit you in. The life of a retired ringmaster with no big top or performers is non-stop.'

Oh he's droll. He's terribly English and his upper lip is so stiff he looks like he's had Botox and his Bryll-creamed hair is perfectly coiffed. He's not unattractive, but he is rather bland, if that makes sense? His hair is non-descript brown and his cold eyes are an indistinct blue grey. Right now he's looking down his long, slim nose at me as if I'm inferior because I'm not some bendy acrobat type or fire-eating bearded lady. I rack my brains for something I could tell him that might make me seem more on his level, more likely to open up to me.

'I could put my foot behind my head when I was five,' I tell him. 'And I learned how to make my thumb disappear for the school talent show when I was ten.'

He's staring at me as if he's trying to decide whether to set his lion on me, but I press on regardless and demonstrate the truly terrible magic trick my gran taught me in an attempt to make me look normal, because telling the talent contest judge that his dead mother didn't approve of his penchant for women's wigs wouldn't have gone down very well.

'Too random,' Marina warns.

'Just warming him up,' I say out of the side of my mouth.

'Is it working?' she asks.

'Nope. In fact, I think I've made him angrier.'

'What exactly is it that you want of me?' he demands, and then he cracks his whip hard against the floor and makes me jump.

'Well,' I say, dry-mouthed because Goliath has just started to pace the floor. I think the whip is a signal for him to do something. Try to rip one of my limbs off, probably. 'Forgive the intrusion because I know this is a bit of a personal question, but did you by any chance cut the ropes on the trapeze in order to try to kill your wife? Or to kill Dino, maybe?'

I know, *I know. Way* too direct. If I had more time or more tact, I'd probably have thrown in a few more social niceties before going for the jugular, but the damn lion is making me nervous and I'm keen to get this conversation over with as soon as humanly possible.

Bohemia stares at me and then he takes a slow step closer. I take another one back and, sure enough, he draws closer again. It's like a very slow, very menacing dance.

'You're going to end up in the wardrobe at this rate,' Marina murmurs, quiet and urgent.

'Check behind the coats and see if you can find Narnia,' I whisper. 'Because this lion is no storybook hero.'

And then Bohemia does something unexpected. His shoulders slump and he drops his whip to the floor. Instantly, Goliath lies down and I breathe a little easier.

'Have you ever truly loved anyone?' he asks, looking at me wearily.

My every instinct is telling me that this conversation is important, so I answer him as honestly as I can.

'I thought I did. But we're not together any more and now I'm not sure I ever loved him as much as I thought I did. He's a bit of an ass, you see, and he broke my heart, but now it's mostly better again and I'm not sure you can feel that way if you truly loved someone. I imagine you'd always be a little bit heart-bruised.'

Bohemia's brow is deeply furrowed, as if he's perplexed by my answer. I'm not surprised. I'm quite perplexed by it myself, to be honest.

'I loved her too much. I told myself that I loved her enough for both of us and that, in time, as she grew older and less ravishing, she'd realise that she loved me too.' He has the bleak eyes of a man who knew he'd never be enough. 'I offered her a good life.'

I listen and try to decipher what he's saying. There's quite an obvious age gap between him and Brittania; he probably had one hell of a game keeping track of her.

'She must have loved you too. She married you, after all,' I say, trying to help.

He huffs. 'Brittania was barely eighteen when she agreed to marry me. Or when she was given to me, if I'm to be completely accurate.'

I go very still. 'Given to you by *who*?'

He looks away from me, out of the window at the busy scenes going on outside. 'They were different times, back then. Simpler, in many ways. Brittania's father was my most brilliant trapeze artist and, in exchange for his livelihood and top billing, he encouraged his daughter to look favourably upon me when the time came.'

'Do you mean she had no choice but to marry you?'

He frowns and shakes his head. 'She wasn't forced at gunpoint or anything so dramatic; I'm not an unreasonable man. It was just an agreeable outcome for everyone concerned.'

I can't disguise my distaste. 'You make it sound so cold and clinical. More like a business deal than a marriage.'

'Isn't that the irony?' he says, grim-eyed, as he shakes his head. 'It may *sound* cold and business-like to you, but for me it was anything but. Britannia was fifteen when I fell in love with her.'

I look down, because I don't want him to see how much his words are affecting me. *Fifteen.* My heart hurts for Brittania.

'And I waited, and I waited, and when she was of a respectable age, I made sure that she came to me. Is that so terribly wrong? To love someone, to wait for them, to make sure that they know how much you're willing to sacrifice to be with them?'

'What did you sacrifice?' I ask, not taking my eyes from his for a second.

He laughs, hollow and empty. 'Besides my sanity?'

I can't gauge if he means that literally. He looks like he might. Is he telling me that he lost his mind and cut the ropes? I don't say a word. I just look at him steadily, hold my breath, and wait.

'I sacrificed everything for her. My reputation. My heart. My lion. And then my life.'

And then he's gone, taking Goliath with him, leaving me staring at an empty space. I know more, but nowhere near enough, and it's frustrating the hell out of me.

'He's gone.'

Marina sits down on the end of the bed and makes notes as I relay the details of our conversation.

'Poor Britannia,' she says, picking at the edge of the eiderdown.

I can only nod. The more I hear about Britannia Lovell's life, the more I understand her. And the more I like her.

'We need to try to find Dino next. I'd like to save Brittania until last,' I say. 'Oh, and I need to talk to Lady Eleanor again too.'

'And Artie,' Marina says, standing up and flicking her hair over her shoulders. 'He never came back with that saucer of milk.'

We pause on the kitchen steps before we round the corner into view, because we can hear Artie speaking and they're the kind of hurried, shaky words you definitely don't want an audience of more than one for.

'So, I was wondering, if you might, possibly, potentially, need someone to take you to the ball on Saturday? I'm very good at holding coats and at making sure your drink is topped up and I'm not too bad at the waltz as long as it's slow and you don't mind me counting in your ear. Unless, of course, you're going with the man who's coming to bong the gong, because that would be totally understandable too. He can probably waltz without counting and everything. And tango. And foxtrot. I can't foxtrot. Or tango.'

Marina winces and clutches my upper arm hard with her face screwed up and I feel the exact same way. It's painful. I want to shout, 'For the love of God, man, stop speaking and let her answer you!' so badly that I fold my lips in tightly on themselves to hold the words in.

'Yes.'

Oh my God, it's like sweet, sweet music. Marina's wince turns into a grin that touches her ears and I feel like a proud mama whose son just got four big fat yeses at the *X-Factor* auditions. Marina and I are his crowd and we give him a silent standing ovation before strolling in and pretending to chat about nothing in particular.

'Everything okay in here?' I look blandly at Artie. He grins at me as if he's just won the lottery and Lestat lifts one eyelid in greeting from his position next to the ovens.

'I was just coming up,' he says. 'I'll be there in one minute.'

It's the closest he's ever likely to come to asking us to leave.

'We'll be in the reception hall when you're ready,' I say, shooting a smile at Hells Bells as I back out. Marina does the same and chucks in a cheesy double thumbs-up.

'You may as well have just told them we heard them and be done with it,' I mutter once we're out of view.

'Ssh,' she says, straining to overhear them again.

I lean my back against the hall wall, knowing that we really should give them some privacy now.

'Umm, Bells, can I just double check something?' we hear him say, agonisingly unsure. 'When you said "yes", did you mean yes, you'd like to come to the ball with me, or yes, you're already going to the ball with the gong man who can foxtrot?'

I close my hands over my ears with my fingers crossed for him. I can't bear to listen. I watch Marina freeze as she waits with bated breath, then punch the air as if she's just won an Olympic gold before grabbing my hand and running us through to the reception hall and flopping down onto one of the sofas. It's thankfully quieter in here now; I'm guessing that most of the preparation is going on in the ballroom.

'Act normal when he comes in,' she says, finger-combing her hair into place. 'She said yes! Well, what she actually said is that she's not keen on the gong, it makes too much noise and that she can't foxtrot either and, yes, she'd like it very much if he'd take her to the ball, thank you very much.'

I laugh and shake my head. 'I don't think I've ever known a couple more suited to each other.'

Britannia appears by the fireplace. 'My Aunt Eleanor and her husband were the most perfect couple I've ever known.' She looks towards the library, where at this moment Lord and Lady Shilling will no doubt be engaged in a ghostly hand of whist.

'Britannia.' I greet her with a cheery smile. 'Do you have any idea where we can find Dino?'

She laughs prettily, pearly teeth against siren-red lipstick. 'Why would you want to do that?'

I shrug. 'I fancy a chat.'

'Dino isn't much of a conversationalist. He's more of a … How can I put this?' She taps her fingernails against her teeth. 'Let's just say he's more of an actions-speak-louder-than-words man. He tends to spend his time in the dungeons. I think he likes to think of himself as a tortured artist, so it suits his sensibilities.'

'Right then,' I say. Artie has just reappeared and Brittania has made her exit through the wall, so I stand up and point towards the exit with both hands. 'This way, troops. I'm reliably informed that Dino hangs around in the dungeons.'

Marina holds a hand out and I pull her up from the sofa to stand beside me.

'Well, isn't *that* fabulous,' she groans. 'Don't go anywhere near the shackles, Artie.'

CHAPTER TWENTY-FOUR

It might seem an obvious statement, but it's bloody dark in the dungeons. There's one measly slat and barred window set right into the top of the wall and it lets in so little daylight that it serves very little purpose. I'm getting horrible flashbacks to being shut in the cellar on our last job by the fembots.

Marina sandwiches herself against me and mutters in my ear. 'Why don't they ever put lights in places like this?'

Suddenly we're bathed in a weak circle of light and I look towards the source and find Artie grinning toothily at me.

'It's on my house keys. My mum bought it for me so I can always find the keyhole in the dark.'

'Good thinking, Artie.'

Even in the dim light, I see appreciation of my praise in his eyes.

'Can you sweep it slowly around the room please? Let's try to get ourselves a measure of this place.' All I really want to do is find out if Dino is in here, but if I say that he'll probably flit away before I can spot him. Of the Maplemead ghosts, he is the least communicative, with me at least. He made a damn fine job of communicating his feelings to Lois and Barty earlier in the week. Britannia's advice that he's an actions-rather-than-words man rings loud in my head. I'm hyper-aware of a couple of things; one, he's quite skilled at moving things when he wants to be and, two, we're in the dungeon again. I walk slowly backwards until I reach the wall, my arms outstretched and touching Marina and Artie either side of me to signal they should do the same.

Artie sweeps the low light around and, although it's really not strong enough to see properly, I can see enough to know Dino's not standing anywhere in this dungeon with us. I can also make out the shapes of the bulky wooden and cast-iron torture equipment bolted onto the walls and I have to work really hard to chase *Fifty Shades of Grey* thoughts out of my mind with Lois and Barty cast in the starring roles. Sexy, it isn't. But what if it were Fletch down here with his sexy eyes and his low-slung jeans? Would I let him lash me to the wall and tickle me with a feather? It's not an instant no. Where was I? Dino. Dino the Dynamo is a no-show in the dungeon, as far as I can see.

And then I realise. I need to look up.

'I need to check around the ceiling,' I murmur as I pull my phone out of my back pocket and click the torch. Yes, I know I could have done that earlier, but Artie was so puffed up about his keyring torch that I didn't want to burst his bubble.

The strong white beam bounces around the dark room and I direct it upwards and move it methodically from corner to corner. I'm about to give up when I see him.

'He's there,' I say under my breath, and then I step forward a couple of steps and smile pleasantly up at him.

'Hi, Dino.'

'You again with your magic eyes,' he says, sounding thoroughly bored by me already.

I file his phrase away. I've never thought of myself as having magic eyes before and, actually, I quite like it even though he meant it disdainfully. I'm just a normal girl with magic eyes. That could work on Tinder. I'm not even on Tinder but, if I was, I think they'd all be swiping left so fast they'd break their fingers. Or swiping right. I have no clue.

'Do you think you could come down here and talk to me please?'

'Why would I do that?'

'Because I'd find it pretty difficult to come up there and talk to you?'

He makes a point of sighing heavily to display how unimpressed he is by my lack of athleticism. We can't all be bendy bloody Wendys, can we, I think, but I don't say it because I don't think sarcasm is going to entice him from his perch.

'Please?'

His old school manners get the better of him and he grumpily executes a graceful double somersault and lands not far from us on the bare earth floor of the dungeon. I track his movement with my torch. I'm not enjoying this shaky white light interview style; it's all a bit too Blair Witch for my liking.

'Would it bother you if we stepped out into the light?' I ask, gesturing towards the doorway.

'Yes.'

'Oh.'

'I take it we're staying in here, then?' Marina murmurs and I nod.

'What do you want with me? I'm busy.'

I decide that, as with Bohemia, it's going to be best to just be quite direct.

'When I watched you and Britannia perform in the ballroom, it looked to me as if someone had deliberately cut the ropes.'

'Are you *investigatore*? *Polizia*?'

I don't know if he's throwing Italian words in to wind me up, but I check in with my Sicilian sidekick quickly before I reply.

'No. I'm not police or an official detective. I'm just an inquisitive woman with magic eyes who tries to help ghosts.'

He folds his arms across his broad chest, making his biceps pop like, well, Popeye. 'I don't needs *aiuto*.'

Help, Marina reliably informs me.

'So what *do* you need, Dino?'

'Only one thing.' His dark eyes blaze with passion. 'To be in the ballroom this evening to catch her when she falls. And again at midnight. And again in the morning. It's all I do, same every day.'

'But… you never catch her, Dino,' I say quietly, trying to understand.

'*Ancora*,' he counters.

Marina translates for me again. *Yet*. Ancora *means yet*.

'But I will. One of these times will be the time she finally chooses me, and that time I will win.'

I stare at him, incredulous.

'You've been repeating your final performance for all of these years and you still think that you're going to be able to save her one day?'

It's mind-blowing, really. He's such a fiery, impatient man and yet, three times a day every day for the last God knows how many years, he's taken his part in the vain hope that the outcome will be different.

'I will save her. She will live, so I will live, and we will be flesh and bone here again.'

He speaks with such certainty, as if he really believes it's true, and I know in that moment that there is very little I can do for Dino right now. He's held here by his undying love for Britannia Lovell and she is the only person with the power to release him. Just not the way he imagines.

'You didn't cut those ropes, did you?'

I ask because I'd like to hear him confirm it but, in my heart, I already know he didn't. Fletch would have a field day with me relying so heavily on my gut instinct again, but I have a good ear for liars and of all the things Dino is, a liar isn't one of them.

'I have her blood on my hands because I let go of the trapeze, but it was not I who cut the ropes. Every time, I try to hold tighter to the bar, but still it flies from my fingers and, every time, she dies. I die too.'

'How did you die, Dino?'

His face shutters down, as if the memory physically pains him. '*Il leone mi ha ucciso.*'

I repeat it to Marina and she winces.

'The lion killed him.'

We sit in a line out on a bench in the garden, each of us holding a strong cup of coffee and glad to be out in the daylight.

'So we've narrowed it down to either Britannia or Bohemia who cut the ropes,' I say, working through the findings from today's investigations.

'And we also know that Goliath killed Dino and Dino didn't kill Britannia,' Marina adds.

I nod slowly, trying to formulate their timeline in my head. 'So the order of their deaths is Britannia falls, the lion mauls Dino, Bohemia shoots the lion, and then… hang on, what happened to Bohemia?'

Artie pauses from scribbling to look up at us to make a suggestion.

'Shot himself?'

I can't see many other possibilities. What a sorry, sorry state of affairs.

'Unless someone else shot him.' Marina picks up a stick and tosses it for Lestat to chase. He's lolling on the grass not far from us, legs akimbo and balls out, and he looks at her as if she's lost her mind.

God. Every truth we uncover reveals a new question waiting in line behind it. I couldn't be an actual policewoman or a real detective, it's mentally exhausting.

'Can we go and play Cinderella with Britannia's dresses now?' Marina asks.

Artie yelps. 'Oh no!'

We both look sideways at him.

'What do I have to wear for the ball?' he asks. The look in his eyes is pure horror.

'Black tie,' Marina says. 'Dinner jacket?'

He frowns. 'I only have my old school blazer.' He looks thoroughly downcast. 'And the black tie I bought for my dad's funeral.'

I'm overwhelmed by the urge to throw my arms around him and hug the life out of him. School was one long round of loneliness and bullying for Artie and the loss of his dad in a freak beer barrel accident is the worst thing that's ever happened to him. I know all of this because Arthur Elliott Senior paid me a visit after he died to plead with me to give Artie a job in the first place. I was dubious at the time, but it's turned out to be one of the best business decisions I've made.

'We'll help you,' I say. 'Won't we, Marina?'

She looks thoughtful. 'You know, my nonno was quite the gentleman in his day. I'm pretty sure we still have some of his handmade Italian suits in his wardrobe at home.'

Artie brightens. 'Really?'

When Marina says her nonno was quite the gentleman, what she actually means is that her grandpa was pretty much a Sicilian gangster. I have no doubt that his suits will be the finest money could buy, that they probably didn't cost him a penny, and that Artie has just unknowingly struck sartorial gold.

'I'll bring some to work for you to try tomorrow.' She nods. 'You'll need to get your hands on a mask though.'

He falls silent while he thinks. 'I've got a Chewbacca one somewhere.'

Marina looks to me with sharp alarm, but I just shrug. 'People only take them off when they get there anyway. Chewbacca will be perfect.'

* * *

So. Here we are again. Or here I am, I should say. It's turned eight o'clock in the evening and everyone has finally gone home. The caterers and musicians and furniture people have cleared out for the evening, Lois and Barty called in for an hour to get a 'ghoul update' and Marina and Artie have left to make their own ball preparations, taking Lestat with them for his own safety.

I'm starting to feel a tiny bit territorial about Maplemead. Like it's mine. I ate alone in the dining room and have retired to the Princess Suite with my after-dinner brandy. Yes, I know I sound like one of the cast of *Downton*. It's this bloody castle.

The sun has settled low and rose gold on the horizon; the murk has cleared through and left a gorgeous summer's evening behind it. I find myself hoping that it holds until Saturday for the ball and then I really *do* feel over possessive about the place, because I experience a frisson of concern in case anyone damages the gorgeous flower frescos on the ballroom walls. And, really, would it be too inconvenient for the ladies to remove their high heels so as not to damage the parquet?

I catch myself, give myself a shake. It's fortunate that this is my last night here because I really am starting to have ideas above my station if I'm thinking stuff like that. I need my tiny flat, my dog and my batshit-crazy family back around me.

Being here… it's just messed with my head, that's all. I've been the lady of the house and, Leo is right, I've played some sort of bizarre game of house with Fletch, which is out there by anyone's standards.

He and I are absolutely not relationship material. We live our lives on different pages. If we were newspapers, Fletch would be a broadsheet and I'm the *National Enquirer*. Either way, we're tomorrow's chip paper.

* * *

It's just after eleven and I'm propped up in bed with all of my case notes scattered over the blankets. I've got lists of facts we're sure of, lists of probables, lists of possibles and lists of highly unlikelies. I look from one to the other, trying to figure out the whole story and see the crucial thing I'm missing. The lynchpin to this is in front of me on these notes. It's got something to do with that extra engraved B on the garden wall, I just know it is. I bite the end of my pencil and sigh, because tomorrow is Friday, the day the Americans arrive in Maplemead village. An entire movie cast and crew and it's my job to make this castle welcoming and ghost-free before they start work on Monday. Strictly speaking, it's Leo's job too, although he's rendered himself as useful as a condom with a hole in it by falling in love with Britannia.

The tiny unworn romper. Brittania. Bohemia. Dino. I close my eyes and let them all run through my mind, sifting and sorting themselves in different ways until a startling thought slaps me around the brain.

My phone buzzes on the side table, making me jump and lose my train of thought. I reach for it from the bedside table and the screen informs me that I have a new message. *From Fletch.*

I know what you're wondering. Why do I even have his number in my phone? Believe me, it's not because he put it there so I wouldn't forget him or because I put it there so I could stay in touch. For accuracy's sake, I did put it there, but only so I could text him a pic of Lestat peeing on his photograph in the newspaper. It's a long story, but the fact is we have each other's numbers and he's just sent me a text.

I consider laying the phone back down again on its screen and ignoring it, but my thumb doesn't get the memo and clicks the message open anyway.

You asleep, ghostbuster?

Hmm. Well, if I ignore it, he'll probably just assume that I am. While I'm deliberating, a second message buzzes in.

Or are you ignoring me so I think you are?

God, it's as if he's peeping through my window. I glance out at the still, dark night and then text him back.

You're not about to hammer the door down again, are you? Because I'm working.

There. That's chilly enough to put icicles on his donkey dong.

At ease. I'm at home, feet up and porn on.

I huff. He's such a bloody wind-up.

Which roughly translates as you're drinking coffee and watching Match of the Day.

There's a pause and then:

Beer and football. Close enough.

In my head I see Fletch stretched out and relaxed in a battered leather armchair, feet crossed on the coffee table, a chilled bottle of beer in his hand. I watch him bring it to his lips and take a slug, see him swallow and relax. I enjoy the thought and then I don't like myself for even imagining it. The screen flashes again.

Are you in bed?

Oh. So that's difficult to measure. It's a straightforward question with a sexy subtext.

Am working.

And then, as an afterthought, I add:

In bed.

He doesn't answer and, after a while, I type again.

How's your mum doing today?
Walked out of the hospital and took a taxi to the bottle shop.

If he was in front of me now I'd probably lay my hand on his arm and quietly say I'm sorry, but he isn't here and when I type the words they don't look enough so I delete them. While I'm thinking what to say, he texts again:

I don't think I said thank you for last night.

You don't need to I type, then send *anytime* as an afterthought. Oh bollocks. That made me sound easy, didn't it?

I might just have to hold you to that, ghostbuster.

My fingers want to tell him that I like it when he holds me and I engage in a silent battle with my hands to stop them from typing.

Are you wearing that white nightdress again?

Okay. So we're heading back along those lines. I think he's doing it to deliberately avoid talking about his mum, and that's okay. Glancing down at my green Hulk T-shirt, I type my reply.

Yes.

I tell myself that I lied to help him keep his mind off the tough stuff going on in his life. I'm all heart. I should win the most magnanimous white liar award, which doesn't exist but totally should.

He lapses into silence again and this time I don't waffle to fill the space.

I liked you in it. You looked like a sexy virgin who needed deflowering.

Oh God. What do I say to that?

Thank you.

I press send, then bang my forehead repeatedly against the phone because it's such a lame-ass reply.

It's your turn to say something sexy.

No winky face to soften it.

That's how this sexting thing works.

We're sexting? But I'm in a hulk T-shirt! I go all hot and gather up my papers in a panic.

Have you gone to sleep on me, ghostbuster? I was just kidding about the sexting thing.

A pause and I half smile. He can be pretty funny sometimes.

Unless you want to tell me something filthy.

Do I want to tell him something filthy? I've had three parts of a bottle of wine and a generous brandy to help me sleep, so God knows why I feel so awake and in the mood to shock the pants off Fletcher Gunn. This is one hundred percent the point where I should put my phone down. Why is it still in my hand? Goddamn you, phone! And God-double-damn my thumbs, stop typing! I can barely look! Is it anatomically possible for your thumbs to act independently of your brain?

Umm, I might.
You might what? Want to tell me something filthy? Fucking hell. Never stop being random, Bittersweet. You've just given me a hard-on with three words, and one of them wasn't even an actual word.

Pride blooms unhelpfully in my chest. This is dangerous because the fact that we aren't in the same place makes this feel unreal, less intimate.

Want me to call you?

Oh God! I think he's asking me to have phone sex with him! I need to say something fast to stop him dialling me.

Don't call me, I've lost my voice.

Dear God, I'm rubbish at lying. To cover up, I type:

Unfasten your jeans.

I wait, agonised. Did that count as something filthy? Is it his turn?

Lie back on your pillows.

I don't know what else to do, so I do as I'm told.

And relax. This doesn't count as crossing all of those boundaries you get so hung up about.

I believe him, because I want to.

Have I told you how much kissing you turns me on?

I can practically feel him breathing the words down my ear.

Take your nightdress off.

I am suddenly really quite overwhelmingly hot, so I wriggle my arms out of the Hulk T-shirt and fling it on the floor.

The sheets are cool against my skin

I'm getting into this a bit as I settle back down on the pillows.

Tell me when you're naked.

I lift the sheet and peer down at myself, then clamp it back down again and text him.

I'm naked.

I press send, then add:

Apart from my Wonder Woman knickers.

There's a pause. I turn out the lamps and wonder if he's put his phone down in despair, then my screen illuminates, much brighter now in the darkened room.

You're so very ridiculously sexy, Wonder Woman. You have no idea how much I want to be there in bed with you right now. I wish you were too.

Hand on heart, I really do.
I want you, Fletch.

Let me call you. I want to hear your voice.

I don't tell him no this time and, seconds later, the phone vibrates as his number flashes up.

'Tell me,' he says, ultra-low and raw in my ear when I answer. 'Tell me you want me, Melody. I want to hear you say the words.'

Fletch has a power over me and it's precisely because of the way he hands all the power to me at times like this. He doesn't mess around or play it for laughs or pretend he's not into me. He's not a kid. He's a fully grown, broad-shouldered man with river green eyes and a racehorse-firm chest and I only wish I could feel his weight over me right now, pressing me into the mattress. I think I might have just said that out loud.

His breathing turns shallow against my ear and he's saying incredibly dirty things now about what he wants to do with his hands and his mouth and he's made me take my Wonder Woman knickers off. I am officially delirious.

He's saying things, I'm saying things, and he's breathing so hard I can practically feel his breath warming my skin. And then he's not talking any more because I don't think he can, and that's okay because I can't either. I listen to his ragged gasps, to the way he's murmuring my name over and over like a curse word, and it's enough. It's too much. I stop breathing with how good he's making me feel, and I tell him I'm there, and he moans feverish encouragements that make my whole body shudder and I can't hold my moans inside.

He's with me, heartbeat for heartbeat, and he tells me he can't hold on, and he's so gorgeously, almost painfully raw that I wish he was here and I could hold him through it as he breaks into a million pieces down the phone line for me.

Did I say phone sex felt less intimate? I was wrong. I feel as if he's right here with me.

'You okay?' he whispers. 'I'm wrapping my body around yours and holding you.'

I let his gentle pillow talk settle over me as I curl onto my side and pull the blankets up to my shoulders.

'I'm so tired, Fletch,' I say quietly, imagining he's really here and holding me. It's so vivid that I can feel his hand over my hip and his lips against my ear.

'Close your eyes, beautiful girl,' he says. 'I'll stay with you until you're asleep.'

'Okay,' I mouth, because it's an effort, because I'm already sliding under the coat-tails of sleep. My tired, sex-satisfied brain is shutting down, jumbling up my own complicated love life with Britannia's.

'Don't let me fall,' I sigh into the pillow.

'I'll catch you.'

He says something more, but I don't register his words because I'm already halfway towards mixed-up dreams about late-night kisses and circus lions and life and death and deep, searching late-night kisses. Did I mention kisses twice? I can't help it.

I've just had the best sex I've ever had with a man who isn't even here.

'Melody.'

It's still dark, and I'm ridiculously warm and comfortable. Even better, I'm in the middle of a dream where I'm having dinner with Iron Man and he's just taken off his helmet. Only it's not Robert Downey Jr under there, it's…

'Melody! Wake up, I need to talk to you.'

I sigh and excuse myself from the dinner table because Britannia Lovell isn't going to go away until I've listened to what she has to say.

Opening my eyes with reluctance, I see her perched on the side of my bed. Or is it her bed? I'm alive and sleeping in it at the moment, so I'm going to claim dibs. Reaching my arm out I flail around and flick the lamp on, bathing the room in a soft, creamy pool of light.

'What is it?' I ask, blinking myself awake as I tuck the sheet under my armpits and sit up against the pillows.

'Are you sleeping in the nude?' She arches her eyebrows. 'How very avant garde. I didn't think you had it in you.'

'Have you woken me up to insult me or was there something you actually wanted?' I grump, going pink at the memory of exactly why I'm naked.

She looks down at her hands and I take the moment to study her. She's so striking in her beautiful costume and her dark hair falls forward in perfect ripples as she bows her head.

'I've got a problem,' she whispers, and then sighs heavily.

Frankly, I can't imagine what problem she could possibly have that necessitates me needing to be woken up to be told about it at four in the morning. I searched the castle for her after dinner and couldn't find hide nor hair of her.

'Go on,' I say. I've talked to enough ghosts with problems to know that the best thing to do is to shut up and listen.

She buries her face in her hands and shakes her head.

'I've been such a stupid woman.'

When, I wonder? Today, last week, a hundred years ago?

'How so?' I prompt.

'I know you've spoken to Dino and Bohemia today,' she says, knotting her fingers.

I nod. 'Yes. Bohemia told me how young you were when you got married.'

'He was a decent-enough husband, but not the husband I would have chosen for myself.' She raises her solemn eyes to mine. 'I tried, for my father's sake I tried, but I couldn't love him, Melody. Not in the way a wife should love her husband, anyway.'

'And you couldn't help falling in love with Dino?' I say, filling in the blanks as best I can.

'Well, no, not exactly.' She raises her eyes to the ceiling while she chooses her words. 'Oh, I don't know, Melody. Dino joined the troupe after my father died and he was so passionate and intense and, yes, maybe I did lead him to think that I had feelings for him. I certainly let him… Well, you know.'

'Quite,' I say. For such a sassy one, she's still a woman of her time who doesn't like to go into the finer details of intimate relations.

'It was all terribly difficult, to be honest. Bohemia was suspicious and Dino was pressuring me to leave with him. I was twenty-five and it seemed as if my whole life I'd been passed from one man to another. I never knew what it was to be free. The only time I was ever really myself was up there on the trapeze.' She looks at me dead on. 'I didn't love them, Melody. They both loved me but I couldn't love either of them back, not truly.'

I frown. 'I'm guessing neither of them actually know that?'

She shakes her head, miserable. 'They won't accept it. They're waiting for me to choose. Even now, after all these years, they're still here waiting for me to decide between them, like petulant, duelling schoolboys. I'm not even sure it's about me any more, it's as much about being the victor.'

She looks thoroughly miserable, more so than I'd ever realised.

On the surface it's been easy to make judgments; Britannia is so effervescent and ravishing that it's an easy conclusion to draw that she is leading both of her lovers on. I'm realising now that, as is most often the case with life, things aren't always as they seem. Piecing all of their statements together, a different picture is emerging now, one where Britannia is a victim of circumstance and controlled by two strong, opposing men who each claim to love her the most.

'I was so very tired of it all, Melody.' She wraps her arms tenderly around her midriff. I watch her carefully, turning over the idea that struck me last night in my head before I say it out loud.

'Were you pregnant, Brittania?'

Her face is agonised with pain and I know I'm right. B didn't stand for Bohemia on the cross in the garden. It stood for baby. Holding that tiny outfit in my hands in the tower had felt significant, and now I understand why.

'How could I bring a baby into that situation? I wasn't certain which of them was the father, but I *was* certain that they would both claim to be. I had no other choice. There was no way for me to leave them or the circus and I couldn't bear to stay and condemn a child into that life with me.'

I understand a split second before she opens her mouth again what she's about to tell me and I wish I could hold her hand to comfort her.

'It was the only way out,' she offers quietly, by way of explanation.

I don't sit in judgment. It isn't my place and I can't begin to understand what Britannia's life was like back then. For all of her beauty and her spark, she must have been desperately lonely and distraught to have imagined that suicide was her only way out. I can't bear to think of the baby too; it's all so very terribly sad.

'You think I'm a monster,' she mumbles and I know that if tears were possible, she'd be shedding them now.

'No,' I say, sitting forwards. 'I wish I could hold your hands, or hug you, because I think what you did showed incredible strength and that you did it because you couldn't bear for another child to have the same life that you did.'

Her eyes are glued to mine. She's just confessed to her own suicide, probably the first time she's ever said the words aloud, and my reply matters. I'm not tired any more. I feel wretched for her, for the loss of two innocent lives. I need to find a way to help her.

'I'm so glad you came here,' she says. 'All of you. I've been trapped here in this infernal loop and I'm exhausted by it. I watch how much you laugh with your friends and I am so very jealous, Melody. I never had any real friends. Circus life is transient, there was never the time.'

My heart is in bits for her. 'Come and lie down,' I say, patting the empty bed beside me.

She looks at me, quizzical.

'Come on,' I urge her. 'Lie down and we can talk and laugh and then you'll have had a friend.'

Uncertainly, Britannia makes her way around the bed and lies back on top of the blankets.

'Like this?' She looks at me sideways and I slide down on my pillows so I'm lying down too, much as I did earlier with Marina on this exact bed.

'And now we talk,' I say, matter of fact.

After a minute of silence, she asks me what we should talk about.

'Oh, you know,' I say. 'Work. Actually, not that.' I change tack hastily, because talking about work with Britannia is a really bad idea. She died the last time she was at work and my work involves getting rid of her, so it's a bit of a sticky subject all round.

'Clothes?' I say.

'No offence, but your fashion style is beyond awful,' she says. I don't quibble; she comes from an era of floor-sweeping dresses and women who dressed demurely. Jeans and Converse must look completely alien to her eyes. Right, so fashion is out too.

'Boys?' she suggests.

'Well, yes, we could talk about boys,' I say, wondering where she's headed with this.

'You seem very taken with the newspaper reporter,' she says, and I can hear the note of speculation in her voice. Because she is a ghost and we are temporary bezzies, I decide to be completely honest with her.

'Sometimes I am. He certainly gets under my skin and he knows how to kiss me.'

Britannia sighs, heavy-hearted.

'You're so lucky to know how it feels to be kissed by someone you love, Melody.'

'Oh, I don't love him,' I say, startled. 'In fact, most of the time I don't even like him. We just have this sex thing going on that seems to be totally separate from how we feel about each other as people.' I twist on my side to look at her. 'Maybe it doesn't make much sense to you because times have changed so much.'

'Some things never change,' she says, quietly. 'Can I tell you a secret?'

I nod. 'Anything.'

She moves her hair back from her suddenly sparkling, feverish eyes as she props herself up on her elbow to look at me. 'I've fallen in love with Leo.'

I stare at her.

'I know it's wrong and that nothing can ever come of it but, Melody… I can feel my heart. Even when I was alive I never felt my heart, but him…' She lays a hand over her silk-corseted breast, over the heart that longs to beat faster for Leo Dark. 'It's like nothing I've ever known. All of these years they've been waiting for me to choose and all of these years I've been waiting for *him* and I didn't even know. I didn't want to go without knowing what love feels like and now I'd trade a hundred years for even one minute in his arms.'

Wow.

'He told me that he's fallen in love with you too,' I tell her and she almost cries out. 'Even though it can never happen, please know that he loves you too and, in a different place and a different time, you two could have been the world's most-in-love couple.'

She smiles, wrapping her arms around her body and closing her eyes.

'Love feels so good,' she whispers.

I imagine that it must.

'Thank you for being my friend, Melody,' she says, her eyes still closed.

'You too,' I whisper. To me she looks completely real, as if she's just sleeping.

'He loves me,' she murmurs, full of wonder.

He loves me not, I think. We fall silent and I think about everything Britannia has just shared with me. About her life, her unborn baby, and the bleakest of choices she felt compelled to make to bring it all to its dramatic conclusion. It's a terrible misfortune to go to such dire lengths and then still end up trapped here because her lovers weren't done duelling for her heart, even though neither of them were ever in a position to claim it.

She's different when she's sleeping. She looks innocent, and really young. Because she's been stuck here for more than a century, it's easy to forget that she was barely twenty-five when she died. Younger than me and, God, I feel about sixteen most days. All she really wanted was to experience true love and, even though she's had to wait a hundred and twenty-five years, her relaxed, blissful face tells me that, right here, right now, she feels it. She feels the warm glow of friendship and the deep, abiding joy of romantic love and I'll be for ever glad that, however briefly, Leo and I were able to bring those things into her life.

I close my eyes. The memory of my unexpected late-night phone encounter with Fletch filters through my tired subconscious as I tumble towards sleep. Then I jolt awake again, wide-eyed and heart hammering, because all at once I know exactly what I need to do.

CHAPTER TWENTY-FIVE

'Are you sure about this?' Marina asks, winding her ponytail around her hand. It's half past five in the afternoon and we're conducting a crucial business meeting in Babs because the castle is absolutely overrun with caterers, musicians, waiting staff and any number of other nameless people who've been drafted in to make sure the ball runs like clockwork tomorrow. It's only to be expected on the eve of such a big event but, all the same, it's meant that my own plans have had to go on ice until midnight. I'd hoped to be out of here before nightfall, but it looks as if there's one last nightshift on the cards for me.

'Of course I'm not sure about it,' I sigh. It sounded plausible in my head but, when I outlined it to Marina and Artie, it sounded vaguely ridiculous. They didn't say so, of course, but I could see in their faces that they weren't entirely sure. 'But it's the best plan I've got so I'm running with it like Mo bloody Farah.'

I'm working on pure instinct now, trusting my gut to lead me in the right direction and I'm depending on Leo to turn up and play a crucial part in proceedings too. I haven't told him exactly what he's going to need to do yet, because if he has very long to think about it he'll try to change the plan or attempt to do things differently to change the outcome.

I know things he doesn't now, though; Britannia trusted me last night with her secrets and her hidden heartache and she is the one I've engineered this whole plan around. Leo's still young; he has his whole life ahead of him. Britannia doesn't have that luxury, but I think I know how we can at least give her a few brilliant minutes and I can only hope they'll have been worth waiting for.

'Do you know if Fletch is coming over later?'

I look at Artie sharply. 'Why do you ask that?'

I don't mean to snap at him. It's just that I woke up this morning and remembered my late-night phone call with Fletch and now I feel like I operate some kind of sex line. It's not real sex though, is it? It was only a few words on a screen and hardly any words at all spoken down the phone line. He didn't get to actually see inside my Wonder Woman knickers and I still don't know if he's a donkey dong or a piggy willy. It's business as usual as far as I'm concerned, although I've turned my phone off for most of the day as a precaution in case he tries to call me or send me a dick pic or anything. I'm kidding, I'm kidding. I don't think that's Fletch's style at all. He's a words rather than pictures kind of guy and, judging by the things he whispered down my ear last night, he knows ALL the words and exactly how to use them to their greatest effect.

'No,' I relent. 'He's not coming over later, for the exact same reasons you're not staying.' I can't think of anyone less appropriate to be in the ballroom tonight and, if all goes to plan, our days of playing house are over. I packed up all of my belongings from the Princess Suite earlier and flung them in the back of Babs, along with the holdall Fletch left in the Knight Suite. I figure it won't kill me to be neighbourly and return them to him at his grotty flat on the High Street.

Artie looks crestfallen, so I throw him a bone. 'I think Lois has invited Fletch to the ball, but I'm not sure if he's planning to attend or not.'

'You mean he hasn't asked you to be his date?' Marina says, leaning forward in her seat to peer around Artie at me.

I pull an 'as-if' face. 'Fletch and I don't date.'

She makes a noise that sounds suspiciously like a laugh.

'What?' I look her directly in the eyes.

She shrugs, then lifts her knee to her chin so she can deliver a sharp jab with her heel to Babs's glovebox.

'You'll dent the paintwork doing that,' I moan, even though the glovebox is already a mass of dinks and kinks from a lifetime of being opened by brute force.

She ignores me and passes me my magic-8 ball.

'Check if you should ask Fletch to be your date at the ball.'

'Have you lost your mind?' I bark. 'There's no way on this entire bloody earth that I'm asking Fletcher Gunn to the ball.'

I'm glad at this moment that I haven't told Marina about my brief spell as a phone sex-worker last night. She'd just make more of it than there is. I make a mental note that I should probably think about a date for tomorrow and refuse to take the magic-8 ball when she holds it out across Artie's lap.

'Shall I do it?' he asks, taking it from Marina and giving it a few turns. After it's cleared, he looks at me out of the corner of his eye.

'Your magic ball says "yes, definitely".'

Marina takes it from his hands with a nod of self-appreciation.

'See? Your ball, your rules, Melody. Make the call.'

'Am I the only one whose mind is on the actual job at hand here?' I snap. 'I'm more worried about helping Britannia Lovell tonight than about what dress to wear tomorrow night.'

Marina looks at me. 'Which dress *are* you wearing tomorrow night?'

'I'm not sure,' I say, with a saccharine smile. 'Would you like me to ask the magic-8 ball that, too?'

She grins and slams it back into the glovebox.

'I wish you'd let us stick around tonight,' she says, changing the conversational tone from joke to deadly serious. 'I could make some calls, rearrange Nonno's care?'

Both Marina and Artie protested when I told them that my plan called for a closed ballroom; it's just me and Leo once all of the caterers and party planners have cleared out of the castle tonight. If I'm right, then what happens in there will be pretty intimate and I want to afford Brittania as much privacy as possible.

Marina knows there is little point in pressing the point when I've made up my mind.

'Text me as soon as you're done?'

'Me too,' Artie says. 'Although I'll have to put my phone on silent because my mum's a light sleeper and I'm a heavy sleeper so I might not feel it vibrate.'

'It's good to know you're just at the other end of the line if I really need you,' I tell him and he nods as if he thinks I'm being perfectly genuine.

Marina reaches into her bag and pulls out a Mars Bar. 'Emergency sugar supply,' she says, pressing it into my hand. 'Be brave, grasshopper.'

I tuck the chocolate into the side pocket of the door and she fist-bumps me as if she thinks we're American homies.

'Come on then, Chewbacca.' Marina rolls the passenger door open and digs her car keys from her bag. 'We need to get out of here.'

I watch them climb into Marina's little Vauxhall and pull away and I feel as if she's packed all of my bravado and certainty into her boot and taken it with her. Everything is riding on this. I called Lois earlier and pretty much gave her my cast-iron guarantee of success. Failure is not an option. I breathe deeply. In and out. In and out. I tell myself that I've got this, that I'm the best damn ghostbuster in town, that my business is going from strength to strength, that my plan is solid gold rather than built on evershifting sand. It's going to be just fine. Better than fine. Fine and dandy. I give myself a pep-talk worthy of the aforementioned Mo Farah, and then I go and ruin it all by wolfing down Marina's emergency Mars Bar in three giant bites, then lying down on the front bench seat for a panic-induced nap.

* * *

Someone's tapping on my window. I struggle awake and stretch awkwardly across the seats, then remember where I am and grab for my phone to check the time in case I've slept past midnight. Half eleven. God! I must have zonked right out, probably my on-board self-preservation system kicking in to protect me from having an attack of the vapours. Still, it's just about right.

Whoever is outside taps again and I look up to see Leo standing there with his jacket collar turned up even though it's summertime.

I give him a bleary-eyed thumbs-up and roll the door open.

'Feeling okay?' I say, a tiny bit awkward and aware that I probably have the lined imprint of Babs's seat across my face.

He shrugs. 'Hard to say, seeing as you haven't told me what we're doing.'

All I've told Leo is that we both need to be in the ballroom at midnight to watch Britannia and Dino perform, as they do every night at midnight. They usually have a maximum audience of one; Bohemia. Tonight there will be three of us and, if my plan works, then I'm very much hoping that this will be their final performance at Maplemead Castle.

The castle door is locked and I let us in with the key I'm to hand back in tomorrow. Barty and Lois are spending their final night down in the village with the newly arrived cast and crew of the movie and tomorrow they will return here in the full hope and expectation of it being the safe ghost-free castle they thought they bought unseen over the Internet. I can only cross my fingers and hope for the same thing.

It's so incredibly still in here at night; that is when the ghosts aren't making their presence known. Moonlight guides our way along the shaded passage, our echoing footsteps the only sound.

Outside the ballroom door, I pause and turn to Leo.

'Listen,' I say quietly. 'I know this goes against the grain for you but, please, can you do exactly as I say when we're in here?'

His brow furrows, as if he might protest, and I put my hand on his arm. 'Trust me on this one, okay?'

Our eyes meet in the shadows and, after a few seconds, he nods slowly. 'I do.'

The irony of our conversation doesn't escape me; there's no reason he shouldn't trust me. I didn't break his heart.

Turning the door handle, I push the door open and step inside the dark ballroom.

'You're a regular Girl Guide,' he says, a couple of minutes later, when I pull a lighter from my pocket and walk from deep stone window sill to window sill, lighting the creamy fat candles Marina and Artie helped me gather up from the bedrooms and place in here earlier on. I'm kind of glad now that I insisted that they couldn't stay for this; it feels right that it's just Leo and me.

'Be prepared and all that jazz,' I murmur, even though I think that might be the Scouts' motto rather than the Guides. I'm hazy on the details; I've no idea what Girl Guides actually say, because the thought of being a Girl Guide was about as appealing to me as homework or church on a Sunday when I was a kid. I'm a Bittersweet; we see things with our magic eyes and convention has little place in our unconventional lives.

I glance at my phone. Eleven forty-nine. The ballroom is transformed by the flickering candlelight from dark to atmospheric and portentous. It's different in here tonight; the room has been set out by the caterers for tomorrow's spectacle. Round tables laden with tall vases of trailing fresh flowers and silver glinting cutlery surround the parquet dance floor, which has been buffed and polished to a mellow golden hue. Spindly silver chairs surround the tables and glittering crystal glasswear awaits the pop of champagne corks and tell-tale red lipstick marks. The whole place smells of summertime gardens and of anticipation and dreamy excitement, a stage set for laughter and dancing and merriment. It strikes me in that moment how perfect a setting it is for tonight's performance too; it's entirely fitting that Britannia Lovell's final show should be surrounded by beauty and fragrance and light.

I haven't briefed her on the full details of my plan, either. I don't know if it's because I don't want to get her hopes up or because I don't trust myself enough to feel certain it's going to work, but all I've asked of her is that she makes sure that Bohemia and Goliath are present for the midnight performance too. It's not a difficult task for her; he's there most nights anyway to watch the woman he loves.

On cue, a by-now-familiar prickle of cold fear runs down my spine and I hear the low, intimidating growl that heralds Goliath's arrival. That's good, I tell myself, because it means that Bohemia can't be far behind him.

Our attention is drawn upwards, because the quiet ballroom is suddenly no longer empty and serene. I can almost smell the circus, the sawdust and greasepaint, and I can almost hear the slide of a big band trumpet. Britannia and Dino have arrived bang on time. I'm so bloody nervous I can barely swallow and I glance over at Leo to see how he's doing. He's stripped off his jacket and has his top button open and his shirt sleeves rolled back, a cross between a politician and a tango dancer as the candlelight plays off his glossy, raven hair. He's a movie-star-handsome sort of man and, right now, he's about to step up and play the part of his life.

I watch him for a moment. He has eyes only for Britannia and his hand lays flat over his heart as he watches her begin to perform. She is more beautiful than ever thanks to the atmospheric candlelight, her flight all the more effortless and joyously free. It isn't difficult to see how all three men in this room have fallen under her spell; I'm halfway there myself because she is so startlingly mesmerising. As she steps into her hoop and begins to spin, I take Leo by the arm and steer him to the centre of the dance floor.

He looks down at me, surprised, as if he'd forgotten I was even in the room and, when his eyes question me, I quietly remind him that he agreed to trust me.

We are beneath her now and, across the room, I watch Dino prepare to send the fateful swing across to her outstretched arms. Those ropes; how did he not spot the deliberate cut? Perhaps if she'd have survived her attempt to end her own life, it would have been enough to strengthen her resolve to find another way out of her desperate situation.

'I can't bear to watch her die again.' Leo's quiet anguish fills me with fear that this won't work. 'What do I do, Melody?'

'Catch her,' I whisper, as Dino releases the swing with a flourish. 'You just need to catch her, Leo.'

I hear his sharp intake of breath as he understands what I'm asking of him and his murmured, panicked mantra of oh-my-God-oh-my-God-oh-my-God reaches my ears as she holds her hands out towards the bar.

'Please let this work,' I whisper, my hands clamped flat against the sides of my face in pure breathless, heart-clenching fear. 'Please.'

And then it begins. Britannia reaches out to catch the trapeze and, as always, the tattered rope cannot stand her weight and it slips sickeningly from her fingertips as if coated in greasepaint. She cries out, a hideous, keening sound, and then she is once more tumbling from the high ornate ceiling like a beautiful rag doll in freefall.

Oh God. *It's not going to work.* What was I thinking? How could I have imagined it would? I can barely look. Leo stands, riveted, doesn't take his eyes from her as he yells her name, an anguished roar as he holds out his arms.

And there, right there in front of my eyes, the most beautiful, spectacular thing I've ever seen happens.

She's real. She's flesh and blood and bone.

I know she is, because she isn't in a crumpled heap on the floor this time around, she's cradled safely in Leo's arms and she looks perfectly alive. In fact, she looks more than alive because there is a faint glow around her, an aura that only adds to her outlandish beauty.

Somehow, miraculously, my plan has worked. They're staring at each other in absolute, silent wonder and then she reaches out her shaking hand and lays it on his cheek.

'You saved me, Leo,' she breathes and cut-glass crystal teardrops shimmer on her lashes. 'After all of these years, you saved me.'

He is as shocked as she is and I catch my breath as he lowers his face to hers and kisses her lips for a few tender moments. It is as if Sleeping Beauty has finally been kissed by her prince and awoken from her long, long sleep. Leo's chest heaves as he gathers her protectively in before setting her carefully down onto her feet in front of him.

I'm aware of movement on the periphery of my vision and then both Dino and Bohemia close in on them. They're staring at her and she is staring at her hands, turning them in front of her as if they are the most amazing things she's ever seen.

'How?' Dino cries, falling to his knees at her feet. 'How can this be? It was I who should have saved you.' He's a man given to dramatics and, to be fair to him, this is quite a dramatic turn of events.

Bohemia steps forward, staring at his wife. 'Britannia?'

Leo places a hand on her shoulder and a tear rolls down her cheek as she covers his fingers with her own.

'How did you…?' Bohemia manages. He's gaping at Leo. 'How can you touch her?'

Leo glances momentarily towards me on the edge of the dance floor, and then uncertainly back towards Britannia. He falters, as if unsure what to say, and Britannia herself decides to speak up instead.

'Dino, I'm so sorry. I should never have allowed anything to happen between us. Performing with you set my blood on fire, but I never loved you as you loved me.'

Dino reacts as if this is news to him, as if he's sustained himself over the decades on hope alone. He scrabbles at her ankles as he releases a string of tearful Italian that even Marina would have a tough time deciphering. It doesn't matter; I don't need to understand his words to know he's begging. It's undignified and Britannia bends to lay a hand on him but, of course, it passes through him as fresh air and she withdraws it again slowly.

He lifts his head, his face a picture of grief, and then he is surrounded by blue light, as if an emergency ambulance has arrived to ferry him away because he is so overwrought. It hasn't, of course but, nonetheless, he is leaving us. The blue haze around his edges intensifies as he begins to fade and Britannia covers her mouth in shock and reaches out instinctively for him.

'Let him go,' I say softly and tears roll freely down her face as she watches Dino fade from her eyes and from her very long life.

They all look at me then; because they are suddenly aware of how this is going to play out.

Britannia turns to her husband, a statue beside her, the huge lion silent at his side.

'I'm sorry, Bohemia,' she says, holding out her hands towards her husband. 'I tried to love you. I really did.'

I watch as the circus master's shoulders fall and he bows his head. Even though Britannia's words can't truly have come as a shock, they must have been a crushing blow.

'It was always you, for me,' he said. 'My heart has no purpose without yours.'

In front of us, his scarlet coat fades to grey, as if the loss of his love has leeched all the colour from his soul. He lays a hand on

Goliath's head and the huge animal turns its fearsome face up to gaze sorrowfully at his master.

'Time for us to go, my dear friend,' he says and the lion seems to understand the gravity, because he lays his velvet head against his master's jacket. And so that is how they leave us, an image of man and beast that fades slowly from colour to black and white and, finally, to nothing, as if someone turned off an old TV set. That's how it appears to me, anyway. I've seen ghosts depart in many ways, all of them individual and fitting of the person leaving us. I've seen ghosts leave the earth in an angry, ugly burst of fragmented red energy and I've watched pure souls leave in a shimmer of beautiful rainbow colours.

Britannia covers her face with her slender fingers and Leo's arms move to hold her to him. His eyes meet mine over the top of her head and I see questions there that I know he isn't going to like the answers to. But there's nothing I can do now. The wheels are in motion, I cannot change things any more than I already have. Britannia's timeline has to end tonight.

'How long?' he mouths.

I shake my head. I don't know for sure, to be honest. 'Five minutes? Ten? Not much more.'

He closes his eyes for a moment, as well he might. What do you say if you only have a few minutes with the love of your life?

I'm about to give them some privacy when Britannia turns from Leo's arms and crosses the dance floor to me.

We look at each other for a quiet moment and I see her for who she truly is; my friend, Brittania Lovell. A great gulp of tears comes from nowhere because she is hugging me fiercely and crying too.

'Thank you for everything, Melody,' she whispers. 'You're the best friend I never had.'

I want her to leave with joy in her heart, so I step back and smile and laughter lights up her lovely face. She's full of dizzy joy and, for a moment, she clutches my hands tightly in hers and we just look at each other across the years and decades; two twenty-something women who really just want the same thing as pretty much every other twenty-something woman. To find that one person who makes your heart race and soar in your chest or, in Britannia's case, makes it beat again, however briefly.

'Go.' I loose her hands. 'Go to him. Go for those French kisses you've missed out on and for the warmth of his arms and for a love so big it's literally made life worth living again.'

She sighs, glancing around the ballroom. 'I can smell the flowers,' she whispers. 'I'd forgotten how lovely they are.'

She gives my hands one last tight squeeze before she turns and half runs, half skips back to Leo in the middle of the dance floor.

He holds his arms out to her and they embrace like long-lost lovers on a train station platform. I walk away and step outside the door, because these precious minutes are so deeply intimate and private, beautiful and heart-breaking.

'I have to leave you now, my darling,' I hear her say after a while and I can tell by her voice that she is peaceful with it. 'But know that I loved you with all of my heart and that you have been the most wonderful thing that ever happened to me. I've always known I was waiting for someone. I'm so very glad it was you, Leo.' They fall quiet and I try not to think about them kissing.

'It's so much more than I ever imagined it would be.' I turn back into the room as she holds his face in her hands. 'You're the love of my afterlife, Leo Dark.'

'I'll always hold you in my heart,' he tells her and already I can see that she's less solid than before. Ethereal, like a fairy-tale princess.

If I'd been asked to guess how Britannia would leave the earth, I'd have said in a gleam of solid gold. I wouldn't have been far off the mark; she's a streak of utter brilliance, a firework flash of glittering rose gold stars, a laugh and a blown kiss as she takes her leave.

A tiny pure white star over her abdomen is last of all to wink out and I catch my breath with relief to think that wherever Britannia travels on to next, her child travels alongside her.

I turn to Leo and he's ashen in the pale candlelight; a man who has loved and lost again, all in the space of ten minutes. The huge shadowed room echoes with our heavy silence. It's over.

'Why don't you go on outside and wait for me,' I say quietly. 'You look as if you could use a breath of fresh air.' I watch him leave and then I take a seat for a few minutes on one of the spindle-backed silver chairs around the edge of the dance floor. Tomorrow will see this room transformed into a place of jollity, of dancing and carousing; I feel sure that wherever Britannia is now, she'd heartily approve. She was one of life's good-time girls, someone who loved to laugh, a woman who knew how to live life with passion and a mischievous glint in her eye. I came full circle as far as she was concerned, from intimidation to admiration. I'm really going to miss her.

I haul myself to my feet, weary and relieved.

I've done it. I've bloody well done it. Come daylight, I think I'll probably be able to take some pride in that but, right now, I'm feeling reflective and melancholy. As I move to snuff out the candles around the room, something catches my eye in the middle of the dance floor. I pause and bend to take a closer look. It's a rhinestone, a flint of diamond shine that must have fallen from Britannia's costume as she performed. I pick it up and lay it in the palm of my hand, watching it catch the light as I rock it with the tip of my index finger. My fanciful heart wants to believe that she left it behind as a tiny reminder that she was ever here. I hold it tight as I look up, blow a kiss towards the chandeliers overhead, and let myself out of Maplemead Castle for the final time.

* * *

'Hey you,' I say, dropping down next to Leo on the stone steps after I've locked the heavy castle doors. It's a balmy, still, summer's night and the moon hangs full and vibrant silver-white over the trees in the distance. I can smell the fragrant honeysuckle that winds around the balustrades and I'm reminded of Britannia's earlier words in the ballroom.

'She told me she could smell the flowers,' I say, my voice clear in the quiet night. 'I'm so glad we were able to give her that.'

He stares out into the distance.

'How did you know what to do?'

I think back to my late-night phone date with Fletch and his promise to catch me if I fall.

'Just something someone said.'

Leo has his elbows resting on his knees and he pushes his hands through his hair. He's dishevelled and real and I can't help but notice how much better he looks for being a little less groomed and a little more vulnerable. He's guilty of many things; he can be ridiculously vain and completely thoughtless sometimes, but I've known Leo Dark for a very long time both as a friend and a lover and, right now, my heart hurts for him, not because of him.

'I know it seems ludicrous because it was only a few days, but it was real, Melody. I loved her.'

'I know,' I say, because I don't have a shred of doubt. If there is such a thing as love at first sight, theirs was it. Those brief, dazzling days together are imprinted on his heart for ever.

'You'll be okay,' I say, scooting closer. He slings an arm across my shoulders and I lean into him. It's after one in the morning and somewhere in the trees around the castle grounds an owl hoots. 'It'll get a bit better every day, until one night you'll get into bed and realise that you haven't thought about her once today.'

He laughs sadly and looks at me sideways. 'When did you get so wise?'

I scuff my Converse against the edge of the stone step. 'Heart-break does that to a girl.'

He lets my words sink in before he speaks. 'Have I ever said sorry to you?'

I bite my lip and concentrate on the moon rather than looking at him.

'You don't need to say it now.'

'I don't think I'll say it to you any other time, so take it while you can.'

He's probably right. He's raw right now and has had a taste of how it feels to be the one left behind. Given that he taught me my life lessons in heartbreak, I have every right to feel a smidgeon of satisfaction but, hand on heart, I don't.

I unfurl my fingers and we both gaze at the rhinestone glittering on my palm. A shaft of moonlight illuminates it brightly and I twist my hand so that it catches the light. It's bright and beautiful, as if the essence of Britannia is distilled in its many facets.

'I found this on the ballroom floor just now.'

I place it in his hand and fold his fingers around it and that's how we sit for a while, quiet and contemplative. His arm is a warm, comforting weight around my shoulders and I let myself rest against him and sigh deeply. My relationship with Leo Dark is one of the most complex ones in my life. We'll for ever be connected by our tangled romantic history and now also because we were both lucky enough to have had our lives touched in one way or another by the spectacular, magical, spell-binding Britannia Lovell.

Waking up in my own bed, or rather being woken up in my own bed by Lestat shoving his face into mine, feels like finally waking up from a long, rambling, bizarre dream about castles and princesses and phone sex and how love truly does conquer all. It's all over bar the shouting, otherwise known as the grand ball at the castle tonight.

I still don't have a superhero date, but that's kind of okay because what I do have is a killer dress courtesy of Britannia, a kickass business and a bunch of friends who love me which, in my book, makes me a pretty lucky girl.

Lestat is giving me that menacing look he reserves for six in the morning, the one that suggests I have five minutes tops before he piddles in my Converse, so I drag myself from my warm bed and throw a huge baggy jumper over my PJs so I can take him out to the cobbled alleyway at the side of the building.

'Is it your birthday?'

I take my eyes off Lestat and see Dwayne, my postman, ambling up the cobbles towards me.

'No.' I frown.

'You're sure? Because I have a kiss here waiting for you if it is.'

He puckers up and closes his eyes and I cross my arms across my chest and sigh pointedly. I've known Dwayne since senior school and he's never been one to knowingly miss a chance for a cheeky snog. His life goal was only ever to be a postman; it's the only legal way he can call on women unsolicited every morning and try to charm his way into their house for coffee and a quick game of hide the sausage, a career goal that eludes him for the vast majority of the time.

'Just hand it over.' I'm brisk with him, because it is by far the most effective way of getting him to give up the goods. He opens his eyes and unpuckers with a 'your loss, love' shrug. Neither of us are particularly offended by the exchange; it's our accepted method of communication.

'Happy birthday anyway,' he mutters, shoving a parcel towards me. I turn it over in my hands to look for clues. It's shoebox size and it rattles as if it contains shoes, which is odd as I haven't ordered any. The paper is plain and brown, tied with old-fashioned parcel string, and my name and address is handwritten across the top in confident black script.

I murmur, 'It's not my birthday,' as Dwayne heads off down towards the High Street whistling and I look around for Lestat and find him about to cock his leg up a potted plant that wasn't there when I went to bed last night.

I shove the parcel under my arm and dash towards him flapping my hands, rather like I'm trying to shoo seagulls away from a picnic on the beach. He shoots me a filthy look, but all the same he shuffles further on down the cobbles to pick himself a different spot.

Well, that's perplexing. The new plant is in a terracotta pot and it's sort of like a little tree that reaches up to my hip. On closer examination I see that it has fruit on it. Lemons.

An inkling of understanding whispers in the back of my mind, but I can't quite catch it. Luckily, I spy a little envelope strung from one of the lower branches.

Laying the mystery parcel down for a moment, I detach the envelope from the plant and lift the flap.

A healthy snack in case you get hungry again. Rhubarb was out of season. X

I stand there in the alley and hug my big old jumper around me then, as if I'm in some cheesy American movie, I pluck one of the lemons and take a bite. If this was a cheesy American movie, I'd smile and go all soft-focus and faraway, because the girl got her guy and they all lived happily ever after. But this isn't a movie and, oh farts, this is the sourest lemon in the entire goddamn world so, for the second time this week, I lean over and heave out a mouthful of vile fruit I've eaten because of Fletcher bloody Gunn.

My eyes are streaming and my head feels as if its been turned inside out. I head inside with Lestat at my heels and chuck the lemon in the kitchen bin before brushing my teeth to get rid of the bitterness in my mouth. As gift-givers go, Fletch is up there with the most random. A while back he gave me a lime green plastic pooper-scooper and now he's given me lemons.

I could not have a sweeter tooth if my teeth were made of actual candy. Lemons are pretty much my nemesis, unless they're in a meringue pie or one of Nonna Malone's biscuits.

Me and Fletch really are the most unlikely match. He can make my veins swim with acid and then flood with honey. Because he is so good with his mouth, it's easy to forget sometimes that he is intent on proving that my family and everyone like us, or not like him, are a bunch of crackpots. It must pain him greatly that he's wildly attracted to me. I like that thought.

Don't stick with this in the hope you're going to find 'reader, I married him' anytime soon. Reader, I murdered him is highly likely though.

Lestat has taken a shine to Fletch's holdall. I flung it down with mine in the corner of my living room when I got home this morning, and now my disloyal pug seems to have claimed it as his new bed and arranged his pudgy ass on top of it.

'Come on, fur face,' I say as I wait for the shower to fill the bathroom with a relaxing fug of heat and steam before I go in there. 'Shift it.'

He doesn't move a muscle, so I give him a little nudge with my toe until he lifts his eyelids at me in lazy question. He clearly doesn't have any intention of moving. I consider leaving him there to carpet Fletch's bag with loose hair, but then I panic that Fletch might be secretly asthmatic and die a wheezy, hairball-induced death in his grotty flat and then come back to haunt me for ever. At least I'd be able to gloat about being right about ghosts all along.

He'd probably still try to deny it.

Resigned, I bend down and annoy Lestat as much as I can with a combination of tickling and double-handed ass shoves until he looks at me reproachfully and kind of commando rolls off the bag towards his own bed three feet away.

I haven't looked in Fletch's bag. What sort of person do you think I am? It's zipped-up, anyway. I go to straighten, but then I notice a black notebook poking from the open, very unzipped side pocket. It's practically dropping out, so I poke it back in again and, while I'm there, I fan the pages a tiny bit and see that it's full of notes.

Well, he is a reporter. Taking notes is his job. When I stand up, I find that the notebook is somehow in my hand now and I have one of those moments where you know what the right thing to do is and have a bit of a mental breakdown. I know the right thing is to put this book back without looking inside. And I also know that I'm going to look.

I should never have looked. I've slumped down against the wall and read his fancy Moleskine book from cover to cover, and I wish I could rewind the clock and never lay eyes on it. They say that no good can come of snooping and they're bang on the money because I can't unsee the notes Fletch has written about me and mine.

The Bittersweet family built their reputation in a simpler age and they stubbornly continue to peddle their outdated Victorian trade in this modern, scientifically astute world.

Our outdated trade? I don't know if he wrote this last week or last year, there is no date. It rings a bell as something from an article he ran last year. Yes; he makes a habit of taking pot-shots at us whenever the opportunity arises. And at Leo, or anything else that leans even slightly towards unscientific.

I flick through notes about other people and other stories he's covered, reminders to himself about meetings and events, occasional side rants about things that have pissed him off. There are lists of clinical treatments noted beside the details of a centre in Birmingham, presumably medical options for his mum. It's like looking inside his head and I feel distinctly shabby about myself for doing it.

I cannot help but want to believe that she is genuine, but to set aside everything that is rational flies in the face of all common sense. How can that be wise? How can someone be so plausible, and yet so implausible at the same time? At best, she is deluded and, at worst, she is a charlatan.

There's more of the same further towards the back; an article written in note form about the case at Maplemead.

In brackets underneath he's made rougher pencil notes, more of a personal lament as an aside to the professional piece, definitely not words for his article.

(Why can't she just be a normal fucking girl? A nurse or a secretary or a dentist? A fucking loo cleaner, even. Anything but a ghostbuster. How can someone be insanely fucking gorgeous seventy percent of the time and just plain insane the other thirty? She laughs her way through life like an accident waiting to happen and, every time I see her, I have to wonder how much of her is real, because the one thing I know is that ghosts categorically are not.

I'm screwed. I'm screwed because she isn't a shag and shake hands kind of girl, and I don't think once will be enough. Or twice. Shit.)

You know what? I'm not angry. None of what I've read is news to me and, God knows, I'd have written worse about him in a notebook if I kept one. That doesn't make it hurt any less to see it in black and white though, even though he called me insanely gorgeous.

The fact is that Fletch and I have an inexplicable connection and it's bloody inconvenient for both of us. He and I are too fundamentally different to ever have a meaningful, lasting relationship but, equally, we are too fundamentally in lust to let a small thing like life incompatibility stop us from dancing around each other. It was easier to categorise before Maplemead, because I could tell myself that it is purely a chemical reaction.

Now, though… God, I don't know what it is. We insult each other and then he kisses me and makes me feel like the only woman in the world. We pour scorn on each other, then he holds me as if I'm made of spun sugar. It's push me, pull me, love me, hate me, kiss me, leave me, then kiss me again because it felt so mind-bendingly good. It's confusing as hell.

He's right. I'm thirty percent insane. I must be, because I'm still going to the ball and, if he's there, I'll no doubt let him kiss me stupid all over again.

I'm as ready as I'll ever be. I've bathed, shaved and slathered, I've primped, smoothed and spritzed; even my flicky eyeliner has gone to plan.

'Mum? Gran?'

They're both sitting at the scrubbed pine kitchen table and look up when I pop my head around the door to say hi before I go.

'I'm off,' I say, half hanging into the room. I'd sort of wanted to show them my dress, but now I'm here I feel a bit ridiculous so I pretend to be in a tearing hurry.

'Er, not so fast, young lady,' my mother says, standing up and beckoning me in. 'Let's have a proper look at you.'

Bashful but secretly glad, I pretend to roll my eyes and then step into the warm, cinnamon-scented kitchen. They both look me over appraisingly and I style it out by doing a slow twirl and dropping a curtsy to finish.

'Where did you get that dress?' my mother asks.

'Maplemead,' I say. 'Britannia said I could help myself from the wardrobe there.'

'1950 or thereabouts,' my gran says, sipping from her champagne flute. 'And expensive.'

I'd guessed vaguely the same, going purely on hazy knowledge gleaned from various Audrey Hepburn movies Marina has made me sit through. I'd intended to wear the purple dress I'd loved on sight, but when I pulled it out of the wardrobe I spotted this one next to it and fell head over Converse in sartorial love. I imagine it must be like when you find your perfect wedding dress. Except it's black.

The fitted bodice is crafted from heavy silk and it has a wide off-the-shoulder boat neckline that makes me feel all saloon girl sophisticated. My arms and shoulders are bare and the skirt flares to three-quarter length with a couple of tulle layers beneath it for added volume. Or else it would be probably three-quarters on a normal height woman. On me it's an ankle skimmer.

I feel like Danny Zuko might turn up and collect me for the prom in his big old American muscle car and then fling me around the dance floor when we get there. We'd bop. Bop? Who even says that word? God, I've lost the plot. I don't want to bop with Danny Zuko or slow dance with Fletcher Gunn. Scrap that last thought. It should have stayed in my head. It shouldn't even have been *in* my head.

Anyway, I'm in this glamorous fifties dress that probably belonged to Britannia's aunt and I've used the fancy body lotion that my gran gave me for my birthday that makes me look as if I've walked through a cobweb of fairy dust and my hair is sort of up in a messy bun in a way I'm hoping looks cool and underdone rather than like a bird's nest. This is me on a really good day. In fact, it's me on one of my best days.

'You look every inch the princess, darling,' my mother says softly and I can't be sure but I think she's gone misty-eyed. To be fair to her she doesn't get many chances to see me look this girly, so she might as well grab it while she can.

'And have you a Prince Charming?' Gran enquires archly.

I pause, unwilling to answer. 'Maybe.'

'Didn't you say it was a masquerade ball?' My mother gestures vaguely towards her own eyes. I could kiss her for her timing because I don't need to elaborate on my date now. I just shrug, because I haven't gotten around to sorting the masquerade bit of my outfit out.

'It doesn't matter.'

'I may have one of those full-face rubber masks upstairs,' Gran says.

'Do you mean a gas mask, Gran?' It's not really the look I was hoping for.

'No!' She bats the air as if I'm an idiot. 'One of those you buy from special online shops. Bit like a balaclava with a zip up the back.'

My mother covers her mouth as if she's been taken unwell.

'Gran, are you offering to lend me your gimp mask?' That's a sentence I never expected to say.

She looks thoroughly unrepentant. 'Don't judge me, darling. I've been married for over sixty years, how else am I to keep the spice in our marriage?'

The fact that my grandpa has been dead for the last twenty of them clearly hasn't held them back from moving with the sexual times.

'On second thoughts, you'd better not. The talc would ruin your hairstyle.'

I can't even begin to articulate an answer that doesn't involve me losing my dinner into the sink. Thankfully my mother saves me again by sending my gran a reproving look and passing me a slender package from the dresser.

'What's this?'

'Open it and see.'

I'm beginning to wonder if Dwayne was right about it being my birthday. I slide a velvet pouch out of the package and inside it I find a wispy black lace eye mask. It's perfect for the dress and perfect for me because I couldn't see myself with one of those fancy feather and gold ruffled things on a stick.

'It's perfect, thank you,' I say, standing on my tiptoes to give my mum a quick peck on the cheek. She isn't a hugger, but she pats me on the cheek all the same and then kisses me on the forehead.

'Go on then, Cinders. You better get going.'

'Don't come back with one shoe!' Gran calls as I open the door and they both peer down at my feet. I see a look of disbelief cross my mother's face and I hotfoot it out of there before she can say another word.

It feels appropriate that Marina, Artie and I arrive at the ball together with Babs as our pumpkin coach. We belch and fart our way over the drawbridge and are greeted by a very different sight to the one we've become accustomed to. The expansive drive has become a car park full of dark saloons and flashy coupés and we're directed to park up towards the back by a guy in a high-vis jacket.

'I think he wants us to hide Babs in the bushes,' Marina says, offended. 'Rude.' Her hand gesture is equally rude in response, and totally at odds with her appearance tonight. She is drop-dead gorgeous in the vintage silver mermaid dress, a Hollywood siren with rippling waves, curves to die for, and a glittering crystal eye mask.

Chewbacca howls his annoyance beside her and we all fall about laughing. God, it feels so good to relax. I watch Artie clamber out of Babs, dapper in Nonno Malone's retro suit, and I feel a clamour of affection for him and his ridiculous Chewbacca mask. I can only afford to pay him peanuts as our trainee and, in return, he gives us everything. I like to think that he gets far more than just his small wage from us, though; he's blooming by the day from a painfully shy, lonely young man into a quietly confident trainee ghostbuster. It's a career path he probably never expected to take, but one that is turning out to be just his cup of tea.

He turns and offers Marina a hand down and, uncharacteristically, she accepts his assistance without complaint. It strikes me that we are all a little bit different tonight, all a little bit affected by the costumes we've chosen to wear and the personalities we've chosen to assume.

Artie is a confident Italian wookie and Marina is a glamorous starlet. I'm not sure what I am. I'm more niche B movie than mainstream blockbuster, but all the same I'm happy in my own skin tonight and that feels good enough for me.

'Oh God. There's gong man,' Marina hisses as we thread our way through the parked cars towards the stone entrance steps. I follow the direction of her finger and find myself looking at someone who looks like he's just strolled off the set of one of those cheesy American blockbusters I mentioned. He's all brawn and teeth and she squeals with delight when he bounds down the steps and whisks her off her feet. I see her wave at me over his shoulder as he kidnaps her and I laugh softly. He might think he's whisked her off her feet, but he'll be the one bowled over by the end of the night.

'Ready, Artie?' I say. He's slowed his step and, when he lifts his Chewbacca mask, I can see that he's a seething mass of nerves and self-doubt.

'What if she isn't here?'

He sounds downcast, already forecasting being stood up on his first-ever date. 'What if she's changed her mind?'

I look at the castle doorway and see Princess Leia emerge in small, uncertain steps.

'Put your mask back on, Chewbacca,' I whisper and he looks across and catches sight of Hells Bells standing at the top of the steps. She looks pretty as a picture in her white dress, a dead ringer for Carrie Fisher. I'm not kidding. She's a doppelgänger, mostly because she's wearing a Carrie Fisher mask.

I watch as he makes his way up the steps and offers her his arm and they head on inside, already laughing as if they've known each other for ever.

I stand at the bottom of the steps, in no hurry to go inside just yet myself. The summer evening sun is warm on my shoulders and I glance at my date and I can see that he feels the same. It's obvious from the way he's just lifted his leg up to pee against someone's fancy-shmancy Jaguar.

'You brought your dog as your date.'

I glance down at Lestat, who looks really rather splendid in his black satin cape and then up at Leo, who looks equally well turned out in his formal dinner jacket. Thankfully he removes the freaky beaky feathered bird mask he's wearing before I answer him.

'He asked me. I couldn't refuse him,' I say and then we both laugh.

He's flanked, as always, by the fembots, who have chosen to wear identical candy floss pink dresses in exactly the same design as those hideous dolly loo-roll-holders from the nineteen seventies. They watch Leo laugh privately with me and although their smiles are wide, I can tell they are thinking stabby thoughts inside their heads. I note they've opted for little Lady Gaga pink veils that cover their eyes rather than masks and I wonder if they'd go all *Hunger Games* and try to kill one another in order to become Mrs Leo Dark. It's an entertaining thought, if somewhat macabre, but then despite my pretty dress, I'm no Disney princess inside my head either.

'I'll see you inside later,' Leo says and before he leaves he does something he hasn't done in a very long time. He leans in and kisses me on the cheek. I smell the old, familiar scent of his aftershave and, before he straightens, he tells me quietly that I look gorgeous tonight, even if my shoes are a tad on the ridiculous side.

I know. *I know.* It's Leo. He was in love with someone else yesterday and he broke my heart yestermoon. The thing is, when he broke it, I think he caught a loose shard of it and kept it with his own and now he and I are linked for always. It's a loose link, mind. It won't stop either of us from loving other people, but it's a part of him and a part of me and, every now and then, the link between us tightens and there's the outside chance we might shag.

There isn't. I'm kidding. Or else, I'm at least ninety-seven-and-a-half percent sure that I'm kidding. I just yearn for that feeling of being someone's girl again, or of someone being my man. That sounds pathetic. Forget I said it. I just want someone to boff my brains out and say rude things to me sometimes.

I watch Leo disappear inside the castle and am momentarily amused by the fact that the fembots cannot get through the doorway in their dresses. One of them gives the other a shove, then she turns back and hauls her twin in behind her.

'Nice shoes, ghostbuster.'

I turn around and there he is, the last man to say very rude things to me.

'Thanks. They match my knickers.'

In a sea of dinner jackets and black ties, Fletch is in midnight blue, the fathomless colour of the night sky when you are on holiday somewhere wonderful. His clothes fit close against his racehorse-firm body and his white shirt is open-necked. He looks as if he's just stepped off a yacht in the Med, suave and confident, and his only nod towards the masquerade element of the evening is a plain slender black strip across his eyes.

'Very Lone Ranger,' I say, gesturing at his eye mask. In truth, it makes me a tiny bit weak at the knees because he looks like a real live actual superhero.

'Very sexy,' he says, looking me over from head to toe, then glances at the upstairs windows of the castle. 'Want me to deflower you in the Princess Suite for old times' sake?'

I bite my tongue to stop myself from telling him that he already did.

'I'd settle for a drink.'

He glances down when Lestat sits on his foot, then looks at me and half laughs, half sighs.

'I see the dark overlord has joined you.'

'He's my date.'

Fletch bends to fuss Lestat's ears and then, as he straightens, he looks me in the eyes. 'Pity. I was kind of hoping that was my job.'

My stomach flips over slowly because the sun catches his eyes and makes me wonder if I'll ever find treasure in those rock pools.

'He's pretty territorial,' I say.

We both look at Lestat, who has assumed the dead dog pose on the steps to get the late evening warmth of the sun on his belly.

'He won't kiss you like I do,' Fletch says.

No one does, I think. 'Thank you for the lemon tree,' I say.

He shrugs. 'Life gives you lemons, make lemonade. Or gin and tonic. I prefer the gin myself.'

I look at him and I see a man who has been given a whole orchard full of lemons in his lifetime, and although it's made him a little bitter and an acquired taste, he's also pretty damn good at making sweet lemonade. Or sex. It's a euphemism.

'I prefer the lemonade,' I say.

'We'll always be very different people, Bittersweet,' he says and I nod because it's an inescapable truth.

'Someone recently called me just a normal girl with magic eyes,' I tell him. 'I'm not that different from everyone else.'

I guess I'm trying to make myself sound like a regular Joe in the hope of being more appealing, but my heart gets heavier in my chest as I say the words. I've spent my life trying to fit in, to dull down, to hide.

Fletch stares at me.

'Of all the horseshit things I've ever heard you say, that's just about the biggest pile of crap yet. You'll never be a normal girl. You wouldn't be normal, even without the ghosts.'

'That wasn't a compliment, was it?'

He looks genuinely perplexed. 'I don't even know. It wasn't meant to be an insult.' He runs his hand lightly from my shoulder to my fingertips, catching casual hold of my hand.

'Normal's pretty overrated,' he murmurs. 'And they were right about your magic screw-me-slowly eyes.'

And there he is. I may be the girl with magic eyes, but he's the man with the magic words.

'Just because we live on different sides of the fence, it doesn't mean we can't be grown-ups and lay our weapons down every now and then,' he reasons quietly, because people are milling around drinking champagne and chatting on the stone terrace. 'I'm all for a battlefield truce. I'm prepared to lay down my arms sometimes and hold you in them instead.'

He trails his finger across my collarbone as he speaks, and I swear to God I feel like Black Widow being seduced by Bruce Banner. It's heady stuff. I understand his proposal for what it is, all the more clearly after reading his notebook. He's offering to be my summer fling, but not my winter coat. My fair-weather lover. Can I do that? I worry that my heart cannot withstand him, but then I also worry that he will for ever be my missed regret. The man made me orgasm when he was ten miles away. That isn't a skill to be passed up lightly.

And then he tugs me by the hand and tucks me behind the stone portico, out of sight of the well-heeled party people.

'What are you doing?' I breathe. My heart is hammering.

His eyes are hot on mine and he brackets my body with his own. 'Helping you decide to say yes.'

I can't even remember what the question was. The band are playing in the ballroom, accompanied by the distant clink of champagne glasses, and the late evening sun bathes the whole scene rose gold.

And then, inevitably, Fletch kisses me. He kisses me as if I'm Cinderella and he's a really dirty version of Prince Charming. It's not a polite, 'can I have this dance' kiss. It's a 'don't even think about dancing with anyone else because you're my girl tonight' kiss, open-mouthed and turned on. For a couple of mesmerising minutes, I can't think about anything but him. He holds me close, as if we're dancing beneath the crystal chandeliers in the beautiful ballroom rather than hiding behind the porch, and I can almost hear Britannia's laughter as she soars free and forever joyful over the castle rooftops.

'I don't know what to do about you, Bittersweet,' he whispers, sliding his hand down my spine, moulding me into him as he kisses my hair, my face, my mouth. 'I tell myself, no, that we both know it's the worst idea in the history of bad ideas, and then I see you and all I can think is yes.' I laugh against his mouth and then he slides his hand over my breast and I stop laughing and sigh instead. 'And wonder if I'm ever going to get you naked.'

'Well definitely not tonight,' I say. 'It took about an hour to get into this dress.'

He rests his forehead against mine and groans. 'You're killing me,' he says, then steps back. 'Let's go and get that drink.'

I nod. 'I'll find Lestat and be right behind you.'

In truth I just need a minute alone to get over him.

Lestat is moseying around down by the cars again and I call him to me. Taking a few seconds to breathe in and out slowly, I look up at the façade of the castle and reflect on the week that's just passed by. Somehow, with a little bit of luck, magic and instinct on our side, we've tucked our second job successfully under our belts. And, you know what? I'm so bloody proud. We've done what we came to do here but, more than that, we set three tired, beleaguered souls free from their eternal love triangle.

In an abstract way, I see the romantic overlap between Britannia's tangled love life and my own, and I thank my lucky stars that I have my family and friends around me to keep me grounded. They drive me around the bend, but they are the best part of me and me of them. I know that whatever happens, they'll always catch me when I fall.

And then there's Fletcher Gunn. He isn't a roses and chocolates man. He's a lemon tree and pooper-scooper kind of guy and he makes me eat raw rhubarb and he's just laid his cards on the table for me to pick up, or not pick up, as I see fit. Perhaps I'll ask my magic-8 ball in the morning.

Inside my dress my phone buzzes and I fish it out of my bra in as dignified a way as I can muster. Marina has taught me many valuable life lessons, including how to carry all of your vital possessions in your bra when your outfit doesn't have any pockets. For me tonight, that means my phone and my cherry lip-gloss. I click the screen on and see I have a message from Marina, all in shouty capitals.

GET YOUR BACKSIDE IN HERE, PRONTO. CHEWBACCA IS WALTZING WITH PRINCESS LEIA AND GONG MAN IS TRYING TO GET HIS HAND DOWN THE BACK OF MY DRESS. I MAY HAVE TO HEADBUTT HIM.

I laugh softly and call Lestat. It's time to go inside.

* * *

There's one last thing I need to do before I find the others. Stepping inside the castle I accept a glass of champagne from a circulating waiter and slide into the library rather than heading to the ballroom.

'Melody, dear. I wasn't sure we'd see you again.' Lady Eleanor smiles in greeting and rises from her customary table by the window to meet me. 'Isn't it marvellous to see the castle come to life like this again? It reminds me of the good old days.'

I nod and taste my champagne. 'This is my last night here,' I say. 'I wanted to say goodbye.'

She bows her head for a second and, when she looks up, I see her mouth is quivering as if she's finding it hard to keep herself together.

'Thank you for helping Brittania. I'll miss her terribly, but it was for the best.'

'I hope so.' I smile sadly. 'Can I ask you one last question?'

Her fingers flutter against the pearls around her neck as she glances back nervously at her husband. Lord Alistair seems engrossed in a book, so she leans in to whisper.

'There was no sense in involving the police. It would have been a terrible scandal and for what end? We heard gunshots and came running and they were all there on the ballroom floor.' She pauses and heaves in a great, shuddering sigh at the awful memory. 'Britannia's name would have been dragged through the mud. I couldn't bear that. Far better for people to just think that the circus moved onto another town, that she was still out there somewhere performing.'

I'd pieced most of this together lying in bed last night.

'Are they buried in the gardens outside?'

Checking her husband isn't coming over, Eleanor nods bravely. 'Brittania is. I'm not ashamed of what we did, Melody. Alistair struggled with it for the rest of our lives, but it was the best thing to do. This way she stayed where she belonged. Where they *both* belonged.'

I smile sadly and nod. Eleanor's right; there was no more fitting resting place for Brittania and her baby than at Maplemead with her family.

'What happened to the others?'

Eleanor looked pained. 'The circus folk look after their own, they dealt with it. All we knew is that the bodies were taken away.'

I can only imagine the horror scene that must have greeted the Shillings in the ballroom that night; the fact that they dealt with it at all and then managed to keep their secret for all of these years is nothing short of a miracle.

'I think I'd have done the exact same thing,' I say, and Lady Eleanor covers her mouth as if to cry at the validation. For all her brave words, I've no doubt that her guilty secret has weighed heavy on her shoulders all these years too. In the ballroom, the band strikes up a waltz.

'Eleanor?' Lord Alistair has crossed the room to stand beside us, and he's holding his hand out to his wife. 'Shall we?'

A shaky smile touches her lips as she slips her hand into his and she nods farewell to me as she lets him lead her into the middle of the parquet library floor. I remember Brittania's words about her aunt and uncle being the most-in-love couple she'd ever known. As I pause at the door for a second to watch them dance, I think they might be the most-in-love couple I've ever known, too.

I've learned many things about romance in my brief time at Maplemead. I've learned that love can arrive unexpectedly and all at once, like a swift blow from a sledgehammer. I've learned that fickle hearts can be steadfast for the right person, and that the right person is worth waiting for, even if it takes a hundred years. I've learned that love has a dark, twisted side; it can kill you, but I've learned that it can save you, too.

I've learned that love makes lion hearts of us all, whether shy teenage boys or fiercely protective family. And, most of all, I've learned that love endures, that it finds its path wherever it chooses, like a river snaking its way around obstacles and blockades because it is the life force and can overcome anything.

I click the library door shut as my text alert trills again, this time from Glenda Jackson.

Well done on a case successfully resolved, Melody. Call just in from a disgruntled hotel owner over in Blackgate. Something about mass hysteria breaking out at breakfast this morning because of ghosts in the dining room. I said you'd call him on Monday.

Onwards and upwards, I murmur, and then I shake my foot because Lestat has reappeared and is tugging on the lace of my new sparkly Wonder Woman Converse. There was no accompanying note with them in the shoebox, but then there didn't really need to be, did there?

Come Monday, I'll be back in my trusty jeans and Converse at my desk chomping at the bit for the next case, but just for tonight I'm going to be a princess in my own fairy-tale castle.

A LETTER FROM KITTY

Thank you so much for reading this, the second book in the Chapelwick Mysteries series. I hope by now that you're coming to view Melody and co. as old friends, and that you'll be glad to hear that there are more crazy adventures in the pipeline!

If you did enjoy it, I would be very grateful if you could write a review. I'd love to hear what you think, and it makes such a difference helping new readers to discover one of my books for the first time.

I'd love to chat to you about the books – I'm always around on Facebook and Twitter. If you'd like to get in touch, my details are at the bottom of the page.

Would you like me to let you know when there is a new Melody Bittersweet book out? Please click the link below to sign up for my newsletter – your details will never be shared and you can unsubscribe at any time.

Until the next adventure,
Kitty xx

www.bookouture.com/kitty-french

kittyfrenchauthor

@KFrenchBooks

www.kittyfrench.com

ACKNOWLEDGMENTS

Thank you to my editor Natalie Butlin for your thoughtful, considered advice and for caring so much about this story. Wider thanks to the whole team at Bookouture for your support and assistance, and to Emma Graves for the eye-popping cover. Special thanks to Kim Nash – your unwavering love for Melody means the world, as does all of the brilliant work you do to spread the word.

Huge thanks to my very lovely agent Jemima Forrester, your unstinting help and guidance is so very appreciated.

Much love and gratitude to all of the bloggers and readers who take the time to read, review or tell others about the Chapelwick Mysteries, your support is invaluable and goes neither unnoticed nor unappreciated.

I must thank the other authors at Bookouture – what a fabulous, funny, inspiring bunch you are. I feel honoured to be amongst you.

I'm really lucky to have a great gang around me on Facebook and Twitter. It makes a huge difference knowing that you're all there ready to chat, even if it's the middle of the night and I feel like the only person awake in the world. You make me laugh and you keep me writing. I'm grateful for you all.

Special thanks to Kathrin Magyar for coming up with one of the phrases in this book on a FB post. I won't single it out as it's a bit sweary, but you know which one it is Kathrin and it was entirely perfect!

Love as ever to my family and friends for unerring support and being endlessly proud, and an extra thank you to my youngest son Alex for coming up with the name Chapelwick. There you go Al, your name in print as promised!

Printed in Great Britain
by Amazon